To [illegible]

with best wishes,

PASSING THROUGH

david penhale

David Penhale

Cormorant Books

The publisher gratefully acknowledges the support of the Canada Council for the Arts and the Ontario Arts Council for its publishing program.
We acknowledge the financial support of the Government of Canada through the Canada Book Fund (CBF) for our publishing activities, and the Government of Ontario through the Ontario Media Development Corporation, an agency of the Ontario Ministry of Culture, and the Ontario Book Publishing Tax Credit Program.

LIBRARY AND ARCHIVES CANADA CATALOGUING IN PUBLICATION

Penhale, David
Passing through / David Penhale.

ISBN 978-1-77086-053-7

I. Title.

PS8581.E55325P38 2011 C813'.54 C2011-904033-6

Cover art and design: Angel Guerra/Archetype
Interior text design: Tannice Goddard, Soul Oasis Networking
Printer: Solisco Tri-Graphic

Printed and bound in Canada.

FSC C003594

This book is printed on 100% post-consumer waste recycled paper.

CORMORANT BOOKS INC.
215 SPADINA AVENUE, STUDIO 230, TORONTO, ONTARIO, CANADA M5T 2C7
www.cormorantbooks.com

For my father,
the good man at the centre of this story.

"Surely," thought Rip, "I have not slept here all night."

— WASHINGTON IRVING, "RIP VAN WINKLE"

[ONE]

IT WAS FRIDAY, the beginning of the weekend in the Middle East, a day to lace on a pair of boots, stick a map in your pocket and head for the desert.

But Daniel Foster was in Toronto, not Dubai. In his daughter's townhouse, not the apartment in Golden Sands. Tall and tanned, he had dark hair with a touch of silver at the temples. His business suit, tailored by Frazier & Sons of Savile Row, had won the respect of many a maître d'. The box of Froot Loops on the counter belonged to his granddaughter. He tugged open the fridge and frowned at the empty shelves.

Out for breakfast then. Foster put on his raincoat and patted for the keys to his Mercedes. He felt a jolt of panic. He had no keys. The sheiks had cut him loose. Bracing himself against the mild September day, he stepped out the door and spun around to inspect 27 Mazurka Street.

His heart emptied as he stared at the bird's nest on the electrical meter, at the discarded tire with a burdock growing from its centre. Turning away, unbuttoning his raincoat, he started up the sidewalk, amending with each step the plan he had made during the whispering, airborne hours on KLM. With an allowance coming in, Mary and Shawna, his only living relations, could move into one of those barn-sized houses he had flown over on the final approach to Pearson Airport. Four bedrooms, three bathrooms, Scarlett O'Hara staircase. The works. Cheered by this thought, Foster went up the sidewalk with his coat billowing behind him like a magician's cape.

Mazurka Street, a jumble of Victorian cottages and cinder-block duplexes, connected two major roads. Yet it seemed hidden, half-forgotten. A puddle shimmered in the sunlight. There had been a rumble of thunder in the night, Foster recalled, a crack of lightning, a rattle on the roof. When had rain last fallen in Dubai? Two years ago? He sniffed the air, savouring the scent. Toronto's weather could be pleasant, he had to admit. In Dubai's perpetual summer, he had remembered Toronto as a winter city, a city trapped under a low, grey sky. Lucky thing, a fine day like this. *And you need the luck, Danny*, Irv, his father, would say, leaning on the hood of the Studebaker and writing an order for stove bolts.

Mazurka ended at Dundas Street. Foster glanced to the right and stepped over the curb, locking his eyes on a row of rusty metal letters spelling out *Elite Restaurant*. Tires shrieked, a horn blared. Bewildered, he turned to see a delivery van hurtling toward him. Was this how he would die, struck down in the roadway like a stray camel? For a serene moment it seemed right that he would perish here, his life come full circle.

The bumper of the van dipped to a stop centimetres from his knee. A tangle of dreadlocks flew from a side window. An angry face followed. "Asshole!" the driver yelled. Chastened, he had looked the wrong way. This wasn't London. Foster hurried across the road and pushed open the door of the restaurant that seemed to have waited twenty-five years for him to return.

How had The Elite survived? The curved counter, the spin-top stools, the high-backed booths, the chromed napkin holders whirled him back to a childhood Sunday. He had trooped to the Baptist Church to hear

Miss Rebecca Wilson tell Bible stories in her quavering voice, and here he was at his grandmother's side, clean and combed and correct in his blue blazer, hungry for his reward for loving Jesus. The memory carried the scent of camphor. Foster perched on a stool and picked up a menu. What would he order if his grandmother were at his side? A hot chicken sandwich with mashed potatoes and peas. Rice pudding topped with cinnamon. A glass of milk.

"What can I get you?"

The voice had a familiar cadence, and Foster looked up, half-expecting to see Ghuman peering down at him. But Ghuman, Foster's friend, the ace programmer he had met in Riyadh, had perished when an airliner overshot a runway and exploded in flames. Perhaps this relic of a restaurant catered to the dead.

"Are you from Karachi?" Foster smiled. Bit of a diva, Ghuman. He could make a computer sing.

The waiter looked stonily down. "Anybody looks like me must be a Paki. Is that what you think?"

"There's a cadence to a Karachi accent, and I guessed —"

"You couldn't guess Mississauga?"

Foster's smile froze. Rule one of expatriate life: never argue with the locals. "Can I get two boiled eggs? Brown toast and coffee?"

The waiter walked away.

"Three minutes for the eggs," Foster called after him.

For a busy executive, a wait is a gift. Foster slipped a hand into his jacket and drew out the photographs Mary had sent him. The first was a school picture of Shawna. His eleven-year-old granddaughter had latté-brown skin and springy, copper-coloured hair. "A Jamaican guy I knew for a while," was all Mary had told him of Shawna's father, years ago, over a scratchy long-distance line. From last night's chat, Foster knew Shawna was clever. It seemed a shame that he was off to Chiang Mai, that he wouldn't get to know her.

Turning his attention to the second photo, he pondered the mystery of his only child. Mary wore a black uniform with silver lightning bolts embroidered on the shoulders. She stood with a group of security guards, beaming like a teenager meeting her favourite rock band. The last man in line was leaning on Mary. Foster slipped the photos into his pocket and stared at the cloudy front window. A mailman came through the door and took a seat at the counter.

Breakfast arrived. The coffee tasted of acid. The toast was burnt. The eggs were hard. Foster chewed in moody silence. With the allowance coming in, Mary could quit her dead-end job. Go back to school. Once she was on her feet, he would send the airfare and she would visit him in Chiang Mai, the paradise he had chosen for his retirement. He pictured himself ushering Mary and Shawna into a villa set among thick, green coconut trees. There was something fishy about this mental picture. He traced the bug to its source. The villa came from his grandmother's bookcase, from "Rain," a short story by Somerset Maugham. Foster pushed his sorry meal aside and checked his watch, the Rolex Oyster Perpetual that in the Gulf had been a badge of office. Mary would be home in an hour. The waiter trudged past in offended silence, toting a bag of milk.

Milk. Mary's empty fridge. He would go grocery shopping. What better peace offering for last night's fiasco? Mary had thrown his offer of an allowance back in his face. Foster got to his feet, drew out his wallet and stepped to the cash register, snapping a thumbnail over his credit cards as he went. Put on your plastic armour, you shall not suffer loss.

When the waiter ignored him, Foster cleared his throat noisily. The mailman shot him a knowing look. The waiter dawdled over, stationed himself behind the register and glowered at the money in Foster's hand. "A hundred? Can't take it."

"It's the smallest I have. Will you take a credit card?"

"No credit cards." The waiter rapped a thick finger against a hand-lettered sign.

"Traveller's cheque?"

The waiter shook his head. "Bring the money later. By four o'clock."

"Thank you," Foster said, forcing himself to smile. "Is there a grocery store nearby?"

"Cut Cost," the mailman said, keeping his eyes on the sports pages. "Two blocks west."

Down the street Foster strode, past Dollar Heaven and Lou's Pawn Shop. He was eyeing the greasy stoves in the window of Appliance Wonderland when the sky darkened and rain pattered down, spreading rivulets of grime over the sidewalk. He hated Canada.

The surprising thought slowed Foster to the easy, ground-covering lope that had carried him through the *wadis* (the dry river beds) of the Arabian Peninsula. How could anyone hate a country as bland as processed cheese? In the Arab world, his Canadian temperament had been his stock-in-trade. Canadians are competent, consistent. Canadians have a calming effect, like goats stabled with nervous horses.

The neighbourhood had fallen on hard times, Foster saw. It was no place for Shawna to grow up. When he was Shawna's age, the Junction was a brash and busy crossroads made prosperous by railroads and stockyards. In the night you heard the boom of shunting, and on a north wind you caught the sad, charnel smell drifting from the slaughterhouses. There were pyramids of oranges in the greengrocer's, suits with phantom lapels in Cohen's tailor shop. And, Foster suddenly remembered, a fluoroscope in Dixon's Shoes.

With a fat shoe clerk looking on, Foster would run to the fluoroscope wearing a new pair of Sisman Scampers, and peer into a netherworld where the bones of his feet glowed. His grandmother would hook her purse over her arm and toddle over to see for herself. Only a fool paid good money for shoes that didn't fit, and grandma was nobody's fool.

Grandma and her Bible, her Shakespeare, her *Stevenson's Garden of Verse*. Grandma in her mission chair, watching wrestling on TV. Not that Foster could count on seeing the matches. His father might turn up to claim him, as if his son were a sentimental item he had pawned. A week, ten days on the road and Foster was back with his grandmother. People once believed the sun, the moon and the stars rotated around the earth. The notion made a wonky kind of sense. His grandmother had been the gravity that held him and Irv, his flimflam father, in orbit. And for all Foster knew, invisibly guided the shoe clerk and Cohen the tailor.

The rain stopped, the air grew heavy. Foster walked on, his nostalgia cooling into dread. With his working life over and his death the last major item on the agenda, he found himself reaching for, if not his grandmother's granite faith, then some explanation. A higher mathematics. A cosmic algorithm. It was a waste of time, he knew. Musing about his purpose on this planet scarcely counted as thinking.

Cut Cost, a decaying building of concrete block fronted by a glass wall, seemed familiar. His grandmother had brought him, a child of six, to the store's grand opening. Across the parking lot went Foster, dodging a pickup truck bristling with ladders. At the entrance, he watched a woman of startling beauty — she might have been Somalian, her regal stature, her large, shining eyes, the bright tie-dye of her gown — slip a quarter in a slot and pull a cart free.

A gaunt woman materialized at his side. She took his hand, placed it on the handle of an unfettered cart and mutely held out a palm. She was Eastern European, Foster thought, a survivor of the Soviet Era with melancholy pooled in her eyes. Seized by an impulse to put history right, he yanked out his wallet, snapped out a hundred-dollar bill and pressed it into her hand. Before she could protest or thank him, he was off, clattering the cart through the doors.

The store was a swirl of saris, abayas and the cheap slacks and shirts he had seen from Cairo to Kenya. Where would these people find jobs with the air clear of slaughterhouse smoke? You're going about it all wrong, he longed to tell them. Nowadays money is a stream of electrons, an arc of wealth that flies high over Canada. His life savings, for example — the 1.3 million American dollars winging their way from AMEB to the Cayman Islands.

It had been years since he had set foot in a grocery store, but Foster plunged in gamely, snatching up bags of apples, bunches of bananas, boxes of mandarin oranges, then lettuce, parsnips, carrots. He swung down another aisle and spotted a package of Froot Loops. He would buy a box for Shawna. The breakfast food aisle made him happy — every carton carried the promise of a new day. When a vacant checkout loomed into view, *You need the luck, son!*, he swung his cart up to a counter.

A teenager with spiky red hair gave him a blank look. According to the badge pinned to her smock, she was Tina, and was committed to his shopping experience. The scanner beeped. Groceries tumbled down a stainless steel ramp. From a display rack Foster took a comic book for Shawna, a copy of *Canadian Homemaker* for Mary, the *Toronto Star* for himself.

"You've got kind of a mountain," said Tina. "You want bags? They're five cents each."

Kind of a mountain. "'The mountain, and the deep and gloomy wood, their colours and their forms,'" Foster recited, smiling at Tina, "'were then to me an appetite …'" And a something, something. Fragments of the poems his grandmother had made him memorize still ran through Foster's head. It pleased him to recall these lines of Wordsworth.

Tina rolled her eyes, whacked the total button and announced the damage. The amount seemed a pittance. Foster handed Tina his AMEB credit card. He looked through the window, spotted a taxi and waved until a portly driver clambered out and began a dignified stroll to the front door.

"Declined," Tina said.

Foster looked at her. "Nonsense. Try again."

She tried the card again.

"Declined."

"Why?"

"It doesn't say. It never does."

"American Express?"

"We don't take those. Sorry."

Sorry. Why were Canadians always saying sorry? As if you had to apologize for being alive. The balance on that card was high enough anyway. He had put his airfare on it, and the expenses from the week he had spent in London, consulting with Cedric Richards-Henderson, his financial advisor. Reluctantly, Foster handed over three of the crisp hundred dollar bills he had bought at the money exchange in Heathrow. The money he had hoped to present to Mary.

"All this?" the cabbie asked.

"Yes," Foster said.

"Your change," Tina said.

"Aren't you going to pack this for me?"

"You bag your own, sir."

Fine. The sooner he was in Thailand, the better; he had had his fill of Canada. Foster snapped open a bag. The *Toronto Star* came gliding down the conveyor belt. The headline read, *MIDDLE EASTERN BANK GOES UNDER.*

There was a picture of a bank tower.

The tower was in Dubai.

The bank was AMEB.

His bank.

MUSIC, ONE OF the new rhythmical styles, boomed from Mary's house as Foster picked his way up the front walk with the cabbie a step behind carrying grocery bags. Was Mary home? Foster knocked, hesitated, then pushed open the door, searching his pockets for his cellphone — until he remembered that he had cancelled the service before he left Dubai. Mary's phone was an old, wall-mounted model. He reached for the handset, forcing himself to think. A fragment of Kipling floated through his mind. *If you can keep your head when all about you / Are losing theirs and blaming it on you …* The papers had exaggerated the story. No one trusted the Arabs, not since 9/11. An urgent beat thumped from the living room. Foster stuck his head in the doorway, waiting for Shawna to take the hint and turn the music down. She was at her computer desk, swinging her legs, bobbing her head, slanting her shoulders side to side. She waggled a remote control at a wall unit and the room fell silent. No, a tinny beat leaked from her earphones. She had a gadget clipped to her waist. Was she old enough to be left on her own? "Where's Mary? Where's your mother?"

"Mama back soon," Shawna sang, "back soon, back soon, back soon."

If you can keep your head … Cedric's business card had a reassuring heft. The sheiks wouldn't let AMEB fail, Foster told himself as he tapped in the number. The line buzzed. The cabbie went back and forth like the sorcerer's apprentice. Foster tilted the card, mesmerized by its holographic mantra. *Plan the future / Live the dream, Plan the future / Live the dream, Plan the future / Live the dream.*

"Appalling taste, of course," Cedric Richards-Henderson had said when he handed Foster his card. "Meant to pull the Yanks." The breezy Brit-slang was part of Cedric's act, Foster had decided. Foster was "the wild colonial boy." Managing money was "a doddle." A stock tip was "a Chinese Whisper."

"Run the lolly through the eye of the needle," Cedric said. "Best route to the Caymans."

"Eye of the needle?" Foster said.

"If we send the lot through AMEB, we save the transfer fee."

We, though the money was Foster's. That week — the week the sheiks cancelled Foster's contract, handed him his passport, threw his life off course — the stock markets came crashing down. But Cedric, bless him, had seen the downturn coming. Foster's fortune was all in cash. "Maybe we should spread the risk?"

"Oh, there's no risk. Safe as houses, AMEB." Cedric smoothed his tie. The tie was Eton, but was it genuine?

Standing in Mary's kitchen, the phone buzzing in his ear, Foster looked over to see white plastic bags covering the kitchen table like a fall of snow. When the cabbie arrived with yet another load, Foster gestured impatiently at the floor. Sylvia of the silky scarf, pick up the phone.

"Richards-Henderson Financial," Sylvia said, in her rich contralto.

"That's the lot," the cabbie announced at the same moment.

"Sylvia, it's Foster." With the handset jammed against his shoulder, Foster paid the fare and waved the taxi driver away.

"Daniel. Hello."

Call me Foster, he had told the woman, and more than once. *Everyone calls me Foster.* "Put me through to Cedric."

The line clicked and Foster found himself alone with Pachelbel's "Canon in D Major." How Foster hated that repetitious piece! It was music for the elevators of hell.

"Monitoring the line," Sylvia broke in to say.

A roar came from the living room. Shawna had turned the stereo back on. Should he tell her to turn it off? Why had Mary left the child on her own? "It's bad," Cedric said, coming on the line suddenly. No breezy banter. Then it was bad.

"Tell me that my money reached the Caymans."

The din abruptly stopped. A murmur undercut the ensuing silence, as if the phone had turned into a seashell. A Nautilus shell, Foster thought uselessly, the pretty one with the logarithmic spiral.

"The money went down the rabbit hole, Foster."

Rabbit hole? Had Cedric dipped into his stock of single malt scotch? Foster took a deep breath, forced himself to exhale. *If you can keep your head …* "The newspaper says something about derivatives."

"Yes, the twit stuck the bank in all the way, assets, reserves, light bulbs, those little pens on chains …"

"Pens on chains?"

"The market reversed and AMEB went arse over teakettle."

"Arse over teakettle?" Foster staggered back, colliding with the kitchen table. "Twit? AMEB's wonder boy president?"

"The same."

"But how …"

"Bugger fiddled the books."

"Fiddled the books? Explain that."

Foster listened, staring through Mary's patio door. There was a rusty barbecue out there, a swing set with no swings, a basket-weave fence missing its bottom board. As Cedric talked on, jargon swirled through Foster's mind like tinsel in a winter wind. The Yuan exchange bridge. The Yen carry trade. Swap counter-parties. Domino-driven funds. The dark money pool. The global slosh effect. Ripple wrecks. AMEB had been hit by a tidal wave, Cedric told Foster. The bank had simply vanished, sunk like a stone, gone down with all hands. Taking Foster's fortune with it.

"So what happens now?"

"It's early days. There may be some recovery."

"Some recovery? Cedric, I'm on my way to Thailand. I'll be in Chiang Mai next week, shopping for a villa."

"At least I'm here," Cedric said in a flat voice that shook Foster to the core. "I took your call. Kevin's done a runner. Stuck his cellular in the charger and walked out."

Foster closed his eyes. "You're there, Cedric. You took my call. Thank you. You're my advisor. Tell me what to do."

"Forgive me, Daniel."

Forgive me? The line went dead. After a moment, Foster put the handset in its cradle. He stood for a long time gazing through the patio door at the lengthening shadows.

How long had Mary been in the kitchen? In her sweatshirt and jeans, she seemed younger than she had last night. Her face bore an expression of wonder. Mary, I'm in trouble. I'm frightened. Badly frightened. My life has come to nothing. He should tell his daughter this. He should tell her now. But Foster had no words. Every family invents a language, and the Foster version did not include the vocabulary of the heart. He said nothing and the moment passed.

"Hey, you guys!" Shawna called from the living room. "Sam and Dam are on."

"Coming." Mary said. She touched Foster`s arm and moved away.

"Coming," Foster echoed, though he had no idea what Shawna was talking about. He began to walk, and found himself shuffling his feet, fixing his gaze on the floor. At the entrance to the living room, he stopped and looked around, taking in the threadbare couch, the beanbag chair, the mismatched end tables.

Mary settled herself on the couch, and Shawna snuggled up to her mother. The beanbag chair seemed a long way across the room, and then it seemed a long way down. Mary was watching him furtively, Foster sensed as he thunked into the beanbag. He sat with his legs straight and his arms thrown over the sides, staring at the television. The colours were out of whack. The greens quavered, the reds flared, the blues burned. He would buy Mary a new set. As soon as AMEB was sorted out.

On the television, a white-haired man strolled into a locker room with a towel around his neck and a tennis racket under his arm. A younger man ambled in. "You beat me again, Sid."

"That's because I beat my pain." The white-haired man held up a bottle of pills. The bottle was blue, and it seemed to be on fire.

"Foster?" Mary said. "Are you okay?"

"Little problem with my bank." Foster made a dismissive gesture. "Nothing to worry about."

When the commercial ended, a hawkish-looking woman in a white satin gown swept into a room that had red walls and too many mirrors. A bellboy flitted through the foreground. Was this a hotel? It certainly wasn't the Burj Al Arab, the luxury hotel shaped like the sail of a dhow. "He found the receipt," the woman told a brawny youth in a tuxedo. "He knows everything."

"He knows nothing," the youth scoffed. Was he a guest, Foster wondered? The manager of the Burj Al Arab? A client of Cohen the tailor?

"That guy is so-o-o-o screwed," Shawna said.

"You think?" Mary said.

"Samantha and Damian are, like, you know, doing it," Shawna whispered.

"Are they now." Foster nodded sagely. He would have a word with those two. If the sheiks caught wind of that kind of hanky-panky, they would put Samantha and Damian on the next flight out. Very moral, the sheiks. A major bank couldn't just disappear. It's early days. On the screen the words *Restless World* formed in misty letters over a daybreak sky.

"They never open with Sam and Dam," Mary said. "Something's up."

"Totally," Shawna said.

"Um," Foster said, as if he were in a meeting at Duboco Petroleum and had yet to make up his mind about the matter under discussion.

He didn't care much for television, but now the commercials fascinated him. They were punchy thirty-second movies with plots, stars, settings. The last commercial ended. The pretty people disappeared. Well, there it was. People are easily replaced. You learned that in the Middle East and you learned it fast. *You're just a donkey they've rented.*

"Foster?" Mary said. "Thanks for all the groceries."

Were groceries on the agenda? *Restless World* resumed. The scene had shifted. "You stole that formula," said a woman wearing a lot of makeup.

"Yeah? Let them prove it." The man in the white lab coat was a petroleum chemist, Foster decided. He gazed down the length of his body at his bare feet. When had he shucked off his shoes and socks? An Arabic proverb came to mind. *Come back with Hunain's shoes.*

It meant to come home with nothing.

[TWO]

THE PLASTERER HAD worked from left to right, Foster concluded three nights later, at four in the morning. The sofa bed was a tight fit, and he lay staring at the ceiling of Mary's spare bedroom with his head and his feet pointing at opposite corners of the mattress. There was a pattern to those whorls on the ceiling. Cedric would jump through the looking glass, follow the money trail through the wonderland of international banking, pop up in the Caymans with the goods.

Night sounds. The click and whirr of the fridge. The creak of a contracting floorboard. The murmur of voices through a thin wall. Had the television been left on? What if the money was gone? The frightening possibility throbbed like a bad tooth. Was he doing enough? He had phoned Canary Wharf twice a day. What else could he do?

His bladder ached. Foster levered himself to his feet, put on his robe and threaded his way to the door, squeezing past an exercise bike and a sewing table, stepping over a duffle bag and a vacuum cleaner. He went down the dark hallway thinking about AMEB, Thailand, Cedric Richards-Henderson, ran into someone and reeled back in surprise. A pair of boxer shorts seemed to float in mid-air, then attach themselves swimmingly to a lanky man. He grinned at Foster, raised his fists and bobbed and swayed with comic menace. Foster flattened himself against the wall to let the phantom fighter pass. When Foster reached the bathroom, he glanced back to see the door to Mary's bedroom close. He had seen that man before, but where? An hour later, on the edge of sleep, Foster's data-savvy mind came up with a match. The picture of Mary and the security guards. The man leaning on Mary.

When morning came, Foster showered and shaved, got dressed and went to the kitchen. Mary stood at the stove, peering down at a saucepan. She had on her Secure-All outfit. A black ball cap hid her hair. Foster scarcely recognized his daughter in that paramilitary getup. But then, with the vapour rising from the saucepan, she brushed her forehead with a bent wrist. She had done that as a baby. Her Irish salute, Kathleen, Mary's mother, had called it.

"Hey," Mary said. "You're up."

"I don't usually sleep this late."

"Sleep okay?"

"Fine."

Something — an egg? — rattled in the pot.

"Those pink sheets are really old. When I get home I'll find the other pair."

Were the sheets pink? Foster couldn't remember.

"I meant to change them. No one's used that room since Mom. Can you move around with all that stuff in there? I'll move it when I get home."

Kathleen had slept in that bed? There was a bright spill of Froot Loops on the table. Foster sorted the circles with a fingertip. They made five groups: red, yellow, green, orange, purple. Or two groups: primary and secondary colours. Or …

"You just missed her."

Foster looked up, startled. Kathleen was dead.

"Shawna. She just left for school. She says hi." Mary put an egg cup and a plate of toast on the table. "So, how's it going?" She looked at him.

"Fine."

"With the bank, I mean."

"Fine."

"Fine. You'd say that if both your legs were broken."

Was this sarcasm? Foster picked up a spoon and knocked the end off the egg.

Mary leaned over his arm to take a look. "Did I do it right?"

"It's a bit runny." Why had he said that? "I like them that way."

"No, you don't."

"Sometimes I do."

While Mary busied herself at the counter — was there something on her mind? — Foster made a start on his breakfast. He looked over to see his daughter sitting opposite him, a coffee mug cradled in her hands. He raised his eyebrows, inviting her to speak.

"Foster, are you going to be here for a while?"

So that was it. If Mary wanted him out of the house, why didn't she say so? "Was the water boiling when you put the egg in?"

"They crack if you do that. Reason I ask, they want me on nights next week and I thought … maybe you could babysit Shawna?"

Babysit Shawna. An old sadness came over Foster. *Oh, you'll get the knack of parenting,* people had assured him when Mary was born. But he never had. He picked up the pepper shaker. Put it down again. What if Shawna took sick? There were pills in the medicine cabinet. But Shawna might be allergic to them. Children were, these days. What if she invited her friends over, threw a wild party? "Once AMEB is sorted out, I'll be on my way."

"Terrific." Mary got to her feet.

Terrific that AMEB would be sorted out, or terrific that he would be on his way? Foster looked down. The pepper shaker was in his hand.

The egg was black with pepper. Problem solving was Foster's expertise.

"The fellow I met in the hallway last night, could he babysit Shawna?"

"Tyler?" Mary spun around. She had been staring through the patio door. "You met Tyler?"

"We didn't exactly meet," Foster said. Could he make the bump in the night seem funny? "We ran into each other on the way to the bathroom."

Mary stared at him. "You what? Oh. Listen, don't say anything to Shawna."

"Tyler is a secret?"

"He's not a secret. It's just that he's not official."

"I'm not following you."

"Know what?" Mary said, switching to a bright voice. "You bought all this great food, so we'll have a special dinner to welcome you and Tyler into the family."

"I'm already in the family." If you want to make good decisions, you have to keep the facts straight.

"I didn't mean … Look, Tyler has to go away for a while. A week, maybe. He's got this terrific idea for a new business. You'll be here next week, won't you?"

Next week. With AMEB up in the air, with the cash in his wallet dwindling, it was difficult to think that far ahead. "I hope to have things sorted out before then."

"Whatever." Mary grabbed a windbreaker from the back of a chair.

The front door slammed. After a moment Foster picked up the phone and called London. Sylvia's recorded voice told him that his call was important and that he should stay on the line. Today's hold music was Debussy. "Prelude to the Afternoon of a Faun." When Cedric came on the line he told Foster that very good people were working on the AMEB problem. Results were expected any day now.

Within a week. Two weeks at the most. Foster said goodbye and stood lost in thought, staring at the breakfast dishes in the sink. Then, remembering his unpaid bill at The Elite Restaurant, he emptied his pockets of change, and counted the coins. There was enough to settle his debt. Just enough.

A WEEK WENT by, seven sparkling autumn days of blue skies and white clouds. You noticed clouds after years in the Middle East, Foster reflected, studying the sky through the window of the spare bedroom, waiting for the moment to swing his legs out of bed.

At 7:00 a.m. he took his turn in the bathroom. The trick was to nip in after Mary was out, and get out before Shawna wanted in. Which gave him six minutes, most days.

At 7:20 a.m. he trooped to the kitchen, where Mary made eggs and toast for him, cereal and toast for Shawna, toast and jam for herself.

At 7:45 a.m. Shawna peddled off to school on her mountain bike. Mary left for work soon after. Secure-All had assigned her to a plant that made kitchen cabinets, she had told Foster.

At 7:50 a.m. he trudged up the street to buy the *Toronto Star*, *The Globe and Mail*, and the *National Post* at Corner Convenience, a little store that smelled of apples and fresh bread. A couple by the name of Park ran the store. If Mrs. Park was on the cash, she would beam at him, her eyes almost disappearing into the folds of her smile, and ask about the family; smiling and nodding, she had grilled Foster on his first visit. If her stone-faced husband stood behind the counter he would take Foster's money without a word. Foster preferred Mr. Park.

At 8:05 a.m. Foster was back in the townhouse, where he spread the papers on the kitchen table, slipped off his suit coat, loosened his tie and settled in to scan the newspapers and sip the coffee Mary had left on the stove. If there was a story about AMEB he clipped it and set it aside to discuss with Cedric.

At 9:10 a.m., early afternoon in London, he made the first call of the day to Richards-Henderson Financial. "Nothing new," Cedric would say. Best people working on it." Cedric sounded more optimistic with each passing day, Foster thought. More like his old self. After the phone call, Foster put on his raincoat and set out on the first of the day's long walks.

Mornings he walked down High Park Avenue, past the old mansions and the willow trees, past the apartment towers with bicycles on their balconies, across Bloor Street and through the gates of High Park. At the park's entrance lurked a squad of old men in baggy pants and ancient sports coats. Pensioners from a nearby retirement home, Foster supposed. The living dead, taking the morning air. Foster ignored them. He focussed his attention on the women jogging along in outfits of chromium yellow, lime green, electric blue. They quickened his heart, these prancing beauties, and the glances they threw his way boosted his morale. He could still turn a head. Not that he was in the market. Gloria Nelson had been his last lover — if their practical arrangement counted as love. A no-nonsense Brit in her late forties, she worked for Emirates Air, living small and saving her money. Every expatriate has a dream, and Gloria's was to return to Yorkshire and buy a restored longboat. Cruising up and down the Rochdale Canal wasn't Foster's idea of paradise.

High Park didn't fit the bill either. The lawns and shadows, the many tones of green and the odour of loamy decay unsettled a man who loved the desert. But walk he must. It was only when he was in motion that his predicament fell into perspective. Cedric wouldn't let him down. The sheiks would bail out AMEB. Thailand would still be there in a week or two. Foster's route led him past the soccer field and the baseball diamond, down to Grenadier Pond and over to Colborne

Lodge, the restored home of John Howard, the eccentric architect who in the nineteenth century gave the city the vast park and lived out his days in the solitude of its woods.

At noon Foster made his way to the park's little zoo, where, in the shade of an enormous maple, a grumpy Croatian in a greasy black suit sold him a hot dog; on the other side of a chain-link fence, a llama slept in the sun. When Foster sat on a bench to eat his meagre lunch, the llama swivelled its nappy head and fixed him with a belligerent stare. As if to say, you don't belong here. The llama was right, Foster knew. He didn't belong here. Not with crimson leaves pinwheeling down. Not with winter coming on.

At 1:00 p.m. he hiked back to the townhouse and sorted through the messages on Mary's answering machine, eager to hear Cedric's voice. But Cedric never called. Tyler, on the other hand, left long, rambling messages for Mary. The man couldn't think in a straight line. Foster left Tyler's messages for Mary to make sense of. The other calls were for Shawna, urgent communications from children named Benny and Alisa and Mohammed and Kayla. These messages Foster summarized — sender, action required — and left the pink slips in a neat line on the kitchen counter.

At 1:15 p.m. he made his second phone call to Cedric. "Nothing new," Cedric would say. "Best people working on it."

At 3:00 p.m. Foster walked east on Dundas, north on Keele, east again past factories with windows covered with weather-beaten plywood. In the oblique light he could make out the chalky lettering on the brick walls: Harris & Co., Empire Seeds, British American Steel. Relics of the industrial past, oxidizing into oblivion. His own past, the memories of his grandmother and his father that had pressed upon him so strongly that first day in Canada, had likewise faded. The old neighbourhood now seemed only vaguely familiar, like a book read long ago and re-encountered on someone else's bookshelf.

At 4:00 p.m. he strolled back to Mazurka Street, arriving just before Shawna came racing home from school and banged through the house with her rather daunting high spirits. While Mary made dinner — they were working their way through the groceries he had bought at Cut Cost — Foster would pick up the remote and surf the channels, hoping for something — anything — about AMEB. It worried him that the stories were less frequent.

At 5:00 p.m. he was in the beanbag chair, watching *Restless World* with Mary and Shawna. Why did he, a man who had never cared for television, sit through a soap opera? Because Shawna might give him a high five when something especially good happened — the day Paul got his comeuppance for stealing the goop formula, for instance.

In the evening, while Shawna multi-tasked through her homework and Mary watched police shows, Foster dozed in his chair. If there was no police show to watch, Mary would mute the television and pick up a romance novel.

At 10:00 p.m. Foster would walk down the hall and drop into bed. On the edge of sleep, a wish, a plea for deliverance would form in his mind. It wasn't a prayer. He had put all that business behind him long ago.

"AS IT TURNS out, I may be with you for another week or so. If that's all right."

"Yeah. No problem." The cover of *Larrisa's Longing* hid Mary's face. The young woman on the cover was hurrying down a road. Behind her, a mansion burned.

"So if you need someone to stay with Shawna …"

Mary didn't look up from her book. "I told them I couldn't do nights."

The television played unwatched, filling the room with its flickering light.

"Do you like fish?" Mary lowered the book. "I was going to make fish on Sunday."

"Dresana had a way with fish," Foster said, to keep the conversation going. "She'd saute onions and garlic and make a delicate —"

"Who?"

"Dresana. My maid."

Mary goggled at him. "You had a maid?"

"Everybody in Dubai has a maid. Well, not everybody. Most people."

"Lucky them. Tyler's coming for dinner on Sunday. It won't be anything fancy. Mom was the big cook. Not me."

Foster nodded. There would be pots steaming on every burner, grand opera pouring from the stereo, *Celeste Aida*, *Caro nome*, Kathleen flitting from counter to counter, sipping wine, slicing and dicing, conducting the music with a chef's knife. Was Mary reliving the tension, wondering if tonight the opera and the wine would sweep Kathleen into dark waters?

"FOSTER?" MARY SAID, turning away from the stove. "I need the table."

Foster gathered the business sections of four newspapers. There was nothing in any of them about AMEB. He was about to settle himself in the beanbag chair — he was still experimenting, but it seemed best to hit the thing dead centre — when Shawna skipped past and flipped on her computer. Barred from the kitchen, Foster gazed at the phone like a lovesick teenager. Cedric might call, even on a Sunday. It was possible.

"Hey!" Shawna said. "There's a website about AMEB."

"AMEB?" Foster hurried over to peer at the screen. He saw nothing about AMEB. Shawna must have closed the window. "What did it say?"

"There's going to be a meeting."

"A meeting? Really? Where? When?" Foster fished his glasses from his pocket. "Can you show me?"

"No problemo." The computer, a bulky antique, took long, agonizing seconds to respond. His granddaughter had three chat sessions going, an email client open, a web browser loading, a war game raging; bullets hammered from an enormous machine gun.

"At a library. Wait. I'll print the page."

A library? The venue puzzled Foster. He had expected AMEB to face its shareholders in a conference centre or the ballroom of a hotel.

Mary dashed into the room. "We need space in here." She shoved the couch closer to the wall. "Shawna, your computer goes in your room. We talked about that, remember?"

"Hel-lo? I was going to do it."

"I'll put the newspapers away." Foster was closing the door of the middle room when Shawna staggered by with the computer monitor in her arms. "Need some help?" Shawna nodded and he took the monitor from her.

"You can't come in!" Shawna said when they stood outside her bedroom. The door was plastered with signs. *Trespassers Will Be Electrocuted! I'm Standing Right Behind This Door and I Have a Gun. Alien Autopsy in Progress.*

Puzzled by these warnings, Foster put down the monitor and went back down the hall pondering what Shawna had told him. A meeting about AMEB was a positive development. But why hold the meeting in a library? What questions should he ask? Foster took his raincoat from the closet. He needed to think.

"If you're going out," Mary called over her shoulder, "apple juice? And hey, a movie."

"Yo, I'll come too." Shawna gave Foster a sly look and threw her voice into the kitchen. "Is *Shrek* okay?"

"What? No! Get something with Johnny Depp in it. Or Vin Diesel, if it's a new one."

In Corner Convenience, Mr. Park glared at Foster, tracked him with his eyes past the shelves of snack food and the display of household batteries. Did Mr. Park take him for a shoplifter? Foster kept his hands in plain sight while Shawna led the way to a rack of movies. He stood at his granddaughter's side, scanning the titles, recognizing none of them. He was the adult. Was the choice up to him?

"They've got the new Bond. But forget that. Benny says it's lame." Down the aisle Shawna paraded, inspecting the movies like a general reviewing a regiment. "The lady wants a guy flick. And we all know what that means, don't we, boys and girls? New dude coming in. Got it! *Total Terror II.* The stupidest blow 'em up ever made."

"I'll get the apple juice," Foster said. Evidently the dinner was an important occasion. What role was he expected to play?

When they walked back into the townhouse, Mary was slapping down cutlery. A thin blue haze hung in the air.

Shawna gawked at the table. "Candles?"

"Is something burning?" Foster put the apple juice on the counter.

"Oh, shit, shit, shit." Mary ran to the stove, juggled out a pan, dropped it in the sink and turned on the tap, filling the kitchen with hissing steam.

It wasn't going well. Foster wanted to help. He stepped into the kitchen. "If we open the patio door and put on the bathroom fan, the cross draft —"

"Everything's fine." Mary pushed him away.

When the doorbell rang, Foster was hunkered down in the beanbag chair studying the printout Shawna had given him and picturing a room full of AMEB investors. Who, in all likelihood, would howl for blood. Which would be unproductive. Counterproductive, in fact. Much better to focus on a settlement. Ask for percentages. Ways and means of payment. Foster heard Mary say, "Oh! These are lovely."

"Dad? This is Tyler." Mary came into the living room with a bouquet of long-stemmed red roses in her arms. Mary's beau had a smile that came and went. He had on a pair of jeans and an expensive-looking Toronto Maple Leafs hockey sweater. There was something incomplete about him, Foster sensed, an eagerness to please. He wanted to be fair. Tyler had dressed to impress.

"Very pleased to make your acquaintance, Mr. Foster."

"Nice to meet you," Foster said as they shook hands. "Call me Foster."

Tyler turned to Mary. "Isn't that his last name?"

"That's what he likes to be called."

"How come he's all dressed up?" Tyler said.

Shawna answered this question. "He doesn't have any other clothes."

A feeling of unreality came over Foster. He might have been a mannequin.

"I'll put these in a vase," Mary said, giving the roses an admiring glance. She took the bouquet to the kitchen.

The candles had disappeared, Foster noticed when everyone sat down for dinner. The fancy napkins seemed familiar. He had brought them home from New York City, a gift for Kathleen. Mary had pulled out all the stops. He looked at his daughter and wondered why she had arranged this dinner party. She hadn't made up her mind about Tyler, he decided. She wanted her father's guidance.

A plate of fish sticks went around the table. "There might be some burnt ones." Mary handed the plate to Shawna, who passed it untouched to Foster. "I left them in the oven too long," Mary said.

"Long as you haven't got one in the oven." Tyler winked at Foster.

Oh my, Foster thought. He slid a blackened fish stick onto his plate, loyally taking the burnt offering out of circulation.

"Shawna, take some peas," Mary said.

Making a face, Shawna scooped a handful of peas onto her plate.

"Shawna?" Mary frowned at her daughter.

"I wasn't going to listen to it." Shawna dropped the iPod into her lap.

"What tunes you got on that thing, little lady?" Tyler asked.

Shawna shrugged, avoiding Tyler's eyes.

"Fiddy Cent?" Tyler prompted.

"No-o-o-o-o."

The serving plates went around again. If Mary wanted his opinion, Foster thought as he took another fish stick, he should learn more about this young man. "What kind of music do you like, Tyler?"

"I'm a grunge guy. Nirvana, Malfunkshun."

"Grunge. Really." Grunge was a style of music, Foster supposed. Whatever it was, he knew he wouldn't like it.

Tyler looked thoughtful. "Screaming Trees. They're okay too."

"I so hate that group," Shawna said. Catching her mother's warning glance, she picked up her fork. An awkward silence settled in.

"Let me think," Foster said, looking at Mary. "You used to like Rod Stewart." It pleased him to have come up with this.

"That was Mom."

"Oh. Well, what kind of music do you like these days?"

Tyler was looking at Mary with interest.

"All kinds," Mary said.

His daughter's evasive answer saddened Foster. The summer he and Kathleen had separated, what was the name of the boy who had hung around the house, mooning after Mary? Brent? Bradley? His father was a doctor. Foster felt a nagging guilt. He had been there for Mary's puppy love period, but for her teen years he had been half the world away, a voice on the phone, a cheque in a birthday card.

Shawna gave Mary a look of disbelief. "You don't like my stuff."

"Sure I do," Mary said.

"Yeah, right. You just adore 78violet."

Mary seemed uncomfortable. Foster wanted to rescue her. "What album would I take to a desert island?" No one had asked him this question. "Stan Kenton's *Artistry in Rhythm*." He smiled at Shawna. "It goes like this: *dee*, dah … dah dah dah *dee* dah."

Shawna looked stricken and stiffened in her chair. An air raid siren softly wailed. Tyler pulled a cellphone from his pocket. "Hi. No way! Listen, can't talk now. Catch you later. Yeah."

"Mary tells me you work for Secure-All," Foster said.

"Just part-time," Tyler said. "I have other opportunities."

"Can you be more specific?" Foster ignored Mary's glance. She should see Tyler for who he was.

"Detailing cars. Landscaping. Bar security."

Bar security. Foster nodded. This explained the mock fisticuffs the night he had bumped into Tyler in the hall.

"Are you a hockey fan?" Tyler asked. "Follow the Leafs?"

"Um," Foster said.

"Bet you played when you were a kid," Tyler said with a grin.

"Oh, it's been years since I laced on a pair of skates," Foster said with the modest smile he had used to parry similar questions in the Middle East. Hockey held no interest for him. He had learned to keep that truth to himself. Everyone in the Middle East believed Canadians were crazy for hockey, just as they believed Canadians opened their front doors to a calendar-art paradise of snow-capped mountains, rushing rivers and towering pines.

"The Leafs invited me to training camp, Mr. Foster. Okay, not their camp. It was a pre-training camp deal. I'd been playing Junior B, best season I'd ever had and I got this phone call."

"Really," Foster said. Tyler seemed too old for the hockey dream.

"They were looking for a grinder. I knew that going in."

"Grinder?" Foster said.

Tyler wiggled an imaginary hockey stick. "Dig the puck out of the corner. Knock a guy on his ass. Get the crowd into the game." Tyler's expression turned wistful. "If only I'd been a little taller, a little heavier."

"Benny and me?" Shawna said. "Last summer when we went to soccer camp? We —"

"The coaches liked me," Tyler said. "If only ..."

"Oh, well." Foster tried to look sympathetic. "You gave it your best shot." Foster had never allowed himself this excuse. Tyler's gaze slid away.

"Keep your forks." Mary snatched up the dinner plates.

They were having chocolate cake and ice cream when Mary said, "Tyler? Tell Foster your idea." Tyler shrugged. He didn't look at Foster. "Go on," Mary said. "Maybe he can give you some pointers."

Foster raised his eyebrows.

"You're giving this party?" Tyler spread his hands. "And you have wall-to-wall? And it's, like, an hour before the party and your girlfriend knocks over a glass of red wine. It's white, the carpet? Or maybe your dog takes a dump. Whatever."

Tyler handed Foster a business card. No, it was a fridge magnet.

"Party Angels! We're in and out in less than an hour, guaranteed. We clean the carpet and you rock on!" Tyler grinned at Foster.

Foster studied the fridge magnet. If Mary was in high school and Tyler turned up at the door, he would send him packing. They were looking at him, all of them, Mary with an expectant expression, Shawna with precocious intelligence in her eyes, Tyler with a hopeful grin. The hush of anticipation took Foster back to the staff meetings he had chaired at Duboco Petroleum. He was the man at the head of the table: it was his job to make people think harder. He made a tent of his fingers and said, "A carpet gets stained just before a party. How often would that happen?"

"All the time," Tyler said.

"How do you know that?" Foster picked up his knife and leaned forward. "Statistics? Surveys? Market studies?"

"Well, pretty often." Tyler said.

"Julia Roberts?" Shawna piped in to say. "In this movie? She had this apartment? And there was this white rug and Hugh Grant, he —"

"Even assuming a high frequency of occurrence," Foster said, with a nod to Shawna. She was trying to help. "How can you guarantee the one-hour response?"

"I keep the machine in my car."

"What if another call comes in while you're cleaning a carpet?" Foster pointed his knife at Tyler. "Do you have a backup plan?"

"Backup plan?"

"A second crew?" Foster leaned back in his chair. "A mutual arrangement with another carpet cleaner?"

"Yeah, that's an idea," Tyler said. "Another cleaner."

"Oh?" Foster leaned forward again. "What would this firm charge? How soon would they get there?"

Tyler said nothing. He looked hurt. Well, too bad, Foster thought. It was a tough world.

"I'd cover the call," Mary said.

"Really?" Foster turned to his daughter. "Do you know how to operate a carpet cleaning machine?"

"Yes." Mary met Foster's eyes. "I think so."

"Tyler, do you have two machines?" Foster asked.

"Not yet."

Foster put down his knife. "So this is what you have." He spread his fingers to count the points. "No market research. No backup plan." Foster looked at Mary. "And yet you're willing to quit your job and —"

"Who said anything about quitting my job?"

"But Mary, think it through." Shawna was watching him intently,

Foster noticed. She was a smart girl. "What if you're at work when the second call comes in?"

"I wouldn't be at work!" To Foster's astonishment, Mary's eyes filled with tears. She jumped to her feet and strode out of the house. Tyler went after her. Foster stared at the open front door. He had been trying to help. He looked at Shawna. His granddaughter pushed away from the table, went to the living room and clicked on the television. Leaving Foster sitting alone.

[THREE]

THE LIBRARY HAD wide steps, tall windows, a nook over its doors where pigeons sat huddled with their heads tucked under their wings. Foster stepped along the sidewalk, leaning into the wind, cursing the cold. The library had seen a hundred winters. To Foster, it seemed ancient. The sheiks thought nothing of tearing down a ten-year-old skyscraper to erect something higher, more fantastic.

Why, he wondered as he went through the front door, would AMEB hold a meeting here? A library was a place to read Dr. Seuss. The rows of computers reassured him; behind its gilded age facade, the library had gone high tech. A computer-generated sign directed him downstairs. Down the steps Foster went, into an overheated room buzzing with chatter.

The audience sat on folding chairs. The men wore expensive-looking safari outfits bristling with flaps and pockets. Many of them had neatly trimmed white beards. The women wore ski outfits, stretch pants and Alpine sweaters. Snapshots were passed from hand to hand. As Foster walked up the centre aisle he glimpsed a photo of a Shih Tzu wearing a pink ribbon, a photo of children playing on a lawn. Foster stumbled along a line of knees and took a seat.

A wavering shape coalesced into a spill of brown hair, a glint of silver, a woman's attentive face. A beauty once, and attractive still, she was tall — his height, nearly — and she wasn't dressed for après-ski. Her black camisole swooped down to reveal the tops of her breasts. Her silk jacket, red — Chinese, judging by the cut and calligraphy — came to the middle of her thighs. She wore black tights, Capezio dance shoes. Her earrings, intricate gadgets of stars and moons, spun in all directions. Her perfume had an orange scent.

"Cold out there," Foster said, taking off his raincoat. He glanced at the front of the room. "Has the presentation begun?"

"Not yet. We're supposed to introduce ourselves to our neighbour. My name is Jessica Vivara." Jessica shook her head sadly. "I started teaching right after art school. Just a scared kid, not much older than my students. I threw myself into my teaching. My art could wait, I told myself."

"Um." Foster scanned the room for bankers.

"A year ago I'm in the common room and there's a notice on the bulletin board. Don't you love bulletin boards? Last year I did a series of found collage. Anyway. 'Live your dream,' the notice says. So I go to the seminar. 'Cash in your pension,' the guy says. 'Let the pros invest your money. Don't miss the best stock market in history.' He made giving him my money sound like a moral duty. Hey, I'm doing all the talking."

Foster looked down. Jessica's hand had settled on his arm. She had long, slender fingers. Glossy fingernails with pearlescent half moons. There was a trace of yellow paint in the whorls of a knuckle.

"So I packed in the teaching and I cashed my pension and I let this guy handle the proceeds. What do I know about investments? He put it in this AMEB thing, and poof! It's gone." Jessica tilted her head, setting her earrings in motion, altering the orbits of the moons and stars. "You know something?" She looked at Foster thoughtfully. "Maybe he did me a favour. I'll have to take my art seriously now."

"It's good to take things seriously." Foster looked around again.

"You know what really bugs me? The little prick who did the seminar? He's selling oceanfront property in Nova Scotia. God save the widows and orphans. The lots he's peddling are probably underwater."

"Is that Coco you're wearing?" Foster turned in his chair. In the Gulf you noticed a woman's eyes, and Jessica Vivara had lovely eyes, brown with flecks of jade. "I lived in the Middle East. Scent is unisex over there. One of the men I worked with wore Chanel No 5."

Jessica looked at him in surprise. "Really?"

As they went through the icebreaking exercise, she told him she had been married. Her husband had died two years after their wedding. She had no children. Foster kept the personal information to a minimum. Jessica listened so attentively that he went on to tell her she would like the desert: the sand, the shapes, the silence. "The light changes just before sunset," he told her. The watchful part of his mind sounded a warning, a blast like an air horn. Why was he chatting this woman up? "The dunes change colour."

"Shh!" hissed someone sitting behind them.

Jessica spun around. "Oh, shush yourself."

At the front of the room, a man with a serious demeanour stood waiting for silence. When silence came, he waited a moment longer. "My name is Kevin Koch and I want to thank you for coming here tonight." Koch's clear, churchy voice commanded the room.

"I didn't come here tonight to listen to a lot of smooth talk," a voice called. "I put my money in your bank in good faith. I want my money back."

"Yes!" another voice chimed in.

"That's right!"

"Hear, hear!"

The protest swelled to a chorus. Foster felt indignation well up within him. AMEB had a lot to answer for.

"I'm not with AMEB," Koch said mildly.

Not with AMEB? Foster stared in surprise. If Koch wasn't from the bank, why were they here?

"I worked hard for that money," a reedy voice called from the other side of the room. Foster craned his neck. The man who had spoken had leathery skin and a squinting gaze that suggested a lifetime of outdoor labour.

"I'm not with AMEB," Koch said again.

"Know what my financial advisor says?" a voice called. "There's nothing left to divide."

Foster blinked. This couldn't be true.

"As I told Pete when we were doing the icebreaker," Koch said. A man in a safari outfit raised his hand. "I'm just a retired human resources supervisor who lost his money in AMEB."

"The money's lost?" a woman said, in the suddenly alert tone of someone waking up halfway through a movie. A deep hush fell over the room. The data projector's fan cycled on, making a sound like a desert wind.

"Let's leave that to the experts." Koch stepped back and pulled down a screen.

Experts like Cedric, Foster thought.

"I called this meeting to bring us together." Koch bent over a laptop. Words swam into focus: *A Mission Statement for the Victims of AMEB.*

"Oh, my God." Jessica gripped Foster's arm. "He's one of them."

Foster knew what Jessica meant. During his last years in the Middle East, the craze for mission statements — and focus groups and core values — had swept over Duboco Petroleum like a biblical plague. After the company let him go, a counsellor turned up in his office, an earnest little woman named Carol. "What are your goals?" Carol kept asking. "Who is Daniel and where is he going?" To shut her up, Foster told her he was going to Thailand. He was going to sit in the sun for many long years, and then he was going to die.

"Are we actually going to do something?" a woman asked.

Koch drew a Magic Marker from a pocket. "Let's get the mission statement first. Everything flows from that. Who's got the opening?"

"To meet the needs of Canadian investors," someone offered.

"Good." Koch scribbled the phrase on a flip chart.

"How about, 'to aggressively meet the needs of all AMEB investors.'"

"Good." Koch wrote this down.

"'To aggressively and compassionately meet the needs of all AMEB investors everywhere.'"

"Good."

The mission statement grew longer and longer. Good, Koch kept saying, good. There was no help here, Foster decided. He should go back to the townhouse and phone Cedric. He got to his feet. Jessica sprang up at the same instant. Their heads bumped. They made their way to the foyer and stood looking out at the night. Branches thrashed in the wind. Thunder rumbled. Rain rattled down.

WAS THAT DAVE BRUBECK? Yes, the tune was "Take Five." Foster opened his eyes. The complex rhythm came from a paint-splattered radio balanced on a step ladder. He was in a big room, lying on a futon. Jessica Vivara's loft had walls of orange brick and a high ceiling braced by wooden beams. Sunlight slanted through factory-style windows, spilled over a trestle table chockablock with sketchpads and brushes and tubes of oil paint. Jessica was walking toward him carrying a wicker tray. She had on a white terrycloth robe and she was smiling at him in a way that made him nervous. She was halfway across the room when the robe fell open and slipped down her back to trail from her arms. Beneath her feet the floor shone like sunlit water. For Foster, art came down to a handful of iconic images, and here was Botticelli's Venus, the nymph on the half shell, rising from the sea. But Jessica was no Renaissance nymph. She had strong shoulders, ample breasts and a herringbone scar on her abdomen. She slid a hip on the bed and set down the tray and poured coffee into a pair of chipped mugs. Why hadn't the woman fastened the robe? She didn't seem to notice that it had fallen open. Foster glanced at the apartments across the street, at the blinds hanging above Jessica's windows. Had the blinds been down last night? How soon could he decently leave? He looked around furtively for his clothes, saw them hanging on a chair, saw Jessica watching him, saw her smile turn sour. He looked at his watch. "Is that the time?"

"Places to go?" Jessica gave him a twisted smile. "People to see?"

"As a matter of fact —"

"Got a story the lady will buy? Let me guess. You broke a tooth and the dentist is coming in early."

Avoiding Jessica's eyes, Foster reached a hand for his pants. The one night stand was a set piece. A farce. He knew his part well — he had played it often enough — but Jessica was upstaging him, stealing his lines. He dressed quickly. Jessica belted her robe and stared at him.

At the door she deflected his kiss and pressed a slip of paper into his hand. "Call me. Wait, I might be out. Give me your number."

Foster blurted out Mary's number. The door closed in his face.

The air was fresh and cool, the autumn sky streaked with red. Foster had walked a block when it dawned on him that he had no idea where he was going. He drifted to a stop and with strangers rushing past him, took a bearing from the sun and consulted a mental map of the city, a map so out-of-date that in his imagination it curled like old parchment. A pirate's map with galleons on wavy seas and *Here be monsters* written on islands that might or might not exist. But then, in his desert rambles, he had found his way with less to guide him. Jessica's loft was located near the lake, Foster realized. This was the old industrial district near Spadina Avenue, below Queen. The low-rise factories — had he visited one of them with his father, carried a box of carpenters' aprons to the car? — had been converted to chic condos. Fashion District, read the superscript on the street signs. He passed a café where a waiter was arranging wire chairs around marble-topped tables. The whizz of cappuccino makers had replaced the whirr of sewing machines.

On the way to Mazurka Street, Foster rode a bus, a streetcar, the subway. The people around him were young, well-groomed, smartly dressed, and they seemed to look right through him. He was a ghost, lingering in the world of work. He should be in Thailand, savouring an afterlife of leisure. Jessica wouldn't ring Mary's number, he decided. She would leave well enough alone.

WHEN HE CAME INTO the kitchen, Mary was lacing up her boots. She gave him a speculative look but didn't ask about his overnight absence. Foster was grateful for that. The moment he had the kitchen to himself, he phoned London.

"Always good to chat with you," Cedric Richards-Henderson said when he came on the line. "But there's nothing new to report."

"Cedric, I want you to cut me a cheque."

Cedric said nothing.

"I've thought it over. If the recovery is going to take time, I might as well wait it out in Thailand. Send me an advance. It doesn't have to be much." Foster ran some numbers in his head. Airfare. A short-term lease on a flat. Food and drink. A second-hand sedan. Walking around money. "Fifty thousand US should do."

"Can't be done."

"Cedric?"

Today's hold music was "Claire de Lune." Foster was talking to Debussy. Annoyed, he hung up the phone and picked up the newspaper.

The financial page featured a photograph of the man who had brought AMEB down. David Corman, the disgraced president, the ex-whiz kid who had overturned Foster's apple cart, looked like a schoolboy. No, he was too old for that role.

Peter Pan at forty was more like it. Harry Potter without the magic. The sidebar story didn't make Foster any happier: *Not Responsible for AMEB, Say Banks, Governments.* Foster set out on his morning walk, wondering what to do next.

THAT EVENING HE put down the paper, struggled up from the beanbag chair and went into the kitchen. Mary was doing the dishes. She had on a pair of jeans and a sweatshirt lettered, *Toronto Cops are Tops.* Foster took a tea towel from the oven door and picked a mug from the draining board. "I'll be with you a while longer. If that's okay."

"No problem." Mary kept her eyes on the sink.

She seemed to have forgiven him for the night Tyler had come for dinner. Foster opened a cupboard and set the mug on a can of pears. Mary would have more space if she did a little organizing. "We should talk about money."

Mary shook the water from a handful of cutlery. "Don't start with the allowance."

"Oh, we can talk about that later. The point is, I'll pay my share of the expenses. You keep track and when I get a settlement, I'll write you a cheque."

"Don't worry about it." Mary rattled a plate into the drying rack. "You're in a tight spot."

"I don't want to be a burden. Tell you what. Go over your accounts. Let me know how much I should give you for room and board."

"Go over my accounts." Mary dunked a pot in the suds and scrubbed at a blob of burned-on spaghetti sauce. "Yeah, I'll do that."

"Meanwhile, if there's anything I can do to help ..."

Mary gave him a sidelong look. "Like what?"

Like what. Foster thought a moment. "Well, if they put you back on nights and you need a babysitter ..." Mary said nothing. He couldn't read her reaction. "Or, if Shawna needs help with her homework ..."

For the first time in many days, Mary looked at him directly. "She could use a hand with math, Foster. I'm hopeless at math. As if you didn't know."

"Of course. I'll be glad to help." Pleased with the way things were going, Foster went into the living room. Shawna sat before her computer. He gazed over her shoulder. His granddaughter snapped the program window closed.

"As it turns out, I'm going to be staying with you a while longer. You'd like that, wouldn't you, young lady?"

"Oh my goodness gracious yes."

Fair enough, Foster thought. He had pitched that too young. "We could spend some time together. Get to know each other."

"Want me to start calling you Grandpa?"

Grandpa. The idea filled him with horror. "Everybody calls me Foster. Why don't you call me that?" He peered hopefully at the screen. "What homework are you working on?"

"Geography." Shawna giggled. "Foster."

"Are you studying the provinces and their capitals? I learned them when I was about your age. In fact, I made up a little rhyme I can teach you. Victoria lives in BC, Ed Mountain, in Alberta ..."

Shawna looked at him shrewdly. "I've got this report to do for Ecology? We're supposed to visit a public place and measure its impact on the environment. Soil stress, waste generation, stuff like that. Can you take me to Centreville on Saturday? They changed Mom's shift and she won't let me go by myself."

"Centreville?"

"You know. On Toronto Island. Where they have the rides."

Foster glanced toward the kitchen. Helping Shawna with long division was one thing. Taking charge of her for a day was more than he had bargained for.

"Mom!" Shawna shouted.

Mary didn't answer. She was thinking it over, Foster decided, remembering her bumpy childhood, passing judgment on her father.

"Mom? Hellllo-o-o-o-o-o? Can Foster take me to Centreville?"

"Okay," Mary called. "Sure. Fine."

"There was a message on the machine for you," Shawna said in a singsong voice.

Bewildered by the conversation's sudden speed — was Centreville an amusement park? — Foster peered into the kitchen. "From London?"

"No! From your girlfriend."

"My girlfriend," Foster echoed, utterly baffled.

"Jessica."

"Oh, I see. Jessica is a lady that I met at the library."

"Girlfriend lady, you mean. She's sorry and she thinks you're hot."

What had that woman said? Foster went to the kitchen. "There's nothing on the machine."

"I wiped it," Shawna said. "We needed the space."

[FOUR]

THE *SAM MCBRIDE* churned away from the dock in the autumn sunshine. Foster and Shawna stood at the rail, watching the skyline recede.

"So, what's she like?"

Foster looked down at his granddaughter. "Who?"

"You know who."

On the bench that curved around the cabin sat an old couple with binoculars hanging from their necks, a group of spandex-clad cyclists with their hands on their bikes, and a ragged man gazing at the sky with a shopping bag in his hand. The bag held all he owned, Foster was uncomfortably certain.

"So, what's she like?"

Desperate for a change of subject, Foster pointed at the CN Tower, shook his finger and in a reedy voice said, "To a man standing in the middle of the harbour, the skyline of Toronto resembles the 1939 World's Fair."

"Nobody can stand in the middle of the harbour," Shawna scoffed. "Except maybe Jesus."

"Why, that tower looks just like the Trylon." It occurred to Foster that he was imitating Batty Burford, one of his high school teachers.

A trip to the '39 fair had been the high point of Batty's life. Feed Batty a leading question, and off he would go, even on a test day. Foster had his imitation of Batty down pat. Shawna seemed unimpressed.

"Okay, what does she do?"

"Who?"

"Jessica."

"Oh, right. She was a schoolteacher."

"Was?"

"She retired last year."

"Retired? How old is she? Ninety?"

A young woman who seemed scarcely older than Shawna went past with a baby strapped to her chest. She was wearing a backpack and pushing a stroller piled high with bottles and blankets and toys. Scallops of sweat arced down her black tee shirt. Foster watched as she trundled down the deck. She might have been a miner, pushing a cart of ore.

"What grade did she teach?"

Shawna's tone suggested that this was an important question. Foster put his hands on the rail. A sailboat came about smartly and heeled over with a rattle of sailcloth. "I don't know."

"Did she teach math? Music? Phys Ed.?"

The woman with the baby went by again. She was pacing to help the baby sleep, Foster realized. Why had he thought so harshly of this young mother? He leaned his arms on the rail to bring his head level with Shawna's. "Jessica taught art."

"Why did she quit? Did she get fired?"

"She wanted to do something else." Foster gave Shawna a wry smile. They saw the world from opposite ends of a lifetime of work.

"What does she do all day?"

"I don't know. She paints."

"Paints what?"

"Paintings."

"Well, duh! What kind?"

"Big ones and little ones." From the little he had seen, Jessica covered canvases with bursts of colour.

Overhead, a flock of gulls wheeled and cawed. The props reversed, spinning the water to foam. The ferry lurched, throwing Shawna off balance. Foster grabbed her shoulder. What if she had fallen and broken an arm? She shook off his grip. "Do you like her pictures?"

"Oh, sure."

"Do you like them a lot, or just a little bit?"

"Can we talk about something else?"

They walked down the landing ramp. Shawna ran past a line of flagpoles. As Foster hurried after her, he looked up to see the Stars and Stripes fluttering beside the Canadian flag. In his childhood it would have been the Union Jack flanking the Red Ensign.

"Ever been here?" Shawna asked. She had waited for him to catch up.

"A long time ago. My father brought me here."

"Your father? My great-grandfather? That must have been ages ago."

It startled Foster to think of Irv, occasional buyer of ice cream cones and catcher's mitts, as a great-grandfather. On that long ago summer day — the annual picnic of the Wholesale Hardware Association — Irv had a cardboard boater on his head and a name tag pinned to his shirt. *My name is Irv and your business I deserve!* And he was three sheets to the wind. The expression seemed apt to Foster, Irv afloat on a sea of booze, blown where whimsy took him. As he walked along with Shawna, Foster remembered fields of wild grass and streets of decaying cottages, sunburned faces, galvanized coolers sweaty with ice.

Shawna took his hand and started to run. She pulled him under a canopy of maple trees and past a row of wire-mesh wastebaskets. Foster caught a familiar smell, a dead fish and algae scent he recognized as

Lake Ontario in autumn. *CENTREVILLE / IT'S GREAT TO BE A KID!* a sign read. Foster studied the crowd heading into the amusement park. They were too old for this, he and Shawna. He had twenty years on the parents streaming past him to the ticket booth, and Shawna had three years on any kid in sight. Yet here she was, bouncing beside him, clapping her hands in excitement. The business about the homework assignment was a pretext, he thought now.

A bored teenage girl sold him a day pass. Shawna led him down another sidewalk lined with flags. So many flags! Since when were Canadians so crazy for flags? Shawna gestured him on, spinning around, skipping back, running forward again. She whooped and ran to a ride, a giant whirligig. Foster jogged across the lawn after her. A big fibreglass bee came gliding down, a whiskery roustabout with dead eyes lifted a steel bar, Shawna clambered into the bee. Foster climbed aboard and sat with his hands cupped on his knees. Up went the bee. Around it circled, emitting a metallic whine that reminded Foster of aircraft turbines. Well, he thought, as the bee whizzed around and around, at least he was airborne again. If this thing made a stopover in Frankfurt, he could pick up a Cathay Pacific flight to Bangkok. He remembered an old joke about Christ returning to earth — and having to change planes in Frankfurt.

When they were back on the path, Shawna eyed him. He recognized the look. All his life people had made this bewildering demand. It wasn't enough for them to be happy. They needed him to be happy too. For Shawna's sake he managed a grin. "That was fun, wasn't it?"

Shawna grinned back. "Want to go again?"

"The bee? Again? Really? Oh, sure."

They rode the bee three times, the Antique Carousel four times, the bumper boats once, the miniature Ferris wheel twice. They paddled about in a plastic swan and see-sawed through the Haunted Barrel Works. They had lunch in an outdoor restaurant. Foster paid for their order, and with Shawna over at the condiments table slathering mustard on her hot dog, he flipped through his wallet. He was down to his last hundred. Lifting his can of ginger ale, he drank a silent toast to the accountants sifting through the wreckage of AMEB.

"Want another hot dog?" he asked Shawna.

"No, I'm good."

"No, thank you."

Shawna looked across the lawn. "Dex used to get on my case about please and thank you."

"Dex?"

"Dex was pre-Tyler." Shawna put down her bottle of orange pop and thought a moment. "Wait. Pre-Tyler and pre-Percy."

Foster took this in. Mary hadn't told him about any of these men. "Tyler seems very nice." He watched Shawna for a reaction to this trial balloon. The shrug she gave him seemed years too old for her.

"More rides?" Foster asked.

"Yes, please, Mr. Foster, sir!"

By three o'clock he was dizzy from all the spinning, bobbing, swaying. His back was sore. His feet hurt.

"Hey! Miniature golf!" Shawna shouted, and charged off.

Foster trooped after her. He was knocking his ball through the door of a windmill when Shawna stuck her chin on the end of her putter and looked at him. "Does she do anything else? I mean, she's home all day."

"Who's home all day?" Foster watched his ball travel over a green carpet.

Shawna rolled her eyes. "Jessica."

Hadn't they exhausted this subject?

Shawna knocked her ball under a swinging log. She turned to Foster. "Do I look like my great-grandfather?"

The question took Foster by surprise. He smiled. "You're much prettier."

"Come on, really. Do I?"

Foster looked at his granddaughter. There was something of Irv in Shawna, in her eyes especially, an impish intelligence, an off-centre take on things. "Well, sure. I suppose."

Shawna nodded. The link to an ancestor seemed to please her. "Dez and Damian? They look so-o-o-o much like each other."

"Damian?" Was this another of Mary's lost beaus? Foster was losing track.

"Damian! On *Restless World*. Is Jessica a potter? Does she get naked and sit at that wheel thing? Like in that old movie?"

Foster stared at his granddaughter. Get naked? What had that woman said in the erased phone message? Shawna scampered away to join a line of kids waiting to ride the Log Flume. Foster trudged after her. When their turn came, they climbed into a cartoon version of a log. Up the incline clanked the log. Up went Shawna's arms. Foster raised his arms too. The log plunged down, splashing into a trough, sending water flying. The plunge was so unexpected and Shawna's joy so evident that Foster had to laugh. They climbed out of the log and stood again on the path. Foster remembered the reason Shawna had given him for coming here. "What about your research?"

"Benny's got it covered. I have to pee."

"Oh," Foster said.

They circled a sandbox. A toddler sat swatting the sand with a tiny plastic shovel. Shawna ran toward a washroom.

"I'll be over there," Foster called after her. "Under that big willow tree. On the bench. Do you hear me? Over there on the bench."

Shawna spun on a foot. "Fine. Okay. All right. I got it." He seemed to have embarrassed her.

The bench, as he stiffly approached the willow and its patch of shade, was as inviting as an oasis. Not that there was anything fancy about an oasis. They were usually just a bowl of rock where water collected and a few palm trees grew. A young woman was pushing a stroller toward the same bench. She was the circling mother from the *Sam McBride*, Foster realized. What was the etiquette on sharing benches with unescorted women in modern Canada? In the Middle East, it was unthinkable. "Do you mind if I sit down?"

The woman gave him an appraising glance, and nodded. He eased himself down gratefully, slid forward to rest his back and closed his eyes. The early October sun had a thin, accumulative warmth. Very good people were sorting through AMEB's files, finding stray dollars and sending them his way.

"My name is Melissa."

"Foster."

"Can I say something personal?" Melissa had a high, nasal voice.

Personal? Foster snapped his eyes open. Had he offended her somehow?

"I think it's wonderful, the way you're spending the day with your daughter."

Daughter. That was good to hear. Foster set his arm on the top of the bench and turned his head. "Well, thank you. Shawna's my granddaughter, actually."

"It's the best thing about Toronto."

"Yes, the amusement park is fun."

"Interracial marriage. It's the only hope. I wish I'd gone with a person of colour."

"Um." Shawna's background was none of this person's business.

"It's what makes us different from the States. All that prejudice down there."

"Are you from the States?"

"Heavens, no. I'm from a dinky little place north of Toronto."

"Oh? Where?"

"No place you'd know. It's called Flesherton."

"North of Shelburne on Highway 10? Main street set in a valley? Big hardware store owned by the Petersons?" Foster had been there with Irv.

"Never heard of any Petersons, but yeah, that's where I was born."

"Beautiful little place."

"Beautiful!" Melissa snorted. "Try retarded." She arranged the baby on her lap. The infant began to bawl.

Was this the moment to say how cute the baby was? Foster twisted in his seat. Melissa had tugged up her T-shirt and attached the baby to a breast. The child began to suck noisily. Foster stared up at the willow tree. Light flickered through the turning leaves.

"Breastfeeding doesn't bother you?"

"Oh, no." Foster gazed into the interior of the tree.

"I'm so glad you feel that way. That's so unusual in an older person."

"It's a natural bodily function." To be performed behind closed doors.

"Our bodies tell us everything. All we have to do is listen."

Foster studied the sere yellow leaves and the scraps of blue sky. What was his body telling him? *Gather ye rosebuds.* Because death is coming up behind you, fella, and it's gaining ground every day.

"I came here in the third month."

"In March?" Foster was looking at the opposite shore.

"No, in January. My third month. It was really cold. I walked to the far side of the island and I stood in the wind with my hands on my belly so Megan could hear the waves crashing on the rocks."

The woman's odd story touched Foster. "I came here as a child. There was a town here then. A street with shops and a movie theatre. And the most marvellous merry-go-round." He pointed across the lawn. "We played games over there, where the Ferris wheel is now. Three-legged races. Carry the egg on a spoon."

"Your mother made this a special place for you."

"My father brought me, actually. My mother died when I was three."

"Oh, I'm so sorry. About your mother, I mean. Good for your

father."

Yes, good for Irv. Even if he had passed out and fallen through a sling chair.

"Where's your daughter?"

"Mary? She's working today."

"Your granddaughter, I mean."

Startled into alertness, Foster stared at the entrance to the washroom. He scrambled to his feet. Scanned right. Scanned left. Shawna was nowhere in sight. "She went over there to the washroom. She should be back by now."

"Oh, my." Melissa snuggled the baby into the chest carrier. "I'll go and see if she's there. You stay here and watch my stroller." She jumped to her feet. "What's her name?"

"Shawna. Her name is Shawna."

Melissa strutted away, her sandals flapping against her heels. Foster concentrated his gaze on the entrance to the washroom, trying to stay calm, willing his granddaughter to appear. When Melissa emerged from the washroom alone, walking faster, breaking into a run, his heart sank. "She's not in there," Melissa called across the lawn.

"Not in there?" Foster said in a faltering voice. He clambered onto the bench and looked around frantically.

"Every minute counts in these cases. They're likely still on the island."

These cases? They? Yes. Shawna had been abducted. She would be murdered. He had been unforgivably negligent.

"There!" Melissa cried.

"Thank goodness!" Foster hopped down from the bench, giving his ankle a painful twist.

But Melissa was gesturing to a policewoman, a young officer riding a knobbly-tired bicycle. "Yoo-hoo! Over here!"

The policewoman turned her bike and began to pedal over. Melissa took off in a splay-footed run. Foster hobbled after her. She turned and tossed him a cellphone. “I’ll give the cop the description. You phone her mother.”

If you can keep your head when all about you / Are losing theirs … Foster flipped open the cellphone. He couldn’t call Mary. Not yet. How could Melissa give the police a description of Shawna? Of course. She had seen Shawna on the ferry.

“Phone for help!” Melissa yelled, seeing him hesitate. “Every second counts!” She bounced across the grass, cradling her baby’s head with a hand.

Phone who? Cedric Richards-Henderson? Foster fished a slip of paper from his pocket and punched in a number.

The phone rang. Rang again. Rang a third time.

“Jessica? It’s Foster.”

“Foster … Foster … Now let me think … Tall? Good looking? Give me a minute. I slept with a lot of men that night.”

“What?”

“Hello, Foster. Hello.”

“How are you?” Foster asked, and felt like a fool. He had an emergency on his hands.

“Well, now, how am I? I’d like to lose ten pounds. I broke a nail stretching a canvas. Some damn bank swallowed three hundred thousand bucks I sort of needed. One of the sketches I did this morning, I kind of like. The first man I let touch me in three — no, five years — didn’t return my calls, but I’m just jim-dandy. And how are you?”

“My granddaughter has disappeared. We think someone may have taken her. We rode the Log Flume but she’s not in there and we can’t —”

“Foster, slow down. Where are you?”

“Toronto Island. You know. Where they have the rides.”

“You’re there with her parents?”

"No, my daughter's at work. She's a security guard. I can't reach her."

"You mean you're alone?"

"No. Someone's helping me. Melissa. She's from Flesherton. It's all my fault."

"I'll get there as fast as I can. Have you called the police?"

"Yes. They're on their way." The policewoman was riding toward him, standing on the pedals of her bike. Melissa was running alongside. The baby was bawling.

"Don't meet me," Jessica said. "I'll find you."

The phone clicked off and Foster stuffed it into his pocket.

"What's up?" Shawna asked. She was standing beside him with a cone of pink candy floss in her hand.

"Where were you?" Foster took Shawna by the shoulders and gave her a shake.

"Hey!"

"Shawna?" A burst of static issued from the little radio strapped to the policewoman's shoulder. She had a gun in her hand. "Step away from the child, sir. I need you to step away now." The gun was aimed at his heart. Foster's mind cleared. It wasn't a real gun. It was one of those new electrical things. The high voltage would knock him down, scramble the micro-pulses that kept his heart beating. It might kill him.

"Do you know this man?" The policewoman edged between Foster and Shawna. "Sir, I need you to step back and put up your hands."

Foster raised his hands. The policewoman was a looker. He would die at the hands of a beautiful woman. There were worse ways to go.

"Yeah, I know him. He's my grandfather."

"She wasn't in the washroom," Melissa said.

"I went to get some candy floss."

The stun gun was back in its holster. Foster lowered his hands. The policewoman tilted her head and spoke into her radio. The call was a false alarm. She looked at Foster, and then at Shawna. "You need to be more careful, both of you. There's some real crazies out there."

"Yes," Foster said. "Sorry."

"Don't let it spoil your day," the policewoman said. "Just keep an eye on each other."

"I wasn't lost," Shawna said. "And I am careful."

"That's the stuff," The policewoman mounted her bike and cycled away.

For a moment no one spoke. Foster took out his handkerchief and wiped cotton candy from his hand.

"Hiya," Melissa said. She told Shawna her name.

"Hi." Shawna gave Melissa a wary look.

"Well!" Foster stuffed his handkerchief in a pocket. "Why don't we all sit down and catch our breath?"

"I've got to get going," Melissa said. But she stood her ground.

What was he supposed to do? Kiss her? Surely not. Shake her hand? People were always hugging each other these days, Foster had noticed. He put out his arms and stepped forward.

Melissa danced back. "I want my phone. You put it in your pocket."

"Oh! So I did." Foster handed her the phone. "Thank you for your help."

"Yeah. Thanks a lot," Shawna said in a flat voice.

With a curt nod, Melissa clipped the phone to her gym shorts and set off down the sidewalk, pushing the stroller with grim energy.

Shawna gave Foster an amused look. "You must think I'm a little kid or something."

"I'm sorry I shook you. It's just that — where are you going?"

"Over there. To toss this cone in the garbage."

Foster hurried after Shawna. He took her hand. Shawna yanked her hand free. "Were you really going to keep that hippy lady's phone?"

"No, of course I wasn't. Oh. I called Jessica."

"You called Jessica?" Shawna said, vastly pleased.

"We should head for the dock. I'll have to call her back. Tell her not to come." Foster looked around. "You didn't see a pay phone, did you, when you were lost?"

"First of all, I wasn't lost. Second, a pay phone? Hello? Do they even have those anymore? I'm like, the only person in my whole school that doesn't have a cellphone."

"Let's walk to the dock. Maybe there's a pay phone there."

"Betcha there isn't."

"Well, fine. That's where she'll land."

They began to walk, Foster plodding along, Shawna parading ahead of him, crossing her feet, swinging her hips, throwing glances side to side as if she were a fashion model strolling down a runway. The air had taken on a chill. The sun was low in the sky.

"Will she be mad at me, do you think?" Shawna asked.

"What? Who? Jessica? Oh, no. She'll understand. It wasn't your fault."

"Will she be mad at you?" Shawna skipped ahead.

"Shawna, walk with me? Please? Is that too much to ask?"

"Whatever." Shawna fell in at his side.

After a moment Foster said, "Why would Jessica be angry with me?"

"Maybe she was painting this famous masterpiece and now she'll never finish it."

"Shawna — look. She won't be angry."

"Betcha you're wrong. Betcha your girlfriend will be really mad."

"She's not my girlfriend."

"Is so."

Foster said nothing.

"Betcha five bucks."

"Now, see here, Mary!"

"Mary? Mary's my mother. I'm Shawna, remember? Foxy kid? Dresses cool on a budget of like, zero?"

At the dock, cyclists and parents and sleeping children waited for the ferry. Foster shielded his eyes with a hand and peered across the harbour. Shawna giggled. "You look like one of those explorer guys on Discovery. You know, the ones who wear piss helmets."

"Pith helmets." He looked across the water again, and then turned his head to look at Shawna. "Listen, maybe we shouldn't tell your mother about thinking you were lost."

"Keep it a secret, you mean. Okay, but we have to tell each other a secret. Something we did that was awful. I'll go first. One time when Gramma Kathleen conked out on the couch? Her purse was right there and I took some money. Your turn."

"Shawna, this is hardly the time —"

"Here comes the ferry," Shawna sang.

The *Sam McBride*, its engines loudly reversing, had almost reached the dock. Jessica stood in the bow with her shoulders back and her hair lifting in the wind. She had on a painter's smock. A welter of emotion buffeted Foster. Shawna wanted a secret. "I didn't go to my father's funeral. I had an exam the next day. I stayed in my room and studied."

"Okay," Shawna said.

The ferry surged back, skewed to one side, came at the dock again. The gangway went down and Jessica came striding toward them.

"Hi!" Jessica gave Foster a quick hug and slipped her hand under his arm.

"My name is Shawna."

"Oh," Foster said. "Shawna, this is Mrs. Vivara."

"Thank you very much for coming, Mrs. Vivara."

"Call me Jessica."

"Okay," Shawna said with a smile.

"I'm so glad you're all right. What lovely hair you have."

"Thank you. It's a Dutch braid. I'd be happy to show you how to do it. It's pretty easy. You go over the middle first."

Foster looked at Shawna in astonishment. Suddenly, she was Little Miss Manners. He turned to Jessica. "It was just a mix-up."

Jessica nodded. "Melissa told me all about it."

Foster blinked. The cosmos had spun out of control. How could Jessica have talked to Melissa?

"I called that number back," Jessica said, seeing his surprise. "Melissa answered."

Foster followed Shawna and Jessica onto the ferry, wondering if he understood anything at all.

"THERE'S A THAI place that delivers." Jessica was sitting cross-legged on the bed, flipping through a phone book and fiddling with a stick-and-leather gadget in her hair. They had driven Shawna to Benny's house — Shawna had cleared this arrangement with Mary last night — waited for the front door to open and Shawna to go inside, and then driven to the loft in Jessica's little white car with Jessica talking nonstop about Duchamp's bicycle wheel and the Armory Show of 1913, artistic controversies about which Foster knew nothing. He turned his head to look at the windows. The loft, in the afterglow of their lovemaking, was a shadowy realm of easels and tables, easy chairs and chests of drawers. Paintings covered the floor, rows of canvases with aisles between them. Those strange blurry flowers. *And there were gardens bright with sinuous rills, / Where blossomed many an incense-bearing tree;* His grandmother had made him memorize this poem.

"Foster?"

"Whatever you like."

"I can't do this by myself. You have to give me something to work with."

Were they still talking about takeout food? He hoped so.

"This intense physical thing is all I have to go on."

They weren't talking about food, then. He shouldn't have phoned Jessica from Centre Island. He had raised the stakes between them; he was holding a bust hand and she had called his bluff.

Jessica looked at him. "If you have something to say, spit it out."

Another female, demanding his secrets. "Listen. I'm grateful for what you did today."

There was a silence. Then Jessica said, "You're not blowing me off that easily." She reached for the phone. "Mister, you better like pizza."

[FIVE]

"THAT WAS TCHAIKOVSKY," Foster said, staring through the patio door. "Sleeping Beauty Waltz." In the cold sunlight, the swing set was white with frost.

"Point taken," Cedric said. "I'll have Sylvia put you through straightaway next time."

"Cedric, listen to me." Foster inched his chair closer to the table. "I need that advance."

"Can't be done. Not at present."

Foster closed his eyes. "How much longer?"

"Days. Weeks. Months." Cedric's voice had a moony quality. "Difficult to say."

"Months!"

"I'm going to put you back to Sylvia. She needs a word."

"Mail for you," Sylvia broke in to say. "Shall I forward it to Canada?" Before leaving Dubai, Foster had registered Cedric's office as a forwarding address. "A stock prospectus … real estate bumf from Thailand … a statement from American Express … and two statements for your AMEB card."

"Bills from AMEB? How is that possible?"

"The credit card division is a separate corporation. Perhaps you'd like to know the outstanding balance?"

"Yes. Open the statements." Foster sank back into his chair. *I did send to you / For certain sums of gold, which you denied me.* A fat lot of good it did to remember bits of Shakespeare.

"You owe American Express five thousand, four hundred and eight point four nine. You owe AMEB Credit four thousand, seven hundred thirty-one point one seven. That's in US dollars. Shall I give it to you in Canadian funds?"

"Oh, by all means." Alone in the kitchen, Foster made an airy gesture.

"Good news," Sylvia said brightly. "The Canadian dollar is up half a cent."

TYLER TURNED UP at dinner time. Foster shuffled his chair to make room. And bumped into a wall. The townhouse seemed to shrink a bit each day, as if it were contracting with the cold.

"Hey, Fos," Tyler said, plunking himself down. "How about those Leafs?"

Fos? Foster looked at Tyler.

"The Leafs bite," Shawna said.

"Shawna, that's not a very nice thing to say." Mary handed Foster a bowl of mashed potatoes.

"Whatever." Shawna skated a green bean around her plate.

"Elbows off the table, young lady," Mary said.

Shawna made a face and dropped her arms to her sides.

"I saw Frank Mahovlich play," Foster said, to get Shawna off the hook. "At Maple Leaf Gardens."

A platter of pork chops made its way around the table. Tyler heaped food on his plate and gave Foster a grin.

"Sam and Dam?" Shawna said. "They were on this beach? And this old girlfriend of Dam's walks by? And —"

"Beats me what you women see in that stupid soap opera." Tyler winked at Foster.

"Men watch it too," Mary said.

"Girlie men." Tyler gave Foster another wink.

Foster sawed at a pork chop. He never missed *Restless World*.

Shawna looked at Mary. "Can I be excused?"

"You should say, 'May I be excused,'" Foster said.

"Can-I-may-I-whatever?"

"Go," Mary said. "I mean, yes. You may."

"I think I'll stretch my legs," Foster said a few minutes later. Seeing Tyler's amusement, he added, "If you will excuse me."

"You know what they say." Tyler winked at Foster yet again. "Excuses are for losers."

As he walked up the street Foster tried to recall another occasion when strangling a man with his bare hands had seemed a reasonable course of action. Nothing came to mind.

A FEW DAYS later, Mary stood at the stove, boiling his eggs while Foster sat at the kitchen table, leafing through a newspaper. "I got this phone bill."

Why was she telling him this? Foster peered around the newspaper.

"It's hundreds of dollars higher. All those calls to London."

The eggs rattled in the saucepan.

"Foster, I can't pay it."

"Why would you pay for my calls?"

"So, you'll pay it?"

"Of course."

"When?"

"The moment I get some cash out of AMEB."

"I was already behind with the phone bill. Foster, I can't live without a phone. They tell you that when you start at Secure-All. No phone, no job."

"Then I'll pay the bill immediately." It saddened him to see fear in his daughter's eyes. He had never meant to be a burden.

"WANT ME TO check the net?"

Foster looked up from the want ads and gave Shawna a smile. His first in many days. "Thanks, but there's no need. Before I went to Dubai I was a senior systems analyst."

Shawna gave him a blank look. "A what?"

"Systems analyst. Someone who designs information systems."

"Did you always do whatever that means?"

"No. Before I was an analyst, I wrote programs."

Shawna's gaze drifted to her old computer. "You must be really smart."

"Oh, coding is perfectly logical. I can show you sometime, if you like."

"Hey, that would be cool. Jessica called again."

"Thank you, Shawna. You told me earlier."

"She said, 'The pizza lady wants another hot one.'"

A tingle travelled up Foster's spine. What a message for Jessica to leave. Or had Shawna made it up? He scanned the want ads again. Even with the economy so fragile, there should be openings in information technology.

"Sam and Dam? They split up once. That was way before you moved in. They got back together though."

"Did they now? Well, well."

MATTRESSES *$99* ANY *Size! Printer Cartridges Refilled — Save Big $$!!*

Could this scruffy little industrial mall really be the home of Computer Professionals International? Foster pictured himself standing on a sidewalk in New York City, a rising star, a golden boy staring up at the DPC office tower.

A young man strolled past. He had spiky brown hair. He wore a black parka, a green commando sweater and a pair of jeans frayed at the knees.

"I'm looking for Computer Professionals," Foster called.

The kid in the parka gave him an incurious glance. "Follow me."

Clutching the Spiderman briefcase he had borrowed from Shawna, Foster followed the parka down a narrow hallway and into a small, windowless room. A fluorescent fixture buzzed. A partition covered with sackcloth screened a workstation. A barber's chair, a bulky anachronism of chrome and leather and porcelain, loomed over a couch upholstered in yellow vinyl. Between the couch and the chair lay a threadbare carpet. A Bakhtiari from southern Iran, Foster thought — the flowers in the smudgy medallions, the faded blues and golds. On the carpet slumbered a Great Dane, its lips curled over its huge yellow teeth, its long legs quivering in dream.

"Who should I ask?" Foster wondered aloud. There was no receptionist.

"Say what?"

Foster frowned. If this spiky-haired ragamuffin had turned up in his office … "My name is Foster. I have an appointment with Jamie Stone."

"J. Stone, president of CPI, at your service. I answer to Jamie."

It was October 31st. Was Jamie dressed for Halloween?

"Let's sit." Jamie climbed into the barber's chair. Foster unbuttoned his suit coat and settled on the couch. Where could he put his feet? The dog jerked up its head and growled at him.

"Czar," Jamie said, in a warning tone.

The dog bared its teeth. The Spiderman briefcase slipped from Foster's lap and landed on the carpet.

"Spidee," Jamie said, smiling down at the briefcase.

"As I said on the phone, I'm looking for contract work." Foster handed over the resumé he had composed on Shawna's computer.

Jamie peered at the top page. "FRMIS?"

"It's a legacy system, I realize."

"Legacy? Try ancient history. Didn't DPC go belly up?" Jamie tossed the resumé aside and pumped the barber's chair higher. "A cloud programmer I can find a home for. A Precip maven, I'd hire myself. How's your Precip, Daniel?"

Cloud programming. Foster frowned. The cloud was the Internet — your data could be anywhere in the world — and Precip was the hot new database language. Its syntax was vague and in Foster's opinion, annoyingly cute. He had read an article about Precip. To access data, the command was *rain dance*. He looked up at Jamie. "I'm familiar with the concepts."

"Hey, I'm familiar with the concept of getting laid. Doesn't get it done, does it, pilgrim?"

Foster blinked. What was he doing here, talking to a juvenile delinquent? He should pick up his ridiculous briefcase and walk out. He should try other agencies. But he had tried other agencies. "Look. I might not be up to speed on the latest technologies. A manager doesn't operate at that level of detail."

"Manager? Where you have been the last twenty years? It's all run-and-gun now. Czar?" Jamie threw a dog biscuit into the air. The dog caught the biscuit in his stained teeth and wolfed it down.

Foster snatched his resumé from the floor and handed it to Jamie. "Look at the projects I brought in, on time and on budget. Look at the number of people I supervised in Dubai."

Jamie scanned a page. "You were in the Middle East a long time. Do they still need old-style managers over there? Maybe you should go back."

Foster leaned forward. "I'm willing to take a more junior position."

"How much were you making with Duboco?"

"My last contract? A hundred and fifty thousand US. Plus housing and car."

"No shit? How much after taxes?"

"There were no taxes."

Jamie's eyebrows shot up. "And none of that stuck? What happened? Did you take stock options?"

"Something like that." Foster settled back wearily.

Jamie shook his head sadly. "Every sad-assed geek that comes through the door has stock options."

Foster got to his feet. "Look, do you have anything for me or not?" Jamie stared at Foster. He seemed to see him for the first time. "I can upgrade. Take courses." But Foster knew he was being ridiculous. Computing was a kid's game. The very thought of a thousand-page manual made him tired.

"Know what I'd do in your shoes?" Jamie said.

Czar pulled himself to his feet, gave Foster a myopic glance and wandered around the partition, his nails clicking on the floor. Foster listened attentively. If Jamie Stone had anything to tell him, he wanted to hear it.

"Last time I lost my job? I rented a hundred movies. Holed up and watched them one after another." Jamie looked into the middle distance. "Know what I learned?"

Stunned by the bizarre twist the conversation had taken, Foster shook his head.

"A movie is always about someone in trouble. You can learn a lot, watching how a guy like Tom Cruise handles himself when he's in a jam. If I were you, I'd start with *The Time Machine*."

Was Jamie putting him on? No, he was serious, Foster decided. To Jamie, pop culture had the power of scripture.

"Know something?" Jamie said. "Forget the remake. Get the original, the one with Rod Taylor. See what happens to a man who gets thrown out of his own time. MGM. 1960."

"Keep my resumé on file."

Foster walked up University Avenue at a frantic pace, hurrying past the courthouse, where bored jurors sat on benches in the sunshine, gaining speed as he walked past the hospitals, where smokers in dressing gowns stood with IV poles in their hands. A trickle of sweat ran down his back, and he fell into an economical stride. He couldn't afford to take the subway, and it would be a long walk home.

How much of his life had he given to FRMIS, tweaking loops, perfecting subroutines? Fat lot of good that devotion did him now. He was the last speaker of a dead language. Foster cut across the campus of the University of Toronto. Fresh-faced students, the unwitting inheritors of his internationalism, rushed past him, gabbing into cellphones, calling to each other in English and Chinese and Russian and Hindi. Foster sighed. He didn't need *The Time Machine* to tell him what he already knew. He was a visitor from the forgotten past.

WHEN HE OPENED the front door two hours later, a figure in crimson said, "But you promised."

"You are not going out alone," Mary said.

Shawna stamped her foot. "I'm not some dumb little kid."

"I said no."

"They're always changing your stupid shift! You've got a stupid job and I hate you!" Shawna went storming toward her room, a red plastic cape fluttering from her shoulders. Spotting Foster, she stopped abruptly and said, "What about him?"

Foster felt the weight of his daughter's gaze. Mary had always looked at him with that expression of wary curiosity, it seemed to him. As if she was trying to make up her mind about the stranger who claimed to be her father.

"Twenty feet!" Mary said. "Hear me? Don't let her get more than twenty feet away from you."

Mary's vehemence took Foster aback. Did she know about Centreville, about Shawna's disappearance? Shawna took his hand and pulled him to the door.

During his absence from Canada, Halloween had become a big deal, Foster realized as Shawna trooped from house to house with a white pillowcase slung over her shoulder. They walked past red lights burning in vestibules, lacy spider webs dangling on front porches, paper witches turning in the wind. Pirates and astronauts and ballerinas scooted up walkways, rang doorbells and shouted "Trick or treat!" His stomach rumbled hungrily. What would happen, he wondered, if he were to knock on a door in his Savile Row suit? *And what are you dressed up as, sonny?* An executive, ma'am. A has-been. A woman smoking a cigarette fell into step with him.

"Which one is yours?"

"The Spiderwoman with the plastic cape."

"Mine's the second clown on the right. The one with the axe."

Foster and his anonymous companion stopped before a house. Arranged on its front steps, a dozen illuminated pumpkins grinned like severed heads. Organ music oozed from a hidden speaker, long, lugubrious chords counterpointed by cackles of maniacal laughter.

"I dressed up as a clown when I was a kid. Some things never change, I guess." Foster glanced at the woman who stood at his side. She wore a red toque and a green hockey jacket with *Christine* embroidered over a pocket.

"Nah, it's that movie." Christine dropped her cigarette on the sidewalk and crushed it underfoot.

"Movie?" Foster said in a small voice.

"*Death Clown III*. Chloe must have rented it a hundred times. So I said the hell with it and got her the DVD."

Rent a hundred movies. "Do you think she finds some kind of meaning in the movie?"

"Beats me." Christine lit another cigarette, turned her head and hissed smoke from the side of her mouth. "The clown is a good person, basically. The people he kills have got it coming. Chloe and I are going left here. Have a good one."

That night Foster's dreams took the form of long, baffling movies — space adventures, whodunits, westerns. The actors spoke a foreign language everyone seemed to understand. Everyone but him.

THERE WERE AMPLIFIERS and DVD players on one wall of Lou's Pawn Shop, guitars and power tools on the other, watches and rings in illuminated display cases. Lou stood behind a high counter. His thinning hair was dyed black. His old suit hung loose on his frame. He had Foster's Rolex in his hand and sadness in his eyes. "A thousand is the best I can do."

Foster stared at him. "I paid over six thousand for that watch."

"Who wears a timepiece these days?" Lou waved a hand over a hundred watches. "The young people use their cellphone to check the time."

THE NOVEMBER AFTERNOON was cold. Scraps of paper blew across Foster's path. He walked down Mazurka Street with his hands in his pockets, looking up at the sky, at the milky sun and the swiftly moving clouds. Winter was on the way. The *Restless World* theme played as he came into the living room.

"What happened to Paul?" he asked when a commercial came on.

"Who?" Shawna said.

"The guy that stole the patent," Mary said.

"He didn't steal it," Shawna said. "Foster? Jessica left another message."

"But what happened to him?" Foster wanted to know.

Mary shrugged. "Sometimes they just disappear."

"Yeah, this guy Earl?" Shawna said. "He went out to get a newspaper? And he never came back."

A chill passed over Foster. He remembered a childhood superstition. Someone had stepped on his grave.

LATE IN THE hour, Samantha pulled Damian's clothes from a closet and went through the pockets, tossing his shirts and slacks on the bed. The closet was almost empty when she found a key. She stood staring at it. The credits ran. Foster wondered what the key might open. The door to a love nest? A safety deposit box? Another cliffhanger. When Mary went to the kitchen, he followed her and held out an envelope. "Room and board."

"Foster, I never said you had to pay your way. It was just the phone bill."

"I arranged for payments. There will be no interruption of service. Take the money. You can't afford to feed an extra mouth."

Why did this statement of fact anger Mary? She bent over the sink and scraped furiously at a carrot. After a moment, Foster set the envelope on the counter, went back to the living room and picked up the want ads.

WHY NOT WALK to Thailand? The ocean was made of sand and Foster strode along easily. But then the sand turned into water and he sank, deeper and deeper. A submarine sailed by. He hammered on the hull. They had to let him in.

"What the hell?" a voice roared.

Awake now, Foster realized he had been banging on the wall. He opened his door to see Tyler standing in the hallway.

"Are you okay, Mr. Foster?"

"Sorry," Foster muttered. "Bad dream."

THE NEXT MORNING Foster went to the park. He walked under bare trees and over hard ground. When he reached the zoo he found a woman sitting on his bench with a bag of peanuts on her lap. A squirrel, its bottlebrush tail erect, scampered around her shoes. The woman turned her head, and became Jessica.

"How on earth … Oh. Shawna told you."

Jessica got to her feet and watched the squirrel spin a peanut in its hands. "If I came here every day, that poor thing might put on some weight." She gave Foster a challenging look. "Want to walk some?"

They followed a path that led up a hill and past a stand of trees. Jessica walked with her hands in her pockets and her head down, Foster with his hands clasped behind him and his face tilted to the sky. It was a warm, still, autumn day, an echo of summer. Sunlight slanted across the lawns. Grenadier Pond shone like a mirror. The reeds were silver with frost. A gang of Canada geese waddled across the path, honking and swaggering. Foster watched them waddle away. "Shouldn't they be on their way south?"

"They stay all winter."

"Really." Foster looked at the geese with new sympathy.

"How are things?" Jessica asked.

"Fine. I'm thinking of going back to work."

"Computers?"

"No, I'm considering other offers." He turned his head and looked at Jessica. "The last time we spoke, you said something about going back to teaching."

"I thought about that, but you know, maybe this bank thing is a sign."

"A sign of what?"

Jessica lifted her head. "I'm an artist. I'm going to try for a show."

"Well, good for you. I think that's great." Would people pay good money for Jessica's fuzzy flowers? Perhaps they would. He had seen some odd things on the walls of boardrooms.

"Foster, is there something wrong with your phone?"

"The long distance bill you mean? Did Shawna tell you about that too?" Foster frowned. He really would have to speak to his granddaughter.

Jessica gave him a puzzled look. "Phone bill? I was hinting around about your not calling me." She picked up a pine cone and flicked it onto the pond. A goose lumbered into the air, flew a few feet, settled down again.

"I can lend you some money."

The suggestion shocked Foster. "That's very kind of you. But there's no need."

They walked along in silence.

"You've got me stumped," Jessica said. They turned and began walking north, retracing their steps. "Tell me what you want of me."

What did she mean by that? Women were a deeper mystery than modern art. Jessica deserved a response. They had slept together. She had come to his aid when he had lost sight of Shawna, and today she had offered to help him again. "Perhaps we can come to an arrangement," Foster said, trying to sound suave, a debonair character in one of those French films Kathleen liked to watch, Yves Montant strolling beside the

Seine with a Gitane smouldering between his lips. The lovers would set up a tryst, share a baguette and a bottle of *vin ordinaire*.

Jessica stopped in her tracks. "Arrangement?"

"I could come over one evening a week."

She stared at him. "You're serious, aren't you?"

There was nothing for it now. He would have to blunder on. "Would Tuesday evenings be convenient?"

"Convenient. Oh, sure. We'll have a nice cup of tea and a quick fuck."

Dumbstruck, Foster watched Jessica strut away, jump into her car and drive off. On the way back to Mazurka Street, he stopped at an Internet café, a storefront with dusty floors and dirty keyboards, and he searched for sites about working overseas. It was time to move on.

GRANDPA'S TOOLBOX HAD sent him an email? Shawna was teasing him. Two weeks had gone by since his encounter with Jessica in the park, and Foster was sunk in the beanbag chair, scanning the want ads. There were openings for bartenders, house cleaners, hairstylists. He rubbed his three-day beard thoughtfully. Why were there no ads for managers? Did the country run itself these days?

"Honest, they did!" Shawna tapped her monitor. "They sell lumber and stuff and they're opening up this great big store in Toronto."

"Now, why would they send me an email?"

"Because you asked them for a job?"

"Ah. Well, you know, I'm not sure that I did."

"I sort of applied for you."

"You sort of what?"

Parcel delivery, Foster read. *Must have own car*. Shawna was only trying to help. "Listen, I appreciate the thought, but I'm not interested. No harm done. I'll send them a note. May I use your computer for a minute?"

But when he sat in Shawna's chair and read the message from Grandpa's Toolbox, he was interested. They were a legitimate outfit, a big box retail chain based in Florida, about to enter the Canadian market. Their website featured older men demonstrating cordless drills to contractors, showing kitchen cabinets to couples, measuring pieces of wood with a pencil behind an ear. Well, why not? On his boyhood jaunts with Irv, Foster had studied hardware catalogues and poked through sample cases. The hours were flexible. He could earn walking-around money and keep looking for a real job. He had to do something. His wallet was empty. A phone bill payment was coming up. Soon, Cedric kept saying. Soon.

"Will meet with you at your earliest convenience," Foster wrote to herewegrow@grandpastoolbox.com. He stepped away from the keyboard feeling pleased with himself. He had made Shawna happy, if nothing else.

A few minutes later, Shawna called him back to the computer. A reply had come in. Grandpa's Toolbox wanted to know his education, his previous income, his employment history, his hobbies and interests. With Shawna leaning on his shoulder, Foster worked his way through a maze of icons and text boxes. Some of the questions struck him as odd. *From the list below, select an ideal grandfather.*

Shawna grabbed the mouse. Foster was curious. How did his granddaughter see him? She clicked on Yoda. An extraterrestrial. That seemed about right. The next question baffled him. *You're decorating a room for someone you love. From the list below, select a colour for the walls and a colour for the ceiling.*

Foster cocked an eyebrow. "What colours do Sam and Dam like?"

Shawna giggled. "Blue and red. Remember her bedroom?"

Suppose you were in trouble and needed advice. From the list below, select three qualities you'd like your advisor to display.

"I'll do this one," Foster said when Shawna hesitated. Compassion. Humour. Listens well.

"That stuff was on the form I did for Miss Moony."

"Miss Moony?" The name was new to Foster. "Was she one of your teachers?"

"Social worker," Shawna said. "What's next?"

Social worker?

What mistakes should your advisor avoid?

Losing a client's life savings, Foster thought. He typed, "Judging people too quickly."

"Awesome!" Shawna spun around and gave him a high five.

Later that evening, as Foster was drying the dishes — and enduring Mary's silence — Shawna sang out, "Badda Bing!" A tea towel over his shoulder, Foster peered at the screen. *Greetings, Grandpa Candidate Foster! The Here-We-Grow Team can see you at any of the following times.* He couldn't take all this seriously. But to please Shawna, he selected an appointment. The site replied immediately. *See you soon! We'll knock on your door.* The interviewer would come to the house?

"Thank you, Shawna," Foster said. "I don't know what I'd do without you." His granddaughter threw back her head and gave him an upside-down grin. For a moment, his broken, wasted life made sense.

"CHECK IT OUT!" Shawna called from the front door. "They're making a movie on our street."

"Really?" Mary rose from the couch. "Do you see anybody? George Clooney's in town. It was on the news."

Slouched in the beanbag, waiting for *Restless World* to come back on, Foster wondered vaguely who George Clooney might be. They shot movies in Toronto, he knew, American features with the city doubling as New York or Chicago. Would the commercials never end? Samantha had barricaded herself in Jed Creed's penthouse. Creed, with his swaggering arrogance and his bottomless bank account, fascinated

Foster. "That is totally the biggest movie-mobile," he heard Shawna say.

"Samantha?" Jed Creed said. "I know you're in there." Why didn't Samantha answer? Was she watching through the peephole? It seemed so, because Jed flashed his con man's smile and spread his big hands in a gesture of supplication. "Sam? Let me in, Baby. Please."

Baby? Jed and Samantha were lovers? It was possible, Foster supposed. He looked up to see Shawna standing at his side. "O-mi-god. The movie lady? She wants to talk to you."

Puzzled, Foster made his way to the front door. He had on the pants from his suit — they needed pressing — a T-shirt and an old sweater Mary had given him. The legacy of a former boyfriend, Foster suspected.

A tall, trim woman stood on the front walk with a recreational vehicle looming behind her. Foster rubbed his chin. He was down to his last razor blade and he hadn't shaved. The woman was in her early thirties, he thought, and so well groomed she seemed slightly unreal. She had on a black pantsuit and a white blouse. Her hairdo, a chic Joan of Arc thatch, was both sexy and severe. Her eyes were a clear, captivating copper-brown.

"Mr. Foster? I'm Amanda Curtwell, a team leader for Grandpa's Toolbox."

"I've been expecting you." This wasn't true. He had forgotten all about the email exchange. For the first time in his life, he had blown off a job interview.

"This way, please." Amanda Curtwell led him down the walk, up a set of folding steps and into the huge vehicle. A young man sat behind the steering wheel. He slid off his seat and introduced himself as Peter Chen. His suit, a severe pinstripe, had a stiff, off-the-rack look. In his black shirt and white tie, he looked like a teenage boy playing a gangster, Foster thought. Nathan Detroit in a high school production of *Guys and Dolls*.

"You're wondering about the RV." Chen waved Foster down the centre aisle.

"I'm sure it's a very nice way to travel." Foster couldn't take all this seriously. If this were a real job interview, he would be sitting in a proper office, not in the U-shaped dinette of a forty-foot motor home. He looked through a pane of smoked glass. A crowd had gathered on Mazurka Street. Hoping to see a celebrity, he supposed.

Amanda Curtwell reached a hand across the table and snapped down the blind. "The RV fits our staff demographic. Many of our associates own motorhomes. They feel comfortable in one and we get a sense of what they'd be like on the sales floor."

Foster took in the captain's chairs and the banks of gauges, the galley with its stove and dishwasher, the living area with its beige leather couch and flat-screen television.

"This model has SatTrak," Peter Chen said, following Foster's gaze. "On the drive up from Florida, we had CNN all the way."

A copy of *Never Business as Usual* lay on the dinette table. "Think outside the big box," Foster said. He picked up the book and leafed through its pages.

Amanda Curtwell smiled at him. "You've read Gary's book?"

"I heard Gary Garth speak in Dubai." Theorists of Garth's ilk — star professors, fast food moguls, miracle-working chief executive officers — toured the world like the travelling salesmen of bygone days, hawking a modern kind of snake oil, a concoction of slick new ideas guaranteed to cure whatever ails an organization. Garth, a charismatic young billionaire, was from big retail. He had made his billions sweeping away the sleepy main streets Irv had so loved.

Chen nodded respectfully. "The RV was Gary's idea."

"No offices to staff," Amanda Curtwell added.

"No hotel rooms to rent," Chen chimed in.

Did Curtwell and Chen sleep together in this behemoth, Foster wondered? Or had he watched *Restless World* too often? In the soap opera, everyone slept with everyone else, eventually. The characters seemed to change partners as often as square dancers. “An RV is a turbo tortoise,” Foster said, remembering the phrase from the talk Garth had given. He expected Garth’s golden words to earn him another smile from Amanda. No smile came his way. The challenge in those coppery eyes intrigued him.

“I’ve seen your mouse trail,” Chen said. “You went through the entire site.”

“Oh, yes. I scrolled through all the pages.” Or Shawna had.

Chen gave Foster a thoughtful look. “Mr. Foster, why do people come into a hardware store?”

To lean on a counter and shoot the shit. To inhale the sturdy odours of turpentine and linseed oil. To laugh at Irv’s cornball jokes.

“Ever seen one of these?” Chen handed Foster a large rubber disc. Foster rubbed the torn scrap between his fingers, recalling a home repair show he had watched recently. He liked the shows, the genial hosts, the problems presented and solved. “Must be an old tap. They use ceramic cartridges in these now. It might be better to replace the faucet set.”

“Exactly. But someone like me, a third-generation Chinese-American with an MBA, wouldn’t know that. I’m outside my area of expertise and I need help.”

“He needs a grandfather’s help.” Amanda smiled at Foster. Something about her smile made Foster want to please her.

“I have no more questions,” Chen said, as if he were a lawyer addressing a judge. “He’s relaxed. He fits the part. Look how he dressed for the interview. And he’s already on message.”

Amanda Curtwell nodded. “Grandpa Foster, welcome to the Toolbox team.”

You need the luck, son. Foster leaned forward. “A major corporation needs timely, efficient data processing. I retired from Duboco Petroleum as Chief Information Officer, Gulf Region. But a man can only play so much golf. I'm ready to go back to work. Make me an offer. Let's talk terms." To hide his desperation, Foster put on a confident smile.

"We just did, Mr. Foster," Amanda Curtwell said. "The terms of employment are on our website, which, of course, you read. As a graduate of Grandpa School, an associate in training, you'll work twenty-five hours a week in our new Toronto store. You will earn the minimum wage. But if you can turn a seventy-cent bag of tap washers into a fifty thousand dollar kitchen reno, you'll get a few points of the store's net. Opportunity abounds. The wise woo."

The bit about woo came from the gospel according to Garth. Grandpa School? The cute name worried Foster. Soon, Cedric kept saying. Soon.

"You'll travel to Florida and spend a week at Grandpa headquarters, all expenses paid. You'll earn forty hours pay." Amanda Curtwell picked up a pencil and tapped the table. "I need your decision now, Mr. Foster. You're being offered this opportunity because one of our recruits passed away suddenly."

That would happen all right, with the staff demographic. A week in the Florida sunshine. Seven days away from the beanbag chair. Foster looked down at the torn rubber washer. They were grating on each other, he and Mary. What if he called Jessica from Florida, ended it that way? And — it was painful to admit — *Restless World* had become the highlight of his day.

"When do I start?"

Amanda popped open a laptop. Foster had been dismissed.

"You leave tomorrow morning at six," Chen said.

"Which terminal?" Foster was looking forward to flying again.

"You go to Florida by bus. We'll pick you up here."

A bus? Foster stepped down from the RV. The crowd had vanished. Shawna sat on the curb fiddling with her skateboard, or pretending to.

When he came back into the house, Mary was reading a romance novel. Foster looked at the television. "What happened with Sam and Dam?"

"Damian is a jerk. He treats Samantha like dirt. How'd it go out there?"

"The interview? Fine. It isn't a real job. Just something to tide me over."

"But you took it." Mary waved the romance novel in a gesture of exasperation.

"Yes," Foster said slowly. "I took it." Why was Mary so irritable? "I'm going to Florida for a week. For training."

"Lucky," Mary said. "When are you going?"

"Tomorrow." When his daughter said nothing more Foster went to the middle room. He thumped his suitcase on the sofa bed, snapped open the locks and felt a tingle of anticipation. He was on the move, a traveller again. His spirits rose as he packed. He rolled a tie and tucked it under a shirt, and felt an awareness prickling at his attention. He looked around the room. Tyler's stuff had disappeared: the carpet cleaning machine and its paraphernalia, the exercise bike, the hockey bag. Foster's fugitive joy evaporated. He was a rat leaving a sinking ship.

[SIX]

THE BUS LURCHED around the corner, cutting the old houses with its headlights. *Next stop, Grandpa Camp!* read the illuminated sign above the windshield. It was a proper bus, at least. If they had sent a school bus, Foster would have gone back inside; he had promised himself that much. Grandpa Camp. He was ten years old. He would sit around a roaring fire, thrill to ghost stories, stick a flashlight in his sleeping bag and read comic books after lights out. Why was he imagining all this? He had never gone to camp as a boy. As the bus hissed to a stop, Foster recalled a video he had watched with Shawna, a saga about three intrepid teenagers and a clever St. Bernard who get on a yellow bus and set off for *Kamp Karefree*. How much of what we seem to remember comes from the movies?

The driver hopped down, flipped up a latch on the bus's belly and tossed Foster's suitcase into a baggage bay with offhand skill. Foster climbed aboard. The bus accelerated and he went stumbling down the aisle to spill down into a seat and land on something hard. Fishing between his legs he tugged out a three-ring binder. *Grandpa Training Manual.*

"Morning," he said to the man beside him. No reply. His seatmate was asleep. *To sleep: perchance to dream: ay, there's the rub: / For in that sleep of death what dreams may come.*

"YOU HAD TO love Joe Carter," Charlie Anderson was saying. "The way he'd hit the ball a ton and smile that big smile of his." It was early afternoon and the bus was rolling through southern Pennsylvania under a slate-coloured sky. Foster and Charlie sat with box lunches on their laps — a cheese sandwich, a carton of milk, a Granny Smith apple. Foster left the milk untouched. A full bladder was a liability. There was a washroom on the bus, but there was always a line up.

His seatmate was a stocky man with a ruddy face. By the time they hit Lexington, Kentucky, Foster knew the essential facts of Charlie's life. Charlie had been a truck driver. He had been married thirty-seven years to Marge, who died soon after his retirement. Charlie had no children. Foster had told Charlie an abridged version of his own story, leaving out AMEB, Jessica, and the cold war with Mary. His thoughts drifted back to Toronto. Tyler could be out of town on business. But that didn't explain the missing exercise bike. Or Mary's irritability. On the evidence, they had broken up. Mary was better off without him. She would realize this sooner or later.

"Did you see the '93 World Series, friend?" Charlie shook a pill onto his palm. "Sixth game. Phillie leading 6 to 5. Bottom of the ninth. Carter's at bat. Count is 2 and 2. Pitcher winds, deals, pitch comes in … Bam! Out she goes. Know what Carter said after the game? 'I was only trying to make contact.' Can you beat that? Only trying to make contact." Charlie looked at Foster shrewdly. "Don't tell me you follow the Yankees. Anybody but the Yankees."

"Um."

"You didn't hear a word I said, did you?"

Foster shook his head. "Baseball is Greek to me."

Charlie sighed. "You want the window seat, friend? It's your turn."

"No, stay where you are." After all, what was there to see? Only the billboards and the stilt-legged signs, the ads for lawyers and antique malls. Foster closed his eyes and tried to sleep.

THE BUS WAS rolling through darkness when Foster snapped on his reading light and opened the training manual. He stared at the bookmark, a miniature denim apron, and then he began to read. An hour later, Charlie glanced over and asked, "You make any sense out of that thing?"

"Big company. Prescribed sales method."

"Bunch of bullshit, if you want my opinion."

"Well, I'm not sure they do."

"True, friend. True." Charlie shifted his bulk, leaned a shoulder against the window and looked into the night. "Driver's booting this rig right along. Hope he has sense enough to feather it through Georgia. They got speed traps there."

"You drove this route?"

"And every other route they got. You can't win, I guess. Twenty years I spent on the road. Last five, I couldn't hardly stand it. And here I am, back on an interstate." There was a silence. "Know what I thought about all those years?"

Foster looked up from the training manual.

"The shop I was going to set up in the garage. Had it all laid out in my head. Contractor quality table saw. Band saw. Planer. Good bench, proper lights. I must have planned that sucker a thousand times."

"Is that your hobby, woodworking?"

"Was."

When Charlie said nothing more, Foster asked, "What did you make?"

"Birdhouses. Got so I could bang them together in no time."

"Birdhouses?" Charlie didn't look like a bird lover.

"The birdhouses were Marge's idea. We'd load up the van and off we'd go. Flea markets, antique malls. I'd set up the table. Sit on a folding chair, answer a lot of damn fool questions."

"Met a lot of people, did you?"

"It was Marge they wanted to talk to, not me. You got a hobby, Foster?"

Did walking count? Foster pictured himself tramping through a dry riverbed under the hot desert sun. But Charlie meant something like model railroading. "No hobbies."

"Smart man. I never want to see another goddamn birdhouse. I'd come home and that fool woman would be standing in the driveway, suitcase in hand. Did the Maritimes. New England. Carlsbad Caverns. Must have driven to Arizona a dozen times. Half-brother of mine lived down there. Crazy as a woodpecker on a hardwood tree. Tail gunner in World War II. B-17s. Walter's dead now." Charlie talked on and on. Foster didn't mind. It was like listening to the radio. They were cruising past Fayetteville, North Carolina, when Charlie fell into pensive silence. Dozing in his seat, Foster thought about AMEB. What if they announced the settlement while he was at Grandpa Camp? He would phone Cedric from Florida. Sylvia would have to accept a collect call.

In South Carolina, Charlie talked about his childhood in Ontario's tobacco belt, about the farms of Norfolk County with their rich soil, roadside kilns and drafty shanties. "Rich? One old farmer I worked for had a barn full of Cadillacs. Took me in there one day and showed me. Must have been a dozen of them sitting around in the gloom, covered in dust. Said it broke his heart to trade a Caddie in. Heard that he hanged himself in there, years later."

North of Savannah, asleep with a box lunch on his lap, Foster dreamed that he was in a kitchen, crawling across a floor, looking up at the walls. It was time to call Cedric. But where was the phone? The linoleum had a sweet smell and it was patterned with diamonds. A radio softly played. His mother stood at the sink; her back was to him. She was washing dishes and singing along with Bing Crosby. Asthma, the disease that would soon stop her heart, made her voice thin and pure. The song was about land, starry skies, cottonwood trees. The bus lurched, jolting Foster awake. Charlie was snoring softly, his barrel chest rising and falling. Foster looked away. He couldn't bear to watch people as they slept. Closing his eyes, he tried to picture his mother's face. As always, he drew a blank. Shortly before her own death, Foster's grandmother had told him that — maddened by grief — Irv had thrown his late wife's clothes on a fire. Pictures, letters, keepsakes — everything went up in flames. Foster fell asleep again. He was on his way to Thailand, riding an AirBus out of Stepol. Mary and Shawna were on the plane; they were coming for a visit. He would need to buy a villa, choose furniture, hang pictures on the walls. He would need only a few minutes to do all this. In the dream, the idea seemed perfectly reasonable. He should tell the pilot to let him off the plane first. A skeleton sat in the pilot's seat, rags streaming from its bones. Foster made a desperate grab for the controls. He missed and went cartwheeling into the void, flailing his arms. A hand seized his wrist.

"Whoa," Charlie said. "Take it easy, friend."

They came to a rest stop just after midnight, and Foster walked past the gas pumps with Charlie at his side. The restaurant smelled of fried meat. There was a lineup in the men's room. Foster counted the urinals, then the men in line; when a man in a tan jacket took his turn, Foster timed him and ran an algorithm in his head. "We should have a urinal in just over three and a half minutes."

Charlie looked at him.

"Queuing theory."

"You got a lot of stuff like that in your head?"

"I guess I do."

Four minutes later, when two urinals came available, Charlie planted his feet, arced his back and sighed with pleasure. Foster felt oddly intimidated. Had he ever known a man so completely at home in his own skin?

"Baseball is all about numbers," Charlie said as they were washing their hands. "Batting average. RBIs. Walk-to-strikeout ratio. They're always thinking up new statistics. Linear run estimators. Total chances."

"Total chances. For a moment I thought you were talking about life." Foster meant this as a joke.

"Friend, baseball is life."

A man with a greying buzz cut looked over from the hand dryer. "It is in Atlanta."

Charlie turned his head. "You like the Braves' chances for next season?"

"They'll be in the hunt," said the man from Atlanta. "Four months to spring training."

"Everybody finishes first in February," Charlie said with a smile. He shook a pill into his hand and bent to drink from the faucet.

Outside the restaurant, as they were walking slowly back to the bus, a transport rig aglow with running lights crawled past them, heading for a lane where a herd of eighteen-wheelers had gathered for the night. Charlie watched the truck move away. "Must be fifty big rigs back there. Volvos. Whites. Peterbilts." When they reached the bus and saw the door open and the driver's seat empty, Charlie and Foster lingered in the balmy night, leaning against the bus and looking up at the sky. Charlie sniffed the air like an animal picking up a scent. "Warmer."

"A little warmer at each stop," Foster agreed.

"Must have been a humdinger."

"I beg your pardon?"

"That dream you were having. For a while there you had your hands up like you were knitting something." Charlie looked into the distance. "Marge used to get bad dreams. I'd sit beside her to see if she was going to settle down or if I'd have to wake her up. She's sleeping okay now, I guess."

After a moment Foster said, "My wife's dead too."

"Sorry to hear that."

"Kathleen and I split up long before she died. Never should have got married, I suppose."

Charlie rubbed against the side of the bus, scratching his back like a bear at a tree. The bus was parked on a hill, and from where the two men stood, the Interstate was a stream of light. A transport truck burbled down the entry ramp. A couple left the restaurant and started across the parking lot, the woman slanting forward, an infant in her arms, the man leaning back, carrying a sleeping child.

"My wife was Catholic. I had to guarantee that our children would be raised in the faith. They made a big deal of it in those days." Foster looked up at the night sky, wondering why he was telling Charlie all this.

Charlie followed his gaze. "How did that work out?"

"It wasn't an issue in the end. Kathleen stopped going to Mass." Saying this, Foster felt a lingering guilt. Had he pulled Kathleen away from her church with his rationalism, condemned her to a lesser station in the complicated Catholic hereafter? No, that was her business. And God's, if God came into it. What, then? He found himself remembering the day Mary telephoned to tell him that Kathleen had been found dead in her rooming house. There was a big flap on at Duboco. Two systems were down and Houston was screaming for blood. He took the call in the conference room. He thanked Mary for calling, hung up the phone, picked up a printout and wept like a wounded child. Why had he cried for a woman who had grown to hate him? Why had all this come to mind, in the middle of the night, at a rest stop in Georgia? With growing impatience, Foster traced the impulse, as if it were a bug hidden in a thousand lines of code. Ah. The notion of Charlie watching over his sleeping wife. What good did it do to remember the dead? And yet, Kathleen was as real to him now as she had been in life, even if, on the evidence, he and Charlie were just two widowers leaning against a bus, looking up into the Georgian darkness.

THE BUS CROSSED the Florida state line at first light. An hour later, under a red sky, it left the expressway, rolled down a secondary highway and passed under an arch lettered in silver. *Welcome to Palmerton / Home of Grandpa's Toolbox!* At Charlie's insistence, Foster had taken the window seat. De Soto Street was a no man's land of abandoned buildings, vacant lots, piles of rubble. An old commercial block stood empty, its signs advertising defunct businesses — Hansler's Shoes, Willamon's Men's Wear, Coridan's Drug Store. The sight made Foster wistful. The stores suggested a vacant movie set. *Rent a hundred movies.* Abandoned scenery litters the landscape.

The bus moved past motels and fast food outlets, used car lots and strip malls. Speedee TV Repair. Whole Food & Meditation Center. The Biblical Church of Revelation and Truth. A line of old men shuffled along a sidewalk. They wore sports shirts printed with palm trees, baggy slacks with double pleats. Where were they going so early in the morning, these wan ghosts? The bus entered big box country, crossed a vast parking lot, turned and came to a stop in a numbered space. The men got to their feet, stretched their arms, gathered their belongings and bumped toward the door.

Foster stepped into the sunshine. How wonderful the sun felt! He tucked the training manual under his arm and patted the cover. If the Grandpa rigamarole was the price of escape from the claustrophobic townhouse, the routine of walking and waiting, Jessica's baffling presence in his life — the bargain seemed fair. A line of buses stood with their windshields at an acute angle to a blank wall. Foster counted them. Nineteen buses. Had each of them arrived with forty trainees? If so … Foster glanced at the bus that had brought him from Toronto. The driver was unloading the luggage bay, and the men were watching. Except for Charlie. Charlie was looking at him, Foster realized, and suddenly he felt conspicuous, standing apart in his business suit. "I'm trying to figure out how soon we'll get a cold beer," Foster called. Joking had never come easily to him, and he was glad when Charlie gave him a little smile.

They carried their suitcases into a store as vast as an aircraft hangar. Quaintly lettered signs hung from the high ceiling. *Grandpa's Tool Shop. Grandpa's Paint 'n Paper. Grandpa's Nails 'n Glue. Grandpa's Plumbing 'n Heating. Grandpa's Lumber Shed.*

Peter Chen ushered the group through a door marked *Grandpas Only*. Foster put down his suitcase and looked around, his happy mood evaporating. He put a high value on privacy, but there was none to be had. This was a barracks, not a hotel. He would sleep in a bunk bed constructed of rough lumber. "Coffee and doughnuts next door in the Learning Place," Chen said. "We start in twenty minutes."

"You want upper or lower?" Charlie had an eye on a lower bunk.

"Upper," Foster said. He would pretend he was airborne.

The Learning Place had blackboards, a globe in a wooden cradle, a flag with a fringe of gold, wainscot of beaded pine, sash windows with pull-down shades, a pot-bellied stove. On his boyhood travels with Irv, Foster had seen dozens of cast iron stoves, and there was something wrong about that one. He walked over and rapped the stove with a knuckle. Fibreglass. The stove was a fake. He crossed the room again and had just taken a seat next to Charlie when Amanda Curtwell came sweeping into the room with Chen trailing behind her. "Our customers are family," recorded voices sang in the close harmony of a barbershop quartet. "Their satisfaction we guarantee." Foster got to his feet with the rest of the men. First chance he had, he would nip out and buy a copy of *USA Today*. Cedric and his very good people should have completed the audit by now.

"PRETTY SURE WE passed a bar on the way in." Charlie was ambling down De Soto Street like a foraging bear, his thick body rolling from side to side. The sky was streaked with lavender. Steam rose from the road. The air had a damp, tropical scent.

"If I remember correctly," Foster said. "Hernando De Soto landed here in 1539 with six hundred men."

"Six hundred? Not six hundred and one?"

Foster had to smile.

"What did you make of all that guff?" Charlie asked.

"The lecture on inner needs, or the one about the sacred home?"

"Speaking of sacred." Charlie pointed at a small building with a heavy steel door. Venetian blinds with wide slats hung in the windows; neon signs advertising beer tinted the slats red and green. Foster and Charlie walked into a haze of smoke. The trophy head of a deer brooded over a pool table. Billiard balls clacked. The bartender was a lanky, dehydrated man with swooping white sideburns and hooded, closely set eyes.

"Miller," Charlie said, pulling out a stool.

Foster nodded. "Make it two."

The patrons at the bar, roofers and window washers and landscapers, judging from the sun-baked pickups in the parking lot, sat drinking draft beer from thick glass mugs, malt liquor from tall aluminum cans, rye whisky from shot glasses.

"Know what I like about this place?" Charlie looked around. "It's not done up like Neptune's locker or a goddamn 1890 hardware store. It's the real item. A gen-u-ine bar."

The bartender set up their beers and moved away.

Charlie picked up his glass. "Down the hatch."

"Cheers," Foster said. The beer had a clean, crisp taste.

"Let me see if I got this straight," Charlie said a few minutes later. "This guy's at home and one of the burners on his stove is on the fritz. So he gets in his car and he drives over to Grandpa's Toolbox. He's more upset than he knows, because something's wrong with his house and that's his …"

"Central image of security."

"Right. So this threat to his whatchamacallit, triggers …"

"A deep need for connection."

"Right. The doors go whoosh and he's in a big box store, but not really. He thinks he's in a dinky hardware store and then he sees Grandpa and bingo, everything is hunky-dory." Charlie's eyes twinkled with mischief. "Suppose this guy's never seen a hardware store in his life. Suppose he's a Russian from Outer Siberia."

"Latent images, Charlie."

"Oh, yeah. Everybody's seen a million movies and TV shows and if you get them to close their eyes and you say 'hardware store,' they see this nice old guy wearing an apron."

"Right."

"And this nice old guy is standing under a canvas awning and he's sweeping the sidewalk with a broom."

"Right."

"And that's us."

"Right. If we survive a week in the model store, that is."

Charlie gave Foster a crafty smile. "What if Mr. Stove closes his eyes and sees a real grandfather, cranky old fart on a tractor-mower, rides around all day bitching about the government?"

Foster laughed. "Well, now, I don't remember Amanda saying anything about a riding mower."

"No, you got me there. She didn't." Charlie sipped his beer and looked into the haze of smoke. "Do we really need grandfathers this badly?"

Foster had no answer to that. "Is there a pay phone?" he asked the bartender.

"Outside the john."

An archway on the other side of the room led to a dimly lit corridor stacked with beer kegs. The corridor led past a battered payphone to the toilets. The handset reeked of sweat and cigarette smoke. "I wish to place a collect call to London, England," Foster told the operator. "My name is Daniel Foster and the number is —"

"Sorry, sir. That call cannot be made from your location."

A heavyset woman squeezed past, pinning Foster against the wall.

"Can I call Toronto?" There might be a message on Mary's machine.

"Yes, sir."

The call went through. "Hello?" It was Shawna's voice.

"I have a collect call from Daniel Foster. Will you accept the charges?"

"Yeah, okay."

"Hello, Shawna. How are you?"

"Okay."

"How are things at school?"

"Good."

Foster waited for Shawna to say more. She didn't. "May I speak to your mother, please?"

"She's sleeping. Want me to wake her up?"

"No, don't wake her up." Secure-All must have changed Mary's shift. "Are there any messages for me?"

"Yes."

The bartender brushed past, shouldered a beer keg and went by again.

"Did Cedric leave a message?"

"No."

Foster flattened himself against the wall to let the heavyset woman squeeze past again. The call would run up Mary's phone bill. Which he would have to pay. "Is there anything I should know?"

"She didn't let him in."

"Mary didn't let Tyler in?"

"Nooooo. Samantha didn't let Jed in. He's still banging on the door."

A man in a leather vest threaded his way down the corridor. Foster stepped aside and thought for a moment. "Did a woman named Sylvia leave a message?"

"A woman named Jessica left a message."

"Did Sylvia leave a message?"

"No. Who is Sylvia?"

What is she, that all our swains commend her … Foster silently recited. "Thank you, Shawna. It's good to talk to you, but I'd better get off the phone. I'll see you … when I get back."

"Want me to phone Jessica for you?"

"What? No. I'll … look after that."

"Okay. Bye."

For a long moment Foster stared into a garbage can. There was a copy of *USA Today* in there, sprinkled with lemon peel. He plucked out the newspaper and shook it. Sitting beside Charlie again, he put on his glasses, spread the damp pages on the bar and turned to the business section. He looked up from the newspaper. If Gary Garth asked Shawna to imagine a grandfather, what would Shawna see in her mind's eye? Would his granddaughter draw a blank? Foster focused his attention on the newspaper. There was nothing about AMEB.

"TEEEEEEEAM GRANDPA!" FOSTER yelled.

"Teeeeeeam Grandpa!" his fellow trainees shouted back.

With applause erupting around him, Foster went back to his table, burning with embarrassment. Tomorrow it would be someone else's turn to lead this silly ritual, thank God. He picked up the daily schedule, wondering what fresh tortures the afternoon held. The trainees had spent the morning in the model store, practising the model sales method on model customers — a troupe of professional actors ran the role playing exercises — and while a gum-chewing technician operated a video camera, Foster had dealt with an angry customer, a confused customer, an uncertain customer. "Can we give Grandpa Foster some constructive criticism?" Peter Chen would say, kicking off a feedback session that, in Foster's view, had the helpful, corrective tone of the Spanish Inquisition.

"WE'RE SUPPOSED TO do what, exactly?" Sal Croce asked.

"Make something from the stuff in this box," Charlie said.

"Why?" asked Tom Tipperman, the fourth member of the team. A thin, nervous man with a beaky nose, he was getting on Foster's nerves.

"We've got," Sal said, unpacking the box, "pipe elbows, ABS, five. Duct tape, three-inch rolls, two. Nylon window screening, one package. Quarter inch bolts, two inch, one pack of ten. Hex nuts, same size, one pack, also ten. Sign board …"

"Why?" Tipperman said. He reminded Foster of a bird chirping, *Why? Why? Why?*

"Utility knife, one …"

Amanda Curtwell was hovering nearby. Somebody should take charge. Foster pulled the box out of Sal's hands.

"FIVE MORE MINUTES." Amanda Curtwell cruised past the table where Foster and his teammates sat in silence. Foster looked around. The men at the other tables were tinkering with the contraptions they had cobbled together. Table Three had made a wine rack. Table Two had pieced together a weathervane.

"Tell you what," Charlie said. "How about each of us makes something? I can do a birdhouse." He stacked materials with his big hands and turned to Sal. "You pick next."

Sal reached into the box. "I could make a desk set, I suppose." A pile of odds and ends grew in front of him. "But I'd need that little spool you just took."

"Trade you for that hunk of dowel," Charlie said.

"Sure."

"Computers are your line," Charlie said, turning to Foster. "But nobody could make a computer out of this stuff."

"That circuit box could be a CD case," Foster said after a moment.

"Could be at that," Charlie said.

"Why are we doing it this way?" Tom chimed in.

Charlie looked at Tom. "Because if we don't get our ass in gear, we're going to look pretty damn stupid."

THE SKINNY BARTENDER dealt down mugs of draft beer.

"Best table." Sal beamed at his teammates. "I can't believe we won best table."

"Got the trophy right here to prove it." Charlie patted a bundle of ABS pipe taped to a chunk of signboard.

"Did you guys really like the tie rack?" Tom asked in a shy voice.

"The tie rack was great," Charlie said. "Down the hatch. You guys want another one?"

"Not for me, thanks." Sal yawned. "I think I'll head back and catch forty winks before dinner."

"Been a long day." Tom got to his feet.

Foster sipped his beer.

"You guys go ahead." Charlie nodded at the trophy. "Foster and I are going to turn this thing into a laser beam."

"Thanks for pulling things together today," Foster said, after Sal and Tom had left the bar.

"It wasn't just me. There were four of us sitting there."

"I'm the one with executive experience."

"Oh, I get it. And the rest of us are dim-wits."

"No, no. It's not that."

Charlie looked at Foster. "Like I said on the bus, I thought I was a red-hot birdhouse salesman. 'Til I tried it without Marge. Friend, I couldn't give the goddamn things away." Charlie shoved the makeshift trophy aside and held up two fingers. The bartender nodded. Pool balls clacked. A man in green coveralls crossed the floor and leaned on the jukebox. He dropped a coin into a slot. A guitar played a twangy boom-chuck rhythm. Charlie tapped his fingertips on the tabletop. "'Roll, Truck, Roll.' Big hit for Draw-bar Bill. You like country music, friend?"

"Sure."

Charlie gave him a skeptical look. "Did I tell you I was the company's top driver, five years straight?"

"No, but I'm not surprised."

"I'd be jockeying a rig through Montreal, dead of winter, dog tired, rush hour, snowstorm, those crazy Frenchmen doing doughnuts into the guardrail. And I'd just steer around 'em. Nothing was going to slow Charlie Anderson down, no sir. I'd get so uptight about making time that I'd have to pull over and barf."

Foster didn't see the point of this story. "I never liked driving in Montreal."

Charlie shrugged. "Guess we should get a move on."

On the walk back to Grandpa Headquarters, with a full moon shining on the crowns of the palm trees and the dry grass crunching under his feet, Foster sniffed the breeze and caught a hint of the sea. He heard waves breaking, or fancied he did. For a moment, walking in the sultry night, he was back in the Middle East. For a moment, he was home.

THE REST OF the week passed quickly. Foster sat through "Just Enough" seminars — overviews of electrical work, plumbing, carpentry, painting. The idea was to put customers at ease, figure out what they needed and then walk them to the right department. He attended "Get It Right" sessions: specialty training in product knowledge and best practices. When the trainees were bused to an operating store, he stocked shelves and served customers. Some of the customers were ringers, Foster suspected. Did the woman who wanted lag bolts really plan to install a sixteen-foot ledger board? For a second-storey deck? Working alone?

On his last day in Florida, he stepped deftly over the thick yellow cord that connected a motorhome to the gigantic building. Despite the rah-rah nonsense, the songs and cheers, the silly T-shirts *(I'm a Junior Grandpa!)*, Foster had enjoyed the week. Hardware had changed since Irv's day. Cabinet hinges, for example. Grandpa's stocked the old butterfly type, but the new standard was the Euro clip-on, a precision-machined gizmo with six way adjustability. Florida might be suburbia with sand — the strip malls and gas stations and fast food outlets — and God's waiting room — the lizard-eyed octogenarians crawling along in their enormous cars — but a week in the sun had restored Foster's spirit.

Amanda Curtwell stood waiting at the door of her RV. Foster gave her a jaunty wave. She was a fine sight in her pleated black pants and her crisp white blouse. No silly T-shirt for Amanda. She was younger than Mary, he realized as he followed her to the dinette, and here she was holding down a responsible job, a job that required tact and intelligence. It seemed a shame that he couldn't offer Amanda a position with Duboco Petroleum. He pictured her in the ante room to his office, keeping his calendar, screening his calls, dealing with minor matters herself, calling important issues to his attention. It dawned on Foster that Amanda expected him to sit down first. Yes, of course. RV or not, this was her office. She asked him if he had enjoyed his stay, made a little joke about the coffee in the Learning Place. In the soft light coming through the window, she looked younger than her years. Foster wanted to carry her books home from school. He wanted to sit beside her on a porch swing, lean over and steal a kiss.

"Your report card, Grandpa Foster."

The card she handed him, with its stiff pink paper, its sections and subsections, really did look like a report card. Amanda Curtwell picked up a printout. "Your marks in problem solving, creative listening, and customer interaction are satisfactory. Excellent marks in product knowledge. Congratulations."

"Thank you." The situation was faintly ridiculous. He didn't need Amanda Curtwell to tell him he was competent.

"You did not so well in interpersonal skills."

"Oh?" Foster stared at the card.

"And you scored low in leadership."

"Really?" Foster turned the card over, half expecting to see a blank line for a parent's signature. Had his father ever read his report card? Once, Foster remembered. The year he scored 98% in math. Irv had sat slouched in an armchair, in the lobby of an ancient hotel, kitty corner from a railway station, draft beer, ten cents a glass. He hadn't looked at the card. "Never mind, son. That's just what they think."

"I'm not overly concerned about your leadership score," Amanda went on. "Not everybody can be a leader. Leaders without followers are lost."

Foster nodded. The axiom was one of Gary Garth's. Amanda was studying his face. "Is there more you want to say?" Foster said. Tricky thing, a performance review. He would be a model trainee, help Amanda through the process.

"Grandpa Foster, your 360s aren't very good at all."

"My 360s?"

"The performance surveys we filled out about the people we work with."

We? Foster didn't remember filling out a survey about Amanda. "What don't my … fellow Grandpas like about me?" Foster felt miffed. He had given Charlie, Sal and Tom top marks on the survey. This was the loyal thing to do.

"People see you as standoffish. Overly critical. Arrogant."

Foster's good mood faded. He looked out the window, stared at a blank wall. "Well, I suppose that's something to work on."

"It comes up again in the Mystery Shopper's Report." Amanda put down the printout and looked at him. "There's something about your manner, even now …"

His staff at Duboco Petroleum had liked him well enough, Foster wanted to say. The smiles they gave him as he walked by, the little presents on his birthday. If he had given them a survey to complete, the results would have been glowing. But then he thought, would his staff have been honest? Every expatriate in Dubai was there on someone else's say-so. His staff had needed his good opinion. Had he lived for years without knowing what people really thought of him? Amanda Curtwell was studying him sympathetically.

"We'll work together on this, Grandpa Foster. I'll make you my special project."

Special project? He didn't like the sound of that.

Amanda got to her feet. "I'll see you at the graduation ceremony, Grandpa Foster. We have a surprise guest."

"Oh, good," Foster said. As if he hadn't been surprised enough already.

"HOW'D IT GO?" Charlie asked when Foster returned to the dormitory.

"Just fine." Foster hopped on his bunk, stretched out and gazed up at the ceiling. "How did your interview go?"

"Friend, you're talking to the Lead Grandpa of Toronto Fasteners."

"Hey, that's great," Foster said. He liked Charlie.

"All the same to me."

Foster closed his eyes. "That's the spirit."

MEMENTO HALL HAD plush seats, a banked floor, a proscenium stage. Behind the footlights stood a podium worthy of a presidential press conference.

"Get a load of this," Sal said.

Charlie nodded. "They know how to put on the dog."

"Why do we have to wear these outfits?" Tom said.

Why indeed, Foster thought. Like all the men streaming into the hall, he wore the Grandpa uniform: a red-and-yellow plaid shirt and a pair of denim bib-and-brace overalls. He plucked a sleeve and travelled in memory to the fitting room of Frazier & Sons. "I'm not quite happy with the balance," Simmonds the tailor would say, casting an eye over Foster and the suit in progress. "Slip the coat off and we'll put that right." Keep my measurements on file, Simmonds. We shall meet again. The lights dimmed. Foster and his team took their seats.

A hush fell over the room. Beams of light darted from the ceiling and played over the audience. A drum roll sounded. "Land of Hope and Glory" played from hidden speakers. Spotlights stabbed down to illuminate the formal procession in academic gowns and mortarboard hats that was making its way up the centre aisle. The platform party climbed a set of stairs and moved across the stage, then stood at their places while a plump man in a white suit delivered a long, polemical prayer. He gave an account of the week's activities. He gave thanks for this great company, whose outlets were manifold. He asked God to bless the new stores to which the multitude gathered before him would march. He ended with a ringing "Amen."

As the audience took their seats, a gangling man with a cowpoke manner ambled to the podium. He wore a white shirt, a string tie, cowboy boots and a pair of jeans that, to Foster's eye, looked tailor-made. "My name is Dustin Franks. Dusty to my friends. I'm the CEO of Grandpa's Toolbox." Dusty surveyed the room with evident satisfaction. "You know, I've stood here a good many times, and I don't think I've ever seen so fine a group of Grandpas. Dang." Dusty glanced over his shoulder. "Gary heard me say the exact same thing last week." The audience laughed and there was a smattering of applause. Foster studied the platform party. So Gary Garth was the surprise Amanda Curtwell had promised. "After you all get your diplomas, Gary's going to give the convocation address," Dusty said. "We're all anxious to hear from our CVO."

Tom whispered, "CVO?"

"Chief Visionary Officer," Foster whispered.

"But first it gives me great pleasure to call upon our store managers to introduce their graduates. And tonight is extra special. We've got our first ever Canadian Grandpas with us. How about a big Grandpa cheer for our northern friends! Stand up and take a bow, you Canucks! And let's hear it for their team leader, Amanda Curtwell!"

Foster stood with the other Canadians while the audience clapped and cheered. He settled back into his seat and watched Amanda make her way to the podium in her dark formal dress, her dark hair shining as she walked under the lights.

The men made their way to the stage, where Amanda announced their names, and Dusty Franks handed them a diploma, and Gary Garth thumped them on the shoulder. These people love graduation ceremonies, Foster thought as he marched back to his seat toting a scroll bound with ribbon. In the Middle East, his American colleagues were forever showing him pictures of their children holding long stemmed roses, stepping from limos, tossing their hats in the air. They capped every transition with ceremony — kindergarten, elementary school, high school, college, even three-day courses in data modelling. When the last Grandpa had been honoured, Gary Garth stepped energetically to the podium. In his open-necked shirt and rumpled chinos, Garth looked like the president of his high school class. It took an effort to remember that he was thirty-five and a billionaire.

For a moment Garth stood at the podium in thoughtful silence, and then he began to speak. "One Saturday morning not so long ago I got up and went to the kitchen and turned on the hot water tap. Cold water came out. My water heater had broken down." Garth paused. "Now, I suppose I could have picked up the phone and hired someone to fix it."

"He could have picked up the phone and bought General Electric," Sal whispered.

Foster smiled.

"But I like to do things myself. So I took off a panel and found the problem, and then I drove to a big box store, never mind which one, and I showed them the broken thermostat. And what did they say to me in that store? Try electrical." Garth shook his head sadly. "Try electrical? I didn't need directions to another aisle. I needed someone to listen, someone to respond. As I walked back to my car, I wanted to drive over to my grandfather's house, and I pictured a man in a plaid shirt and a pair of overalls. But you know something?" An expression of wonder spread over Garth's face. "Neither of my grandfathers fits that image.

The image sprang from a deeper source." Garth picked up a glass and took a sip of water.

"A generation ago, America's business leaders asked themselves a troubling question. What are our assets? They looked out their windows and they saw aging factories. They sought out the philosophers of business and asked, what are our assets? The answer astounded them. Concepts are your true assets. Concepts. Concepts. Ford, for example. The Ford Motor Company isn't factories and dealerships and it isn't an inventory of cars and trucks. Ford is a collective memory. Ford is Laurel and Hardy riding in a Model T. Ford is the station wagon your parents took you to the beach in when you were six. Ford is the Mustang you drove on your first date. Ford is a concept." Garth paused to let his words sink in.

"It occurred to me that if I had an ideal grandfather, others did too. And I sensed that if we could tap into that powerful flow of meaning, if we could make that icon visible, we would be doing America a great service. We're all here tonight because of that insight." Garth looked troubled. "Some so-called experts have attacked my idea. What about diversity, they say? African-American grandfathers don't wear plaid shirts and overalls. Native American elders don't either." Garth made a gesture that suggested the pain of being misunderstood. Foster leaned forward, listening intently.

"A collective memory doesn't replace individual differences. It includes and protects them. When I picture the ideal grandfather, my own grandfathers are not eclipsed. They become more accessible. The concept opens a door." Garth paused to look round the room. "This could only happen in America, we must remind ourselves. Only in America." He seemed to have forgotten about the Canucks in the audience.

"We face many challenges. Our families are in trouble. Too many of our children live in poverty. Government isn't the answer. Private enterprise must lead the way. We will find our way through concepts.

We will heal our families with concepts." Garth seemed to be looking directly into Foster's eyes. "We will call on collective memory. We will make a difference." Garth pointed at the audience, at Foster. "You can help make that difference."

The audience jumped to their feet, clapping and cheering. Dusty Franks ambled back to the mic. "Gary and I would be pleased to buy you all a drink. We'll see you in the Fiesta Room, right next door."

"Wasn't that a great speech?" Tom looked at his teammates.

Charlie made a sour face. "I could use a beer to wash it down."

The Fiesta Room, with its balloons and paper streamers, suggested a gymnasium done up for a sock hop. Foster took in the scene. A spinning silver ball scattered light across the floor. An electronic organ played the opening chords of "Surfin' Darlin'." They had the demographic nailed, all right. High school a fuzzy memory, hearing fading a little. Surfer music was a concept, Foster decided. But he liked jazz and Charlie liked country and western. Did "Surfin' Darlin'" include and protect all other forms of music? Foster went to the bar. He turned, clutching a bottle of Miller Lite, and found himself nose-to-nose with another Grandpa. "One of the fellas told me you're a computer expert," the man shouted over the din.

"Don't know that I'm an expert," Foster shouted back. "But I worked in the industry."

"My wireless hub is real slow."

"Did you try resetting the router?" Foster shouted.

"Worked fine in the basement." The man moved away.

"Canada, eh?" said a booming voice.

A name tag swam into view, level with Foster's eyes. The man towering over him was Peter Klees. He was from Buffalo, New York.

"Go Leafs!"

"Absolutely."

Klees swooped his head down like a giraffe about to nibble on a tree. His eyes bulged and his breath was boozy. "Like the keynote?"

"Gary Garth? As a matter of fact, I heard him speak in —"

"Know what we call him at our table?"

Foster shook his head.

"Garth Vader!" Another Grandpa grabbed Klees by an elbow and shouted, "Pete got a head start on Happy Hour."

Alone in the crowd, Foster went up on tiptoes to peer over a turbulent sea of plaid, then threaded his way across the room to join Charlie. A cloth partition created an eddy of relative quiet. Foster looked around. "Sal and Tom?"

"Got my eye on them." Charlie nodded at a corner table.

"I need a pit stop."

"There's a can behind that thing." Charlie pointed at a faux-marble pillar. "I'll be over there with Sal and Tom."

Foster nodded, took a breath and plunged back into the crowd. On the other side of the room, panicked by the pressure of bodies, he shouldered his way through a heavy door. The door sealed behind him and he was alone in a brightly lit washroom. He crossed an expanse of white tile floor to a urinal, where he stood cursing his overalls, fumbling with the fly. He relieved himself gratefully, then crossed the room to wash his hands in one of fifty identical sinks. A panel of mirror ran the length of the wall. In the looking glass, Foster saw a grown man wearing an outfit meant for a three-year-old. Toddler-wear for seniors. Now, there's a concept. When he was back in Toronto, he would phone Cedric. Foster thought for a moment. Assume the worst case. A recovery of, say, two hundred thousand, in round numbers. A hundred thousand for Mary and Shawna. A hundred thousand for Thailand. Could he live on that? Wondering about the future, Foster pushed through the heavy door and looked around, startled.

The Fiesta Room was empty.

[SEVEN]

THE TIRES DRONED. The windows cycled from daylight to darkness, darkness to daylight. The median strip shaded from green to tan to white. The hours slipped by.

Waking to an unfamiliar sound, a muffled tick-swoosh, Foster leaned into the aisle to watch the windshield wipers gather strings of snow and flick them to the wind. The bus had joined a convoy of transport trucks that was shuffling along like a line of shackled elephants. Charlie was sound asleep. Foster looked past him, out the streaming window at the blowing snow. A trick of air pressure sent beads of water creeping up the glass, as if by magic.

Magic had fascinated Foster when he was a child, and now he had the drowsy conviction that Gary Garth had cast a spell over him. What would it feel like to be under a spell? Like the freezing the dentist gave you? It might feel like novocaine, Foster decided, a spreading numbness, a tingling rediscovery. With every mile the bus travelled, his experience at Grandpa Camp seemed more bizarre. He put his hand on his chest and touched his wallet through the fabric of his suit coat. He would have to put up with the Grandpa foolishness for a few weeks. Until the AMEB settlement came through. He would think of his time in Grandpa's

Toolbox as a contract, and he had done some tough contracts in his time. That six-month stint in Saudi, stuck all day in a computer centre with a VAX supermini, stranded at night in a compound sixty kilometres from Riyadh, sitting around a swimming pool with the same ten people, washing down their gossip with the hooch that Declercq, a chemist from Brussels, cooked up in his still. While the bus crawled its way northward, Foster recalled the old district of Dubai, the winding streets with their rough perfume of fish guts and garam masala. The streets led down to a jetty where a few *fils* bought a ride on a water taxi. The boats, open craft of rough-hewn mahogany, had seating for fifty. The men — never women after sunset — sat shoulder to shoulder. As he crossed the harbour, Foster would gaze at the super tankers moored under the stars, at the royal yachts docked with their portholes aglow, at the trading dhows, ships from another time with eyes painted on their bows. Each water taxi carried a camping lantern slung on a wooden spar, and when Foster's boat passed another, a line of impassive faces shone for a moment and vanished into darkness.

THE BUS ROLLED into Toronto on the first of December with Foster staring moodily out the window. The sun shone with blinding strength. The sky darkened and rain spat down. The sun came out again and the pavement glistened. He waved to Sal and Tom as the two men picked up their bags and waved goodbye. They had become fast friends, Sal and Tom. They were neighbours, practically, they told Foster; they lived a block apart in the old town of Weston. Their fathers had worked in the CCM bicycle factory, long since torn down. Their fathers might have worked together. Sal and Tom were glad to be back.

Foster wasn't glad to be back. The streets were too straight, the houses too much alike, the weather too cold. The bus wound through a post-war subdivision, street after street of identical bungalows with four-hip roofs. They reminded Foster of the little houses in his grandmother's Monopoly set. Collect a block of bungalows and trade them for a hotel.

"349 Jubilee," the bus driver called. Foster gently shook Charlie's arm.

"See you, friend," Charlie said, suitcase in hand. Foster watched Charlie walk up his driveway. He considered going to the door of the bus and calling out. Charlie could take him through his shop, show off his birdhouses. But the bus drew away and Foster settled back. It didn't matter. He would see Charlie at work.

Twenty minutes later, Foster stood with his bag in his hand, watching the bus drive away. The front door of the townhouse opened and Mary stepped out. She had on a bulky black coat with the Secure-All lightning bolts on the shoulders. She was on her way to work. They would start over, he and Mary. His arrival last September had been a false start. The sky shimmered. Rain dappled the concrete.

"Looks like we're in for a thunderstorm." Foster stepped forward. "I don't remember that happening in December."

"Me neither." Mary snapped open an umbrella and held it over their heads. They stood together in silence, sheltered from the rain.

"We don't get a lot of rain in Dubai."

A flash of lightning lit the clouds. A boom of thunder chilled the air.

"Have a good time in Florida?"

"Oh, yes," Foster said quickly. "Fine."

"I'm really glad."

Rain drummed on the umbrella, streamed down the sidewalk.

"There's something for you on the kitchen table." Mary touched his arm. "I have to get going."

Foster watched her umbrella bob up the street. The sky broke open. He stood in the deluge until Mary disappeared around a corner.

Inside the townhouse he set his dripping suitcase on a scrap of carpet, took off his raincoat and hung it in the closet. It was Sunday. No school today. Shawna must be out. At Benny's maybe. Foster went to the kitchen and picked a newspaper clipping from the table.

AMEB Reserve Revealed as Hoax.

London: David Corman, the whiz kid president who brought down the Amalgamated Middle Eastern Bank last September, exposed more of the bank's assets than anyone suspected, a spokesperson for the Bank of England said today. "The reserve (once estimated at one hundred million American dollars) simply does not exist."

Rain beat against the patio door. Foster picked up the phone and called Canary Wharf.

"Foster," Cedric said. "You were my next call."

"Where's Sylvia? She always answers the phone." The change in routine seemed more ominous than the vanished reserve.

"She's left the firm. Foster, I'm leaving too. Martin will take over your account. There may be some bits and bobs to tidy up. There will be no settlement. But you've had that news already, I expect."

"Yes." Deep in his heart, Foster had known the bank was a lost cause.

"Silver lining. Half an interest point reduction on the credit card debt."

"Well. That is good news."

"Foster, I'm sorry this happened on my watch. I'd like to think we'll always be friends."

He and Cedric were friends? It was possible, Foster supposed. All those hours they had spent together. Factor out the money and you were left with the companionship. "What will you do now, Cedric?"

"I'm going sailing. Around the world, actually."

"That's an adventure, around the world alone." Had Cedric ever mentioned that he was a sailor? Not that Foster could remember. But then he recalled a recent conversation. When could he expect the settlement, Foster had asked. *Fair breeze and nobody tangles the ropes? Six months,* Cedric had said. *Government climbs aboard? God only knows.*

"I won't be alone. Sylvia's coming with me."

Cedric and Sylvia were an item? Foster stared out at the pouring rain. Wasn't Cedric married to someone else? The picture on his desk. The semi in Surbiton. The angular woman leaning on the fender of a Jaguar. Hayley? Yes, Hayley. Cedric and Sylvia? Life was imitating *Restless World.*

"Foster? Will you be okay?"

"No worries. I've already taken a job."

"In computing?"

"In the retail sector, as a matter of fact. Change is as good as a rest."

"I knew you'd land on your feet. You're a clever man."

The phone line went silent. There was nothing else to be said. "Goodbye, then," Foster said. "Take care out there. Give Sylvia my love."

"I will. She's very fond of you, you know."

"What's the name of your boat?" Foster thought to ask.

"*Believer.*"

Foster hung up the phone and settled into a chair. After a lifetime of work, he was starting over. A fragment of poetry floated through his mind. *I must go down to the sea again, to the lonely sea and the sky …*

The phone rang. Good, Foster thought. Cedric had more to say.

"Foster?" It was Jessica. "Have you heard the latest?"

"My financial advisor just called."

"Thanks for letting me know about your trip."

He hadn't let Jessica know. Was she mocking him?

"I told Shawna it was just as well. I need to work on my art."

Shawna had phoned Jessica? Foster frowned. He would have to speak to his granddaughter.

"That flower series, all those pretty-pretty pictures?" Jessica was speaking very quickly. "They're in the dumpster. I'm changing everything, Foster. Everything. Know what time I got up this morning? Five. Me! Listen, about changing everything — I don't mean you. No, I'll change there too. Stop being so demanding. Be more giving. Foster, do you hear me?"

"I hear you," he said, stating a fact.

"Forget what I said in the park. You need to soar. Who am I to clip your wings? Hey, are you free tonight? I'm in this great new art group and we're meeting at The Grease Pit. On College Street. It's a bar. Can you come?"

"No reason not to."

"Honestly, the way you put things … No. Forget I said that. Six o'clock?" She had to go, Jessica told him — she had been painting all day, it was starting to work, it was starting to happen. They said goodbye. Foster hung up the phone. He picked up his suitcase and carried it to the middle room, opened the door, tripped and went sprawling down. He looked up at Tyler's exercise bike, looked back at Tyler's hockey bag. And suddenly it was all too much. He needed to walk. Was Canada the problem, he wondered as he put on his raincoat? America had built the bomb, won the Cold War. Power was the spice of American life. What condiment seasoned a Canadian existence? Road salt?

Off to sail the world, Foster thought as he walked out into the rain. You had to admire Cedric for that. The flowerbeds were swamped, the pavement slick with leaves.

THE FRONT DOOR swung open before he could turn his key.

"No, we haven't forgotten you." Mary held a cellphone to her ear. "Party Angels are on the way." She leaned past Foster and looked up and down the street. Foster followed her inside. "Bring your homework!" Mary shouted.

A carpet cleaning machine lay in pieces on the living room floor, a chaos of cords, connectors, hoses, attachments. Mary dropped to her knees and stuffed the parts into a duffle bag.

"Where's Tyler?" Foster said. Mary said nothing. Foster threw up his hands.

Mary whirled around. "Shawna? Now!" A horn sounded outside. "Move it, Shawna! The taxi's here." Shawna came dawdling down the hall, hitching on her backpack. Mary snatched up the duffle bag. Foster grabbed the handle. Mary yanked the bag from his grasp and staggered to the door, herding Shawna before her. Foster gazed at the beanbag chair, thinking how good it would feel to flop down, snap on the television and surf the channels. He grabbed three jugs of carpet shampoo and hurried after his daughter, hooking the front door closed with a foot.

The taxi stood at the curb, its trunk lid open, vapour rising from its tailpipe. Mary planted her feet and tossed the duffle bag in the trunk. Foster tumbled in the jugs and slammed the lid. Mary and Shawna climbed into the back seat. Foster slid in beside the cabbie.

"Where to?" The cabbie was a dwarfish man wearing an oversized pair of eyeglasses.

"Foster, please get out of the car," Mary said. "Take a nap. Go for a walk."

"I know how the machine works." At Grandpa Camp he had sat through a "Just Enough" session on carpet cleaning.

"It's a stupid machine," Shawna said.

"Shawna?" Mary said in a voice sharp with warning.

"People? I don't need this," the cabbie said.

"Just go," Mary said, waving a hand.

"Go where?"

"Do you have the address?" Foster said. "Because if Tyler didn't —"

"I've got it. No, I left it inside. No, wait," Mary peeled a yellow sticky from her sleeve and handed it to the cabbie.

"Queen's Quay," the cabbie said. "In this traffic."

"My daughter made herself perfectly clear."

"Fella?" the cabbie said. "I don't need this."

Mary pulled an instructional brochure from her pocket, flattened the crumpled paper on her thigh and began to read. The cab wove through heavy traffic, the meter pinging, Shawna fiddling with her iPod, Mary studying the brochure, Foster trying to remember the "Just Enough" session, wishing he had paid more attention. He swivelled to face the back seat. "Did they say what they spilled on the carpet?"

"Red wine." Mary kept her eyes on the brochure.

The cabbie shook his head. "That's a bad one."

The taxi's radio crackled into life. A voice barked out an urgent, unintelligible message.

"For a wine spill?" the cabbie said. "You get a bottle of club soda and you shake it. You want the soda to foam? Then —"

"That's not the right thing to use," Foster said.

Shawna looked up. "What's the right stuff?"

"The jugs in the duffle bag," Mary said. "Oh, no. I left them on the coffee table."

"They're in the trunk," Foster said.

Mary glanced at him.

"Or, you get a bottle of white wine," the cabbie said. "And you pour the white wine on the red wine — on the stain — and then —"

"I know what to do," Mary said, emphasizing her words.

No one spoke for several blocks.

"Salt is good too," the cabbie said.

Foster shook his head. "You can't leave salt on the carpet for very long."

The cabbie nodded. "Five minutes. Ten, maybe."

"Wine is acidic," Foster said. "You need an alkaline. Hydrogen peroxide, for example."

"Alkaline," the cabbie said thoughtfully. "Is salt an acid or a base?"

The question whisked Foster back to high school, to Batty Burford's science classroom, its lab counters, high stools and homey chemical stink. *Is salt an acid or a base?* This was one of Batty's trick questions. "Salts are neutral. They are the anhydrous result of an acid-base combination." *Cor-rect! Mr. Foster.* Foster looked over his shoulder to see if Shawna had taken in this bit of science. She hadn't. Eyes closed, she was silently singing.

"Excuse me?" Mary leaned forward and tapped the cabbie on the shoulder. "We just went past the address."

A few minutes later, the cab pulled up before a tower of marble and glass. Mary paid the fare and threw open her door. Forty dollars, with the tip. Foster climbed out of the cab. He would see that Tyler paid Mary back. Foster grabbed a bag and started for the door.

"Foster?" Mary took a deep breath. "I could use some help. But don't take over?"

Foster nodded. Why would he take over?

The lobby had piped-in music, peach-coloured walls, a high ceiling washed with light. Behind a teak counter a white-haired woman sat knitting, a skein of wool in her lap. She had a kind smile, and she wore a blue uniform with padlocks embroidered on the arms. A greeting card grandmother working security. Gary Garth might have invented her.

"Party Angels," Mary said. "We're here for 2048."

"I already buzzed the door." The granny-guard kept her eyes on her knitting.

"Listen, can I leave my daughter here with you for a few minutes?"

Shawna stamped her foot. "Mom!"

The knitting needles clicked. "It's against the rules."

You had to be firm with these people. Foster stepped forward. Mary waved him back. She pulled an ID card from her pocket and showed it to the woman behind the desk. "I'm a security guard too. With Secure-All. Look, I couldn't get a babysitter. It's a spill call. We'll be in and out fast. Shawna will sit and do her homework. She'll be good as gold."

Wind whistled around the doors. The white-haired woman frowned, nodded almost imperceptibly and went on knitting. Shawna kicked a planter. A *ficus benjamina* trembled.

"Honey?" Mary knelt and put her hands on Shawna's shoulders. "Can you do this for me?" The tableau of mother and child touched Foster. The AMEB crash had stolen the future he had planned for Mary and Shawna. Why had he put all his eggs in one basket? He watched Shawna walk sullenly to a chair, spin around and plop down.

In the elevator, Foster looked up at a mirrored ceiling. "Why isn't Tyler looking after this?"

"He forgot his phone."

Forgot his phone. When would Mary wise up to Tyler? The elevator doors slid apart to reveal a corridor panelled with blond oak. Light sparkled from crystal sconces. Mary grabbed a bag and went right. Foster glanced at a brass plate and went left.

The woman standing in the doorway of 2048 had the sheen of the aging, well-tended rich. She wore a slinky, iridescent dress and, Foster thought, too much gold: necklaces, bracelets, bangles, rings. With the practised eye of a single man, he tried to guess her age. It wasn't easy. Under that golden armour she could have been forty, or seventy. "We're here to clean up the mess," Foster said.

As Mary hurried past him with the carpet cleaner, one of the machine's casters left a wiggly black mark on the wall. The woman walked across the room, jewellery jingling, and pointed at a purple blotch that reminded Foster of the time that Duboco, in the throes of a trendy management theory, had dispatched a psychologist to test its senior managers. *What do you see in this shape?* the psychologist asked. *An ink blot*, Foster replied, and then he threw the man out of his office.

Mary pulled a bath towel from the bag and began blotting up the wine. "We'll have this looking as good as new."

Foster peered down. The towel had a border of embroidered roses. It was Mary's best. She handed him the sopping towel. What was he supposed to do with it? He turned to the client. "Could you get me a garbage bag?"

"I have one right here." Mary pawed through the duffle bag and handed Foster a bag and a spray can. She snapped hoses together while Foster stood frowning at the can. He looked at the client. "Do you have a bottle of hydrogen peroxide?"

"Hug-a-Rug is a miracle product." Mary said, snatching the can from Foster's hand. "Watch Hug-a-Rug work its magic." She spritzed the stain with one hand and pointed frantically at the carpet cleaning machine with the other.

Foster plugged in the machine and pushed the "on" button. Nothing happened. "Did Tyler test this thing?"

Mary shoved him aside and jiggled the wall plug. The machine roared into life, and she went to work, drawing the cleaning wand over the stain. Foster watched as a murky liquid swirled into the machine's transparent reservoir. After a moment he wandered over to a pair of sliding doors, opened them and stepped out. He stood on a balcony, staring at the night sky with the cold wind snapping his clothes. The wind, the dark lake, brought Cedric and Sylvia to mind. AMEB had gone to the bottom but they were venturing on, sailing the oceans in *Believer*.

"Come away from there at once!"

"Hmm?" Foster turned his head. The woman in the iridescent dress was glaring at him, her hands on her hips. Mary hurried over and pulled him back inside. "Take the equipment to the truck."

"Truck? We came in a taxi."

"Take this downstairs." Mary thrust the duffle bag into his arms, turned him around and gave him a little shove.

Down the hallway went Foster, into the mirrored elevator, his steps uncertain, his mind blank. He might have been one of those amnesiacs who wander into police stations. You saw their pictures on the news. "Do you know this man?" the announcer would say. The woman on the security desk glanced at him, went back to her knitting. Foster looked around. Shawna was flipping through her math book, bobbing her head to soundless music.

When Foster sat down beside her, she popped out her earphones and said, "Math is stupid."

"What?" Math was Foster's pole star, the fixed point from which he took his bearings. "Show me what you're working on."

Shawna made a face and began to read. "Carla has ten dollars in her pocket. She takes her little brother to the candy store, and she buys a chocolate bar and a bag of jelly beans. The chocolate bar costs twice as much as the bag of jelly beans. She gives her little brother half of what she has left and she puts the remaining three dollars in her pocket. How much did the jelly beans cost?" Shawna shook her head. "See what I mean? Stupid."

"It's simple algebra." Foster picked up a pencil. "Let x equal the price of the jelly beans. That's what we want to know, isn't it? The chocolate bar costs twice as much, which is 2x."

"It's a candy store, right?"

"Yes, a candy store. Carla puts three dollars in her pocket. Therefore —"

"So, wouldn't they put the price on the bag of jelly beans?"

Foster looked at his granddaughter. "That's not the point."

"Don't we want to know the price of the jelly beans?"

"Well, yes." Foster thought a moment. "But suppose the price isn't on the jelly beans."

"So we ask the guy behind the counter."

A strange, sliding sensation came over Foster. It was as if he were walking on ball bearings. "Let's stick with the problem. x plus 2x —"

"When you were out? Jessica called. She said she'll pick you up at six." Shawna looked at the textbook. "Carla's a dork. Nobody thinks like that."

"But can't you see …" Foster took a deep breath, began again. "We have to go below the words. We have to find the numbers."

"Mom told me about the bank. Are you moving in for good?"

"Oh, no. Not for good." *Foster has zero dollars in his pocket. He owes several thousand dollars to credit card companies. His granddaughter baffles him. His daughter has an annoying boyfriend. Let x equal … what, exactly?* Buffeted by a blast of cold air, Foster looked up to see Tyler strolling toward him. The security guard knitted on. Shawna stared down at her book, wiggled in her earplugs and took out her iPod.

"How did you find us?" Foster asked. Cause and effect seemed desperately important.

"I called my cell. Does Mary need any help?"

The elevator doors parted and Mary came marching out. Before Tyler could react, Foster got to his feet, wrestled the duffle bag from Mary's hand and lugged it to the curb. Tyler's car was a flattened-looking subcompact. The wheels looked expensive, frivolous.

They drove back to Mazurka Street with Foster and Shawna crammed in the back like a pair of children. Shawna went into her shell, closed her eyes, lost herself in her music.

"Did the customer pay cash?" Tyler asked.

Mary stared out the side window. "I made it a freebie."

“A freebie? How come, Mare?”

Foster stiffened. Mare. As if his daughter were a horse.

“The wall got scratched,” Mary said.

“Who scratched the wall?” Tyler asked.

“I did,” Foster said, staring at the rear-view mirror.

“Hey, no problem,” Tyler said. “I just wanted to know.”

“YOU’LL LIKE FRANNIE.” Jessica spun the steering wheel and swerved around a bus. “She works in oils. She’s gay, so don’t hit on her. Not that you would. Oh, you know what I mean. Daphne’s a sculptor, mostly. Patricia’s a photographer. Hates digital. She’s got this ancient Nikon. Buys old film on eBay. Wanda does watercolours. When she does them. Holly said she’d come but you never know with Holly. Are you warm enough in that coat?”

They were hurtling toward a traffic island. Foster closed his eyes. Yesterday he had been in Florida. He had the impression that an essential part of him had yet to arrive. They parked the car on Queen Street and started walking east.

“It’s so good you’re here.” Jessica hugged his arm. “Mister, we’re going to do things together.”

“Um,” Foster said, taking in the surroundings. They were in Parkdale, on a defeated-looking street that had once been grand. A frowsy movie theatre sold cleaning supplies. A faded grocery store hawked second-hand books. Lingerie dangled in the windows of an old bank, bras to the left, panties to the right. What would become of the AMEB building in London, that lovely old mansion on Threadneedle Street? Would they hang jockey shorts in the fanlights? Jessica pulled him into a bar.

The Grease Pit had started life as a garage, Foster thought: the oil-stained concrete, the lithographed signs offering service for defunct brands of cars: Packards, Pontiacs, Studebakers. Jessica led him across an empty dance floor — she had him by the hand — and into a room decorated with hubcaps. Hubcaps had vanished from cars years ago. It seemed to Foster that, like old elephants tramping to their proverbial graveyard, the hubcaps had come here to die. A man wearing cowboy boots, blue jeans and a shiny red shirt stood chewing on a toothpick and looking down at a jukebox. When he stepped away, a woman sang, in a twanging, recorded voice, "He's got a busted ol' truck and he's a-driving me to dee-vorce ..."

Jessica stopped abruptly at a large, round table. "People, this is Foster." She pointed around the table counter-clockwise, rhyming off names: Frannie, Patricia, Daphne, Wanda, Belinda and Holly. Who, it seemed, had shown up after all.

"Hello," Foster said. In the shadowy bar, the women were a blur of colour, a gleam of teeth, a flash of eyes. He squeezed in beside Jessica and sat with his hands folded on the table. The Blue Jays cap on Frannie's head reminded him of Charlie and his baseball stories. With AMEB a lost cause, Foster knew he would have to find a job — a real job; he would have to stay in the game for a few more innings. What had Charlie told him about some old pitcher? Nolan Ryan, that was the name. Still playing when he was forty-six. Pitched the way an old dog hunts. Didn't move a whit more than he had to. Got the job done and went home. A waiter appeared. Fatigue was catching up with Foster. The women ordered drinks, their voices blending into an impromptu harmony.

"White wine spritzer. Bloody Caesar. What's your poison, Frannie? Vodka martini with a twist. What have you got in single malt? Glenlivet, Glenfiddich, Highland Park ... Double Glenlivet and a Perrier. What's the house red? Yellow Tail Shiraz. Oh, and there's a Merlot. French or Californian? I'm not sure. Want me to find out? Nah. I'll have a glass of Shiraz. Me too. Me too. Wait. Let's get a bottle."

The best jobs were offshore. Which was where he belonged. The headhunters were in London. Canary Wharf, London Bridge. Hammersmith, some of them.

"Sir?"

"Hey, Jessica, I've got this great idea for a series. Can I bounce it off you? Ready? Cadavers in a morgue. Pre-Raphaelite style. Colour, detail, complexity, but instead of Ophelia floating downstream looking too hot to be dead, it's an accident victim, or an old guy that died on the street. Naked, I mean. Huh. Kind of, Botticelli does an autopsy? Interesting. Want me to come over, do some sketching with you? Sure. Count me in. When it comes to playing dead, I'm the best. A Pre-Raphaelite sisterhood. I like it. Can I come too? Guys … Look, I should work the idea before I open it up like that."

"What do you want to drink, sir?"

"Beer," Foster said. How could he get to London?

"What kind of beer, sir?"

"Whatever's on draft." Fly to Amsterdam, catch a train?

"We have thirty kinds of beers on draft, sir."

Foster looked up. The waiter was a lanky young woman in mechanic's overalls. All these people wandering around in costume. When had North America turned into a theme park?

"Anything on special?"

"Uh-huh, we have our own microbrewery and —"

"Fine. I'll have that."

"Foster just got back from Florida," Jessica announced. The table went silent. All eyes turned to Foster. Jessica smiled and asked, "Did you have a good trip?"

"Fine." Drive to Buffalo, fly to London from there?

Jessica looked at him. "Good fine or bad fine?"

"The trip was fine."

The waiter was back with a tray on her arm. The jukebox stopped in mid-song. Spotlights illuminated an alcove where four musicians in fancy cowboy outfits were tuning guitars, fiddling with amplifiers, clipping sheets of paper onto music stands. Foster sipped his beer. The drummer looked a bit like Charlie, a little bear of a man. The bass player had swooping sideburns and long, boney fingers. The slide guitar player had a cowlick and rimless glasses. The man who had been leaning on the jukebox lifted a mic from its stand and said, "We're going to kick this set off with a Draw-bar Bill classic: 'Double-Wide'!"

"Ladies?" Jessica said. "If you ask this man something and he says, 'fine,' let me know and I'll translate."

The lead guitar player, a tall, earnest-looking youth, counted the band in and picked a complicated intro on his Telecaster. Country and western wasn't Foster's cup of tea, but he had to admit, these guys could play. The music was fast, expert, stirring. "Gonna hitch my heart to your double-wide, gonna take your lovin' for a long, long ride … Rollin' down the road, down the road …"

The women were looking at Foster with cool speculation. Jessica gave him a catty smile.

"And when you're a-sittin' by my side, you'll know my affection is bona fide."

Foster didn't have the energy to cross swords with Jessica. It had been a long day and, all things considered, it had been about as much fun as snake bite.

"Towin' our load, to a new abode."

A new abode. Draw-bar Bill had the right idea. Foster drained his beer, slammed the glass on the table and got to his feet. Everything was wrong. Wrong country. Wrong music. Wrong woman. He took Jessica by the hand and led her to the dance floor. She was goggling at him. He had taken her by surprise. Good. But now what? He hadn't danced in years. The band was laying down a strong beat. Under the spotlights, in the deafening din, Foster lifted Jessica's hand. He stepped back, stepped forward, stepped back again, picking up the rhythm. The kid on lead guitar egged him on with a showy riff. One of Jessica's friends (was it Frannie?) began to clap, and then the whole table was clapping, and then everyone in the room was clapping. Jessica laughed and twirled under his hand. The steel guitar soared. Jessica danced away from him; he felt the answering snap of their arms and brought her close. Can you jive to a song about a double-wide?

Foster didn't give a damn.

[EIGHT]

ON A COLD, snowy morning a week before Christmas, Foster sat at the back of a bus, looking out at the houses on Keele Street, the strings of lights and inflatable Santas. Under the raincoat he wore his tropical weight suit, a dress shirt and a silk tie. The paper bag on his lap held his Grandpa outfit and a tuna sandwich.

The bus jerked to a stop at a windswept intersection three blocks north of Highway 401. He stepped down, tucked the paper bag under an arm, jammed his bare hands in his pockets and started across a vast parking lot, slanting forward to shield his eyes from the snow. It was a long walk to the front doors of Grandpa's Toolbox, and he glanced up occasionally to take a bearing on the sign over the doors. A maple leaf had replaced the apostrophe in *Grandpa's*. A minivan cut in front of him and swerved into a parking spot. Thrown off balance, Foster did an impromptu dance, three steps left, two steps right. The driver got out and stared belligerently at him. Concept, Gary Garth would say. Concept. The hoodlum in the hockey jacket was a fellow human being with a deep need for community and connection. Foster fell into step beside the man who had nearly run him over. "Can I help you find something?"

The man pulled a small plastic box from his pocket. "Took this off the florescent in my shop. Damn thing started buzzing."

"That's a capacitor. They're easy to replace. I'll walk you to the electrical department." Foster led the way through an entrance done up like an old-time hardware emporium, complete with barrels of brooms and pails of toilet plungers, a galvanized washtub hanging in a fake window like a prize turkey. A man wearing the Grandpa outfit and a Santa cap shook their hands and said, "Welcome back to Grandpa's!" The tail of the Santa cap covered the man's name badge. What was his name? McKenzie, McDougall, MacDonald — a name like that — had trained for Electrical in Florida.

"I work here." Foster held up the paper bag.

The greeter nodded happily. "I'll know you next time."

There were signs everywhere: *This Christmas, come back to Grandpa's! Wondering what to give? Ask Grandpa!* Foster led Mr. Capacitor — the trainees had practised this mnemonic trick in Florida — past table saws and microwave ovens and closet storage systems. Men in plaid and denim unpacked light bulbs, worked tinting machines, walked around with hand tools in the pockets of their overalls. "Grandpa Wilson," Foster said when he and Mr. Capacitor stood in Electrical. "Can you help this gentleman?"

In the locker room, Foster punched the time clock and changed into his uniform. He felt self-conscious as he made his way to Nails 'n Glue wearing the Grandpa gear, but, with so many men wearing the same costume, no one paid him any mind. It was, he supposed, like being naked in a nudist colony.

"How's business?" Foster said.

"Slow, friend." Charlie was leaning on a counter. "Contractors, mostly. We're low on two-inch drywall screws. A skid needs to come down. I put in a toe-motor request." Charlie looked thoughtfully over the sales floor. "I had to walk the guy over to tools. We should have the drywall guns in this department."

Foster smiled. Charlie had never really bought Gary Garth's concept of an old-fashioned hardware store. "You might be happier in tools. You know a lot about them."

"I'm okay here. How's your daughter?"

"Fine."

"And the little girl?"

"Fine." Foster ran a hand over the counter. Like all the props in the store, it was fake. In Florida, he had stuck his head in the fixtures department and watched a man beating a board with a length of chain. *Best way to age pine*, the man had said. As if the world wasn't aging quickly enough.

"Get a load of this."

Foster followed Charlie's gaze. A tall man was coming through the front doors carrying a contraption that looked a bit like a tuba.

"Plumbing assembly," Foster said. "Kitchen drain?"

"Looks like he brought the whole damn kitchen. Probably just the trap that's bad."

"I looked up the players you told me about. Rickey Henderson holds the record for stolen bases."

A faraway look came into Charlie's eyes. "1406 career steals. 130 in a single season. That's a record too. The man could break a catcher's heart."

"How do you steal a base?" Foster liked to hear Charlie talk baseball.

"Trick is to get a good jump." Charlie crouched and put his hands on the tops of his thighs. "Say that's second base where you're standing, and I'm going for third." Charlie stared down the aisle. "The pitcher commits himself to throw and I'm off." Charlie straightened up and looked at his watch. "I better be on my horse. Doctor's appointment."

"Nothing serious, I hope."

"Nah. I'll let the doc say his piece. Then I'll go to Food Way and buy all the stuff he said I can't eat. Saves making a shopping list. You hardly see a good base stealer these days. Everybody swings for the fences. See ya."

"See ya, Charlie."

"Good King Wenceslas" played on the overhead speakers… . a poor man … gath'ring winter fuel … Foster's thoughts drifted to the villa he had planned to buy in Thailand. He couldn't seem to hold the demise of AMEB in mind. His thoughts would break free and race along, only to pull up short like a dog running to the end of its lead. He walked to the end wall and ran a critical eye over the bottles of glue. The bottles seemed to touch their curved handles to their cylindrical caps in salute. Foster gave them a parade ground nod, his mind on other matters. There had been no response to the resumés he had posted online, no answers to the emails he had sent to headhunters in London. But there wouldn't be, with Christmas around the corner. He went behind the counter and stood at the nickel-plated cash register. Manufactured by the Duckworth Cash Register Company, Foster read. He put a finger on the Total key, played with the springy resistance and thought of his father. Irv, if you could see me now. I'm a hardware man after all.

"Grandpa Foster?" Foster looked up to see a Grandpa guiding an old woman toward the counter. She was half Foster's height.

"Ida needs your help with a loose toilet seat," the greeter said. "Grandpa Foster will look after you," he told Ida in a loud voice, and walked away.

"Damn fool thinks I'm deaf." Ida plunked her ancient purse on the counter, pulled out a plastic bag and upended it. Nuts and bolts rained down on the pine.

"The seat slides all over the place when I'm trying to do my business."

"The threads are stripped, ma'am." Foster picked up a bolt. "See where the threads have gone fuzzy? The material is very soft. You have to be careful not to over-tighten them."

"I didn't over-tighten them. Jim did."

"Oh. Well, then." *If a customer reveals a family conflict, stick to the technical issues.* Foster opened a bin, picked through the contents, plucked out a brass washer and set it aside. How could he keep his section in order when people took items from one bin and dropped them in another? "See how easily the nuts spin on? Tell Jim finger-tight is fine."

"Jim is dead."

"Oh, I'm sorry."

"Why? Jim lived down the hall. He drank too much. And that old dog of his! I wouldn't let him bring it through the door. They found Jim dead in his kitchen. Makes you think."

"Can someone put these on for you?" Foster could imagine the rest of the story. The dog whining behind the door. The super letting himself in with his pass-key. Had Kathleen died this way?

"Can I do it myself?"

"Sure you can." Foster explained the procedure. "I've marked the price on the bag."

Ida toddled away. The recorded music switched to "It Came upon a Midnight Clear." Horns and woodwinds. Harps of gold. Angels bending near the earth.

"Nicely done, Grandpa Foster."

Foster spun around. His heart skipped a beat. Where had Amanda Curtwell come from? The woman could haunt a house.

"You handled that client with tact and skill."

"Thank you."

"Tom and Sal will be in at —"

"At seven," Foster said. "I read the schedule."

"Yes," Amanda said. "And at eight —"

"The search function will be offline for two hours. A database push shouldn't take that long. You should speak to the systems people." Amanda had a great figure, Foster couldn't help noticing. He felt like a child with a crush on his teacher, standing next to her in his overalls.

"You were five minutes late this morning, Grandpa Foster."

"Oh. Well, the bus schedules aren't well thought out, I'm afraid."

"Grandpa Foster …" Amanda frowned and began again. "Grandpa Foster, your work is satisfactory. Your lateness won't be a Clean Slate issue."

Foster nodded. The training manual devoted a page to Clean Slate. The first two infractions of store policy would be forgiven. An employee who committed a third offence would be fired. "That's very kind of you, Amanda. You're doing fine work too."

She blinked at him and turned on her heel. Foster watched as she crossed the sales floor, went up a flight of stairs and disappeared from view like an angel who had bent near the earth and was now vanishing into the heavens. It couldn't be easy for a woman her age to manage such an experienced staff.

RESTLESS WORLD WAS over. The credits rolled. Jed Creed wouldn't have to face a Grand Jury after all. Samantha kept begging Damian to take her back. Foster glanced at his daughter. She usually had something to say about Jed Creed. But Mary was in a mood. Slouched on the sofa with the remote in her hand, she was flipping between a game show, a National Geographic special, a cop show, a second cop show, a sitcom. Shawna was lying languidly on the floor, reading a book and peering up at the TV from time to time. Foster hoisted himself from the beanbag chair and went to the kitchen. He noticed that Shawna was watching him. Did she want something from the fridge? No, she was heading off to her room. He picked up the phone and called Jessica.

"Change of plans, I'm afraid. I can't make Tuesday this week. Have to work. Would Thursday do?"

"Thursday? Can I go that long without sex? You know, I'll have to think about that. I really will. If you don't show up, I might have to send out."

"I beg your pardon?"

"Joke, Foster. I've been a bit giddy all day. Paint fumes, I suppose."

"Is your art going well?"

"Well, you know, art is kind of a fancy word for what went on here today. My art is going really, really shitty, thank you very much for asking. I just tossed another hundred bucks of stuff in the dumpster."

"Oh."

"But wait, there's more. I gouged myself with a frame. Now I have this scratch on my boob. Too bad you're not here. You could put a Band-Aid on it."

She had a wild streak, this woman. Said the strangest things. "See you on Thursday. Goodbye." Foster listened carefully and heard a click as Jessica hung up. Then a second click. He strode down the hall and tapped on Shawna's sticker-plastered door. The door cracked open and Shawna peered out at him.

"Shawna, were you eavesdropping?"

"Eve who?"

"Were you listening in?" He knew she had. Her phone was sitting on her bed.

"Listening to what?"

"You know perfectly well to what."

"No, I don't."

"Yes, you do."

"How would I know if I wasn't listening?"

"Shawna, I heard the line click."

"Oh, yeah. I picked it up for a second. I wanted to call Benny."

"Look. Suppose you had an older brother. How would you like it if he listened to your private conversations?"

"I don't have an older brother."

"Well, suppose you did."

"Yeah." Shawna narrowed her eyes. "You're kinda like an older brother. You sleep in the next bedroom. You hang around the house. Mom cooks for you. I have to wait for you to get out of the bathroom."

"When did you ever have to wait — now see here. Eleven-year-old girls couldn't have brothers my age."

"Sure they could."

"No, they couldn't."

"They could if they had the same father and different mothers. I saw a program about that. This eighty-year-old guy in Africa?"

"We don't have the same father!"

The door slammed in his face. Foster stood in the dark hallway, his anger turning sour. He hadn't meant to say that. Not to a girl who had no idea who her father was. He turned slowly, and found Mary standing before him, blocking his way, her eyes brimming with tears. "You're not going to put her through all that stuff, Foster. You hear me? I won't have it!"

His daughter's words fell on him like blows. All that stuff? What old grievances did Mary have in mind?

Shawna's door popped open. "Hey, Mom, it's okay."

"No! It isn't. It is not okay." Mary stalked away. Foster watched her go, his heart emptying. Shawna closed her door.

THE NEXT MORNING Foster waited until Mary had gone to work and Shawna was off to school, and then he got up, shaved, showered, put on his suit, pulled on his silk socks, knotted his Burberry tie and walked up the street.

When he came through the door of Corner Convenience, shaking with cold, Mrs. Park beamed at him. How's your daughter? And how's the little girl? And how are you? Fine, Foster told her as she sold him the newspapers. Everything is fine. What else could he say? That his daughter hated him? That he had to get out of her house?

Coffee in hand, he sat at the kitchen table, reading the papers. *Executives Eat with Homeless*, read a headline. Foster studied the picture. The men wore suits. They were his age, or younger, and they were sipping soup in a church basement. There was nothing suitable in the want ads. Foster gazed longingly at the phone, picturing *Believer* heeling at a picturesque angle, Cedric at the wheel, tanned and smiling, Sylvia at his side, her face tilted to the sun.

The Elite had folded, he noticed as he walked along Dundas Street. Newspapers covered the windows. The old restaurant had waited for him to return and then given up the ghost. The neighbouring store, a former five-and-dime, had a new tenant. Exotic Finds sold mahogany furniture, brass fireplace screens, marble knick-knacks. Foster peered through the window, watching a stock clerk lift a green-and-white vase from a nest of excelsior. In the villages of Pakistan they made those things from marble chips, turned the composite block on a foot-powered lathe. In Dubai you could buy a trinket like that for a couple of American dollars.

What was her name, Foster asked himself as he wandered through High Park, thrashing his dress shoes through the snow, the name of the woman who'd bought the marble table? Swiss. Blond. Taught at an International Baccalaureate school. They had met at the Marine Club and had a brief fling, two weekends and a national holiday. The table, a slab of creamy dolomite, shone under her chandelier like a lake under the stars. Ilse. That was the name. One night Isle went to a dinner club and worked her way through a pitcher of daiquiris. She was dancing on a chair by closing time. The next day, the police put her on a plane. You can't carry on that way in public, not in an Arab country. And you can't stick a marble table in your suitcase. Foster kicked at a chunk of ice. Fat lot of good his expat lore did him now.

"BUSY TIME OF the year," Mary said from the kitchen. She was at the sink, washing the dinner dishes. Shawna had gone over to Benny's. Foster was in the beanbag chair, sheltering behind a newspaper. Mary hadn't spoken to him in days. He wracked his brain for something to say. "It's been busy in the store."

"Been busy, has it?"

"Very busy."

"Busy in your department?"

"Oh, you'd be surprised how many people need fasteners at Christmas."

"Yeah? People need fasteners at Christmas?"

Foster lowered the newspaper. This was marvellous. They were having a conversation.

"I love Christmas. But Shawna hates the commercialism."

"She'll go vegetarian next," Foster said, trying for a joke.

"She has, Foster. Well, on and off."

"Ah," Foster said. He should have noticed this.

Mary came into the living room. One of her romance novels lay tented on the table. She picked it up and began to read. Foster waited a moment, then went back to the paper.

"But I don't know. I'd miss opening presents."

Screened by the want ads, Foster listened attentively. Where was she going with this?

"So Shawna and I? We'll do the Dollar Store this year."

"Oh?" Foster put down the paper. Do the Dollar Store?

"So here's the deal. We'll spend ten dollars each. No cheating."

Had Shawna really gone anti-commercial or was this about his cash flow problem? Foster remembered his Christmas ritual, the two cheques he had written every year, both for five hundred Canadian dollars, both made out to Mary but with different memo lines — Mary/Xmas, Shawna/Xmas. His arms trailing over the sides of the beanbag chair, he pictured his office — the white Berber carpet, the onyx desk set, the glass wall facing the Gulf. He thought a moment. Chose his words carefully. Rehearsed them silently. "Mary, go ahead and get Shawna whatever you like," he said. "Something nice."

"You don't get it, do you!" Mary slammed the romance novel on the table.

"Ten dollars," Foster said quickly. "Okay. Fine."

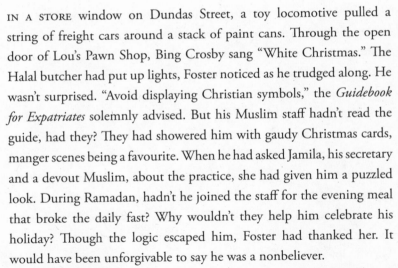

IN A STORE window on Dundas Street, a toy locomotive pulled a string of freight cars around a stack of paint cans. Through the open door of Lou's Pawn Shop, Bing Crosby sang "White Christmas." The Halal butcher had put up lights, Foster noticed as he trudged along. He wasn't surprised. "Avoid displaying Christian symbols," the *Guidebook for Expatriates* solemnly advised. But his Muslim staff hadn't read the guide, had they? They had showered him with gaudy Christmas cards, manger scenes being a favourite. When he had asked Jamila, his secretary and a devout Muslim, about the practice, she had given him a puzzled look. During Ramadan, hadn't he joined the staff for the evening meal that broke the daily fast? Why wouldn't they help him celebrate his holiday? Though the logic escaped him, Foster had thanked her. It would have been unforgivable to say he was a nonbeliever.

Cloudy today, cold, damp and overcast. If the weather held, Toronto would have a white Christmas, Foster thought, peering up at the clouds that hid the sun.

He strolled the aisles of Dollar Heaven with a red plastic shopping basket dangling from an arm. Harrod's, it wasn't. Would Corman, the little rat who had brought down AMEB, shop at Harrod's once he had been rehabilitated into show business? The entertainment section of *The Globe and Mail* had carried the story. Corman was the new host of *Limelight*, a talent search program. He had already signed a six-figure book deal. Foster shook his head, remembering the disgrace that had ended his father's life. Irv, you died too soon. In the age of celebrity, disgrace is rocket fuel. Finding himself in the cosmetics section again, Foster drifted to a stop. How could anyone find a gift worth giving in this bazaar of junk? When a stout woman bustled past, he gave her basket a surreptitious glance. She had a comb and brush set in there, little bottles of shampoo, a fancy nail file. Mary was always short of that sort of thing. He peered up at a pegboard wall, duplicated the woman's choices and dropped them in his basket.

Which left five dollars to spend on Shawna. A display of batteries caught his eye. She had been looking for batteries the other day, for one of her many gadgets. He took two packages and wandered on. Oven mitts? Not for Shawna. He pondered a screwdriver with interchangeable bits. Shawna didn't need a screwdriver. He hefted a package of mysteriously labelled herbal tea. He didn't want to poison the child. He wandered into the stationery department. Envelopes? A paper punch? Pencils? Pencils! Yes, he had seen Shawna sharpening pencils. The yellow HBs seemed the best value. Twenty pencils in a package, pliable eraser tips. But no child wants a boring gift. Pencils with the Canadian flag on the barrel? Pencils made from shredded American money? The idea made Foster wince. Happy face pencils? Stars? Ah! Shawna loved stars, and here were pencils bright with red stars, silver stars, gold stars. His shopping done, he went to the cash desk and unpacked his basket. Ten gifts for ten dollars. Plus tax. Did Mary mean ten dollars with tax or without tax? He wanted to play by the rules. Without tax, he decided.

After dinner he helped Shawna pull Christmas boxes from the attic, unpack an artificial tree and set it up in the living room.

"Awesome," Shawna said when the tree was assembled.

With its metal spine and its strange plastic needles, the tree resembled a hoary television antenna, Foster thought. "It looks great."

Shawna beamed at him. She picked up a box and yanked out silver garlands, strings of lights, pasteboard sleds, plastic snowflakes. Foster pictured himself trudging to the coal yard to buy a tree with the coins his grandmother had given him. The old woman had encouraged him to haggle with Mr. Johnson — Black Johnson, she called him because of the sooty tint his trade had given his skin. Had Grandma ever met a person of another race?

"My fave!" Shawna cried, interrupting his reverie. She was standing before him with a plastic angel cradled in her hands. Foster stared at the ragtag figure, and remembered Kathleen hanging it on a Christmas tree. He vaguely remembered tossing away the box of decorations after the divorce. Had Mary rummaged through the discards he had set at the curb?

FOSTER KNEW THE gift-giving ritual from the snapshots that had arrived in Dubai year after year. Mary was playing Santa. Foster stared at his gifts, a stapler, a letter tray made of wire mesh, a glue stick, an oversized eraser. Mary and Shawna had put some thought into this.

"Hey, Foster?" Shawna adjusted her clip-on antlers. "I really like the batteries."

"Thanks for the shampoo," Mary said. "I didn't know they made Lavender."

"I'll do better next year," said Foster. "Next year I'll buy proper gifts."

"Oh, for God's sake," Mary said.

"When's dinner?" Shawna said quickly.

"We'll eat at six." A warning had come into Mary's voice. "Or whenever Tyler gets here."

Tyler was coming for dinner? Foster stared at the television. Shawna grabbed the remote. On *Restless World* the sets were done up with red bows and twinkling lights. Jed Creed sat before a crackling fire with a glass of eggnog. Sam and Dam held hands. On the soap opera, a Christmas truce had been declared.

FOR DINNER THEY had turkey with all the trimmings. After dinner, Tyler, Mary and Foster sat around the kitchen table, drinking a liqueur that Tyler had given Mary. The liqueur tasted like mouthwash, Foster thought. Shawna had gone over to Kayla's to show off her present from Tyler — a video game console, the latest model with all the bells and whistles. To Foster's annoyance, Tyler had ignored Mary's Dollar Store rule. He had given Mary earrings, a bracelet, French perfume. He had given Foster a pair of cufflinks, a silk tie and a matching handkerchief. It was generous of Tyler to give these presents, Foster supposed, but could Tyler afford them?

Mary picked up the remote. "Maybe there's something on television."

"Okay if I put on the game?" Tyler said. "The Leafs are playing the Habs."

Mary glanced at Foster.

"You two go ahead," Foster said. "I'll stretch my legs."

The sidewalks were empty. He had the street to himself. It worried him that Mary seemed serious about Tyler. Or was it just a crush? That would be fine if she were sixteen … Where had he been when Mary was sixteen? Foster counted back through the years, contract by contract. He had been in Kuwait. It was a little late to play the protective father.

“THERE WAS SOMETHING in the paper this morning about the Blue Jays, Charlie. They acquired a new pitcher.”

“Yeah, I saw that. A leftie.” Charlie looked around the sales floor. “Keeping busy?”

“Returns, mostly.”

“Who’s on with you?”

“Sal just went home.”

“Tom’ll be on with me, then.” Charlie glanced up at the mirrors that concealed the store’s office. “What’s the word from on high?”

Foster smiled. “Miss Amanda came through about an hour ago.”

“Did we pass the inspection?”

“It’s me she’s keeping an eye on.”

“Maybe so. But a guy in seasonal said I screwed up the Grandpa song yesterday.” Charlie ran his thumbs under his suspenders. “You up for a beer later? I’m off at nine.”

“Can’t tonight.” Foster waved goodbye and strode toward the change room. The bus left at six, and Jessica was making dinner for him. As he hurried down the aisle, he saw a Grandpa demonstrating a snow blower to a woman in a sari, a Grandpa showing a mitre saw to a man in a shalwar kameez, a Grandpa explaining fibreglass insulation to a Sikh family. Smart man, Gary Garth.

WHERE HAD THE bedsheet gone? Foster was lying on his back with a leg drawn up, naked as a newborn. He looked over to see Jessica sitting at an easel, wielding a stick of charcoal. It was past midnight. The loft was brightly lit. Jessica glanced at him and then frowned at whatever she was drawing. In the condo across the street people moved to and fro. He looked around for the bedclothes.

"Oh, don't move," Jessica said. "I'll make tea in a sec. I bought a box of that Earl Grey you like."

Foster settled back uneasily.

"Pull your knee up the way you had it."

"You're drawing me?"

"Relax. It's just a sketch. Talk to me. You sent out more resumés."

"Yes. Over a hundred." Foster looked dubiously down the length of his body. The hairy chest, the pale paunch, the muscular legs — nothing matched. A suit completed him. Armani made the man.

"For computing jobs?" The charcoal stick darted about.

Foster wrapped himself in a sheet, stepped off the bed and tramped across the room toga style.

"All done," Jessica said brightly as he came near. She went to the kitchen, taking the drawing with her.

"MY GRANDFATHER IS very brave," Shawna said two weeks later, in Mary's kitchen. "You'd have to be, living with all those terrorists."

"Dubai isn't dangerous," Benny scoffed. He was a serious boy with green, sceptical eyes and a mop of straw-coloured hair.

Foster tied his apron and reached for the dish soap.

Shawna gave Benny a puzzled look. "That's not what Danny Deakens says."

"Danny Deakens is a total moron."

"That's what everybody says."

"Then they're all morons."

"Well, there's very little crime in Dubai," Foster interrupted. Seeing Shawna's disappointment, he added, "But I was there during both Gulf Wars."

"Wow," Shawna said. "Hey, can you be our resource person?"

"Resource person?" Foster shook the water from a plate and set it in the drying rack.

"We have this big presentation to do for Geo-Issues? And we picked the Middle East? Benny's doing the wars and I'm doing religion and stuff."

What could he tell a room full of children? Foster rinsed another dish, set it in the rack. He pictured himself at the Marine Club, under an umbrella, sipping a daiquiri, watching the supertankers transit the Gulf. Shawna was looking at him imploringly. "Okay."

"Yessss!!!" Shawna pumped a fist at her side.

"What do you want me to talk about, exactly?" Foster called as Benny and Shawna trooped toward her room.

"Just the important stuff." Shawna said. "Don't worry about pictures. We're going to post stuff on Piperline."

"Piperline?"

"Yeah, you know." Shawna cupped her hands and spun her thumbs over an imaginary object. "The micro-blog."

Benny looked at Foster with sudden suspicion. "Didn't you use to work with computers, Mr. Foster?"

Foster hung up the dish towel. I sure did, sonny. And it's just as well you're on the other side of the room.

[NINE]

SHAWNA HAD BEGGED him not to be late. She needn't have worried, Foster thought as he tramped through the snow clutching the collar of his raincoat. He was always on time. What would the children want to know? The question took him back to a snug room with clinking radiators, streaky blackboards, desks with inkwells. He slipped on a patch of ice, regained his balance and found himself remembering Janet Latimer. His first crush. First girl he kissed. Hazel eyes. Tall. Sat in the front row. A white blouse, a plaid skirt, barrettes in her hair. Always the first to put up her hand.

Why did you stay so long over there, Mr. Foster?

Because the Arabian Gulf is the fountain of youth, Janet. The real McCoy. The genuine item. Swim in that sea, and you never grow old.

What did you do over there?

Now, that's a very good question. My job title was Head of Information Technology, Gulf Region. But you can't go by that, Janet. I was the tall man in the tailored suit, the source of gravity that kept expatriates from twenty countries spinning in harmonious orbits. Like a solar system, an enterprise needs dead weight at its centre; otherwise, it would fly apart.

What did you do when you weren't working?

Weekends, you mean? I'd go south, into the desert, or north, into the wadis. A wadi is a dry riverbed, Janet. Imagine a canyon with high, sheer walls. Rainwater cut those walls through solid rock. You thought it never rains in the Arabian Peninsula? Well, it doesn't rain often, and some years it doesn't rain at all, but when it does rain, girls your age run from their classrooms. They hitch up their abayas and they dance in the downpour.

Isn't the desert bleak?

The desert is beautiful, Janet. Imagine a sea of dunes, rising and falling to the horizon. Imagine sand curling from the tops of the dunes like spray.

You make it sound wonderful.

Do I? Then you must never forget an important rule of expatriate life. Never fall in love with a foreign landscape. Because one day you will have to leave, and leaving will break your heart.

Janet faded away as Shawna's school came into view. The school, with its redbrick walls and its rows of windows, dated from the sixties, Foster thought. Opening the front door, he saw Shawna running down the corridor toward him, her footsteps echoing on the terrazzo. He slipped off his raincoat, adjusted his tie and smoothed the lapels of his suit.

The classroom was a sunny space with artwork taped on the walls, pictures with the bright colours and bold lines of poignant optimism. The desks were arranged in a circle. Mrs. Patterson, a slender woman of forty or so with the straight blond hair Foster associated with female folk singers, took his coat, thanked him for coming and introduced him to the class.

Benny was up first. The boy gave a ten-minute talk that ranged from Lawrence of Arabia to the most recent invasion of Iraq, a litany of murder and mayhem that left the class dazed and Foster feeling as ancient as Ozymandias; it seemed incredible that so much of that sad history had happened in his own lifetime.

Shawna walked to the front of the room. In the months he had been back in Canada, Foster had paid scant attention to his granddaughter's clothes. But now it occurred to him that she wasn't dressed like the other girls. She had on a purple blouse braided with glass beads, a pair of taupe slacks with pleats and a wide waistband. The clothes were stylish but decades old. Foster gave her a nod of encouragement. Shawna's subject was Islam. She rhymed off the pillars of the faith: Profession, Prayer, Fasting, Almsgiving and Pilgrimage. She talked about the Qu'ran, and she named the major sects, Sunni and Shi'ite. She said that Islam was a major religion, like Christianity and Buddhism, but that people should learn to live together. The class clapped. All eyes turned to Foster. He stood up and looked at the children's open faces.

"Well, then, where should we begin." He began with the geology of the Arabian Peninsula. "The Precambrian gneiss ..." No, he should begin with plate tectonics. "The grand scale motions of the lithosphere ..." But to understand tectonics, the children needed a working knowledge of subductions. He cited statistics about the oil industry. Yields, metric tons shipped. Destinations. Gross revenues. Time went by. There really was a lot to cover. "Fractional distillation —"

"Thank you," Mrs. Patterson said, springing to her feet. She turned to her class and asked, in the light, desperate tone of a hostess whose dinner party has teetered into disaster, "Are there any questions?"

Shawna fidgeted in her chair. Benny took off his glasses and polished them on his shirt.

"Surely there's something." Mrs. Patterson looked round the class. "Jeremy, you always have interesting things to say."

Jeremy had on a hockey sweater. "If the Arabs made all that money selling oil, why don't they just buy land from Israel?"

"Yeah," said another boy. "That would be fair."

Fairness. The Canadian trump card. Foster glanced at a girl wearing a head scarf. Her eyes grew wary. "I'm not sure it's quite that simple."

"Why can't they get along over there?" said a boy wearing shiny orthodontic braces.

Foster stared at the boy, flummoxed by his question. These children seemed to think that he had a solution to a major geopolitical dilemma when the truth was, he didn't even have an opinion. His expatriate years had boiled his political views down to a distillate of self-interest. He had made his money and kept his mouth shut. What could he have done? Walk into some sheik's palace and say, "Now, see here. I want you people to settle this thing with Israel?"

Jeremy seemed to read his thoughts. "Did you tell them about Canada, Mr. Foster? We don't have wars and stuff."

The boy's earnest words touched Foster. He met Jeremy's eyes, wanting to say something true. "Canadians live behind an armed perimeter too. I'm not sure there's any way around that."

The children exchanged puzzled looks, and Foster wanted to explain himself further. But Mrs. Patterson was on her feet, thanking him, handing him his coat, ushering him to the door.

Outside the school, Foster stood with his hands in his pockets, waiting for Shawna. Snow accumulated on his shoulders as if he were a statue in a park. The bell rang and children came through the doors.

"I thought it went rather well," Foster said, walking beside Shawna.

"Oh, yeah," Benny said, with impenetrable irony. "It was awesome."

Shawna said nothing, spurted ahead. Foster let her go. She was right to be angry with him. He was a hollow man, an empty suit.

A WINDLESS STORM stalled over the city, filling the air with a weightless snow that hushed the world. It was like being inside one of those little glass domes the Swiss sell to tourists, Foster thought, staring at the patio door. Shake the dome and see the little village disappear.

"I think we'll go to the mall this aft." Mary spooned a boiled egg onto Foster's plate.

Foster cracked the egg with a knife. "This is perfect."

"Really?" Mary peered over his shoulder. "No, it isn't. The yolk's hard." She walked to the stove. "Shawna's got her heart set on a DVD, so I thought we could make it an outing," Mary said with her back turned to Foster. "They have all the winter stuff on sale. Half price on coats and boots."

"Grandpa's has a special on snow blowers." Foster had earmarked the afternoon for a job hunting session. "But you can't take a snow blower home on the bus."

"Tyler will take us." Mary scraped back a chair and sat down opposite Foster. "Why don't you come along, make it a family outing? We can have lunch in the food court."

Spend the afternoon playing happy families with Tyler. This was not a good idea. "Another time, maybe."

"Tell you what. We'll find you a parka. My treat."

"Mary, that man … You can do better."

"Oh, yeah. I'm a real prize. Men are just lining up. Haven't you noticed?"

It pained him to hear his daughter talk this way.

Mary looked at him. "You can't go through the winter in that raincoat.'

Foster stared at the frost creeping up the patio door. The raincoat was a Burberry. He had paid £500 for it in London. True, the coat was thin, but surely he wouldn't be in Canada too much longer. All those resumés he had fired off by email. It was a battle, finding a job. A battle he intended to win. Replacing the Burberry would be like running up a white flag.

Mary looked away and shook her head. "I can never get through to you."

"No, you're right. I need a coat."

UNIVERSAL SURPLUS SMELLED of wool, gun oil, the pine-scented sweeping compound scattered on the floor. Knives gleamed in a display case. A cabinet bristled with crossbows. Uniforms dangled from the ceiling, flight suits, frogman outfits, flak jackets. Foster nodded at the woman behind the cash. Though it was early morning, she was dressed for better things than peddling military leftovers. A party perhaps, in that tight dress.

"Good morning," Foster said, smiling and brushing the snow from his Grandpa overalls. The woman didn't seem to see him. Miffed by this lack of response, he made his way to a clothes rack and began flipping through the garments. Old soldiers fade away, but their clothes live on. His hand stopped on a greatcoat. Quilted lining. Grey wool exterior. Eagles and anchors on the shoulders. His size, or near enough, and only twenty-two dollars. He could afford that. Barely. A bin of hats caught his attention. With the greatcoat on his arm, he pawed through hats with golf tees glued on them, joke hats with rude sayings and, amidst all this junk, of all things, a deerstalker. Bemused, he picked the hat and turned it in his hands. Made in England. He clapped the hat on his head and became not Daniel Foster, the stranded expatriate, but Sherlock Holmes, the great detective … *When you have eliminated the impossible, whatever remains, however improbable, must be the truth*. He drew an umbrella from a barrel, bent a knee and struck a fencing pose. The umbrella popped open. The woman in the party dress stared out at the blowing snow.

Down the street Foster strode, the greatcoat on his back, the deerstalker on his head, the golf umbrella in his hand. The sun came out, and he caught his reflection in a window. His shoulders sagged. He didn't look like the sleuth of Baker Street. A deserter from a defunct army, maybe.

The store was an Internet café. He went through the door, sat at a computer and checked his mail by clicking on a tiny, smiling face. The little icon flashed and reappeared wearing a frown. *Sorry! No messages for you.*

THREE WEEKS LATER, a storm came cartwheeling up from the American Midwest and buried Toronto in snow. Foster ate his eggs that February morning with one eye on The Weather Channel. Projected on the wall behind the weatherman, the massive low pressure system resembled a huge whirling saw blade. More snow on the way, and then the sky would clear and the temperature would plummet to record lows, the weatherman warned. Stay home if you can. Foster went to the front door and peered out. The wind howled. Snow swirled from the roofs. Cars lay hidden under smooth burdens of drift. The sight angered him. The hell with it. He would go to work anyway. Winter wasn't about to clip his wings. He slipped on his greatcoat, tied a tea towel around the collar and clamped the deerstalker on his head.

He struggled through the deep snow, his shoes full of ice water, his feet aching painfully. He was tramping blindly into the wind when, hearing the whine of tires sliding on snow, he looked back to see Mary leaning hard on the back of Tyler's car. Which, of course, didn't have snow tires. Foster high-stepped through a snow bank and thumped on the driver's window. The window came down. Tyler looked out at him. "Don't gun the engine," Foster said. "You're just digging yourself in."

Tyler gunned the engine. The car shirred sideways.

Foster said, "Have you got a shovel?"

"Watch yourself, Mare," Tyler said. "I'll rock the car back."

"I'll get a shovel," Foster said.

The car staggered forward and stopped, stuck again. Fine. Let them do it their way. Foster groped his way to the bus stop. A dump truck chuffed past, trailing a stink of diesel, lashing him with salt.

An hour and a half later he arrived at Grandpa's, plastered with snow, chilled to the core and thoroughly annoyed. His face burned, his legs throbbed, his fingers ached. His surplus store gloves were uselessly thin. Winter had thrown him a sucker punch. On his way to the locker room, Foster spotted Amanda Curtwell angling over to intercept him.

"I know, I know," Foster said when she was twenty feet away. "I'm late. It's a Clean Slate offence. Mark it in your little book. Now, if you don't mind, I'd like to go in there and dry off."

Amanda pursed her lips and stared at him for a long moment. "I was going to thank you for coming in, Grandpa Foster. We're running with a skeleton staff." She gave Foster a tight smile and strutted off.

Foster and Charlie worked a double shift. In the early evening, when his dinner break came, Foster walked past the windows. The storm had finally ended. The snow glistened. The sky was steel blue. The cold stole its way into the store. The heating system couldn't keep up; the wind whispering over the roof seemed to pilfer the warmth. Foster soldiered on. A teenaged boy asked him endless questions about metric bolts. A young couple bent his ear about their en suite bathroom: the lighting was all wrong, no, the lighting was fine, there was no place to store towels, yes there was, under the sink, did Grandpa's carry bolts with porcelain heads, bolts like that would look stupid. When they finally wound down — had it occurred to these people that they disliked each other, not their spare bathroom? — Foster turned them over to Grandpa Dale, an elfin man of seventy who had been a plumber.

"Cold out there," Foster said when he came back to his own department.

"Cold," Charlie agreed. "Good thing I shovelled the driveway before I came in."

As closing time drew near, a deep loneliness came over Foster. He looked down a long, empty aisle. A bored cashier was tidying up a magazine rack. Charlie was over there by a display of threaded rod, chatting with a woman who wore a yellow toque. Foster looked around and spotted Amanda Curtwell wandering the sales floor. Was she headed this way? Foster gazed wistfully at the front doors. He didn't feel up to one of their little chats. If only the big box store were an airport terminal — away he would fly, to a tropical paradise. Winter had hobbled him like a bedouin's camel, narrowed his existence to Mary's townhouse, Grandpa's Toolbox, Jessica's loft. Foster heard someone say, "Hey, are you all right?" He spun around, startled. The woman in the yellow toque was on her knees, bending over Charlie.

THE HOSPITAL WAITING room had muted lighting, green walls, spider ferns, glass tables. Except for the double doors that led to Urgent Care, it might have been a trendy café. People sipped coffee, read magazines, watched the whispering television mounted high in a corner of the room. Foster padded over to a nurses' station. The nurse with the Greek name and the bossy manner must have gone off shift. Her replacement, a languid woman in green scrubs, had streaky blond hair and sparkly polish on her fingernails.

"I need a family member to fill this out." She handed him a form.

"I'm not a relative."

"You rode in the ambulance." The nurse seemed angry. Sick people should come equipped with families.

Foster picked up the form, made his way to a table and sat down beside a woman who was staring at the television with tears streaming from her eyes; her makeup was in ruins. Her hands lay folded on a textbook. With a visceral shock Foster recognized the book. It was Shawna's math text. But it wasn't Shawna's copy, he saw with guilty relief; someone had written "Crystal" on the edge. He turned his attention to the form.

Relationship to patient. Foster printed, *Friend.*

Is the patient taking medication? Those pills Charlie took. *Medication of unknown type.*

Previous medical problems. Unknown, Foster printed.

Contact information. Foster wrote his name and Mary's phone number.

Form in hand, he stepped to the counter. "I'd like to speak to a doctor."

The nurse snapped the form from his fingers. "Take a seat, sir. We'll call you."

Foster walked back to his chair. His neighbour was smiling up at a sitcom. Should he strike up a conversation? He decided not to invade her privacy. Was there anything of interest on the magazine rack? He walked across the room, flipped past *Maclean's* and *People*, and picked up a copy of *Business Week*. Jessica would be wondering why he hadn't turned up tonight. He should find a pay phone and call her. But what if they called his name while he has out of the room? There was no one else here for Charlie.

The nurse called a name. A family got up and went through a double door. Foster walked to the table they had left empty, pulled out a chair and sat down. He read an article about Internet commerce and a feature about the Euro. There were fewer people in the room now. He went to the magazine rack and picked out another copy of *Business Week*. The feature article was about a city in China that hadn't existed five years ago but now had a population of four million. Foster's thoughts drifted. Would Grandpa's Toolbox open stores in China? Probably. Would Gary Garth's concept work in Guangzhou? Possibly. With almost 1.5 billion people in China, there would be a lot of latent images floating around in the collective memory. Foster pictured a store identical to his, staffed by elderly Chinese men wearing the Grandpa uniform. Grandpa's would need someone to train them. Would the company fly him to China, put him up in five-star hotels? No, the company would not. Halfway through the next article, an analysis of French farming practices, he put the magazine down and gazed round the room. The posters on the green walls were vaguely spiritual — a deer standing in a sunlit clearing, dolphins leaping from ocean waves, sailboats racing bow-to-bow. The sailboats brought Cedric and Sylvia to mind, and Foster closed his eyes and pictured himself on *Believer*, a free man, the captain of his fate.

Someone was calling his name. Foster shook himself awake. The man standing next to his chair was Dr. Asgari, according to his name tag. Dr. Asgari didn't have the craggy features, the cap of white hair, the kindly smile that came with Foster's concept of a doctor. In his polo shirt and jeans, with his cool, intelligent eyes, Asgari looked more like the kid who came to fix your computer. He was looking unhappily at the information sheet Foster had filled out. Foster got to his feet. "May I see Charlie now?"

"No visitors tonight." Asgari kept his eyes on the clipboard.

"What's the matter with Charlie?"

"I'll know better when I see more tests. Did your …" the doctor flipped a page, "… friend have shortness of breath? Dizziness? Chest pain?"

Foster thought a moment. "He has chronic heartburn. Takes a lot of antacids."

Dr. Asgari nodded. "It's three in the morning. Go home and get some sleep. We'll call you if there's any change." He handed Foster a leaflet and trotted away.

Sleep. A very good idea. It had been a long day. Foster put on his coat, made his way down a corridor, pushed through the outer doors and looked up at a full moon. The night air was stunningly cold. Foster took a breath and coughed out a stream of vapour. The air had a honed edge, a sharpness that cut his lungs. A bus roared past, its windows opaque with frost, and he hurried after it, slapping his pockets as he ran. After a moment he drifted to a stop and watched the bus rattle down the road. His money was in his wallet, and his wallet was in the antique cash register at Grandpa's. Mary had been quite right. It was good to have a warm coat. Foster wiggled the deerstalker onto his head, lowered the earflaps, knotted the ribbon under his chin and thrust his hands into the pockets of his greatcoat. There was something in his pocket. He fished out the brochure the young doctor had given him and stared at the title. *Understanding Heart Disease.*

HOW LONG HAD he been walking? The cold knocked him sideways, pushed him back, jokingly attempted to trip him. Foster crunched past a row of apartment buildings and tilted his head to admire them. Ice drooped from balconies. Plumes of vapour ghosted up from chimneys; the night sky had a velvety blackness, a tinge of indigo. He trudged past a gas station, past a strip mall. Tears froze in the corners of his eyes.

Everything pleased him: the mounds of snow, the ice on the power lines. Where had his ears gone? They seemed absent. *Friends, Romans, countrymen, lend me your ears.* The sidewalk angled up, and Foster bent forward and swung his arms, lashing out at the cold. He had to be careful, though — his hands were made of glass. If he slapped them together they might shatter. He glanced over a guardrail and saw the ground falling away from him. Toronto might look flat from the window of a bus, but climb a little and you discover a city of rivers and ravines, hills and valleys. Misty light shone through the glistening treetops. Was that a park down there? There was a playground with swings and slides, a serpentine path, a line of lampposts. Every lamp had a halo. Why was he so happy? But then, the simple act of putting one foot in front of another had always pleased him. Downhill went Foster, through a corridor of snow. He felt a dreamy urge to throw himself down, to throw out his arms and make an angel.

How long had that car been at his side, keeping pace? The car darted ahead. Its brake lights flashed. A door flew open and a policeman stood blocking the sidewalk. Foster stopped, swaying in place, staring at the cop with growing concern. The cop was carrying too much weight. Like Charlie. Bad for the heart, friend.

"Going somewhere, sir?"

"Home." Foster gulped the intoxicating air. "Going home."

"And where is your home, sir?"

Foster had to think about that.

A second policeman stepped nimbly from the cruiser. He was younger. Trim and fit. "I need you to sit in the car, sir." The young policeman opened the cruiser's back door. "Would you do that for me? It's nice and warm in there."

It would be good to sit for a moment. Foster climbed into the cruiser. And instantly wanted out. The seat was sticky. The carpet smelled of vomit. A grate separated the front seat from the back. He had been hoodwinked. Where was the door handle?

"Fits the description," the young cop said, looking at a data sheet. "Caucasian male. Tall. Pleasant manner. Disoriented."

"Where does he belong?" The older cop lifted a Styrofoam cup from the dashboard and looked into it sadly.

"It's on here somewhere. Wait a minute. Lyndhurst."

"The retirement home off Bathurst? How the hell did he get way over here?"

"Wandered off. Got lost."

Why were they ignoring him? Foster hooked an aching finger

through the grate. "I live on Mazurka Street. Number twenty-seven."

"Maybe you used to live there, sir?" The older cop drained his coffee and made a face.

"I'm not lost!"

"Of course you're not." The older cop turned up the heater. Warm air swirled into the back seat.

"I was visiting a friend in the hospital." Foster pressed the brochure against the grill.

"Picked that up on the street, did you?" The older cop stared through the windshield.

"My name is Daniel Foster. I live with my daughter. Her name is Mary. Twenty-seven Mazurka."

"Mary?" The older cop hitched around. "Mary Foster? Can you show us some ID?"

"Certainly." Foster touched his pocket. Cold radiated painfully from his thighs. "My wallet is in Grandpa's Toolbox."

The policemen looked at each other.

"My name is Daniel Foster. I'm an employee of a major corporation. My co-worker, Mr. Charles Anderson of 359 Jubilee Street, fell ill today. I went with him to North York General and I stayed there until I knew he would be all right."

"He doesn't sound nuts," the young cop said doubtfully.

The older cop made a sour face. "My mother made more sense after she lost it."

The horror of confinement tightened Foster's gut, set his heart racing. They would lock him away in a gulag for the gaga. "Take me to Mazurka Street. My daughter will vouch for me."

TWENTY MINUTES LATER, the three men stood on Mary's front step. "I've got my key right here." Foster patted his pockets.

In the wallet, is it, sir?" Foster stepped toward the door. The cops yanked him back. "You don't live here, do you sir? Not really."

"My daughter is home." But what if she wasn't? What if Mary was on the night shift and Shawna was staying at Kayla's?

The older cop shrugged. He rapped on the front door. A bus went by on Dundas, the rumble of its engine eerily clear in the cold air. A streetlight blinked off, buzzed, snapped back on. The door opened, and Mary looked out sleepily, gathering the collar of her dressing gown in a hand. She looked at the older cop in surprise. "Pete. Hi." Foster stared at his daughter. Did she know every cop on the force?

"Hey, Mary," Pete said. "Look, we picked up this guy and he says he lives here."

"Foster?"

Shawna was looking at him, wide-eyed. Foster tugged his elbow free and straightened his back. The cops trudged back to their cruiser, and Foster stepped into the hall. Mary closed the door behind him and told Shawna to go back to bed. Shawna said something about a hot water bottle.

"You're trembling," Mary said, coming to Foster's side.

Waving her away, Foster clomped down the hall to the middle room and fumbled at the doorknob. Why couldn't he make his fingers work? Mary opened the door. He stumbled past her and sat shivering on the bed. Mary leaned against the doorjamb, watching him with her arms folded, and then she came into the room, and put her hand on his arm. "You're frozen!"

"Fine," Foster said. "Fine!" He was shaking violently, uncontrollably.

"Oh, for God's sake." Mary pulled him to his feet. He stood quivering like an exhausted horse while she helped him out of his clothes and dressed him in his pyjamas. His daughter tucked him into bed and threw on more blankets. Shawna came in with a hot water bottle, and Foster took it from her mutely. He turned on his side and closed his eyes and clutched the warmth to his chest. He heard Mary's voice, and Shawna's, but soon their voices grew distant. Was Charlie all right? Would Crystal be okay? What about the man from Lyndhurst, the runaway the cops were looking for? Was he still out there in the cold, a bundle of rags lying in the snow? As he fell asleep, Foster longed to find the lost old man, to bring him safely home.

[TEN]

TEN DAYS AND counting of record breaking cold. Water mains had burst. Electrical transformers had exploded. Early on a frozen morning, Foster sat on a lumbering bus, staring lethargically out the window and glancing occasionally at his watch, a one-dollar wonder that vaguely resembled his pawned Rolex Oyster Perpetual. His shift started in ten minutes. The store was still a long way off. He would be late. He couldn't make himself care. His sense of purpose had crawled into a cave and fallen into the deep slumber of a hibernating bear.

Why had the bus swung into a lay-by? There was no one waiting at the stop, no one at the doors, waiting to get off. Foster watched the driver grab his maroon coat, open the doors, dash outside and disappear from view.

Minutes ticked by. The diesel engine clattered. The windshield wipers slashed back and forth. The driver's seat sat empty. It didn't seem to matter. Foster looked around in idle curiosity. His fellow passengers on this slow bus to nowhere were taking their abandonment in stride. A woman flipped the pages of a Stephen King novel. A schoolgirl in a puffy parka dozed. A man wearing a lamb's wool hat studied an Italian newspaper. Foster turned the deerstalker in his hands, remembering

Kathleen's attempt to explain to him the doctrine of purgatory. A place of suffering just short of damnation. He understood the concept better now. A woman in a red uniform stepped aboard, hung her coat on a hanger, adjusted the driver's seat, fiddled with the rear-view mirror. Someone had left a newspaper, Foster noticed. He reached across the aisle and plucked up the sports section. The bus lurched forward, throwing him back in his seat. The handle of his umbrella dug painfully into his back. Squirming to find a more comfortable position, he opened the paper and began to read. With spring training coming up, there were stories about coaches, managers, hot prospects, free agents, minor leaguers worth a look-see. It all meant nothing to him, but Charlie would be interested. It was something to talk about. He came through the doors of Grandpa's Toolbox to find Amanda Curtwell waiting for him. She had stationed herself next to Grandpa Singh.

"You're late, Grandpa Foster," Amanda said.

Grandpa Singh leaned toward the parking lot, looking for a customer to greet.

"Couldn't be helped," Foster said, trying to sound contrite. Amanda Curtwell was an efficient manager and a handsome woman. Under better circumstances, he would invite her for coffee. If he wasn't pinching pennies. If he wasn't wearing a greatcoat and a deerstalker. If he wasn't clutching the skeletal remains of a yellow golfing umbrella: the damn thing had blown apart the instant he'd alighted from the bus.

"We're a team, Grandpa Foster. We depend on each other."

"Yes," Foster said. Amen. Yes, indeedy.

"And with Grandpa Anderson in hospital, we're shorthanded."

As if he didn't know that. Foster nodded curtly. Meltwater drizzled from his deerstalker and puddled at his feet.

"Grandpa Foster, I think we'd better make tomorrow your first Clean Slate day." Amanda pointed across the floor to the locker room. "Now, scoot in there and change."

Scoot? Had this upstart just told him to scoot? Foster mustered his frazzled dignity, turned his back and walked away.

THE OLD LADY in the striped smock peered at a computer screen. "We have a Charles Henderson."

"Anderson. With an *A*," Foster said. Had he spoken to this volunteer on his last visit? She had the same wispy hair, the same trembling hands, the same dithering manner. He couldn't be sure. Like babies, the elderly are interchangeable.

"Oh, silly me. You're perfectly right. Mr. Anderson is in East 303. See that corridor beside the gift shop? Well, you just follow the purple line. And here's something for you to read."

"Thank you," Foster said. As he rounded the first corner he glanced at the leaflet the old woman had given him. *Visiting Someone in Hospital.* In modern Canada there were guidelines for everything. Foster shook his head, scrunched up the leaflet and tossed the ball of paper into a waste bin. The purple line led him through a maze of corridors; nurses in scrubs and sneakers criss-crossed his path. At the end of the hallway he looked up to see plastic hearts twirling in the air. The hearts were plump and they had a comic dip at the top, like the hearts he had noticed on bumper stickers. I heart sailing. I heart my dog. Why stop there? I liver my wine, Foster thought. I lips my lover.

"You just missed my doc," Charlie said when Foster had taken off his coat and settled in an armchair. "Real comedian. Says a heart attack's nothing to worry about. Unless it kills you." Charlie's gaze drifted toward the window. Lacy wires ran from his chest to a panel mounted in the headboard.

"Cold out there?" Charlie gazed at the sky.

Foster didn't want to talk about the weather. Anything but the weather. He looked around. "Nice room." East 303 was a double, but Charlie had it to himself.

"Not if you're stuck in it."

"Did the doctor say when you're going home?"

Charlie made a face. "Can't get a straight answer. First it was my blood pressure and I'd be out of here in a day. Then he said I had some kind of fancy infection and they were going to hang on to me. He did another test and found something else he doesn't like." Charlie hooked a thumb at the empty bed. "From Iraq, Omar was. That's out your way, isn't it?"

Foster smiled. "Yes, Iraq is down the Gulf from Dubai."

"The family that guy had? Kept me busy, dealing with the overflow. Nephews, nieces, uncles, cousins. Thought they were all called Habibi, 'til Omar told me that's just a nickname. Basim, Tariq, Jamila — they all came over to talk to me. It was like being back in the flea market."

"Sell any birdhouses?"

"I could have, friend," Charlie said, smiling for the first time. "How's life at Grandpa's Nuthouse?"

"Oh, same old, same old." Foster told Charlie about his day, exaggerating the encounters with customers, giving the clash with Amanda a comic spin — the way she had brushed off his suggestion for the stock display, the scolding she had given him for coming in late. "'Scoot,' she said. Can you believe it? Ten minutes later she comes barging into Fasteners ..." Charlie didn't seem to be listening. He was staring out the window. Foster followed his gaze. There was nothing to see out there, just an expanse of snow-covered roof and an empty sky.

From the hallway came a soft, electronic bong. "Code Blue," a voice announced. "Code Blue. Code Blue. Crash cart to Room East 207." A nurse in scrubs jogged past the open door.

"Code Blue," Charlie said. "They called that when Omar had the big one."

"Two weeks to training camp," Foster said quickly. "Who do you like for the pennant?"

Charlie shot him a glance. "In the AL East? The Yankees. Who else?"

"Baltimore just signed Duxberry."

"Baltimore!" Charlie shook his head. "Duxberry's coming off a Tommy John. Their whole starting rotation looks shaky. Now, you take last year …"

As Foster settled back to listen, his eyes lingered on the vacant bed. What had gone through Omar's mind when that terrible pressure gripped his heart? *Oh, God. Not now. Not yet.*

"Rivera's a good set up man … but the Orioles don't have a legitimate closer."

Death is the best closer of all, Foster thought as Charlie took him through Baltimore's pitching staff. The grim reaper gets the win every time.

SNOW DRIFTED PAST the windows of Jessica's loft. It seemed to Foster that he would never be warm again. Usually he took his leave at ten, but tonight he stayed longer, huddled in a wicker chair, leafing through Jessica's art books. The books baffled him with their talk of schema, inexhaustibility, *jouissance.* With cold fingers he did up the top button of his sweater, rubbed his hands together and wondered again when to say his piece. There was no point in waiting for the right moment, no way to spare Jessica whatever pain their break would cause. The right moment had come and gone, months ago, and he was accountable for the pain. He had let this affair go on for too long. On the bus that had brought him here, he had cast his mind back through the episodes of *Restless World.* Those people were always breaking up — Jed, Sam and Dam and all the others. There was no help there, of course. They weren't real. They were actors playing to the camera; hurt bounced off them like bullets from the chest of a super hero.

Jessica was working at an easel, brush in hand. Oblivious to the cold, she wore only a pair of spandex leggings and a baggy T-shirt. She walked to a trestle table and stood frowning down at the drawing she had completed an hour ago. Watching her, Foster felt a jolt of desire, felt something move in him. He got to his feet, put on his coat and crossed the room.

"Jessica, listen."

She didn't listen. She kept working.

How could he make this easier? He knew he wasn't playing fair with Jessica. "We're very different people."

"You say the sweetest things." Jessica took the stem of a brush from between her teeth and stretched a hand to touch his face. "Why so serious? Poor baby. You have to work everything out, don't you?"

Foster looked at Jessica. "There's no easy way to say this."

Jessica stared at him for a long moment. "You're dumping me, aren't you?" she said at last. "Why, you rotten, selfish, son-of-a-bitch."

True. He couldn't argue with that. Before Jessica could recover from her shock, he walked out. In the hallway, he slid back a grate and entered the freight elevator. At the front door he stood for a moment, looking up at the ceiling, and then he put his hands in his pockets and went out into the cold.

THE FRIGID WEATHER ended a week later, vanished in the night like a discouraged siege army. It was Sunday afternoon, and Tyler had come for dinner. Foster angled his knife and fork on the corner of his plate. "I guess I'll stretch my legs."

Mary nodded. It pained Foster, the way their communication had dwindled.

"Who do you have to know to get another beer around here?" Tyler didn't look up from the pork chop he was sawing in half. With his fork, Foster couldn't help noticing. Foster was in the hallway slipping his Burberry raincoat over his suit jacket when Shawna appeared beside him and asked if she could come along.

On Dundas Street, the snowdrifts were melting, the sidewalks streaked with sand. A shopping flyer lay in an evaporating puddle, a pale fish marooned by a falling tide. Winter had tried to kill him, Foster thought, remembering his cold walk home from the hospital. He wouldn't give that killer season another crack at him. When winter came around again he would be long gone, working overseas. The resumés he had sent out had drawn no response. Go to London, that was the thing to do. Walk into an office wearing the big suit. Take a recruiter to a pub, stand him a pint of bitter. Chat him up, listen carefully, follow the leads. Foster took a deep breath. The air had a gamey smell.

"I got an A in history."

"An A," Foster said, smiling down at Shawna. "That's something to be proud of." He felt a bit shy; he hadn't seen much of his granddaughter lately. She had on a vintage ski outfit, a style from the sixties, white pants with a high waist, a purple top with knit cuffs. "How are you doing in math?"

Shawna didn't answer this question. She stopped to peer into a store that sold antique radios. Foster cupped a hand against the glass and looked into the dim interior. There were floor models from the thirties, Bakelite marvels from the forties, futuristic portables from the fifties. The silent radios stood huddled together like refugees at an aid station.

"Are things okay at Grandpa's?" Shawna asked when they were walking again.

"Um," Foster said. Grandpa's had kept him busy. He was chipping away at the phone bill, sending the credit card companies enough to keep them off his back. Just enough, because he was also setting money aside for a trip to London.

"So, you like being a Grandpa."

"Oh …" He remembered that Shawna had applied for the job in his stead. "Thank you again for finding the ad, Shawna. You really helped me out there."

Shawna beamed at him, and Foster smiled back. "Have you thought about what you want to do when you're finished school?"

"I'm going to be a forensic scientist."

Forensic scientist? Those police shows made pathology glamorous. He pictured Shawna in a lab coat, running ballistics tests, dissecting the criminal mind. "You'll need to work on your math," he said, putting a parental lilt into his voice.

"They use computers for all that stuff."

"Well, yes, but to get into university — for that sort of program — you'll need good marks in math."

"Why?"

"It's a bit like being a doctor."

"Oh. Being a doctor would be okay too."

Foster felt a tug of love. Shawna was game to give life a go.

"How's Jessica?" Shawna asked, in a lightning fast change of subject.

"Well, now, I don't really know," Foster said carefully. "We haven't seen each other lately."

"How come?"

"Oh, we just haven't."

"Jessica's cool. She's totally into art."

Foster thought a moment, casting about for neutral ground. "People are generally happier if they like what they do."

"You like your job, don't you? Because if you don't, maybe I can find you a better one."

Foster smiled. But then he began to worry. Did his granddaughter feel responsible for him? When his father's care had fallen to him, Foster was still in high school. He had paid his father's rent, bought his groceries and cheap wine, earned the money unloading trucks, ushering moviegoers to their seats, setting up pins in a bowling alley with a textbook propped on the ball return. "We should head back," Foster said. They had reached the bus loop that marked the western boundary of the neighbourhood.

"I don't mind walking a bit more."

"Okay," Foster said glancing at Shawna, a bit puzzled. Was there something on her mind?

"Did you always know what you wanted to be?"

"In a way, I did." Foster detected something new in Shawna's behaviour. She was engaging him in conversation. "I liked math and I was good at it. Math led me into computing."

"Did you like math because you were good at it, or were you good at it because you liked it?"

"That's a false dichotomy."

"Huh?"

"Liking something and being good at it aren't necessarily exclusive … causality is only one connection between any two propositions …" He was talking gobbledegook. Shawna deserved better. She was wondering what to do with her life. As if his dead-end career would serve as an example. "I don't know why I liked math. I just did. It was my favourite subject, all through school."

"My favourite subject is history. Benny and me? We study together. He's really into the pyramids."

"Benny and I," Foster said automatically. Pyramids. The ancient Egyptians knew how to bisect an angle, construct similar polygons. But Shawna wanted to be a forensic scientist. Foster thought for a moment. "Remember that show about the mummies?"

"Yeah, that was so-o-o-o-o-o-o creepy." Shawna raised her arms and staggered stiff-legged down the sidewalk. "I … am … the … mum … my …"

"The scientists used three-dimensional computed tomography … a CT scanner … a camera that sees through things."

Shawna stopped in her tracks. "Like an X-ray?"

"Yes. Exactly. If you combine X-rays with a computer, you get a 3D image."

"That's what I'll be when I grow up. A mummy-X-rayer-computer-person."

Foster laughed and gave Shawna's shoulder an affectionate squeeze. They were on the other side of the Humber River now. "We should head back."

"Okay," Shawna said.

"If you search online, you can learn about computer tomography."

"Can you write it down for me? I'm not exactly the world's greatest speller."

"I can do better than that." Foster stepped ahead, spun on his heel and bowed at the waist. "Allow me to introduce myself. My name is Tom O. Graphy and I can see through people."

"Okay," Shawna said slowly.

"Tomography. Tom O. Graphy. See?"

"Foster, that is seriously weird."

"Spell it for me."

"Tom-o-graphy. Hey, yeah!"

Five minutes later, when they were walking along in companionable silence, Shawna said, "But it's still seriously weird." Foster had to laugh.

When they got back to the townhouse, she went to her room. Foster took off his raincoat and hung it in the front closet. The television threw a flickering light on the walls of the living room. Tyler was sprawled on the couch, a beer bottle cradled between his legs. "Fos!" he shouted. "How's it hanging, you old buzzard?"

Mary was curled up in the beanbag chair, her eyes on the television. Foster stared at the screen. *Crime Streets* had just started. In a back alley, the body of a young woman lay in a pool of blood. A pair of detectives leaned over the corpse, trading wisecracks. Foster shook his head. He liked whodunits — as a boy, he had poured over *The Casebook of Sherlock Holmes* — but the stories on *Crime Streets* weren't about clever thinking. The police had the crime solved by the second commercial break, and then the public prosecutor bent the law to get a conviction — and went for the death penalty. As if revenge didn't poison the spirit. A cup of tea would be nice. Foster went to the kitchen, opened a cupboard and fished out a package of Earl Grey.

"Fos!" Tyler shouted. "Think I'm a loser, don't ya?"

"Tyler," Mary said in a voice sharp with warning. "That's enough."

Foster clicked on the stove, looked into the middle distance, then slowly turned to face the living room. Was Shawna afraid of Tyler? Was this why she had come along on the walk? The counter was littered with empty beer bottles. You didn't need Sherlock Holmes to solve this little mystery. Tyler was drunk. Foster felt a flash of anger. He would throw Tyler out of the house. He started for the living room. Mary blocked his way. She took the package of Earl Grey from his hand and pulled him to a chair. She leaned a hip against the counter and crossed her arms. Puzzled, he looked up, met his daughter's eyes.

"I know what you're thinking," Mary said. "But Tyler's not like Mom. He's just blowing off steam. He had a bad day. He got fired."

Foster stared at Mary. What did Kathleen have to do with this?

"It got so I couldn't trust Mom." Mary glanced at the living room. "Those burn marks on the carpet? Mom would pass out with a cigarette in her hand. We talked about not smoking in the house but then she'd get a load on and she'd forget. I couldn't have that, because of Shawna. Foster, what could I do? Mom wouldn't get help. You know what she was like. Tyler found that rooming house and when I ran short, he paid the rent."

A stranger had paid for the roof over Kathleen's head. Foster took this in. He looked at Mary. "Why didn't you call me? I would have sent you the money."

"I didn't want to bother you."

Neither of them spoke. The television roared. The kettle whistled.

"Mare?" Tyler said from the living room. "Ah, I'm sorry. Mare?"

"Tyler was great. We took Mom there in his car." To Foster's terrible embarrassment, his daughter knelt beside his chair. "Leaving Mom in that room was the hardest thing I ever had to do. Foster? Give Tyler a chance. Please?"

"Mare?" Tyler called. "Mare?"

"Go ahead," Foster said softly. After Mary left the kitchen, he turned off the stove, set the kettle aside and gazed at the package of tea, heartsick. Why hadn't he made arrangements for Kathleen? The burden of care should never have fallen on Mary. Kathleen had been his wife.

RAIN FELL FROM a leaden sky, lightly at first, and then with a lashing fury. The squall swept over the parking lot, driving Foster toward the bus stop. The bus came sloshing down the street, water streaming from its flanks. He paid his fare, swayed down the aisle, fell into a seat and gazed out at the rain, remembering a different storm. He had been on a weekend ramble when a shamal, a swirling sandstorm, sent him stumbling into a wire fence — and nose-to-nose with a camel. The shamal stopped as suddenly as it had begun. The sun beat down from a cloudless sky. The camel curled its lips, hacked a gob of spit over Foster's shoulder, levered itself to its feet and cantered away.

"Damn thing spit at me," Foster complained to his walking companion. Peter was a teaching master at a technical college.

"Good thing you didn't spit back. That's a racing camel. Worth at least a million."

"Dirhams?" Foster flicked sand from his walking shorts. The exchange rate was pegged at three dirhams to the American dollar. A third of a million US seemed a lot of money for a cranky camel.

"Dollars, Foster. And many more of them than the sheiks would pay for thee or me."

"Next stop, Aerospace Museum," said a recorded voice.

Aerospace Museum? Foster made his way to the front of the bus. "Isn't this the 65?"

"65B," the driver said.

The driver dropped Foster at a deserted intersection. On the other side of the road, a disused aircraft hanger mouldered away in the sunlight, its doors streaked with rust. The sky darkened. Hail pelted down. The sun came out again. Ice glittered on the road like tinsel. A bus pulled up. The bus he had stepped off ten minutes earlier. "You might have told me," Foster said as he climbed aboard and paid another fare.

"You didn't ask," the driver said.

The bus jerked forward. Foster swallowed his anger, grabbed a steel pole and hung on. Something else had happened the day of the spitting camel. In memory, Foster returned to a rock cut, walked through a pocket of deep shade, heard a trickle of water, felt the temperature drop. "Did you see what you stepped over back there?" Peter asked in a small voice.

"Stepped over?"

"A saw-scaled viper."

Foster looked back. The path was empty. The venom of *Echis coloratus* is an anticoagulant. A dose of 5 mg is enough to kill you.

At the hospital, Foster followed the purple line that led under the dangling hearts to the cardiac ward. Charlie wasn't in East 303. The woman at the information desk squinted at her monitor. "There's no Mr. Anderson in the system. Maybe they released him early. They often do, you know." Foster glanced at the woman's name tag. *Clara, A Volunteer Angel!* "Wouldn't the system tell you that, Clara?"

"Well, you'd think so, but they don't make these things easy to use."

"Could you look again, please?" Why did people always blame the computer? Foster propped an arm on the counter and surveyed the lobby. A tall woman in a stadium coat strode gracefully into an elevator. A repairman set up a stepladder and clipped on a tool belt. A little girl came skipping out of the gift shop, a tinfoil balloon floating from her hand.

"Oh, dear," Foster heard the old woman say. He met her eyes, and he knew Charlie was dead.

[ELEVEN]

"SHOULDN'T SOMEONE ELSE look after that?" Foster pinned the handset against his shoulder, and lifted Mary's toaster from a cupboard.

"There is no one else, Mr. Foster." The raspy voice on the phone belonged to a lawyer named Malcolm Drummond.

"Charlie said something about a brother." Foster remembered more of the conversation on the way to Florida. "Lives in the states. Arizona?" The phone line clicked. Shawna was listening in. He would have to speak to her again.

"Correct. Half-brother. Mr. Walter Anderson of Tucson, Arizona. His name used to be on the card."

"Card?"

"From the funeral home. Charlie and Marge pre-planned their funerals. People who don't have kids are more likely to do that."

"Then why isn't —"

"Walter looking after this? Died years ago. His wife's dead too. They had no children either. Must run in the family. Sorry. Wasn't trying to be funny."

The sink was full of dishwater. Foster pulled the plug and watched the murky water swirl away. "Marge's family then."

"Marge was a war bride. Cold War bride, if you will. She came from … hang on, it's in the file … Solihull, England. Landed here in '65 to marry a Canadian soldier. The guy dumped her and she married Charlie on the bounce. Nothing wrong with that, of course. Pair of lovebirds, those two. You're not the executor, Mr. Foster, if that's what's worrying you. I'm handling that end. Not that there's much to do. Charlie left everything to Princess Margaret Hospital. That's where they treated Marge's cancer, or tried to."

"Someone in England, then."

"Are you serious? With no money on the table, you think anybody's going to fly over here to bury a man they don't know from Adam?"

"I still don't understand where I come into this."

"Your name is on the card, Mr. Foster. Charlie crossed out Walter's name and wrote yours. Charlie didn't talk to you about it?"

"No."

"Oh. Well. Then you have no obligation."

Foster plugged in the toaster, pushed down a metal bar, waited for the elements to glow. "What did Charlie want me to do?" The toaster buzzed in distress. There was something wrong with the release mechanism.

"Handle the personal end. Visitation, funeral."

Funeral. Coffins. Candles. An open grave waiting for a customer. Foster hated the whole ghoulish business. He hadn't gone to Irv's funeral.

"Mr. Foster?"

"Yes. Fine. If that's what Charlie wanted."

"Got a pencil? I'll give you the phone number for P.C. Penton."

"Who?"

"The funeral director. He's a character."

"Go ahead." Foster copied down the number and said goodbye. After a moment he slid back the patio door and looked out at the

Canadian spring. The lawn had a tinge of green amidst the old growth, blades of grass as fine as down. Daffodils were erupting near the fence, green-and-yellow sprouts shaped like tongues. A robin with a mottled breast hopped past and fluttered into the air. The dead miss so much.

Mary came bustling into the kitchen, buttoning her Secure-All shirt as she walked. She glanced at Foster. "You look like somebody died."

Foster nodded. "One of the fellows I worked with. Heart attack."

"Hey, I'm sorry. I didn't mean …"

"I know."

"Was he a friend?"

"I scarcely knew him," Foster said, looking out at the yard again.

IT WAS LATE afternoon when Foster climbed the stairs that led to Amanda Curtwell's office. She left her chair, went to the one-way glass and stood looking down at the sales floor. Foster followed her gaze. Customers walked the aisles. In the Lumber Shed, a Grandpa was stacking two-by-fours. In Electrical, a Grandpa wheeled a stock cart under a display of revolving fans.

"Mr. Anderson will be missed," Amanda said. "He was one of our best."

"Charlie wanted me to look after the funeral. I'll have to take some time off."

Amanda turned from the window and nodded. "Yes. Of course."

"Tom will work Saturday. Sal can cover —"

"Grandpa Foster …" Amanda closed her eyes for a moment. "Kindly leave the schedule to me. Do what has to be done. Count the hours as work time. I'll initial your time card."

"I'll do this on my own time."

"Count the hours. Is there anything else?"

"This is a personal matter. I'll do it on my own time."

"Grandpa Foster, we'll pay you for your time."

"Is there a policy, Amanda?" Foster asked in a mild voice.

"No, Grandpa Foster, there isn't a policy. I'm the manager of this store and I'm making a decision."

"There should be a policy," Foster said, looking out at the sales floor. "Given the staff demographic."

Amanda Curtwell glared at him, her face reddening. "Oh, you infuriating man!"

THE PENTON FUNERAL Home, a relic from the 1940s, had alcoves and shadow boxes and strange, streamlined furniture. The place seemed to promise an eternity of airships and ocean liners. Charlie would like that, everything in motion.

"Almost done." P.C. Penton turned on his desk lamp, illuminating a nickel-plated nymph with airstream breasts. With his slicked hair and V-shaped moustache, the funeral director looked streamlined too. As if death had a prevailing wind.

"Is the copy suitable? I'll fill in the blanks later."

Foster took the obituary from Penton's hand.

ANDERSON, MICHAEL CHARLES

Passed peacefully away in the presence of his friends,
on [Day] [Month] [Year] at the age of [?].
Predeceased by his loving wife, Margaret. Charlie was born in
Westdale, Ontario. Long-time employee of Triway Transport.
Visitation at the Penton Funeral Home from
2–4 and 7–9 p.m. [Day]. In lieu of flowers,
donations to [Charity] would be appreciated.

In the presence of his friends? Charlie had died alone, a fact that irked Foster, after his faithful visits to the hospital.

"Fine." Foster handed the obituary back to Penton.

"Is Thursday agreeable for the visitation? As chief mourner, it's your call."

Chief Mourner. A job title of sorts. "Thursday will be fine."

"Very well." Penton took out a fountain pen, unscrewed the cap and began to write. The ink smelled of iron. The odour triggered a memory of a bank with a marble counter and a gimlet-eyed manager. *Smile when I hand him the cheque, Danny.* Irv had withdrawn non-existent funds from real banks. Foster had deposited real money in a bank that turned out not to exist. *There's a lesson here for all of us*, Irv would say in that wise guy way of his. *Now, if we only knew what the lesson was.*

"Mr. Foster?"

Foster leaned forward in his chair. "Sorry. I missed that."

"The casket Mr. Anderson selected is no longer available, I'm afraid. If you'll come with me, I'll show you a possible substitute." Penton reached for a cane and limped his way across a carpet patterned with zigzags. When they were in the hallway he turned so suddenly that Foster almost bumped into him. Foster stepped back, startled. Penton rapped his right leg with his cane, producing a metallic clang. "Lost this leg to diabetes," he said in the wry tone of a fisherman reminiscing about the one that got away.

"Oh," Foster said.

"This one will be next." Penton winked and tapped his good leg with the cane. Death was a great fish; it was nibbling at the funeral director, snatching away a piece of him at a time. Foster watched Penton work his way crabwise down a flight of stairs.

"Any casket will do," Foster said from the top step.

"Come along now. This won't take a minute."

Reluctantly, Foster descended the stairs and followed the mortician down a gloomy corridor and into a dark room. The lights blinked on to reveal caskets of oak, mahogany, cherry wood; caskets of steel, bronze, copper; caskets trimmed with crepe, velvet, velour. It was a long, narrow room, and the caskets were jammed together at crazy angles like boats thrown ashore by a tidal wave. Their lids were open, and for a dizzy moment it seemed to Foster that after a wild ride down the River Styx, the dead had jumped out and made a run for it.

"Silver Slumber went out of production last fall."

"Um," Foster said. Good old Silver Slumber.

"This is Silver Sentinel. Also a twenty-gauge sealer. Better value for the same money. These new gaskets prevent —"

"Fine. We'll take it." We, he heard himself say. As if Charlie were standing at his side. The Silver Sentinel looked a bit like the hood of a transport truck. *Friend, I drove every route they got.*

"You don't mind letting yourself out? I have things to do down here." Penton gave Foster a hopeful smile. "Unless you'd like to see the preparation room?"

"I'll let myself out," Foster said quickly.

"Bring the memorabilia with you on Thursday."

"Memorabilia?"

"Photos, keepsakes. That sort of thing. Your guests will find them comforting."

Up the stairs Foster went, across the lobby, through the entrance doors. Down the sidewalk he strode, picking up his pace — as if death, a horrible shark with P.C. Penton's leg in its belly, were snapping at his heels.

"Then you'll need to get into the house," Drummond said when Foster called him. "I can meet you there tonight. Seven o'clock?"

Foster walked pensively back to the living room. He would have to walk through a dead man's house, go through his things. *Restless World* came on. Foster settled himself in the beanbag chair. Mary was perched on the couch, one eye on the television, the other on the powder compact in her hand. She had a new hairdo and she wore a cable knit sweater Foster didn't remember seeing before. Tyler was taking her on a date.

"You just missed the best ever," Shawna said. "Jed and Samantha? They were in bed? Guess who walked in."

"Damian?" Foster glanced at his watch. He was babysitting Shawna tonight. She should start her homework soon.

"No!" Shawna said. "This guy you've never ever seen before! And Jed goes, 'Who are you?' 'I'm your son,' the guy goes."

"Jed has a son?" Foster wondered how he could have missed this.

"The guy's a fake," Mary said. "Damian sent him."

"Yeah, could be," Shawna said. "Wait! They'll do a DNA test!"

The doorbell rang, and Tyler came trooping in with a duffle bag in his hand. Tyler had a key, Foster knew. So why had he rung the bell? Was this formality for his benefit, Foster wondered? The idea made him uncomfortable.

"How's it going?" Tyler looked up at the ceiling.

"Fine," Foster said. They were a pair of alpha dogs. Their hackles were up.

"Okay if I put this in your room?" Tyler hoisted a hockey bag.

"Leave it there and I'll take it down the hall later."

"Thank you." Tyler set the bag down.

"You're welcome." They had growled at each other too often, he and Tyler. But how much of this civility could they endure?

"Seeya." Shawna headed for her room, the sanctuary with warning stickers on the door.

"Shawna?" Mary said, standing at Tyler's side.

Shawna spun around. "Hello, goodbye, have a great time."

Mary rolled her eyes. She slipped a hand under Tyler's arm. The happy couple — if that's what they were; Foster had his doubts — turned to go. "She's had her dinner," Mary called over her shoulder. "The macaroni and cheese on the stove is for you."

A sitcom's bouncy theme played from the television. Foster dropped into the beanbag chair, snatched up the remote, stabbed the mute button and watched a silenced commercial. A shampoo angel floated through a pink-and-blue sky.

The house grew dark. The television flickered. Foster knew he should get up, go to the stove, heat up the macaroni and cheese. He stared at Tyler's bag, fighting the sweet urge to throw it into a dumpster. He had done exactly that with Irv's suitcase. A few days after the funeral, Irv's landlord had turned up with the Gladstone bag Foster had carried into a hundred hotels. *Put it on the bed, son. I'll be in the bar if you need me.* Foster had taken the bag from the man's hand, thanked him for his trouble, closed the front door, walked to the back door and tossed the bag into a garbage bin, unopened. What could the bag have contained, after all? An old shirt. A hardware catalogue. A racing form.

Foster clicked the remote until he hit a game show, some old rerun. He turned the sound back on, very low. "Is the magic word … micro-wave?" a contestant said. Tossing the remote aside, Foster got to his feet and walked down the hall.

Shawna's door was closed. She had added a sign. "*Keep Out! Yes, This Means You!*"

Foster hesitated. Privacy was sacred to him, and here he was, invading Shawna's hideaway. But he couldn't face Charlie's house on his own. Foster knocked. Shawna peered out at him.

"Got a moment?"

Shawna gave him a puzzled look and opened the door.

Her room was basically the same as his — white walls, a swirled plaster ceiling, a closet with mirrored doors, a high, single window with a view of the tiny yard. There was an old office chair, a desk painted red, a captain's bed, also painted red, a Spiderwoman bedspread. There were bookshelves on one wall, posters on another — the strange people looking down at him were pop stars, Foster supposed. On a dresser stood a dollhouse. Inside the dollhouse, a night light burned, the kind that used a Christmas tree bulb. The bulb cast an amber light that set the rooms aglow and gave their miniature furniture a lantern-like gleam. The tiny kitchen held a table with four chairs, and a highchair. The living room had a sofa, a television and a coffee table, the nursery, a rocking horse and a crib. The bedroom had a sleigh bed and a dresser. Shawna had arranged photographs around the dollhouse. There was a picture of Mary in her Secure-All uniform, taken next to the swing set. A picture of Kathleen, looking more worn by life than Foster remembered. A photo of him as a much younger man. The background looked like Canada — the cars, the lawns. He had no recollection of the photograph being taken. Shawna was looking at him in wonderment.

"May I sit down?" Shawna nodded, and Foster sat on the bed. "I like your dollhouse."

Shawna shrugged. "I was a little kid when I did that."

Foster looked up at the bookshelves. "You have a lot of books."

"When I was little? I was really into pop-ups." Standing on the bed, Shawna tugged a dog-eared book from a shelf and put it in his hands.

As Foster opened the book, a castle rose into the air. Damsels slid into windows. Knights glided onto battlements. He smiled. "Very nice."

"Thanks." Shawna put the book away. She sat cross-legged on the bed, watching him with polite curiosity. As if she were an elderly aunt he hadn't visited in many years.

"A friend of mine passed away."

"The old guy that died in the hospital?"

How could Shawna know this? She must have listened in. "Yes. I have to go to his house tonight — to get some things — and I was wondering if you'd like to come along to help. It won't take long. We'll leave a note for your mother. In case she gets home first." It occurred to him that if he was going to Charlie's house, he would have to take Shawna with him in any case. He couldn't leave her on her own.

"I'll come with you," Shawna said, in a voice that startled Foster with its adult tone. "Of course I will."

ON JUBILEE STREET, fog shrouded the houses and hid the tops of the trees.

"There's 359!" Shawna said. "Are you sure nobody's home? There's a bunch of lights on."

"They're probably on a timer." Foster stared at the hulking van that sat in the driveway, forlorn as an abandoned dog. The mailbox overflowed with flyers. The front walk needed sweeping. The dead are neglectful.

"Hey, there's a note on the front door." Shawna went bounding up the steps. "'Left key with neighbour. Drummond.'"

"Does it say which neighbour?"

"Nope." Shawna darted across the driveway and banged on a side door. Foster hurried after her. A light came on. A moment later, a slim woman wearing a kaftan appeared in the doorway.

"*Salam alekum*," Foster said automatically.

"*Wa Alaykum as-Salaam*."

"We're here to get pictures and stuff for Charlie's funeral?" Shawna said. "Charlie and my grandfather? They were friends because they worked together at Grandpa's Toolbox. Charlie had this brother in Arizona but he's dead too. Did Mr. Drummond give you a key?"

Shawna snatched the key from the neighbour's hand and shot away.

Foster stepped across the driveway and walked into the kitchen. The counter was six inches lower than standard. Everything in the room, the cupboards, the china cabinet, the breakfast nook, had been built to the same scale.

"Sweet! I can reach everything!" Shawna threw open a cupboard. "Hey! Oreos!" She grabbed a bag of cookies and tore it open.

What had gotten into the child? She had seemed so mature an hour ago. Foster took the bag from her hand. "Shawna, please. We're looking for pictures. Wait. Where are you going now?"

She sped away, munching an Oreo. The living room had a plush couch with frilly cushions. There were figurines in a china cabinet — a balloon seller, a southern belle with a billowing skirt, an elfin doctor and a pixie nurse. There were signs of masculine loneliness — a baseball magazine, an empty beer can, a recliner with a remote control on its arm. Foster felt spooked. As if at any moment Charlie might come walking back in.

"Here's a picture!" Shawna lifted a framed photograph from the mantle. "Omigod! Mrs. Charlie? She's like, tiny."

The picture had been taken on a beach, Foster saw when he bent to take a closer look. Charlie and Mrs. Charlie — Marge — stood smiling at the camera. And yes, she was very short. Charlie had scaled the kitchen to her height. What kind of woman had she been, to inspire such love? Foster felt a perplexing sense of loss. He would never know Marge, and for a reason that now seemed incomprehensible, his need for solitude, he hadn't spent much time with Charlie.

Shawna plopped down on a love seat and clamped her knees together. "How come it's so cold in here? Can we turn up the heat? The thingee's over there on the wall."

"We won't be staying that long." Foster looked at the picture in his hand. "We need a box."

"There's tons of boxes in the basement. There's creepy pictures of dead people down there. You want those? They're kind of big." Shawna bolted away and went thundering down the stairs. Something crashed to the floor. "Watch your head," Shawna shouted, just as Foster whacked his head on a beam.

Charlie's shop had a table saw, a drill press, a workbench, tools mounted on pegboard. Foster lifted a chisel from its mount and ran the pad of his thumb over the cutting surface. The edge was sharp and true; its keenness took him back to his own workshop, to the house he had shared with Kathleen so long ago. When he had gone to the Middle East, he had given his tools away. He hadn't missed them until this moment.

"I'm totally glad I made Mom get rid of my old stuff."

"What old stuff?" Foster said, remembering the dollhouse and the pop-up books in Shawna's room. He put the chisel back in its place and looked around for a box.

"The stuff we cleared out of your room before you came. She had my baby stuff in there."

Foster took this in. Had his daughter expected him to stay? The idea bewildered him. He felt like a character on *Restless World*. The director had given him only his lines, not the whole script.

"Hey!" Shawna said, standing on a red metal toolbox. "Check it out."

The birdhouses dangling from a joist — a railroad station, a Taj Mahal, an Eiffel Tower, a red-and-white barn — were whimsical, meticulously crafted creations. They didn't fit Charlie's offhand, I-just-bang-'em-together disclaimer. Shawna took a deep breath and blew, setting the birdhouses in motion.

"Did he sell these in Grandpa's?"

"No."

"Then, how come he made them?"

"He'd stopped making them."

"Why? These are really great."

"Yes, they're very nice," Foster said, impatient suddenly with the burden of Charlie's life. It had fallen to him to clean out his grandmother's apartment, to toss away the boxes of letters, the rotogravure of the royal family, the drawings he had brought home from grade school. "We'll take a couple of them for the funeral."

Shawna climbed onto a washing machine. "Which ones?"

"I don't care. You pick."

"How about this farm picture? You want it too?"

Foster walked over to take a look. A country road led past a windbreak of poplars to a farmhouse with a wide front porch. To the left of the porch stood a barn with a tin roof. "Yes, we'd better bring that."

"Check out the whiskers on this dude," Shawna said, cocking a thumb at a portrait.

The man had on a black coat. His hair was parted down the middle and drooped damply over his ears. He had Charlie's bearish build and seen-it-all eyes. "I'm not dead," the man in the picture seemed to say. "I'm right here, looking at you."

"Hello?" a deep voice called. Foster's heart leapt. He stumbled back against the washing machine and looked up the stairs to see a bearded man peering down at him.

"YOU HAVE A lovely home," Shawna was perched on the couch, teacup in hand, every inch the little lady.

"Thank you," the neighbour woman said.

"Did you know Mr. Charlie very long?" Shawna asked.

"Since the summer only," said the man who had appeared at the top of the stairs.

Foster sipped his tea. These people were Iranian, he thought. The spider carpet under his feet had animals on its border, a medallion in its centre. The room had a Persian look, the brass and glass, and enough anonymous North American pieces to suggest the couple had been some years in Canada.

"Is this real leather?" Shawna rubbed a palm over the couch. "It's so smooth."

"Real leather." The man smiled at Shawna.

His wife gave Foster a puzzled look. "When I came to the door, you greeted me in Arabic."

"Foster speaks Arabic," Shawna said.

"A phrase or two. I lived in the Middle East for a while." Foster eyed the box of photographs and keepsakes at his feet. It was getting late. Shawna had school tomorrow.

"Foster was over there for years and years. He had a really important job. He had hundreds of people working for him."

"Where did you live?" the woman asked.

"Oh, all over," Foster said.

"He lived in Dubai," Shawna said. "He knew all the sheiks."

"We were ten years in Qatar," the man said. "We are accountants."

"Foster lost all his money in AMEB," Shawna said. "Millions and millions."

THE BUS CLUNKED from pothole to pothole. Water dripped down the windows. Foster sat with the cardboard box jiggling around on his lap. His nerves were raw, after that excruciating hour. He'd had to tell the whole story to those sympathetic strangers — the ill-fated electronic transfer, the buck-passing by governments and regulators, the terrible moment when he knew his money had vanished.

Shawna sat swaying beside him, squeaking her finger over the wet glass, drawing a swan. He needed his privacy. He had to say something. "Shawna," he began.

"Uh-huh."

"Please don't tell people the things you know about me." He stared at the picture Shawna had drawn on the window. The drawing had flair and precision.

"Can I go over to Jessica's sometime?" Shawna said, frowning with concentration.

"What?"

"She said she'd give me an art lesson."

"Shawna, listen. Don't tell people about AMEB."

"AMEB is a secret? Excuzzzzze me."

"AMEB isn't a secret. But the part about my money is."

"Why?"

"Just because."

"Just because?" Shawna gave him a scornful look.

"Because ..." Foster stared into the box of memorabilia. Charlie and Marge stared back at him. The dead and the bankrupt have something in common — everybody knows their business. "It's private, okay?" Foster heard his voice rise out of control. "It's nobody's business but mine."

"Whatever." Shawna scrubbed the swan from the glass and collapsed in a sulk.

When they reached the townhouse, she went to her room and slammed the door.

[TWELVE]

WHEN FOSTER CAME into the kitchen the next morning, Mary was at the stove, wearing her Secure-All outfit and staring down at a steaming saucepan. Foster pulled out a chair and sat down. Boiling his eggs had become a ceremony.

"Where's Shawna?" Foster said.

"Soccer club," Mary said without turning around. "Just started. Meets before school."

"Oh. She likes soccer, does she?"

"Got her heart set on playing." Mary balanced an egg on a spoon, lowered the spoon into the boiling water.

"Soccer is very popular in Dubai."

The eggs rattled liquidly. "The phone bill is on the counter."

"Is there a problem?" Foster reached for the envelope.

"I didn't say there was a problem. I said the bill was on the counter."

A little more light each morning, Foster thought, looking out at the side yard. A little more warmth from the sun. "Are you going out again tonight? I can babysit."

"I don't know. Maybe."

"Have a good time last night?" Foster knew by now that she hadn't.

"Peachy. Terrific." The water bubbled in the pan. "Tyler and I had a fight, if you must know."

"Mary, if you and Tyler are quarrelling all the time, doesn't that tell you something?"

"It was no big deal." Mary threw open a cupboard. "Where's the toaster?"

"In the middle room. The inside elements aren't working and I thought I'd —"

"What? It works fine. You just have to flip the bread around."

"That's not the way it's supposed to work."

"Oh, make your own damn eggs!" Mary jammed her ball cap on her head and strode away from the stove. Leaving the pot boiling.

AS HE NEARED the front doors of Grandpa's Toolbox, Foster looked up to see an airliner glinting in the sunlight, climbing into a clear sky, banking into a turn to take up its true course.

"Welcome home, Grandpa Foster," a greeter said. The store was running a promotion on appliances; fridges and stoves sat under the front canopy, and the greeter, a man Foster had never seen before, was leaning on a stovetop. The stove wasn't plugged in — the power cord was taped to the backsplash — but the sight jarred Foster, and he hurried past without saying a word. Once, when he was a boy, he had accidentally set his hand on a hot burner in his grandmother's kitchen. The pain had sent him stumbling back toward an open window. His grandmother had taken him by the arm and thrust his hand into a pan of cold milk. Foster inspected the pale white arcs on his palm. He hadn't thought about the scar in years.

Sal was in the locker room. "How's it going?" he asked.

"Can't complain."

"Atta boy."

"See you later," Foster said. They might have been strangers, he and Sal. Training course friendships evaporate as quickly as shipboard romances. In the Fasteners department, Foster sat on a stool, gazing blankly across the sales floor. A stock boy dropped on the counter a carton labelled *Nylon Washers*. Good, Foster thought. He had been waiting for those to come in. A bird chirped, and he peered up to see a flutter of wings. Sparrows had found their way into the store and built nests in the rafters. To a generation of fledglings, Grandpa's would be a forest.

"And how is Grandpa Foster today?" asked Amanda Curtwell.

Maybe Grandpa Foster was someone else. Maybe he was the grump who had scolded Shawna on the way back from Charlie's house.

"Grandpa Foster." Amanda tapped the carton of washers with a manicured fingernail. "I know you're upset about Grandpa Anderson, but work is —"

"— the curse of the drinking class!" Foster threw his head back and laughed. The saying was Irv's. Why did that old wheeze seem so hilarious now? Amanda stepped back, looking like a frightened child. Foster got a grip on himself. "I'll get right on it."

"Do that." Amanda gave him an uneasy look and walked away.

FOSTER SET UP the ironing board and plugged in the iron. He could have told Drummond to find someone else, he reminded himself as he ironed a shirt and put a fresh crease in his suit pants. Someone unfazed by the trappings of death. There was nothing for it now. He would have to go to the funeral home and battle his demons. When he had finished dressing, he stood back from the mirror, looking for chinks in his armour. His white shirt looked crisp and fresh. His necktie hung straight, the tips meeting at his belt. His suit held its drape: Frazier & Sons had done good work. There is no substitute for quality. Foster checked his watch. The afternoon visitation would begin in thirty minutes.

"I'm ready," he heard Shawna say. He turned in surprise to see his granddaughter standing in the doorway in an antique evening gown of maroon velvet. She wore white gloves and she had a small silver purse in her hands. She hadn't spoken to him since the trip to Charlie's house.

"You look very pretty, Shawna." Foster chose his words with care. "I'm very glad to see you. But shouldn't you be in school?"

"I told Mrs. Patterson I had to go to a funeral."

"Oh," Foster said. "Well, then." Charlie had stipulated an open casket. Could Shawna handle that? He kept his expression blank, but his granddaughter seemed to read his thoughts.

"I can help," Shawna said, her voice carrying an appeal. "I did all this stuff when grandma died."

Kathleen. Yes, of course there would have been a funeral. The full Catholic foofaraw. The body present in the church. The priest in black. The casket sprinkled with Holy Water.

"I won't say anything I'm not supposed to."

The apology embarrassed Foster. "Oh, well. That's fine then."

"CHECK OUT THE dance-band zombie," Shawna whispered as Penton came limping across the lobby with the tails of his mourning suit flapping. Foster looked across the room, and stifled a laugh. With his stiff gait, his rigid smile, his ancient clothes, the undertaker looked, well, exactly like a dance-band zombie. Shawna had the right idea. Find the humour in the situation.

"Mr. Anderson is resting in the Rose Room," Penton said with a little bow.

Resting, Foster thought as he followed Penton and Shawna down the hall. As if eternity were a catnap. In the Rose Room, the metal coffin sat on a steel catafalque, illuminated by track lights that reminded Foster of an art gallery. This week at the Penton Gallery: Work by the Grim Reaper.

Charlie lay on quilted white satin with his hands folded on his chest, looking uncharacteristically formal in the blue suit Foster had found in the closet on Jubilee Street. Shawna slipped her hand into Foster's. The gesture moved him. It had been many years since he had held a child's hand.

"What do you think?" Penton asked in an amiable voice.

It took Foster a moment to realize that Penton was fishing for a compliment.

"Um," Foster said. He couldn't make himself say that Charlie looked natural, because it wasn't true. Charlie's nose was waxy, his cheeks powdery, his lips too red. And his lips seemed to have been glued together — as if Penton were afraid the dead would speak out of turn. Announce the dreadful news that everyone already knew.

"An easy restoration. Nothing like the accident victim we had last week. Perhaps you saw the story on television? A construction crane —"

"We'd like some time alone," Foster said firmly.

"Of course." Penton said with a bow. "I'll leave you with your thoughts."

"I'm a little creeped out." Shawna glanced at Charlie and put a hand on her stomach.

"Me too," Foster said. He felt a sudden panic. He should assign Shawna a task, keep her busy. He put the box of memorabilia on a chair, unpacked it quickly and handed Shawna a birdhouse. "Where should we put that, I wonder?"

"Down there?" Shawna nestled the birdhouse under the coffin.

"Yes, that looks fine," Foster said.

"Or maybe on top? So Mr. Charlie can see it?"

Friend, I never want to see another birdhouse. "I think it looks good under there."

"What about this picture of Mr. Charlie?"

"How about on top of the casket?" Foster took the photograph from Shawna and set it on the shiny metal.

"The photo album should go on the table," Shawna said. "So people can learn all about his life."

"Good idea," Foster said. His granddaughter's earnest belief in the power of education touched him.

When everything was in place and there seemed nothing else to do, Foster settled into an easy chair that accepted his weight with a dusty sigh. Shawna arranged herself in the opposite chair. They sat together in formal silence, looking at the coffin. Charlie's face was just visible, as if he were swimming on his back. "Wait!" Shawna said. She jumped to her feet, startling Foster. "We need a grabber!" She picked up the photo album and came to Foster's side, flipping through the pages. "Is this okay?"

"I think so," Foster said. Taken the same day as the framed enlargement that now stood on the casket, the pictures recorded a day on a beach. Charlie and Marge kissing under an umbrella. Standing arm in arm. Kneeling on a blanket sharing a cone of French fries. Running hand in hand, away from the camera, toward the water, into the next moment of lives that had ended.

"Who sent the flowers?" Shawna said, breaking Foster's train of thought. He stared at the floral arrangements flanking the casket. Lilies and larkspur. Roses and daisies.

"This one's from Grandpa's Toolbox," Shawna said. "Mr. Drummond sent the other one."

P.C. Penton hobbled in. "It's two o'clock. Shall we open the doors?"

Foster got to his feet and straightened his back as if he expected to see a firing squad come marching in. Shawna stationed herself at the book of remembrance. She was doing Charlie proud. Foster worried she would be disappointed. Marge and Charlie were childless. Who would come?

To Foster's surprise, people came.

"Hell of a second baseman in his time," Mervin Perry said, peering down at Charlie. Perry had grown up with Charlie in a little town east of Peterborough. He hadn't seen Charlie in forty years. He turned to Foster and gave him a shrewd look. "Who do you like in the AL East for next season?"

The question caught Foster by surprise. "The Yankees will be tough to beat," he said, repeating what Charlie had told him in East 303.

"Think their pitching will hold up?"

"Well …" Foster had no opinion to offer. Not that it mattered, because Perry launched into a monologue. "Huh," Foster said every now and then. "Um." "Really." When Perry drifted away to talk with someone else, Foster looked across the room. Shawna was having an animated conversation with Mervin Perry's wife.

"Might as well tell you straight up. I'm Betty." Foster turned around to face a sad-faced woman wearing a homespun dress.

"I'm the one that sells the cushions."

"Cushions?" Was Betty a street vendor, here to work the crowd?

"At the flea market!" Betty said with a vehemence that startled Foster. "For those stools people have in their kitchens." She looked down at Charlie and shook her head. "That man and I would get into it something fierce. One time in Barrie they gave him my table, and I said, 'Mister, you can put those damn birdhouses right back in that box.' I didn't mean anything by it."

Did Betty want absolution? It seemed so. "Well," Foster said. "I wouldn't worry about it. Charlie wasn't a man to hold a grudge." *Ego te absolvo*, Kathleen would say when the family cat dropped a freshly killed robin at her feet.

"That's good to hear. Because I liked Charlie. I really did."

"Charlie often told me how much fun he had at the flea markets," Foster said.

Betty looked at him. "Bullshit. He hated every minute." She strutted away.

A man stood leaning over the casket, turning a ball cap around and around in his hands. He introduced himself as the dispatcher from Charlie's old trucking company, shook Foster's hand and said, "Easiest man on a rig I ever did see. Clowns I got working now? You wouldn't believe what they do to a transmission."

The Iranian couple from Jubilee Street came in next, then the people who had lived across the street from Charlie, a sturdy old couple who knelt before the casket, softly praying in a language Foster thought might be Ukrainian. When they had crossed themselves a final time they stood immobile, staring into the crowded room like a pair of solemn children. Foster angled over and thanked them for coming. The woman nudged her husband with her elbow.

"Lawn roller," the man said. "What should I do?"

"Lawn roller?" Foster was lost.

"For making flat the grass," the woman said. "Charlie lend him."

"Oh," Foster said, beginning to understand. "Why don't you just keep it?"

"No," the man said, shaking his head adamantly. "Is not mine."

"Charlie would want you to have it."

"No! Is not mine."

Foster glanced at Charlie. His embalmed face seemed to take on a stoic expression. "Tell you what," Foster said. "Keep it for a while. I'll call you when I need it."

Gathering his pride, the old man drew himself erect, took his wife by the arm and walked across the carpet and through the doors, leaving Foster perplexed. Had he offended the man? He was still thinking about this when Sal came walking in with a dozen men wearing the plaid and denim of Grandpa's Toolbox. The Grandpas shook Foster's hand and slapped him on the back. Carrying on like a troop of Shriners, they fussed over Shawna, signed the guest book, told each other jokes. Then, to Foster's horror, they started hugging him. The Rose Room buzzed with a bewildering mix of laughter and chitchat. It seemed to Foster that anything might happen.

"I'm thinking of packing it in," Sal said. He was standing with Foster, gazing down at Charlie.

Foster looked at Sal. Had Charlie's death hit him that hard?

"All the hassle," Sal said. "Little Miss Amanda. The Grandpa song. When I retired, I was supposed to go fishing."

"Oh," Foster said, getting the picture. Tom had already quit. Charlie had died. The news of Sal's departure made Foster lonely.

At four, when Penton came in to say that the afternoon visitation was over, Foster was sitting on the couch between Betty the cushion lady and Perry the baseball fanatic, trying to follow their argument about the '95 World Series. Betty glanced at the casket. "For a dead guy, Charlie throws a hell of a party."

"WHEN WE WERE on the bus?" Shawna said as she and Foster were walking along. "I spied a boutique de cheap."

She had insisted on staying for the evening visitation. But what was she talking about now? Foster buttoned up his coat and stole a glance at his granddaughter. The weather had turned cool. Was she warm enough in that dress? The question seemed out of bounds. In contemporary Canada, only the old bundled up, he had noticed: the young went coatless, jittered around at bus stops with their hands in their pockets.

She led Foster into a dimly lit, overheated store that had the sour smell of old clothes. He looked round in dismay at the cockeyed garment racks, the chipped dishes and dented appliances. This was a thrift shop. His granddaughter was a recipient of charity. The realization hit him hard. He had dropped the ball, let his fortune slip through his fingers, left Shawna to pick over castoffs. She went off to the women's wear section, stranding Foster in an aisle of old shoes.

"SO WHAT'D YOU find?" Shawna dipped a french fry into a pool of ketchup. They were sitting in a McDonald's down the street from Penton's, tucked between a paint store and a dentist's office.

"An overcoat." Foster tugged the garment from a shopping bag. He had bought the coat to please Shawna. She had insisted on him buying something.

"Nice. Looks brand new."

The coat was his size and only slightly out of style — and a terrific bargain at twelve dollars — but buying a proper winter coat seemed to seal his fate, doom him to live out his days in the Canadian snow. Shawna gave him a cagey look. There was a plastic bag on the seat beside her. He didn't want to spoil her fun. "I bet you found something really great."

"Uh-huh." Shawna wiped her fingers on a napkin, fished in the bag and held up a slinky white blouse for Foster to admire. The blouse had padded shoulders, a scalloped collar, yellowing seams. He put on his boardroom face, the thoughtful, interested expression he hid behind when someone's eyes were on him and he wanted to think. Did other young people wear this sort of thing? He wasn't sure. Children seldom came into Grandpa's Toolbox.

"Is that retro, or what?"

"It sure is," Foster said, with an enthusiasm he didn't feel. Retro meant hand-me-down. Mary couldn't manage money. Hadn't he devised the monthly allowance for that very reason? The monthly allowance that had gone down with AMEB.

On the walk back to P.C. Penton's, Foster brooded. He would quit Grandpa's Toolbox, find a job that paid real money, take Shawna on a shopping expedition. "I get a bigger kick out of this than she does," he would say to the sales clerk. Pipe dream, his pitiless intelligence told him.

AS A BOY, Foster had poured over books about the *Lusitania* and the *Titanic*, studied the cutaway drawings of passengers strolling corridors while beneath their feet chefs toiled in galleys and stokers tended boilers. This could be the lounge of some doomed ship, he thought as he walked into the Rose Room. Perhaps the River Styx had widened since ancient times. Perhaps those lost liners were back in service, ferrying the dead. Shawna stationed herself at the door. Foster crossed the room and stood next to Charlie. The man was easy company, even now.

The evening session was slow. A retired mailman came in to pay his respects. Must have trudged up Jubilee Street with the Andersons' mail thousands of times, he told Foster. A mechanic told Foster that Charlie had kept his van in tip-top shape. A smartly dressed woman came striding on high heels, looked at Charlie, spoke to Foster and went away quite annoyed. As if Charlie had played a mean trick, posing as her Uncle Keith.

Then no one came, and Foster sank into an armchair. His eyes grew heavy and he dozed. The armchair slipped its moorings, floated through time, drifted into the lobby of a hotel on Irv's northern route, the run up Highway 10 that ended in Walter's Bay. *Wait here, Danny. Back in a minute.* An hour or two later, Irv would come swaying into the lobby and wave his son to his feet without a word of apology. Thinking again about the allowance he had promised Mary, Foster envied Irv's indifference to breaking his word.

Was Shawna willing to pack it in and go home? Foster got to his feet and started across the room. She shooed him away. He sank impatiently back in his chair. He had had enough.

He must have dozed off again. Shawna was chatting with a stooped, white-haired man wearing a rumpled raincoat. The man crossed the floor and stood looking down at Charlie. He turned to Foster. "I'm Malcolm Drummond. Charlie's lawyer. Marge picked me out of the phone book. Sent me a cake every Christmas. Nice woman."

Drummond seemed to have something on his mind, and Foster titled his head, ready to listen.

"Listen, I hate to ask, but can you go with Charlie tomorrow?"

"Go with Charlie?"

"I can't sit in a car that long, not the way my back's playing up. Unless you've got something on."

"Nothing important," Foster said. It would be good to have an outing. He would leave a message for Amanda Curtwell, tell her he wasn't coming in.

"Thanks," Drummond said. "I'll talk to Penton. The hearse can pick you up."

Foster hadn't counted on a hearse. He walked Drummond to the door and shook his hand. Shawna stood behind the book of remembrance. She ran her finger down a page. "Thirty-seven so far. Forty if we count the zombie dude."

"Zombie dude?"

"Penton. He's been in here three times."

"Shawna, you've been great," Foster said. "I don't think anybody else is coming. We can go now if you —"

"No! There's a half hour left. What if somebody came and no one was here?"

If three men dig a lot of dirt, what time does the train get to Montreal? This was one of Irv's more mysterious sayings. "Come and sit with me, at least. We'll keep an eye on the door." They crossed the room. Charlie was waiting for them to return. The dead are paragons of patience. Shawna sat in a chair and snatched up the photo album. "Hey! I know. That's Sauble Beach. I'm totally sure!"

Foster leaned forward to inspect the photograph under her finger. Marge and Charlie stood on a crescent of sand. Seagulls wheeled overhead. What would become of the photo album? Would it end up in the trash? The thought was unbearable. He would take the album home, Foster decided. Shawna might want it someday.

"See? There's the sign," Shawna said. "The one at the end of the highway."

Foster looked up to see a woman crossing the carpet, taking long, easy strides. She had on a blue dress and a pair of dress shoes with low heels.

"Hi, Mom."

"Mary?" Foster rose halfway in his chair. Mary was on afternoons. She must have changed her shift. Why would she take the trouble? She had never met Charlie.

"Check out these old bathing suits," Shawna said.

"Yeah? Can you show me?" Mary perched a hip on Shawna's chair and glanced at Foster. "Tyler couldn't make it."

"That's okay," Foster said. "It doesn't matter." He settled down slowly, as if Penton's sturdy old armchair might shatter under his weight.

[THIRTEEN]

THE DOORBELL SOUNDED. Shawna sprang from her chair. A moment later she lurched back into the kitchen, walking on her heels with her arms raised. "Your hearse is here," she said, her voice dark with horror.

"BILL SIMPSON. I do transfers," the driver said in the gravelly voice of a television gangster. He was a big man with white hair cropped in a flat-top style Foster hadn't seen in thirty years. He wore a grey uniform with silver buttons. A peaked cap lay on the seat beside him. "Somebody dies. The hospital puts the remains in the holding room and they call the funeral home. The funeral home calls me and I pick up the deceased and take them where they need to go. And that's a transfer."

When they reached the expressway, Simpson flicked on a turn signal and crooned, "Let's open up a nice hole for Mr. Billy." A Honda Civic nipped into the space he was aiming for. Simpson shook his head. "Used to be they'd show a professional car some respect. These days, they'll run you right off the road, even if you're carrying."

Carrying. Foster looked out over the long, black hood. To escape a shift at Grandpa's Toolbox, he was hitching a ride with the dead. But with the sun shining and the highway opening up before him he would put mortality out of his mind. He was a travelling man again, if only for a few hours.

"Should be in Westdale by eleven, Mr. Anderson. An hour at the cemetery, two hours back. Call it five hours. Which is good. Because I've got another transfer this afternoon."

"My name isn't Anderson. It's Foster."

"Oh?" Simpson glanced at Foster. "I thought you were the deceased's brother. Are you his second cousin, something like that?"

"Charlie was a special friend."

Simpson stared down the road. "We get that these days. And you know what? I think it's great."

"Not that kind of special."

"Oh." Simpson's shoulders fell a little.

On the outskirts of the city, the hearse passed a transport truck with *RAPID DISPATCH* lettered on its side. Foster smiled. Irv would have liked that. It was his kind of humour.

"What did the deceased do for a living? Don't mean to be nosy, but I like to know who I'm driving. Makes it more personal."

"Charlie? He was a truck driver."

"Oh, yeah? What kind of rig?"

"Transport trucks like the one we just passed."

"Local, you mean?"

"No, into the States, all over."

"That so? A man of the road, eh? Well, we'll give him a nice, smooth ride." Simpson waved a proprietary hand over the dashboard. "See that little wheel? You got separate climate controls, Mr. Foster. Set it up anyway you like. Make yourself at home."

They slipped along with the sun flashing on the windshield and Lake Ontario winking in and out of sight. As the city melted away and the subdivisions thinned, Foster tried to plan his next move. He had to find a better job. There must be something he hadn't tried. He ran through the possibilities again.

They had been driving for an hour when Simpson turned the hearse north and Foster let his thoughts go where they would. They climbed hills, fell into valleys, cruised past farmland. Furrows striated the fields. Sunlight slanted through the woodlands. The trees were pale green. Something would turn up. His luck was bound to change.

"Tough old winter, eh?"

"Um," Foster said.

"Guess we had it coming. All that hot weather last summer."

"Has this highway been here long?"

"The 115? Years and years." Simpson looked at Foster with new interest. "Been away, have you?"

Yes, I have, Foster thought. In the Middle East. I should be in Thailand but I'm stuck in Canada. I live with my daughter. Her boyfriend is a dreamer. My granddaughter buys her clothes in thrift shops. When things get tough at home she does stand-up comedy. I'm worried about her. "I was in Florida just before Christmas."

"Nice down there, isn't it?"

"Yes, very nice."

"No snow to shovel in Florida."

"That's for sure."

"HIGHWAY 7," SIMPSON said, breaking a long silence.

Irv had travelled 7, Foster remembered, worked his way through Norwood, Havelock, Marmora, Madoc; visited smaller towns with names like Modley, Wilbur Mills, Westdale.

Forty minutes later, Simpson turned onto a two-lane blacktop road. Bullrush lined the ditches. Split rail fences flanked the shoulders. The hearse crested a drumlin, dipped through a gully, climbed past a windbreak of poplars that led to a farmhouse with a silver roof. A loose-stone wall ran off at a right angle. *Some silly bugger found those rocks the hard way, Danny,* Irv would say, *whacked 'em with a plow.* The pavement abruptly ended.

Simpson eased to a stop and drew a map from his pocket. "I took the first left." A red-tailed hawk circled overhead. *We're lost, son,* Irv would announce. *But we're making good time!*

Foster peered down the narrow lane. "Why don't we see where it goes?"

Simpson drove on cautiously, past a farmyard littered with abandoned implements, up a steep hill, down a gradual slope terraced with outcrops of gravel. The road widened. A sign came into view. "Well, what do you know," Simpson said. "Hamlet of Westdale."

When they came to a backwater like Westdale, Irv would sing out, *We're passing through paradise, Danny. Don't blink or you'll miss it!* Through the windshield of the Studebaker, Foster would see a humdrum village with a church, a hardware store, a whirligig figure running on broken legs. *Dead from the ass both ways,* Irv would say, and then he would lead his son through a sort of commercial catechism. *Do you see a railway station, Danny?* No, sir. *Do you see a major highway?* No, sir. *Well, how did the silly buggers expect the place to grow?* In Irv's crank cosmology, failing to grow offended the benevolent power that caused Studebakers to be manufactured and hardware catalogues to be printed.

Westdale, or what remained of it, lay on one side of a short street. The hardware store was long gone. There was a library, a post office, a collapsing building that might have been a livery stable. The Community Centre, a dowdy redbrick building, had once housed a chapter of the Orange Lodge, Foster noticed. The Glorious Twelfth. King Billy's horse. No pope here. After his stay in the Middle East — the land of the living God — all of that long ago sectarian strife seemed quaint.

Religion seemed to mean little to Canadians these days, and maybe that was just as well. And yet, although he wasn't a believer, Foster missed the serious quality that the faith of strangers had lent his expatriate years. The sense that life mattered.

"Which one is Trinity United, do you suppose?" Simpson said. They had come to an intersection with time-worn churches on three of its corners: an Anglican church with biblical scenes in stained glass, a formerly Methodist church with windows of coloured glass, a Presbyterian church with clear windows.

"That one," Foster said, Irv's lookout again. "The white frame building."

Simpson put on his peaked cap, backed the hearse onto a cinder driveway and pushed a button. The door locks snapped open, and Foster stepped out into the sunshine and stretched his arms over his head. A white car sat parked near the church. Wood smoke scented the air. Somewhere nearby a diesel engine chuffed and roared. Foster was staring vacantly at the church when its double doors swung open and a woman came walking out.

"I'm Celia Bailey." She clasped Foster's hand. "I'm very sorry for your loss." She was fifty, Foster thought, give or take a summer.

"Thank you," Foster said. He wouldn't try to explain his tenuous connection with Charlie. It was easier to play along.

Simpson stationed himself at the hearse's rear door. "If we're ready to roll the coffin …"

A wild-haired man suddenly appeared. His coveralls were streaked with grease. He looked at the hearse, shaking his head and slapping his thigh with a work glove.

"Is there a problem, Mr. Fitzgerald?" Celia Bailey said.

"We can't roll a coffin across that yard."

Simpson looked at his watch. "I'm on a tight schedule."

"Can we use the side gate?" Celia Bailey said, releasing Foster's hand.

Foster looked down the side road. A page wire fence separated the graveyard from the world of the living.

"Front gate, side gate, it won't roll."

Celia Bailey said, "Mr. Fitzgerald, please finish preparing the grave."

"She's all dug." Fitzgerald walked to the front steps, sat himself down and pulled a bent cigarette from behind an ear.

"Show some respect," Celia Bailey said. "No smoking, please."

Fitzgerald's smile sent the cigarette tilting up. "Who said I was going to light it?"

"Tell you what," Simpson said. "We'll leave the coffin in the church and you folks can sort this out later." He looked at Foster with an expectant expression.

When there was a decision to be made, people had always turned to him, the tall man in the expensive suit. Foster kept silent, and felt a daredevil pleasure. The jaunt in the country had come his way unexpectedly and he was going to enjoy the day. He was taking a time out from decision making, a vacation from daughters and granddaughters and potential sons-in-law, a holiday from women with claims on his heart.

"I'll round up pallbearers." Celia Bailey walked to the white car, got in and drove away.

Simpson threw up his hands, wandered to the front steps and sat down beside the gravedigger. Foster watched the white car crest a hill and disappear from view. It was a splendid day. The sun shone in a cloudless sky. The air was perfectly still. A farm truck rattled up to a stop sign, slowed, then clattered on trailing a mist of hay. Savouring the moment, Foster eased himself down beside the other two men, leaned back on his hands, tilted his face to the sun and remembered his father.

Irv in the bar of a farmers' hotel with his order book open before him. *We'll have to fancy these numbers up, son. Make them pretty.*

Irv in a hotel room. A bare light bulb dangling from a high ceiling.

A strip of sticky paper, dark with flies. A mickey of rye on a nightstand. A bed, a fold-up cot. *Let's hear that poem your grandmother gave you to memorize.*

Yes, sir. *Elegy Written in a Country Churchyard, by Thomas Gray.* Though decades had gone by since he had committed the poem to memory, its words came back to Foster. *The curfew tolls the knell of parting day, The lowing herd winds slowly o'er the lea, The ploughman homeward plods his weary way, And leaves the world to darkness and to me.*

"I'll give her ten minutes." Simpson nodded at the cloud of dust the minister's car had left hanging over the road. "Then I'm driving the remains back to the city." He glanced at Fitzgerald. "You tell her that."

"You can't tell that one anything." The gravedigger struck a match on the step.

No one spoke for a time. Cigarette smoke curled into the air. A crow flew across the road, alighted on a headstone and folded its wings. Simpson picked up a pebble and winged it at a tree, missing by a foot.

"Are your people buried here?" Foster said, gazing over the pale ground.

"Catholic cemetery is halfway up the third line," Fitzgerald said. "And the ground is just as hard."

The white car pulled back in, followed by a pickup truck, a big one with a crew cab. Five men climbed from the truck. They wore tan pants and plaid shirts and green, quilted vests. They stood together quietly, dust settling around them.

Celia Bailey said, "Mr. Simpson, if you could drive to the side gate, which Mr. Fitzgerald will open …"

The hearse went down the road with Celia Bailey, Foster, and the volunteer pallbearers walking behind it. They were brothers, Foster thought — the line of the jaw, the similar, rhythmic gait. When the impromptu cortége reached the side entrance, Fitzgerald was leaning over the gate with his gloved hands crossed and a cigarette behind an ear. Simpson backed the hearse through the gate, opened the rear door and slid the casket back. Foster took his place with the others and put his hand on a steel rod. "On three," Simpson said in a hoarse whisper. "One, two ..." Foster took his share of the burden. The weight surprised him. The dead are heavy.

The pallbearers carried the casket over the uneven ground, walking with measured steps past slabs of sandstone blurred by a century of weather. The headstones, with their litany of names, recorded the local history; there were settlements of Healeys, Bruces, Wilsons and, at the stone wall that marked the eastern boundary of the cemetery, Andersons. An excavating machine, the diesel Foster had heard running when he had arrived, sat tilted next to a fresh grave, its treads packed with dirt, its hydraulic arm curled like a sleeper's hand.

As Foster bent to set the casket down, he picked up a clump of yellow earth, and while Celia Bailey droned her way through a service of burial, he stood by the grave, crumbling the dry soil between his fingers, his thoughts drifting back to Irv. The desk clerk at The Disraeli had called to say Irv was in hospital, and Foster had come to the public ward of St. Joseph's. Now, as he stared into Charlie's waiting grave, he recalled the narrow ward, its iron bedsteads, its odour of iodine, the gaunt man in the next bed who thrashed about, his eyes wild with supplication. *Silly bugger's for it*, Irv had whispered. And then, with that hungry love in his eyes, Irv had folded his hands on the white sheet like a child waiting for a bedtime story. In the country churchyard, in the springtime stillness, Foster felt the weight of the judgment he had placed on his father. Fraud can take many forms, he thought now. There are falsities of heart, forgeries of love, and of these sins Irv was innocent. Even as he lay dying, a broken man with a criminal record, Irving Percival Foster had conveyed a windfall joy.

The praying ended. Foster raised his head, and felt water leak from his eyes. He cleared his throat and tightened his hands, struggling to bring himself under control. He might have succeeded, if Celia Bailey hadn't gazed at him, if Simpson hadn't laid a hand on his shoulder, if strangers hadn't left their work and come to bury Charlie Anderson. At the graveside of a man he scarcely knew, Foster wept for his lost father.

[FOURTEEN]

THERE WAS NOTHING in the want ads. Foster turned to the sports section and read that the ace of the Blue Jays' pitching staff was working on a slider. He would have to tell Charlie about that. But then he remembered Charlie was dead.

The sun had risen over the basket weave fence by the time Mary came into the kitchen. Keeping his head down, Foster watched her fumble a slice of bread into the toaster, open the fridge and settle opposite him with her fingers laced around a glass of orange juice. Mary surfaced from sleep in stages, like a deep-sea diver avoiding the bends. He stared thoughtfully at his daughter, wondering if there were other things he had failed to notice about her. Their eyes met. Mary started, and juice leapt from her glass. She jumped to her feet and swung open a cabinet. "Where the hell are the paper towels?"

"Under the sink. I did some reorganizing."

"Foster, what the hell!"

He picked up the paper and feigned interest in the weather forecast. Kathleen would blow up over nothing, a pint of cream gone sour, a misplaced set of keys. Once, he had come home to Regent Heights to find her in a rage because an African violet had wilted. He'd had a bad day at work. The fight had gone on for days, gathering strength like a hurricane moving over warm water. That famous donnybrook, Kathleen called it later. Mary brushed past with her Secure-All jacket swinging on her arm. That jacket wasn't warm enough. It would rain this afternoon, the paper said.

"Hi." Shawna sprinted into the kitchen, grabbed a banana and headed for the front door.

A child her age should eat breakfast. The clock radio buzzed in distress. It took Foster a moment to remember why he had put it on the counter. The alarm didn't seem to be working properly. That was it. He was staring at the clock radio when the phone rang.

"Mr. Foster? Malcolm Drummond speaking. Charlie's lawyer. Thanks again for everything you did. Remember that old van of Charlie's?"

"Yes." Foster had seen the van in Charlie's driveway.

"Three dealers looked at it but they didn't want it. Great shape, run for years, they said, but there's no market for anything that old."

Did Drummond want his advice? Foster flipped to the classifieds. Perhaps there was a similar car for sale.

"Tell you what. If you want the van, it's yours, free and gratis."

Foster felt a jolt of excitement. If he had a car, he could chauffeur Mary to work, ferry Shawna to her soccer practice, drive himself to Grandpa's. He could kiss the bus goodbye. Gas, insurance, repairs. He couldn't afford to run a car.

"Mr. Foster?"

"Yes, thank you. I'll take it."

"Good. You can pick up the car at my office. Got a pen? I'll give you the address."

GRANDPA MCCRINDLE HAD glossy dentures and a belly that bulged his overalls. He gave Foster a puzzled look. "What's your paint and paper profile?"

"Well, just the basics. I'm in Fasteners."

"Fasteners?" McCrindle lifted his eyes to the one-way mirrors. "Why does she do this to me?" He looked at Foster and sighed. "You know the colour wheel? Mix and match? Base and tint?"

"We did two hours on tints in Grandpa Camp."

"I need a good swatch man and Curty sends me a guy from Fasteners. No offence."

"What do you want me to do?" Foster wanted to help McCrindle. He wanted McCrindle to like him.

"Field the easy questions. Oil-based versus water-based. Alkyd stain, acrylic solid," McCrindle looked sadly at a tinting machine. "If a custom colour walks in, come and get me."

"Custom colour?"

"Yesterday this ditsy woman hands me a brown velvet cushion." McCrindle picked up a paint stick and snapped it in his hands. "You can't match velvet. Which I tell Mrs. Cushion. And what does she do? Marches straight to Curty and complains, that's what she does." McCrindle stroked his sleeve. "Rub the nap this way, it looks like RT-456 with maybe a drop of chrome yellow. Rub it that way and it's a dead ringer for FG-982."

"Tough to match, was it?"

"Tough? Picasso couldn't match that cushion. Want to see six different shades of shit?" McCrindle waved a hand at the bargain table. "Now Curty's on my case about mis-tints."

"She's the manager. She has to control her costs."

McCrindle gave him a pitying look. "Yeah, right."

"Excuse me? Can I get some help?" A man wearing a windbreaker was beckoning from a display of paint samples.

“I’ll take this,” Foster said. McCrindle went off to help another customer.

“Do you have sea island green?” asked the man in the windbreaker.

“Sea island green …” Foster scanned the samples. “Sap green? Willow green?”

He tried to remember what Jessica’s art books had to say about colour … primary, complementary, secondary, tertiary … “Nile green? April green?” … primitive, neutral, cool, harmonies, discords … “Apple green? Gremlin green?”

“Grandpa Foster, why did you leave your station?”

Foster turned. Mr. Sea Island had wandered off. Amanda Curtwell stood in his place.

“I’m keeping an eye on my station.”

“You’re not assigned to Paint ’n Paper, Grandpa Foster. You’re assigned to Fasteners.”

“McCrindle is run off his feet and I just thought — ”

“Grandpa Foster, let’s make tomorrow a Clean Slate Day.” Amanda gave him a tight smile. “Your second.” She turned and paced away.

He could make Amanda understand, Foster knew, if she would only listen. He followed her past the barbeques, down the aisle of light bulbs. He watched her ascend the stairs, and then he walked slowly back to Fasteners.

LATER THAT WEEK Foster was in the lunch room eating his tuna fish sandwich when a bulky man eased himself onto a bench. *Grandpa Carey* read the badge pinned to his work apron. He peered at Foster’s badge and grunted. “You got a first name?”

“Call me Foster.”

Carey set down a lunch bucket. “Works for me. I got a rule at home: if you kids call me Grandpa, you better run.”

Was Carey new? Foster didn't remember seeing him in Florida. "Live with your grandchildren, do you?"

"Me? Nah. My grandchildren are in Vancouver. If my son's still out there."

"I see," Foster said. Should he ask Carey about his son? He decided to leave the question unasked. He could imagine Carey's answer. A broken family, with its severed connections.

"What's with that Curtwell broad?" Carey jerked a thumb at the sales floor. "She's been watching me like a hawk ever since I transferred in."

Grandpa's had opened three more stores in Toronto. Staff were being transferred back and forth, Foster knew. "Busy in your department?"

"Not with that storm going on out there. Frigging rain won't quit."

"Warmer, though."

"Know what she's got me doing? Sorting off-cuts." Carey shook his head. "The last guy who had the plywood area was some kind of pack rat. The shit he saved."

"Off-cuts?"

Carey looked at him.

"I want to put up some shelves for my daughter."

"Follow me," Carey said with a shrug. "I'll give you the royal tour."

When they reached the back of the store, Foster wandered to an open loading dock and stood looking out at the rain. Carey walked by, toting a sheet of melamine toward a dumpster.

Foster said, "Are you throwing that out?"

"Yeah. It's warped."

"Can I have it?"

"Grandpa Foster, that's against the rules," Carey said in a prissy voice.

"Can you set it aside for me?" Foster ignored the parody of Amanda Curtwell.

"Suppose I could, if I had a place to put it." Carey looked around. "You want to help me shift that pile of eleven millimetre? We could stick it under there." He held out a pair of work gloves.

"Grandpas," a recorded voice announced over the PA system. "It's safety sweep time! Check your area and mark your charts."

"Ah, shit," Carey said. "That's a listed procedure."

Foster snatched the gloves from Carey's hand. The shelves would free up floor space in the middle room, tidy up the mess. Why had he come to Canada, after all? To help Mary. Foster fell into a rhythm, picking up a sheet of plywood, dropping it, tucking the corners into alignment. It was good to see one pile shrink and another grow.

STRIP PLAZAS AND gas stations went by. Foster changed buses, changed again, trudged past a row of fast food outlets with a pair of licence plates in one hand and Drummond's address in the other. Forget cliffs and crags, pines and rivers, Foster thought as he crossed an expanse of pavement, heading for a characterless office block. This was Canada's true wilderness.

Drummond's reception area, a discretely lit room done up in brass and oak, reminded Foster of Cedric's private club in London, and the receptionist, with her silk scarf, reminded him of Sylvia. As he waited for Drummond, Foster wondered where Cedric and Sylvia and the good ship *Believer* were now. Pounding through the roaring forties south of Cape Town, perhaps, with the wind shrieking and the spray flying.

"Sorry to keep you waiting." Drummond led the way out of the building and across a series of parking lots. In the last of these, Charlie's van loomed like a mammoth on a treeless plain.

Foster stared at the dinosaur he had inherited from Charlie. It was a heavy duty van, painted muddy brown. It had fake wood on its flanks, a luggage rack on its roof, a sun visor over its windshield, a ladder on its rear door. There were souvenir decals on its windows: Maine, Florida, Prince Edward Island. More truck than car, it was much larger than the minivans that brought customers to Grandpa's Toolbox, with their signs jiggling on suction cups — "Sexy Soccer Mom!" "I'm Driving My Kid Somewhere. Again."

Drummond dropped the keys in Foster's hand and walked stiffly away.

"Thank you," Foster called after him. For a man with a taste for fine cars — in Canada, he had owned Jaguars; in the Middle East, Mercedes — the van was a comedown. The thought was ungrateful, Foster felt, and as he sorted through the keys, he worried that he had hurt Charlie's feelings. The dead are always within earshot.

A tug of a handle sent the rear gate sighing open. Foster stared. The cavernous interior held toolboxes, crates, boxes, a stepladder, extension cords. He crawled in and poked around, discovering hammers, saws, screwdrivers, chisels, tape measures, a power drill, a crate containing a belt sander and a pair of work boots, a box holding five volumes of *The Handyman's Encyclopedia* and a set of novels about the Napoleonic navy. Drummond had passed all this along. That was good of him. But then, what else could he have done with this stuff? Charlie had died without issue. A man without children was nothing, the Arabs said. You were somebody, Charlie, Foster thought, reaching for a screwdriver. There's more to kinship than flesh and blood.

The bolts for the licence plates had been greased and they spun off easily. Good old Charlie. When the new plates were on Foster climbed into the driver's seat and slipped the key in the ignition. The steering wheel felt strange in his hands; he hadn't driven a car since he had left Dubai. There were many storage compartments, and they were all full. Poking through them, Foster unearthed road maps, music cassettes, little bottles of hand sanitizer, a bag of butterscotch candies, a cosmetic bag containing a lipstick case. There was a fingerprint on the case, and Foster glanced at the empty passenger seat, half expecting to see Mrs. Charlie sitting there.

Spooked by the thought, he turned the key. The engine started with a roar and country and western music erupted. *Gonna hitch my heart to your double-wide, gonna take your lovin' for a long, long ride ...*

Why was that song familiar? As Foster drove around the parking lot to get the feel of the van, he ran a memory trace. Hubcaps on a wall, women sitting around a table. Dancing the swing jive, Jessica laughing and twirling. The van was no sports car. The steering was vague, the brakes mushy. This was no accident, Foster suspected. The engineers who had designed this behemoth back in the Reagan Era knew their customers. The idea was to keep the world — a pothole in the road, a revolution in Iran — at a comfortable remove. Foster preferred crisp, competent cars. "No offence," he said aloud, as if Charlie were riding along.

On the drive back into the city, while a woman sang "I Was Bettin' on a Pair and Got Three of a Kind," an insistent bonging interrupted the music. Foster switched off the radio and peered at the dashboard. The needle of the fuel gauge rested on E. When a gas station came into view, he glided up to a pump, switched off the ignition and waited for an attendant.

No one appeared, and he looked around impatiently. In Dubai, a crew of uniformed men would be swarming over the car by now, filling the tank, cleaning the windscreen, checking the tires, handing him a complimentary copy of *The Gulf News*. He climbed down and looked up at a sign. *Self-Serve.* Of course. He unscrewed the gas cap, fumbled with the pump, inserted the nozzle and squeezed the trigger. Nothing happened. The door of the cashier's hut popped open and a teenage girl came trotting over and flipped up a lever.

Back on the road, Foster tapped the gas gauge. Twenty dollars — almost the last of his cash, with payday a week away — hadn't lifted the needle very far. He shook his head, remembering that during his early years in the Middle East, gas had been free. You pulled in and you drove off with a full tank, compliments of the sheiks. At least he wasn't on the bus. Things were looking up.

He wanted to show the van to somebody. Why? He was a grown man driving a beater, not a boy with a brand new set of wheels. He should conserve the gas he had just bought, not squander it joyriding. Show the car to whom, exactly? Mary was at work. Shawna was in school. Foster pictured himself at the door of Mrs. Patterson's classroom. I realize you're in the middle of a math lesson, but I need to show my car to my granddaughter. No, that wouldn't do. It occurred to him that he was on the verge of a panic attack. They had started that day in Westdale and the first sign was a sudden feeling of loneliness. Exactly what he was feeling now.

Soon he was standing in the lobby of Jessica's building, pressing the button beside her name. Would the loneliness he felt pass for love? He studied a safety poster on the wall. A quaint souvenir from the building's time as a working factory, the poster warned against using ladders near power lines. The elevator doors slid open, and Jessica stepped out, dressed in her painting smock. His heart fluttered. She gave him a blank look. He might have been a delivery boy. Why hadn't he thought this through, rehearsed his lines? "I brought my new car to show you," Foster said, feeling like a fool.

"Boys," Jessica said. As if this one word explained everything.

"A friend of mine died. He wanted me to have the car." Was this true? Perhaps it was.

Jessica nodded. "Shawna told me about Charlie."

Shawna and Jessica were in communication? "Let's go for a ride," Foster said, blundering on.

"Now?" Jessica looked down at her clothes. "I'm all painty."

"Oh, that doesn't matter," Foster said magnanimously.

They would pick up where they had left off, he decided as he steered the van down Spadina Avenue. Tuesday evenings in the loft. Dinner. Conversation. Bed. The sun broke through the clouds, as if to confirm this happy plan. In the park that ran parallel to Lake Shore Boulevard, joggers bounced along a boardwalk. Teenagers in shorts and T-shirts tossed around a Frisbee.

"Listen, I'd better get back," Jessica said.

"That radio was the top of the line," Foster said. "AM/FM. Cassette. Six speakers. Try it." Why was he babbling away like this? He wasn't trying to sell her the van.

Jessica bent to fiddle with the radio. "What kind of music do you want?"

"Anything. Whatever."

"I can't figure this damn thing out," Jessica said, pushing buttons at random. An electric guitar boomed out an insistent rhythm.

"That's fine."

"Country and western?"

"It doesn't matter."

A crossing guard wearing a red safety vest held up an octagonal sign. Foster eased the van to a stop and watched the guard lead schoolchildren across the road. Jessica snapped off the radio, leaned back in her seat and laced her arms over her chest.

Foster glanced at her. "What kind of music do you like?"

"My turn again, is it?" Jessica rattled her fingertips on her thigh. "Dave Matthews."

"Never heard of him."

"See? There you go."

"There I go what?" The guard waved Foster on.

"It's like Dave Matthews doesn't exist. It's like I made him up."

LAST U-TURN BEFORE EXPRESSWAY, a sign announced.

"I simply said that I hadn't heard of him." Foster put on the turn signal, mystified. Why was Jessica so annoyed? It was a simple statement of fact.

They drove back to the loft in silence. A taxi pulled away from the curb, and Foster swung into the vacant space. Jessica stepped out, leaned into the open window and said, "I'm going to have a show. The date isn't firm. I'll let Shawna know."

"Want me to come over next Tuesday?"

"No, I don't." Jessica turned and walked away.

Fine, Foster thought as he drove off. The hell with it.

A block from Mazurka Street, it dawned on him that he couldn't deal with Mary or Shawna or Tyler at the moment. Not so early on such a fine afternoon. He wanted to think; he needed to walk, and when a blinking traffic signal suggested a left turn, he swung the van south and drove to High Park. He stepped down from the driver's seat and stood in the sunshine. A pack of old men shuffled past, filling him with dread and sending him striding away. There were faces missing. Winter had thinned the herd.

After walking its paths so often, Foster thought he knew the park well, the oak savannah, the shaded ravines. Yet the sudden explosion of growth took him by surprise: the vibrant green lawns, the showy dogwood blooms, the stalks of purple lupine and the carpets of white sweet-clover. A convoy of nannies came into view, giggling and gossiping and pushing fancy baby carriages under the flowering cherry trees. They were as lovely as the pink-and-white blossoms, these women, and they looked right through him.

The llama had returned to the little zoo, and the Croatian was back behind the hot dog cart. Where had they spent the winter, the llama and the hot dog man? Foster pictured them hibernating together in a cave, in the manner of a bear and a bat. It occurred to him that he had hibernated at Grandpa's Toolbox. It was time to think outside the big box, he told himself as he stepped around a Canada goose. Think outside the big box. Irv would have liked that one. But since the day Charlie had entered the yellow earth, Irv had seldom come to mind. He seemed to have moved on. Foster looked up at the wispy sky. The heavens were wearing thin.

What now, Mr. Foster? What's the plan? An interim plan will do. A carefully considered course of action that somehow includes a gigantic brown van, a complete set of woodworking tools and a hundred books about the naval battles of the Napoleonic Wars. Foster strolled on. When the park gates came in sight, he walked to a bench, sat down and stretched out his legs. He stuck his chin on his chest and watched a soccer team in blue jerseys sprint from goalpost to goalpost. How much in the war chest, Admiral Foster? He took out his wallet. Enough for a tank of gas. Maybe. Foster got to his feet and started toward the van. There was a yellow slip on the windshield. He lifted a wiper and stared at the ticket. "Park 3 Metres of Fire Hydrant — $100."

Yes, there was a hydrant. With the van's rear door hanging open, Foster fished through a toolbox and found a tape measure. He stretched out the tape. The van was 2.75 metres from the hydrant. He had parked just a little too close. He bounced the tape measure in his hand, and then he cocked his arm and threw the tape as hard as he could, watched it sail through the air, saw it disappear into a stand of white pine, heard it strike a tree. Then he jumped into the driver's seat and slammed the door, hard enough to rock the van. He closed his eyes and gripped the steering wheel with both hands, squeezed the wheel until his arms trembled. When he felt calm enough to drive, he moved the van to another parking spot, jumped down from the cab and walked into the stand of pines.

An hour later he gave up looking. He was sorry he couldn't find the tape measure, because it had belonged to Charlie.

AS FOSTER WAS inching the van down the lane behind Mary's townhouse, he saw that Tyler had put his car in the only parking space big enough for the van. Typical, Foster thought as he reversed up the lane. There was an empty spot on Mazurka Street. Foster stood on the sidewalk, looking up in puzzlement. There were three parking signs, and it took him a moment to piece together their meaning. It seemed that if he went to a machine, paid an extortionary fee and displayed the printed receipt at the correct angle on the driver's side of the dashboard, he might leave the van there for a couple of hours. Should he fail to meet any of these conditions, the vehicle would be towed away at his expense. And, the signs implied, best of luck getting it back, fella.

The house was silent, or almost. Foster tiptoed down the hall, past the closed door of Mary's bedroom. A few days ago the door to the middle room had begun to stick. Which made sense — the dew point had risen, humidity was higher. He pushed down on the doorknob; the door opened and he stared in dismay. The room was piled high with paint cans, stepladders, painting trays, rollers, brushes, drop sheets.

"You're home early." Mary stood in the doorway, tying the belt of her dressing gown. "We were going to put all this stuff away."

Tyler came into the room.

"What's all this about?" Foster tossed a compressor hose aside, ignoring Tyler's outstretched hand.

"Mary-Tyler Enterprises," Tyler said. "Get it? Like that old TV show."

Foster picked up a paint sprayer. The reservoir was cracked, the nozzle clogged with paint.

"This guy I met at the bar sold me his business," Tyler said. "Paint, equipment, business cards — the whole enchilada." He looked at Foster. "You're walking down the street, and you see a house and it's got this old aluminum siding, looks like shit."

"It's gone chalky," Mary said.

"Yeah, Mare," Tyler said. "That's right. Chalky. So you knock on the door and you give the guy a price." Tyler grinned like a kid with a new pair of skates. "And the guy can't believe how low it is. Because to replace the siding —"

"Is this the paint?" Foster tilted a can to read the label.

"Just enough to get started," Tyler said. "The guy threw in a garage full."

"Twelve different colours," Mary said.

"You have to wash the surface and apply a binder coat," Foster said, frowning down at the can. Tyler had been hoodwinked.

"No, see, you don't," Tyler said, a little desperately. "That's the beauty of it."

"This is the wrong paint," Foster said patiently. "It has ammonia in it, and ammonia reacts with oxidized aluminum to form a gas. The paint will bubble and peel off."

"That's just your opinion," Tyler said.

It had been a long day. Foster banged the paint can on the compressor. "It's not an opinion. It's a fact. At Grandpa Camp —"

"Oooo, Grandpa Camp," Tyler said.

"I gave the guy cash," Mary said.

Foster looked at his daughter. "You paid for this junk?"

"You know something, Fos?" Tyler said, staring at Foster. "Maybe you should mind your own business."

Foster stared back. "It is my business when my daughter is concerned."

"I could phone the guy," Mary said. "Tell him we changed our mind."

"You and daddy have a nice talk." Tyler started down the hall.

"Tyler?" Foster called after him. "Can you move your car, please? I have a vehicle now and I need that space."

"Yeah, yeah," Tyler said over his shoulder. "Whatever."

That night, with the van tucked in beside Tyler's car and Charlie's tools stuffed in the closet, Foster lay on the sofa bed surrounded by painting equipment, pretending not to hear the quarrelling voices coming through the wall. He forced himself to think. He could double back, check old leads. Cedric, for instance. No. Cedric and Sylvia were at sea. What about Jamie Stone, the kid who ran Computer Professionals International? No. Movie recommendations, he didn't need. Maybe it wasn't all Tyler's fault, Foster thought, looking around the room. What was there left for Canadians to do? Unpack the containers that arrive by the thousands on the decks of leviathans. Sell each other insurance. Do each other's hair.

THE BELL CHIMED as Foster came through the door of Corner Convenience. Mr. Park glared at him from behind the counter. What was his problem? Was he pining for the red forests of Mount Seoraksan, the green tea fields of Boseong?

When Mary and Tyler came into the kitchen, Foster was sipping coffee and scanning the want ads. Mary filled the kettle and put it on the stove. Tyler slumped into a chair, gave Foster a glance, said nothing.

"What's with the suit?" Mary said. "Aren't you going to Grandpa's?"

"Fired your ass, I bet," Tyler said.

Mary put a hand on Tyler's arm. Tyler grunted and picked up the sports pages.

"I'm going in later," Foster said. "I have a job interview." This wasn't exactly true. Kalesh Computing wasn't expecting him. For two weeks now he had been walking into offices and asking for the person in charge.

"Foster?" Mary touched his arm. "My boss said they might be hiring."

What would Shawna think if she came to breakfast and saw her mother and her grandfather decked out in Secure-All outfits? It was the stuff of sitcoms. "Thanks, but I'm looking for something better." Foster felt sick. He knew he had said the wrong thing. Mary thought she had a good job, even with the lousy pay, the shift work, the supervisor barking down the phone.

"This guy I know?" Tyler said. "He's looking for a helper. Spraying driveways."

Foster closed the newspaper with a snap. "I can make a living without cheating people."

"Sponging off your daughter. Call that making a living, do you?"

The kettle shrieked. Mary lifted it from the burner and slammed it on the counter. Boiling water leapt from the spout and splashed her hand. Foster jumped to his feet. Tyler got to Mary first. "Hey, Mare," Tyler said. "Hey."

"I'm fine!" Mary shouted, shaking her hand. "Okay? Okay?"

THE SECRETARY SWIVELLED her chair in Foster's direction. "Who have you come for?"

"Mr. Maharashtrian." Foster had been waiting in this shabby office for three hours.

The secretary told him Mr. Maharashtrian wasn't coming back today.

"CURTY WANTS TO see you." Grandpa Taylor picked up a utility knife and slit open a box of contact cement.

Foster looked up at the shining mirrors. "Did she say why?"

"Nope."

Amanda Curtwell was at her desk, reading a printout. Foster felt a tug of sympathy. All those reports to go through. She didn't ask him to take a chair. It was nothing serious, then. She had on a black pantsuit, but her blouse was daffodil yellow. The colour suited her. Foster decided against telling her this. She looked up at him and stated a date and time. "Did you perform that safety sweep, Mr. Foster?"

Why was she asking? The sweeps were routine. "Yes."

"No, Mr. Foster, you didn't."

"Oh. Well, I must have been with a customer."

"No, you were on the loading dock, arranging to take home a piece of store property. I've already spoken to Grandpa Carey. Tomorrow will be his first Clean Slate Day."

The melamine off-cut. Foster had forgotten all about it. Now that he had the van, he could run the sheet through the panel saw, take the shelves home and put them up. "I keep my area neat as a pin. Perhaps you can't see my area from here, Amanda." He knew perfectly well that she could. "If you'd like to come down to Fasteners ..."

"A rule is a rule."

That was perfectly true. He couldn't argue.

"Now, where would we be, without rules?" Amanda turned to face the one-way glass. "Without rules, things would fall apart."

"It won't happen again, Amanda. I'm sorry if I caused you any concern."

"Did you mark the sweep on your calendar?"

"Of course."

Amanda spun her chair to face him. "You recorded a sweep you didn't perform. The policy is clear, Grandpa Foster. You've had your Clean Slate Days. Your last paycheque will come in the mail."

Last paycheque? "You're firing me? Why?"

"I've just told you why."

"For missing a sweep? It happens. You know it does."

"The policy —"

"I do a good job." Foster shook his finger at the mirrors. "A customer asked for me yesterday." Foster knew he should lower his voice. "I helped him find —"

"I'm not going to argue with you. You're through."

Foster glowered down at Amanda. Her eyes shone with fear. She was afraid of him, he realized suddenly. The revelation astounded him. It didn't fit his self-image. For a terrible moment he had no idea who he was. She reached for her phone. "I'm calling security."

A security guard in a baggy brown uniform — Trilby, a man Foster had said hello to a hundred times — escorted him to the change room and watched as he cleaned out his locker. Trilby led him across the sales floor — they didn't go through Fasteners, at least — walked him through the front doors, nodded and left without a word.

Foster sat behind the steering wheel, bouncing his keys in his hand, listening to the faint jingle the keys made when they were in the air. He couldn't remember walking to the van, had no recollection of opening the door and climbing in. Near the main entrance, a garden centre was going up, a row of metal arches covered with clear plastic. A payment on the phone bill was due this Friday. The first instalment on the automobile insurance as well. A stock boy walked past lugging a gaudily painted garden gnome. *It's all downhill from here, fella*, the gnome seemed to say. *You'll never hold a job again.*

On the way to Mazurka Street, the low-fuel warning chimed. Foster stared through the streaky windshield. It was starting to rain. The fuel warning sounded again, and he gave the gas gauge an irritated glance. How many billions of barrels of oil had Duboco pumped from the sands? And here he was knocking on empty, a lifetime late and a litre short.

The rain intensified as he came down Mazurka, feathering the gas, nursing the van along. He threaded his way down the lane, stopped and sat staring through the arc of the windshield wipers. Tyler's car was in the wrong space again. Foster reversed up the lane. There were no empty parking spots on Mazurka Street. He drove up to Dundas Street, parked, craned his neck and read the parking signs with the rain stinging his eyes. He ran back to the townhouse, glancing at his watch as he ran. In three minutes the van would be fair game for the parking police and their tow trucks.

The house was dark. Mary's door was closed. Foster listened and heard a murmuring voice. "Tyler? I need you to move your car."

Silence.

Foster knocked on the door. "Tyler? I'm in a tow-away zone."

The door burst open and Tyler sprang past.

It was raining harder now. Foster moved the van and walked slowly back inside. Soaked to the skin, he slumped in the beanbag chair and stared at the television. The *Restless World* theme played. Jed Creed was living in his ex-wife's garage. His Lincoln took up one side. On the other side was a loveseat, a fridge, a dresser with a TV on top.

Mary came into the room. Her feet were bare, her hair tousled, her Secure-All shirt askew. She looked around, hurried to the kitchen, came back. "Where's Tyler?"

Foster kept his eyes on the television. Did Jed sleep in the Lincoln?

"Foster, what did you say to him?"

Foster looked up.

"Tyler?" Mary called. "Tyler?" She threw open the front door and ran barefoot down the front walk, into the rain.

She came back alone.

EARLY THE NEXT morning Foster went down the hall dressed for a day at Duboco. With the sleepless night behind him and a suit on his back, it was almost possible to think of himself as a man with prospects, opportunities, irons in the fire. He was putting on his raincoat when he spotted an envelope leaning against the coffee maker. The envelope had the Secure-All lightning bolt in one corner, and it was addressed to him in Mary's handwriting. An application form, he decided, slipping the envelope into his pocket. Hadn't he made it clear he wasn't interested?

It was a fine morning, warm with the promise of summer. Mary was only trying to help. On the way to Corner Convenience, Foster took the envelope from his pocket and read the letter it contained.

Dear Foster,

Tyler and I are going away together. We need to be by ourselves for a while so I'm taking some time off. Don't try to reach me because I'll be out of range. The house expenses are covered and I talked to Shawna. She will be okay with you.

Mary

P.S. I know you mean well.

A horn blared. Foster looked up from the note. He was standing in the middle of Dundas Street.

"HEL-LO?" SHAWNA SANG over the thumping music. They were having breakfast, Shawna her Froot Loops, Foster his boiled eggs. "Don't sweat it. We'll be fine."

Why was the jazz station playing that awful hippity-rock? Foster glanced at the radio. Shawna had switched the station. He snapped the radio off. Then, remembering the day he had picked up the van, the argument with Jessica, he turned the radio back on and lowered the volume. The child was upset. Of course she was.

"Shawna, do you know where your mother is?"

"Ah just cain't think about this now!" Shawna jumped to her feet, draped a wrist over her forehead and stared dramatically through the patio door at the tiny backyard. "The la-and. That's all that mat-ters! The la-and!"

"Yes, of course," Foster distractedly agreed. His mind clicked into debugging mode. Last week Shawna had rented *Gone with the Wind* from a video store. She was doing Scarlett O'Hara. Shawna would make a fine scientist, with her magpie mind. You need a PhD to publish research. Which meant — ten years of university? Tuition costs kept going up. He had read that in the papers. How would he pay for her education? He rallied his scattered thoughts and looked at his granddaughter. "Did you have enough to eat?"

Shawna clutched the box of breakfast cereal to her chest. "I'll never be hungry again!"

Was she angry? Afraid? Worried? It was difficult to tell, with all the play-acting. He was hopeless at parenting. Mary should never have left him in charge of Shawna. "I want you straight home after school, young lady."

"Why, Sah! Ah never dah-reamed you-all cah-hared."

"Straight home."

"Fiddle dee dee!" Shawna grabbed her backpack and flounced away, slamming the front door after her.

Up and down the hallway Foster paced, kitchen to bathroom, bathroom to kitchen. He would establish a routine. Dinner at six. Homework. Sign off on tasks as he had done with computer projects. A reasonable period of television. Something educational. Should he inspect Shawna's room, see that she kept it tidy? That yellowing blouse she had yanked out of the bag in McDonald's — she had paid for that herself. She would need a weekly allowance. Foster walked thoughtfully into the middle room, the cluttered space he had camped in for nine months. Tyler's painting paraphernalia had disappeared. Had Mary gone off to paint houses with that idiot? Foster picked up a pad of lined paper and went to the kitchen.

Goals and objectives had shaped his life. He sat at the kitchen table, sharpening a pencil. Then in capital letters he printed:

SHORT TERM TASKS:
1) Find Mary / Convince her re Tyler
2) Take Charge: Of A) Meals B) Laundry C) Errands
3) Create for Shawna: A) Schedule B) Allowance C) Goals
LONG TERM TASKS:
1) Earn Money for Shawna's Education

Foster thought for a moment, then wrote

2) Obtain Overseas Contract

Which meant travelling to London. Which he couldn't do with Mary out of the house. There was another problem. He hadn't saved enough to pay for the trip. With Grandpa's Toolbox out of the picture, he would have to find another job. He needed to think about that, but Shawna came first.

At the top of a new page he printed *Shawna Schedule*. Most problems can be solved with a two-dimensional matrix — he had learned this in data processing. He drew rows and columns, labelled the columns with the days of the week, the rows with the hours of the day. He tapped the pencil on the table and stared at the empty grid, and then he added an item to his task list:

Interview Shawna.

He stared at item one: FIND MARY, and then he picked up the note she had left and read it again. He went to the counter, lifted out a drawer and upended it over the table. Paper clips, erasers, tape dispensers rained down, coupons, cookies, plastic twists, business cards, a medal on a ribbon, a set of starry pencils. Foster stirred thoughtfully through the bric-a-brac. He had given Shawna the starry pencils for Christmas. She had outgrown her fascination with stars. That was worth knowing. He picked up the medal. Shawna had won a swimming event, the 200-metre medley for junior girls. No, the year was wrong. He turned the medal over and saw Mary's name. The medal grew heavy in his hand. Who had driven his daughter to swim meets, sat in the bleachers and cheered her on, wrapped a towel around her shoulders when she stood shivering with cold? Not him. He had been in Saudi. After a moment he put the medal down and picked up a phone list. The numbers weren't properly identified. What did Sec Office mean? He reached for the phone.

"Secure-All. Malloy speaking."

"My name is Daniel Foster. I'm calling about Mary Foster."

"Is this an emergency? This is the emergency hotline."

"It's ... a family emergency,"

"Family emergency. Nice try. Her mother already died."

"I'm Mary's father."

"Father? There's nothing about a father on her personnel record."

"I've been out of the country."

"You're calling from the airport?"

Calling from the airport seemed close enough to the truth. "Can I speak to Mary?"

"This is the emergency line. I'm going to hang up now."

Jerk, Foster thought, crossing off Malloy's number. Mary had jotted down the second number several times. Was it Tyler's? Tyler came from Northern Ontario, and this was a local area code. But Tyler had a cell-phone, and it might have a local code. Foster called the number.

"Metro Police."

Foster hung up the phone and stood in pensive silence, facing the melancholy truth that he knew very little about his daughter. She had a thing for policemen. She had won a swimming medal. He turned his attention back to the list and worked his way through the numbers, talking to a drugstore, a shoe repair, a pizza parlour, a video rental store. *Gone with the Wind* was a week overdue; otherwise, he was none the wiser.

After a moment Foster slid a starry pencil behind an ear and began to inventory the food on hand. Every cupboard he opened was a shambles. He shook his head in dismay. How did Mary expect to find anything? He set a tin of shoe polish on the counter — and felt a tingle of interest. He might as well organize as he took stock.

"DINNER'S READY," FOSTER called, untying his apron. No response. He went to the living room. "Shawna?"

The television snapped into silence. Shawna came to the table, peered down at her plate and crinkled her nose. "Eew! What is this?"

"Kidney beans with toast."

Shawna looked at him. "You heated up kidney beans?"

"Try it."

"Nobody heats up kidney beans."

"It's good."

"There's no way I'm eating that."

"Shawna, we're pretty good friends, aren't we?"

His granddaughter looked at him skeptically.

"Well, your mother is counting on us to work together during this … emergency, and —"

"Hel-lo? You put kidney beans in three-bean salad. You don't heat them up."

"Three-bean salad. That's a terrific idea. I'll make that next time."

Foster dipped a spoon in the steaming broth and smacked his lips, mugging delight. "Hmm, hmm."

"Foster?" Shawna looked at him with flint in her eyes. "I'm not four years old." She pushed back her chair.

"You should say, 'May I be excused from the table.'"

"May-I-can-I-should-I-start my homework? I mean, if it's okay."

"Why don't we tell each other about our day? I vacuumed the house, and then I went for a walk. Do you know there's a zoo in High Park? They have capybaras, wallabies …"

Shawna stared at him.

"What did you do today?"

"Went to school."

"What did you did learn?"

"Stuff."

There was a silence, and then Shawna said, "After school tomorrow? There's an information session about soccer."

"Do you like soccer?"

Shawna shrugged. "How come you didn't go to work today?"

Sharp cookie, his granddaughter. Didn't miss a thing. "I'll keep this warm for you." Foster slipped a plate over Shawna's bowl. He watched her walk down the hall to her room. A thumping rhythm erupted, setting the bubble-glass animals jittering around in the wall unit.

After he had washed the dishes, Foster went to the living room and picked up the newspaper. The science page caught his eye. The CERN Collider was up and running. The biggest physics machine in the world, sixteen years and ten billion dollars to build, 175 metres under the Franco-Swiss border, a high tech tunnel with a circumference of twenty-seven kilometres. The scientists were searching for dark matter. There was a picture of the control room. Two of the scientists were women. Now that was something for Shawna to shoot for. Foster clipped the article and slipped it into the folder he had used for Charlie's baseball stories. He glanced at his task list. Was *Gone with the Wind* in the DVD player? He snapped open the tray and took out the disc. After a ten-minute search, he found the case wedged between the cushions of the couch, along with a hair brush and one of Mary's romance novels. Foster stared at the cover. Perhaps the book would help him understand his daughter. He slipped on his glasses and settled in to read the first novel he had tackled since high school.

Larissa's Longing, the work of Emma Jayne Hillman, opened in Twittington Manor, "a vast estate a day's ride from London." While Napoleon rampaged through Europe, Larissa slaved away in a kitchen run by the evil-tempered Mrs. Blackthorne. Larissa was eighteen and very beautiful. She had an independent spirit and a mass of wild, chestnut brown hair. Foster turned the book in his hand and studied the author's picture. Emma Jayne Hillman had a lot of hair herself.

Foster read on. Peter, the heir to his father's title and the youngest captain in Nelson's fleet, was home on leave, and a banquet was in full swing. Lord Twittington got blotto and picked a quarrel with his son. Larissa, eavesdropping on their conversation, leaned over the table. She locked eyes with Peter, who leapt to his feet, smitten with love. Larissa fled the room, and Foster closed the book.

He picked up Mary's note and read it again. The writing had a romantic tone, it seemed to him. If Mary had mistaken Tyler for Prince Charming, then God help us all.

Later, when Foster was reading the want ads, a shadow flitted through his peripheral vision. The fridge door clicked open, spilling light on the kitchen floor. Shawna made a beeline for her room, carrying a plate piled high with the chicken he had cooked for tomorrow night's dinner. He wouldn't say anything, Foster decided. He kept his eyes on the ads he had circled, jobs he wouldn't have considered twenty-four hours earlier. What did a telephone sales representative do, exactly?

[FIFTEEN]

"HELLO. AM I speaking to ..." Foster squinted at a foggy computer monitor. "Mr. or Mrs. Welsh?"

"Who is this?"

"My name is Daniel Foster and I represent Galaxy Heating and Air ..."

The line went dead.

"You're off script again," Sam Skinner whispered.

Foster fiddled with his headset. Sam had an unnerving way of popping into your head. "I have the script before me. And I read it verbatim."

"You read it what?"

"I read exactly what it says."

"*Am I speaking to?* isn't in the script."

"Well, I just thought —"

"You thought? Who cares what you think! I'm not paying you to commune with the cosmos."

Commune with the cosmos. This was one of Skinner's pet phrases.

"Follow the damn script or I'll fire you."

A bittersweet nostalgia came over Foster while he waited for the computer to dial the next number. At Grandpa's Toolbox, discipline was sugar-coated. Skinner served it up raw.

"Mr. Janga? My name is Daniel Foster and ..." Mr. Janga wasn't in the market for a new, high-efficiency furnace. Nor was Mrs. Jefferies. Thirty no-pickups, five hang-ups and two tirades later, Mrs. Chow, miraculously, wanted to talk. Foster took her through gas-on-demand, electronic ignition, temperature sensors in flues. She asked him about air conditioning and he took her through condensers and compressors and cooling cycles. After forty minutes she thanked him for the language practice and hung up. Foster waited for Sam's voice to whisper a reprimand, but the boiler-room god had fallen silent.

At break time, Foster threaded his way through the cubicles, wondering again if he should go back to the want ads. It was a lonely business, talking to strangers from this seedy hole-in-the-wall. The storefront had been a beauty parlour in a previous incarnation: the cracked mirrors, the stubble of pipe poking through the floor. The lunch room, if you could call it that, had a wobbly card table and a pair of patio chairs. An overheated coffee machine emitted an industrial stink. Foster sorted through the coffee mugs. There were mugs with photos of babies, mugs with funny sayings — *Foxy Gramma!*, mugs for long-ago bowling tournaments. The mug marked *IndTemps* seemed reasonably clean. He poured himself an inch of rancid brew and looked around for the creamer. He was peering into a filing cabinet when a young man came walking in.

"Hi, Dimitri," Foster said. "How's it going?" They were veterans, he and Dimitri, after a week on the phones. Most of Skinner's recruits lasted only a day or two.

"Good. I listen to Mr. Sam, try to do what he tells me."

Foster nodded. Like Dimitri, he was facing Skinner's deadline to make quota.

"So last night I practise on my wife."

Foster kept his eyes on his coffee.

Dimitri glanced over the cubicles to the far side of the room, where Sam Skinner sat entranced with his eyes closed and his feet on his desk, listening to twenty operators.

"Milena says, read the words like a love poem."

How do I love thee? Let me count the advantages of a new furnace. I love thee to the depth of my heat exchanger ... How did that really go? Foster had once known the poem by heart, but now he could remember only fragments.

"This is my Milena." Dimitri held out a picture.

"What the hell are you two doing back there?" Sam roared. "Communing with the cosmos?"

ON THE WAY back to Mazurka Street, Foster stopped at a red light and watched a pack of boys go skylarking down the sidewalk in the early May sunshine, jostling for position and punching each other on the shoulder. When the light changed, he hit the gas and rocketed past them with a chirp of tires. And then he wondered if he was losing his mind, showing off like that.

He parked the van behind Mary's townhouse, went inside to make a shopping list and walked up to Dundas Street, pulling a bundle buggy behind him. Summer was on the way. On the window ledge above Corner Convenience, pansies bloomed in planters. Outside the dollar store, an inflatable shark turned in the breeze. The mannequin in the window of Universal Surplus had swapped her camouflaged parka for a camouflaged bikini, Foster noticed. The plaster figure was missing a foot, a secret a winter boot had concealed. There was something brave about the mannequin's stance.

Perhaps Dimitri and Milena could live on love, but it would take cold hard cash to give Mary and Shawna a better life, Foster thought as he entered the Internet café. There were no replies to the resumés he had fired off. What should he make for dinner? He searched the Internet for simple chicken recipes. Chicken parmigiana seemed a safe bet. While he waited for the printer to churn out the page, he stared out the window at the beach toy shark and, worrying about Cedric and Sylvia, searched for "Cedric Richards-Henderson." To Foster's surprise, the search returned a hit. He clicked the link and saw a banner scrolling over the battlements of a castle. *CRH Staffing Solutions / Get the Royal Treatment / An Aphlan Group Company / CRH Staffing Solutions / Get the Royal Treatment …* Foster stared in bewilderment. What had happened to *Believer*? And then a different thought occurred to him. His old friend had resurfaced as a headhunter.

"Perhaps you remember me," Foster typed in an email message. He put his finger on the backspace key. Of course Cedric would remember him. Foster began again. "Happened across your website. Many pleasant memories of our chats in Dubai. Hope you and Sylvia are well. Regards. Foster."

CUT COST HAD chicken breasts on sale, Foster was pleased to see. He picked up a tray, set it in his cart and went down the aisles looking for Dijon mustard. Was Cedric running his new business on his boat? From the middle of the Pacific Ocean? Lost in thought, Foster swung in behind a burly man who was wearing a pair of cut-offs and a white T-shirt advertising African Lion Safari. It dawned on Foster that he had stared at the man's neck from the back seat of a police car. The night he had tried to walk home from the hospital. The cop behind the wheel. "Percy? My name is Foster. You and your partner picked me up last winter."

Percy gave Foster a blank look. "Did we now."

"I was walking south on Keele Street. You drove me to my daughter's place. I want to thank you for that."

Percy's expression softened. "Glad to see you're okay."

"There's something I've been wondering about. When my daughter opened the door that night, you knew her name."

Percy set his forearms on the handlebar of his shopping cart and looked into the distance. An uneasy silence settled in.

"Mary is away from home," Foster said. "I need to talk to her."

Percy said nothing. A stock boy wheeled a skid of ice cream down the aisle.

"I don't know my daughter very well. I should, but I don't. If you can tell me anything ..."

Why was Percy looking at the tray of chicken breasts? He seemed embarrassed. Perhaps it would help to make small talk. "I'm making chicken parmigiana for my granddaughter."

"Shawna doesn't like chicken parmigiana."

Foster stared.

"She likes chicken cordon bleu."

"How do you know that?"

"It wasn't meant to be," Percy said. "I have to think of it that way."

The conversation had taken a bizarre turn. Foster was lost.

"Look, Mr. Foster. Mary's sort of in love with the whole police force." Percy looked pained. "Mary is special." He shook his head. "I'm saying this all wrong. She doesn't go with just anybody. I'm not saying that."

"No," Foster said. He had no idea what Percy was saying.

"Maybe that's why it didn't work out between Mary and me. The police thing, I mean. She couldn't see past the uniform."

Foster was beginning to understand. There had been more between Mary and Percy than he had thought. It was his turn to be embarrassed. He hadn't meant to pry.

"Discovery had a show about aboriginals," Percy said, taking the conversation in another unexpected direction. "There comes a time when they have to take off, go wandering around."

"Yes, I saw that. Walkabout, they call it," Foster said. "They follow songlines, the paths of their ancestors. But they do that when they're adolescents, not when they're adults with responsibilities."

"You know what I liked about that program?" Percy said. "The way the community understood why their offspring had to take off. We have to find out who we are. Sometimes we have to go off on our own."

What was Percy trying to tell him now? That he knew where Mary was, but wasn't about to tell him? Foster studied Percy's face. He might have been looking at a statue.

"You got the wrong chicken breasts," Percy said, looking into Foster's shopping cart again. "You want the boneless, skinless ones."

"Oh?" Foster said in bewilderment.

"Put the chicken between two pieces of waxed paper." Percy made a fist and held it over a palm. "Pound it down. Put Swiss cheese and ham on top, roll it up. Mix eggs and bread crumbs in a bowl, dip the chicken, cook it in butter. Five or six minutes is all you need. Then pop it in the oven for thirty minutes and you'll have chicken cordon bleu."

For an odd moment, Foster was certain the recipe contained a secret message.

"Get the real Swiss," Percy said. "Shawna doesn't like the fake stuff."

The two men exchanged a nod and walked away, pushing their carts in opposite directions.

THE PHONE RANG as Foster was pulling the bundle buggy up the front walk. He fumbled his key into the lock, shoved the door open, stepped into the kitchen and grabbed the handset. "Mary?" Foster said. "Mary?"

"No-o-o-o-o-o."

"Shawna. Hello."

"Can I stay here for dinner? It's okay with Kayla's mom."

"Stay for dinner." Foster peered down the hallway. Was Mary's door open? "Did Kayla's mother invite you?"

"I just said."

"So you did. When will you be home?"

"Is seven okay?"

"Seven will be fine. I'll pick you up. What's the address?"

The phone line took on a gargling, underwater tone. Shawna must have covered the mouthpiece with her hand.

"Kayla's dad can drive me."

"Oh. Don't forget that you have homework to do. We'll work on those word problems together."

"Kayla's dad is helping me."

It was absurd to feel disappointed. Shawna was learning her math. That was all that mattered. "Shawna? Have you been talking to your mother?"

"Huh?"

"I mean, has she phoned, or … dropped by?"

"Behind the breadbox? There's a thing you have to sign for soccer. Bye."

Foster said goodbye and hung up. There was a stash of papers behind the breadbox, including the consent form Shawna wanted him to sign and a notice about a parent/teacher night coming up soon. And a puzzling letter from a social services agency. Written three years ago, the letter informed Mary that her file had been marked inactive. If she felt the need for further counselling, she shouldn't hesitate to call. Social services? Counselling? Foster marked the parent/teacher night on his calendar, signed the consent form and set it on the counter, picked up his notepad, went to the living room and switched on the television. When Shawna came home, he would give her an update on *Restless World*. It had been more than a week since he had found time to watch the show. Where had the story left off? Sam and Dam were together again, but that wouldn't last. In another switcheroo, Jed Creed had been indicted for embezzlement after all.

A show called *Life — Your Style!* came on. A banner travelling across the bottom of the screen reminded viewers that *Restless World* had been cancelled. It was just a television show, Foster told himself. There was no reason to be upset.

A FEW DAYS later, when Foster came trudging down the aisle, coffee mug in hand, Sam Skinner looked up and said, "Coming in tomorrow?" Sam had a shiny face, country-and-western sideburns and withering halitosis. His pink-and-yellow shirt might have been cut from an awning.

"I don't know, Sam. Maybe not."

"Too rough on you back there, was I?"

Foster shook his head, trying to stay upwind of Skinner. He wasn't quitting because Sam had hurt his feelings. It went beyond that. Sam's boiler-room mind control, Foster sensed, tossed a monkey wrench into vital parts of his mind. It would be difficult to explain this idea to Sam, and Foster didn't intend to try, because Sam would reduce the half-formed thought to communing with the cosmos.

"This is important work." Sam waved a hand toward the cubicles, the flickering screens, the murmuring operators. "People need their rugs cleaned. They need their furnaces adjusted."

"True."

"Say we're promoting timeshares. Say it's February and a guy answers the phone and it's us," Sam said, gathering steam. "Guy's had a bad day and we offer him two weeks in Jamaica. Haven't we made his life better?"

"Um," Foster said.

"I know what you're thinking. How do we know this timeshare is a good product? Survival of the fittest, that's how. Companies compete for business. Take the dodo. Damn bird got fat and lazy, forgot how to fly, and bam, it's extinct." Sam tilted his head and looked at Foster. "Know what you need, my friend?"

Airfare, Foster thought. A residence permit for an oil-rich emirate. A big, tax-free salary. Five years to sit in the sun and tuck away money for Shawna's education.

"Killer instinct." Sam counted out the daily allowance. "That's what you need, my friend."

"I'll put the coffee mug back." Foster looked at the logo printed on the ceramic. *IndTemps — The Temporary Replacement Dream Team!*

"Do me a favour? Keep it." Sam tapped his finger, showing Foster where to sign. "There's too many of them back there. Beats me where the damn things come from."

As he drove along in Charlie's van, Foster felt a troubling kinship with the dodo. The long, lulling Middle Eastern years had specialized him. He was superbly adapted to the expatriate life. Well, what was wrong with that? The dodo was doing just fine on Mauritius, waddling around the rain forest on its jaunty yellow feet, dining on windfall. Until humans turned up, with their dogs and rats, their clubs and spears. The interior of the van had grown stuffy, and Foster sent the window whirring down and turned his face to the fresh air. He had to stay on his toes if he wanted to land a job overseas. He might have to fly off to an interview at a moment's notice. Which he couldn't do until his daughter took charge of Shawna again. He had given Mary time. It was time to find her and bring her home.

SECURE-ALL CENTRAL HAD the urgent atmosphere of a command post. Security guards watched computer screens, murmured into phones, hurried past with clipboards in their hands. Foster spotted Malloy's name on a door and started across the room. A security guard with chevrons on his sleeves blocked his path. "Sir? You can't go in there."

Foster explained his mission.

"Penny?" the security guard said, keeping his eyes on Foster. "Ask the Chief if he wants to talk to anybody about Mary."

Mary's supervisor had delicate hands and soft, expressive eyes. A concert pianist, Foster thought. Or a poet. Malloy's uniform was more comic than impressive, but he seemed to take himself very seriously, sitting at a steel desk under a florescent glare, staring at his visitor as if Foster were an enemy soldier brought in for questioning. He heard Foster out and said, "Mary is on vacation. Now, if you don't mind, I have a business to run."

"Yes, I know," Foster said, hiding his surprise. Vacation? Mary had planned her absence? "I need to speak to her."

"Simon? My flight leaves at three." The woman who had sashayed into the room wore high-heeled sandals, an orange tank top, a white miniskirt and a lot of perfume. She had the craggy features of a tribal elder. She was at least eighty, Foster thought.

"Yes, Mother, I know," Malloy said patiently. "As soon as a car comes in."

Malloy's mother gave Foster a salacious wink and tottered away on her high heels.

"Did Mary leave a phone number with you?" Foster said.

"You're her father," Malloy said. "And you don't have her phone number."

"Chief?"

"Yes, Penny?"

"Bernie says his A-4 won't hold a charge. Can I give him an A-6?"

"Swap the radios in the field. No, wait. We need the frequency on the A-4. Tell Bernie to bring it in."

"Will do."

"She's one of my best," Malloy said. "Reliable. Well-organized."

"Penny?" Foster said.

"Mary. I'm thinking of moving her up to sergeant." Malloy gave Foster a sharp glance. "Keep that to yourself."

"Of course." Mary, well-organized?

Malloy's mother put her head in the doorway. Malloy ignored the intrusion.

"Chief?"

"Yes, Penny."

"Bernie's here to swap the A-4 but there's this ratty old van parked in his spot."

"It's my van," Foster said. "I'll move it."

Malloy looked at Foster with sudden suspicion. "Mary said her father was a big deal executive. Lived overseas, she said."

"I'm going overseas again very soon," Foster said, regretting now that he had come here.

"You and Mary should get your stories straight." Malloy picked up a pen and made a note.

"Simon? I need to go. Now."

"Yes, Mother, I know."

"I can drop you at the airport," Foster said, eager to escape. "I go right by it on my way home." In fact the airport was in the opposite direction.

"Okay, big boy." Malloy's mother looked Foster over approvingly. "Call me Erma."

She was off to Las Vegas, Erma told him on the way to the airport, third trip this year. Slots, blackjack, Texas Hold 'em. "Like to gamble, big boy?" she asked him. Foster smiled. How many men had Erma left spinning in her wake? At departures, as Erma trotted off on her precarious heels, Foster watched an AirBus roll down the runway, lift off and climb into the sky. That twerp Malloy. Did he think the world couldn't get along without him? Of course he did, Foster realized as the plane vanished from sight. Everybody thought that.

A TWISTER HAD touched down in Southwestern Ontario. "We have exclusive News Tracker Video," said the newscaster. Foster punched up the sound and leaned forward. A tornado blew a farmhouse from its foundation, sending timber and metal soaring into the dark sky. The sky cleared. A fluke of air pressure had left one wall standing. The phone rang.

"It's for you." Shawna held out the phone.

"Let's watch that again," the newscaster said. The house blew up a second time.

"You should start your homework."

"Yeah, yeah." Shawna picked up the remote.

"Hello," Foster said, gesturing for Shawna to turn down the television.

"How's the wild colonial boy?"

"Cedric? Are you and Sylvia all right?

"Never better. Speaking for myself."

"You sailed around the world and you're back?"

"Not quite. We made it to Gibraltar. Where the lovely Sylvia walked off the boat and out of my life."

"Oh. I'm sorry to hear that. Did *Believer* … lose a mast or something?"

"Last I saw of her, *Believer* was shipshape and in all aspects ready for sea. Looking for a boat, are you? Apply to Barclay's Bank. One of their reps slapped a lien on *Believer* before I could get the dock lines sorted. Never saw him coming."

"You're calling from Spain?"

"Steady on. Gibraltar's part of the Empire. No, I'm back in Blighty."

Same old Cedric. "No more sailing, then." Cedric had escaped disaster. Like the farmhouse wall.

"Weekends. Dinghies on a reservoir. Wonderful boats. Small, cheap, light on their feet. That's what you want these days. How are you, Foster? Still in retail? They have you running the company by now, I imagine."

"I'm working independently." Did Cedric wear his captain's hat when he sailed his dinghy on the reservoir? The idea saddened Foster.

"Smart man. That's what you want these days. I've set up shop in my back garden. My ex-wife's back garden, I should say. Always a good sport, Hayley. Not that she's speaking to me."

Cedric's rapid fire revelations set Foster's mind reeling. Hayley was Cedric's wife. "Back garden?"

"My new office is a shed with a five quid coffee maker. Keep the overhead down. That's what you want these days."

"You're calling from a shed?"

"Mini-office, they call them on this side of the pond. I'm on the cellular. Hayley put me on her plan."

"I sent you an email."

"Which I duly received, courtesy of the neighbour's Wi-Fi."

If Cedric was freeloading on a wireless connection, his recruitment business wasn't up to much. Foster seemed to hear Erma say, *Like to gamble, big boy?* "Cedric, I'm thinking of working overseas again."

"Had enough of Canada, have you?" Cedric said after a moment. "It must get tiresome, having a moose chase you down the street."

"Well, now, we don't get too many moose in Toronto. There's a llama in the zoo." A silence settled in. What could he say to Cedric? The man had lost his wife, his lover, his house, his money, his livelihood, his boat.

"Daniel? Are you okay? Is there a problem?"

"Oh, no. Things are fine." There was another silence. Why was this conversation so awkward? There's a llama in the zoo and there's an elephant in the room. A pachyderm named AMEB. "Let's just say, if something international came up, I'd look at it seriously."

"I see. Well, I'll keep an eye out. Don't get your hopes up."

"It was just a thought." After another silence, Foster said, "I should let you go. Listen, I'm glad you called."

"How's the family?"

"Mary and Shawna are fine."

"You're a real family man, Daniel. I envy you that."

Foster closed his eyes. "Thanks."

"Let's keep in touch."

"Of course," Foster said, though it seemed unlikely that they would speak again. He said goodbye and stood for a moment staring at the swing set. When he came into the living room, Shawna looked away. Had she heard that conversation, Mr. Family Man?

LATER THAT EVENING, Foster looked up from the want ads to see Shawna standing at the entrance to the living room. She had on an ancient bowling jacket. She had an essay to write, she told him, and she had to go to the library. Would Mary let her go alone? Foster mulled this over. If that were the case, Shawna wouldn't have asked his permission. "I'll come along."

Shawna rolled her eyes.

"We can take the van," Foster said, to sweeten the offer.

When they walked into the library, Shawna affected an airy indifference, as if Foster had just happened to come through the door at the same time. Keeping an eye on her, he went to a counter and spoke to a librarian. "Cooking? That's non-fiction. On the left, past Young Readers."

On his way through the study area, Foster saw Shawna sitting at a table, her face hidden behind a volume of *The Canadian Encyclopedia*. He eased around a book cart, working his way along the stacks, glancing at Shawna, scanning the section headings.

The Food Preparation section overwhelmed him with its categories. French cuisine, Italian cuisine, Bulgarian cuisine. Vegan diets, cleansing diets, heart-smart diets. Foster flipped through *Hate to Cook?* and *The Grumpy Gourmet*. Lugging the cookbooks, he turned a corner and stared at books on parenting.

For an hour he sat at a study carrel with a view of Shawna's table, trying not to think about Cedric and his shipwrecked life. Spontaneity, counselled the author of *The Tweeny Years*, a relentlessly cheerful woman who had raised three preteens while enduring a string of catastrophes: a near-fatal illness, a sudden job loss, the abrupt departure of her husband. Foster made notes. Leave a little wiggle room. Don't take over. Listen and learn. Go with the flow. At closing time he made his way to the circulation desk.

"Library card?" asked the librarian.

"I don't have one, I'm afraid."

Shawna had a card, and she was standing right behind Foster, but she was pretending she didn't know him.

"If you have a piece of identification, I can issue you a card," said the librarian.

When his books had been stamped, Foster walked outside to wait in the van. For five long minutes he sat watching the doors. There were jobs overseas. He had to put Cedric's sad fate out of mind.

As they drove through the dark streets, Foster was glad he had come along. He didn't like the look of the neighbourhood they were passing through, the vacant stores, the lingering shadows. At a red light, he peeked at the books on Shawna's lap. *Fashions of the Forties. All about Weddings. The Threat of Global Warming.* "Is that your essay topic, global warming?"

"Yeah. Climate change and stuff."

"Want some help?"

"Yeah, right." Shawna said without looking at him. "You used to work for a gimongous oil company and now you drive this monster car."

Oil company? Monster car? Did Shawna see him as an eco-criminal? "We don't know for certain that human activity — people — are causing the change," Foster said.

"So, who else?"

Casting his mind back to the reports he had read in Dubai, Foster recalled charts and tables, the inconclusive results. "The science is complex, Shawna. The rise in temperature may be part of a long-term cycle. There are very good people working on the problem." A compass-spinning sense of déjà vu came over him. Very good people working on the problem. Hadn't Cedric said exactly that after the AMEB crash?

"Yeah, but temperatures are going up."

"Well, it seems they are."

"And the ice caps are melting?"

"It seems so."

Shawna stared into the night. "We're going extinct. Like the dinosaurs. That's what Benny says."

"The dinosaurs were doing just fine, Shawna. It wasn't their fault. Their environment changed catastrophically. The dinosaurs couldn't adapt fast enough."

"Stupid dinosaurs. Now they're all dead. Same as I'll be when the floods and stuff happen. All because of stupid cars."

Why hadn't he seen where this conversation was going? The issue was personal to Shawna. "Oh, I wouldn't worry about it."

"So, you think everything will be okay?"

No, he didn't. The human race was using up the earth, faster and faster. He had seen ramshackle factories pouring filth into the rivers of

China, tracts of rainforest smouldering with fire in Brazil. The world would last long enough to see him out. His selfishness shamed him. "You're right. Cars hurt the planet."

It was a troubling admission. Cars were freedom machines. Turn the key and escape. How he had loved Irv's Studebaker! But Shawna was right. The party was over.

"Hey! There's a Sally Ann. Can we stop? It's still open."

Spontaneity, *The Tweeny Years* counselled. "Sure we can," Foster said. Anything to change the subject. He glanced at the rear-view mirror and met his own eyes. Daniel Foster, the ideal parent. Yes, sir, the man could write a book. Here's a tip! Scare your tweeny out of her wits, then take her to a thrift store.

Armed with the allowance he had given her that morning, Shauna scooted away and began pawing through racks of clothes. Foster wandered over to a display of vinyl records. In the house he had shared with Kathleen and Mary there had been a hi-fi — a low, glossy cabinet with speakers behind glittery cloth. Kathleen had loved that thing, Foster remembered as he flipped idly through the discarded albums. He would come home to find her bobbing and swaying, drink in hand, eyes closed, dancing solo to some moody instrumental. Here they were, Kathleen's favourites, "Tijuana Taxi," "The Lonely Bull," "The Girl from Ipanema." Foster picked up an album and read the liner notes. Stan Getz. He had forgotten that Getz had played bossa nova. He set the album aside and flicked through the records. The Dave Clark Five flashed by, then Brenda Lee, then Miles Davis. Spotting a record by Draw-bar Bill and the Long Haul Boys, Foster pulled the album from the bin and read the song titles. "Double-Wide Love," "Your Gear Jammin' Heart," "Where the River Jordan Meets the Mississippi." On the back cover the quartet stood in a recording studio. They wore cowboy boots, blue jeans, red satin shirts, string ties with silver tips. The photographer had captured them in full song. They had been holding that note for fifty years.

"Whatcha got?" Shawna said.

"Oh, just some music I used to like." Foster put the albums back.

"Yeah? Then get it." She picked the records from the bin and held them out to him.

"We don't have a record player."

"So? They're like, fifty cents and it saves the environment."

Though the logic of this escaped him, he bought the albums to please Shawna. While they stood together at the cash register, waiting for a weary-looking woman to ring up their purchases, Foster gazed across the store. There was something ominous about the obsolete typewriters and the outdated appliances. He tried to laugh off the feeling — the store was a Valhalla for vacuums — but a chill came over him. The thrift store dealt in grave goods.

He paid for the records, and the scarf Shawna wanted, with a five dollar bill. Mary had prepaid the house expenses and left money to buy groceries, but he was down to his last twenty dollars, and the van was knocking on empty.

[SIXTEEN]

"FOUR GUYS! SOUTH Etobicoke! Nice little inventory job!" Freddy Wilkinson boomed out, waving a clipboard over his head. "Count the bolts, shake your nuts, give the stock sheet to the lovely Stella, and who knows, maybe you'll get lucky!" Freddy looked expectantly at his audience, the men and women who gathered outside IndTemps every morning, hoping for a day's work stacking boxes or unloading trucks or counting widgets. After several days of this routine, Foster knew he had to move fast. He stepped out of the crowd wearing a thrift store T-shirt and a pair of Grandpa's Toolbox overalls.

"Damn, gramps!" Freddy's vulpine face split into a grin. "You think Stella wants your sorry ass?" He blew Foster a kiss and said, "Get your butt in the pie wagon, you lucky bastard."

As Foster trudged across the parking lot to a chorus of guffaws, he remembered the labourers who came to Dubai by the tens of thousands, the men from the villages of Pakistan with calluses on their hands and henna in their beards, the workers who built the highways and the office towers, toiling in the heat and humidity for a hundredth of the salary he had earned at Duboco. They sent their pay home to their families and some of them died on the job. And, Foster had to admit, he would look at a busy construction site and not see them at all. He climbed into the IndTemps van and took a seat, wedging himself against the window to ease the pain that had plagued him since he had lifted a heavy crate yesterday afternoon. He was leafing through *The Globe and Mail* when a young man sat down beside him. What was this about? There were plenty of empty seats.

The driver climbed aboard and the van pulled away. The young man looked at Foster expectantly. Foster went back to his newspaper. There were big projects underway in China. Would one of these companies — the newspaper story mentioned several — have a legacy application running, a payroll program written long ago in FRIMIS? It was a thought.

"It's Ken, right?"

"My name is Foster."

"Didn't you share at a meeting? You've been sober for five years."

"You're mistaking me for someone else."

"I could've sworn …" the young man turned thoughtful. "I really liked what you said about GOD standing for Good Orderly Direction. That really helped me get my head around the higher power idea. And I liked what you said about working with a grateful attitude. That meant something coming from a guy like you that had his own business and ended up doing day work."

"I'm not Ken."

The young man gave Foster a troubled look. "Then why are you here?"

What could Foster say to this Nosy Parker? He liked day work. Yesterday he had operated a sheet metal brake, the day before a drill press. The money he had earned would pay Shawna's soccer fee, buy her a uniform and shin pads and shoes — and leave a little for the London trip. Freddy Wilkinson played the fool, but he didn't make you sing the Grandpa song. "A bank went bust," Foster said evenly. "And I lost a million dollars."

The young man got to his feet. "When you're ready to get honest, I'll be sitting over there."

Suppressing a smile, Foster turned to the window and looked out at a field littered with bricks. A railway spur ended at a stump of concrete. The van rounded a corner and rolled down a street of old houses, storey-and-a-half cottages with partitioned porches and carpet-sized lawns the intense green of early summer. Television satellite dishes projected from chimneys. Was Jessica still painting those out-of-focus flowers? No, she had changed her style. She had told him so the day he had picked up the van. Foster craned his neck to read the street signs — Foch and Vimy, Somme and Ypres. Every little town along Irv's sales route had a memorial to the Great War with a long list of the dead. Did a name like Passchendaele mean anything these days? *Old men forget: yet all shall be forgot.*

The van ran parallel to a wire fence, swung through a gate, splashed through puddles and stopped before an old factory. Foster stepped down and stood in the soupy mud looking up at a rambling building with ramparts and lancet windows, a castle with loading docks and railway spurs. Above the windows was a frieze with *North Star Electrical Company* in *bas relief*, above the frieze, a parapet wall flanked by towers. The factory reminded Foster of the pop-up book Shawna had shown him the night they went to Charlie's house.

The morning went quickly. Foster sat in an ancient swivel chair behind a massive counter while temps criss-crossed the floor, carrying fuses wrapped in red paper, circuit boxes bristling with wires, bulky knife switches with porcelain terminals. Freddy was right: it was an easy gig. A stock-taker handed Foster a tally sheet. Foster checked the addition, initialled the tally sheet and passed it to the woman sitting beside him. She had a solid, potent body, a round, florid face, a mass of candy-floss hair.

A mechanism creaked and clanked, and Foster looked up to see a murky skylight crack open. Long chains hung from an I-beam. The old factory was a movie set, Foster fancied. They would make a movie about Frankenstein in here, and then they would tear the place down. A horn blew. Through an open loading door Foster saw a catering truck slew into the muddy yard. He got to his feet and followed Stella outside. She strutted to the catering truck. When she turned with a cup of coffee in her hand, Foster said, "Freddy said to say hello, Stella."

Stella walked past without a word. The men standing around the catering truck turned their heads in unison as she picked her way through the mud, egging them on with her saucy walk. Foster picked up a coffee cup and lifted a lever. A snippet of verse came to him. *I met a lady in the meads, Full beautiful — a faery's child* ... The coffee tasted of tomato soup. Foster poured the coffee on the mud. A finger jabbed his back and he turned around. It was the young man from the bus and he looked terrified. *Oh what can ail thee, knight-at-arms?*

"I knocked over a stock unit. I didn't mean to, I swear to God I didn't."

"Slow down," Foster said. "Tell me what happened."

"They sent me for a box of staples and now there's stuff all over the floor." The young man slammed a fist into the side of the catering truck. The corrugated aluminum thundered. Doughnuts spilled from the racks. Sandwiches tumbled into the mud.

"What the hell!" the driver shouted.

"Show me," Foster said. He knew this terror. He had lived with an alcoholic. "What's your name?"

"Andre."

Reluctantly, Foster followed Andre deep into the old factory, walking through corridors that stank of mildew, past cobwebbed doors and dusty machines. The light was dim, the air damp and cool. They turned a blind corner and entered a big room piled high with transformers and switch cabinets. Foster felt a sudden impatience. Why bother with an inventory? Everything here was obsolete, useless. A shelving unit lay on the floor with galvanized staples scattered around it. Foster recognized the staples. They were used to secure electrical cables. Grandpa's stocked them.

"I reached for the top shelf and everything went flying," Andre said. "I tried to get the unit back on its feet, but it just slides. Jesus, I didn't mean to pull it over."

"Take it easy." Foster kicked a path through the staples and stood for a moment, considering. "We'll push the base against the wall and hoist the unit up."

Andre looked at him with shining eyes. Anxious to escape his gratitude, Foster bent and locked his hands on a metal shelf. "On three," he said. "One, two …"

In his eagerness Andre missed the rhythm. Foster put his back into the lift and the shelf unit rose into the air. But then it teetered alarmingly, and began to fall. Foster tried to stop it. This isn't the usual sort of pain, he thought as he went down. It's more like an explosion of light. He was lying on the concrete floor with the shelf unit on top of him and blood streaming into his eyes. This won't do, he thought before he blacked out. Shawna would be coming home from school. He was going to make chicken cordon bleu.

WHITE SHEETS. WHITE curtains. White ceiling. The odour of iodine. He was lying on a gurney. There was something clipped to his finger, a white plastic sensor. Lifting his other hand, Foster explored his head with tentative fingers. There was a ragged region up there, remote as the North Pole. Somewhere in this hospital there was a room where they kept the remains. *They phone the funeral home*, the hearse driver had said. *And that's a pickup.*

The curtain slid aside. Foster's vision cleared to reveal a woman wearing a green smock. She had wiry grey hair, dark fleshy arms, a stethoscope in her pocket, a pair of glasses on a length of red string. She shone a flashlight into Foster's eyes, asked him his name and nodded at the answer. "Do you know why you are here?" She was watching him intently.

A trick of memory took Foster back to Batty Burford's science class. This was a trick question. Foster hummed up some spit and told the doctor about Freddy Wilkinson, the ride in the van, the old factory that looked like a castle. The doctor's head acquired an aura. Why had he gone to the old factory? Now, that was a very good question. He had to think about that one. "A shelving unit toppled over. I was trapped under it."

His answer seemed to please the doctor. Foster was glad about that. He was a bright boy. He had done his homework. She would sew up his wound, she told him. She pricked his scalp with a needle. He had taken a good knock on the head, but he could go home in a few hours, if there was no change in his condition.

A few hours. There was something wrong with that. Light glinted from the needle. A loop of transparent thread dangled before his eyes. "I have to get home. My granddaughter is coming back from school."

The doctor pulled the thread, and Foster felt an eyebrow lift. She had him hooked. She was playing him like a trout.

"What is your granddaughter's name?"

"Shawna."

"How old is she?"

It was hard to think. He had a dull headache. He couldn't feel the stitches going in, but he could hear the sound travelling through his bones. How old was Shawna? He had to answer correctly or the doctor would yank him out of the water and mount him on the wall like a trophy fish. "Shawna is eleven."

"Are you the sole caregiver?" The doctor had a pair of scissors in her hand.

Sole caregiver. He liked the sound of that. "Yes, I am."

"How do you feel?"

"Fine."

The doctor tilted her head and scrutinized him. "Headache? Blurred vision? Nausea?"

"No, nothing like that."

"Let me see you walk." The doctor stepped away. She wouldn't help him, Foster knew. That was part of the test. He slid his legs from the bed and set his stocking feet on the cold floor. His head throbbed. He felt ten feet tall, and for a bad moment he wanted to throw up. Mastering all that, he walked a little way down the hall, turned and walked back.

"The muscles in your back are strained. You must rest. After six hours you can lie flat." The doctor took a pad from her pocket and scribbled out a prescription. "These are painkillers. You may take them tomorrow, not today. You may have a concussion. Concussion is very dangerous. You must stay awake for six hours. If you feel sick you must come back here immediately. Do you understand?" She looked at him carefully.

"Yes."

"You can go home if someone can pick you up. Is there someone you can phone?"

"Yes." Foster planned to take the bus home.

"An orderly will take you to the lobby. There are telephones there. He will stay with you until your person collects you. Only then are you discharged. You may get dressed now." The doctor stepped away and closed the curtain.

Leaning against the bed, Foster put on his shoes, fumbling with the laces.

"How are we doing in there, Sunshine?"

Sunshine? Foster slid the curtain aside and stared at the man who stood behind a wheelchair. His blue scrubs were patterned with teddy bears. "I can walk."

"Afraid not. Hospital regs. Sit yourself down, Sunshine, and we'll put a blankie on your lap."

The lobby had curved walls, pot lights, soft chairs, pictures of waterfalls, mountains, dolphins. The orderly wheeled Foster to a pay phone and gave him the handset as if it were a lollipop. "And who shall we call?"

He had no right to call Jessica, Foster knew. But there was no one else he could call. It was a simple fact. A bond had formed between them. If he failed to honour this bond, both he and Jessica would be diminished. It wasn't an easy concept to understand, and he wanted to be on his feet when he explained it to Jessica. He started to rise and nearly toppled over.

"Oopsie-daisy!" The orderly caught him under the arms and set him in the wheelchair.

It occurred to Foster that murder can be a blameless act. He muttered out the number. The orderly punched it in.

"Jessica? It's Foster."

"What do you want?"

"Is your art going well?" *You're off script*, whispered Sam the telemarketer. Or so Foster imagined.

"Foster, what do you want?"

The orderly was watching him approvingly. Look at our little man, using the telephone all by himself.

"I'm at the hospital. I've had an accident. It's nothing serious. I'm okay." Foster waited for Jessica to say something sympathetic. She didn't. "Can you pick me up and drive me home?"

"You want me to come and pick you up."

"You have to come. I'm the sole caregiver. I have to get home."

THE HOSPITAL DOORS parted and the warm June day came rushing at Foster. The little Toyota sat waiting at the curb. Jessica yanked open the passenger's door and marched around the car with her painting smock fluttering. The orderly plucked Foster from the wheelchair, set him in the front seat, fastened his seatbelt, patted his arm and said, "Bye-bye. Be a good boy."

"What was that all about?" Jessica asked as she jockeyed through the hectic traffic.

"All what?" Foster squirmed in his seat. His pain had abruptly returned, found its way back to him like lost luggage. The world had the sharp colours and garbled sound of deteriorating film stock: the sky was an intense blue; the radio announcer seemed to be speaking a foreign language composed of English words.

"Mr. Cuddles," Jessica said.

"Mr. Cuddles?"

"The orderly. Didn't you see the button on his scrubs?"

"Watch out!"

Jessica hit the brakes. "What?"

"That red truck is moving this way."

"I see it."

For several minutes neither of them spoke.

"Thank you for coming," Foster said.

Jessica said nothing.

"The light is about to change. You should slow down."

"Way back here? What is your problem?"

"You make me nervous," Foster heard himself say. "I never know what you'll do next."

"The way I drive makes you nervous."

Foster glanced at Jessica. Were they talking about her driving? The car hit a bump. He experienced a weightless, floaty delay that was a bit like jet lag — and then agony. "There's someone on that crosswalk."

"They haven't pushed the button yet. Relax. I'm an excellent driver."

"No, you're not," Foster said. It seemed very important to tell the truth. "You don't anticipate."

"I'm a good driver." Jessica glanced at him. "What's wrong with the way I drive?"

"You should look farther down the road. Think things through."

They drove in silence for several blocks, Jessica tapping the steering wheel with her fingers, Foster staring out at the world. How wonderful the world was, how easily it could slip away.

"Okay, I'm a rotten driver," Jessica announced. "Is there anything else wrong with me you'd care to point out? Am I a rotten artist too?"

"I don't know anything about art." Foster looked at her in surprise. "Why are you crying?"

"I am not crying."

She was crying. A wave of fatigue swept over Foster. His pain registered now as an absence; his back had gone missing. His stitched-up head seemed to belong to someone else, as if he were Frankenstein's monster, a creature sewn together using the parts of better men.

How had they reached Mazurka Street so quickly? Jessica jumped out of the car, threw open the passenger door and helped him to his feet. "You had to come," Foster said, trying to explain the certainty he had felt when he stared at the pay phone. "It's a simple fact."

"Had to come? Had to come!" Jessica threw up her hands. "Why did I answer the phone?" she said in a wondering voice. "I had something going. An acrylic. Something good. Something new." She gazed down the street, then looked at Foster. "I can't handle your negativity."

The conversation was a train wreck, Foster realized with a feeling of desperation. They needed to talk. "Can I come over next Tuesday?"

"No!" Jessica marched around her car, thrashing a hand before her face as if she were swatting away a hornet. "You have to make up your mind." She jumped in the Toyota and sped off, leaving Foster staring at the disappearing car.

Make up his mind? What did the woman want of him? Hadn't he made his decision in the hospital lobby? Foster looked at his daughter's townhouse. He didn't belong here, and he had no business lying on concrete floors with shelf units on top of him. He should be overseas, earning the money that would see Mary and Shawna right. Shawna would be home soon. He started up the front walk.

[SEVENTEEN]

THE TWEENY YEARS hadn't covered this eventuality. For days Shawna had talked of nothing but her first soccer game; she had on her red-and-gold uniform, her equipment bag was on the back seat, they had driven an hour through heavy traffic from the city to the suburbs — and now she wouldn't get out of the van.

Wondering what to say to his granddaughter, Foster stared through the windshield at the athletic complex. There were tennis courts, jogging tracks, soccer fields. On one field, a team of boys sprinted along with their coach trotting behind them. On another, a double row of girls zigzagged a soccer ball back and forth. In the parking lot, minivans came and went. On the sidelines, parents sipped coffee, stood next to strollers, stroked the heads of dogs.

"It's a beautiful game," Foster said. "In fact, that's what they call it — the beautiful game."

"Who's they? The legion of morons?"

"I played soccer when I was in university. And I scored a goal." He had Shawna's attention now. "I gave the ball a header." Foster slapped his head with an open hand. "The goalkeeper lunged, and in it went. Why are you looking at me like that?"

"You're bleeding."

There was blood on his hand. He had slapped his stitches. Taking the tissue Shawna offered him, Foster said, "Did Kayla sign up?"

"Yeah. She's really good."

Foster thought for a moment. Was Shawna feeling shy?

There was a silence. And then Shawna said, "Why do you hate Tyler?"

"Why do I …? I don't hate Tyler. Whatever gave you that idea?"

"I heard you and Mom talking one night and you called Tyler a doofus."

"Shawna, I don't know. Maybe I said something that sounded like 'doofus.'"

His granddaughter looked at him. "What if Mom and Tyler get married?"

"If your mother and Tyler were to get married — and we don't know that they will — but for the sake of argument … then it would be … important for you and Tyler to get along." Foster felt queasy. It would be a terrible mistake for Mary to commit herself to that … doofus.

"If I play tonight, can you go away for a little while? This is my first game. You can watch next time."

The children would be supervised, parents were not required to stay; the letter he had found in Mary's kitchen made this clear. But he couldn't help feeling disappointed. He had been looking forward to watching Shawna play.

"Kayla's dad said he'd sign me in."

Kayla's dad. "All right. If that's what you want."

Shawna grabbed her equipment bag and ran to join Kayla and her family, who had parked nearby. Foster noted the time and drove away slowly.

The athletic centre lay only a few blocks from the house he had shared with Kathleen, Foster realized when he consulted the street guide. He hadn't planned on going there. Now there seemed no reason not to. No imprint is deeper than the way home, and he made the turns automatically, the windows of the van open, the scent of lilac drifting in, the drone of lawnmowers stirring his memory. A few minutes later he glided to the shoulder of the road, switched off the ignition and stared at the house he and Kathleen had once owned, a split-level with angel stone on the lower storey, aluminum siding on the upper. Paradise for eighty-nine thousand dollars, appliances included. The double garage had a new door. A wind chime tinkled in the breeze way. The apple sapling he had planted on the front lawn had become a tree.

It was a modest house, he thought now, remembering the first time they had walked through the echoing rooms, wondering at the enormous space. They were solemn with each other that day: the house had made the marriage real, raised the stakes between them. But once he was past his jitters, Foster liked Regent Heights. That first summer the simplest things made him happy: a patchwork of sod, a whirling sprinkler, the resistence of the starter cord when he fired up the lawnmower. One morning he stuck his head into the attic to see sap oozing from the spruce rafters. It was as if the house were still growing.

Kathleen hated the suburbs. What was she supposed to do with herself, for the love of God? She wasn't working; they shared the decaying notion that this was the proper thing to do. Kathleen stopped drinking when she got pregnant. It was her turn to be happy. Of course he wanted children — he remembered this conversation vividly, the paint tray on the speckled newspapers, in the bedroom that would become the nursery — but hadn't they agreed to wait until they were on their feet financially? Then Control Data promoted him and his objection was moot. His new job took him to New York for weeks at a time. When he came home one spring day, the glass was back in

Kathleen's hand. He felt responsible for Kathleen and it offended him when people told him this was nonsense.

The light was waning. The west-facing windows had taken on a conclusive glow. For a terrible moment Foster was convinced that the soccer game had ended hours ago, that Shawna was sitting on the curb with her equipment bag on her lap. Alert suddenly, he looked at his watch. No, there was plenty of time. There was no point sitting here. He might as well head back, park by the bleachers, wait for Shawna in the van.

There was a turning circle at the end of the street, and as Foster went around it for the first time in twenty-five years, a sign on a garage caught his eye, and he went around again like a tourist in a British roundabout. It was a rustic sign, one of those hand-burned things people buy at flea markets. Chudzik. Mary had a friend when they lived on this street. Anna? Ella. Ella Chudzik. Foster parked the van, hesitated a moment, then walked up the driveway, stopping next to a gleaming Lexus to ease his back. The open porch had iron railings, aluminum chairs with red plastic seats, flowerpots of geraniums. A moment after he rang the doorbell an old woman appeared, a shadow on the screen. She hobbled away, calling in rapid-fire Polish. A younger woman replaced her at the door.

"My name is Foster."

"I know who you are."

Foster nodded, hiding his surprise. He hadn't expected Ella to recognize him.

Somewhere in the house a television roared. Ella closed her eyes for a moment. "She's got the remote screwed up again." She turned her head and called, "*Tak, Drogi matka! Tak!*"

Ella was a link to Mary. Foster asked, "Can you spare me a minute?"

The door swung open, and Foster followed Ella to the kitchen, where she waved a hand at a table, a chrome-and-laminate dinosaur from the fifties, and walked away, a willowy, well-groomed woman in expensive clothes. He pulled out a chair and sat down. The kitchen smelled of boiled cabbage, just as it always had. On top of the fridge the same golden figure crouched on a dusty trophy, about to release a bowling ball. Above the table, Jesus and Pope John Paul II stared past each other. An orange tabby — the Chudziks always had a cat — tracked across the floor and vanished down the basement stairs. As Foster gazed through the screen door at the shaded lawn, it seemed to him that he could walk down the street and find Kathleen in the living room, dancing barefoot to Stan Getz. Ella came back into the room and went to the stove. "Would you like tea? I'm making tea for Mother."

"Yes. Thank you."

Ella sat down and looked at Foster. There was a challenge in that look, a trace of the precocious child she had once been. She wore a wedding ring with a large diamond.

"Is your mother well?"

"She has her ups and downs." Ella kept her gaze on Foster. "My sister and I take turns looking after her. What happened to your head?"

Foster touched his stitches. "A little accident. Nothing serious."

"Mary said you were in Dubai."

"I'm back in Canada now." Of course he was. Well, duh, Shawna would say. "Ella, do you know where Mary is?"

The kettle broke into a shrill whistle. "We'll go around back," Ella said. "It'll be quieter."

She made the tea, then led him out the back door and onto a patio. They were about to sit down when her mother shouted. Ella left him and went back inside. The lawn was dotted with dandelions. There was a dogwood tree, a bird bath, a small statue of the Madonna. He stood in the warm evening, studying his old house from a new vantage point, remembering the last summer of his marriage. When Ella returned, she handed him a lawn chair, snapped out a second chair and settled on it in a ceremonious way that suggested she had decided how much to tell him. "Mary has my address. She's welcome anytime. She knows that."

Ella had said her piece. She would tell him nothing further, Foster decided. An oriole flew over a rock garden and disappeared into a tree. "Is your father …"

"Papa died ten years ago."

"Oh. I'm sorry to hear that." Foster pictured Mr. Chudzik opening the garage door, camping on a chair and looking out at the street with a flyswatter in one hand and a glass of rye in the other, the bandy-legged king of all he surveyed.

"You made a big impression on him. 'Smart man,' my father would say. 'University man.'"

"Um," Foster said, remembering more. When he came outside, Chudzik would get to his feet and trudge to the property line — to the limit of his English, Foster thought now — salute with the flyswatter, turn around and trudge back to his throne. The tribute had embarrassed Foster. A smart man wouldn't have to go looking for his daughter. He looked across the backyards. Mary would flit over the lawns like a phantom. You had to look twice to be sure what you were seeing.

"They were friends, Mary and my father. That's how I got to know her. I'd find Mary in the garage, sitting on a piece of cardboard listening to his war stories." Ella gave Foster a wry smile. "To hear that man go on, he and three other guys defeated the entire German army." Following Foster's gaze, she said, "The Boskers filled in the pool. They've owned your house for years now." A shout came from the house. Ella shook her head. "I'll be back in a minute."

Staring at his old backyard, sipping his tea, Foster remembered the pool parties. They began on Friday night, gained momentum all weekend, spilled from backyard to backyard. The scent of chlorine. Charcoal smouldering. Beer in a tub of ice, the labels floating off the bottles. Women in bikinis tottering down the street on high heels. Kathleen holding court in a lounge chair, her legs crossed at the ankles, a sandal hanging from a toe, Howie Carruthers or Randy Wilson stepping in to top up her glass with white wine. "Whatever's on the go, provided there's a nun on the bottle," Kathleen would say in a stagy Irish accent. She had lost herself, become a cliché. Foster remembered the day Kathleen threw a glass of wine in his face. It was all his fault: their broken marriage, her struggle with the bottle, Mary's troubling behaviour. Ella was back in her chair. She handed him a book. Foster stared at the title. *The Expatriate's Guide to the Middle East.*

"I found it last week, when I was cleaning out the garage,"

The slim volume had disappeared from his desk late that final summer. With the divorce in the offing, Mary had become a magpie. When Foster went looking for her in the Chudzik garage — Mary had made a nest of cushions under a workbench — he would find a spatula or a screwdriver or one of Kathleen's CDs waiting for him in the cardboard box Mr. Chudzik had labelled *YOU TAKE*.

"Do you know what Mary called herself, after you went away?"

Foster shook his head.

"The Expatriate's Daughter." Ella stirred her tea thoughtfully. "You know the way some people pick up vibes? Mary's like that. If I'm upset about something she picks it up. It's weird, the way she does that. We hardly need to talk."

"Um." Ella seemed to see Mary as some sort of mystic. Was there anything to this? Foster had never believed in that sort of thing, but for a moment, in the fairy light of the backyard, he wondered if he had misunderstood something fundamental about his daughter.

"She met someone. A really great guy. She'll be fine."

"I'm sure you're right," Foster said, although he was sure Ella was wrong. Tyler was dead weight. He would drag Mary down.

"I've got to get Mother to bed." Ella reached into a pocket and handed Foster a business card. "Ask Mary to call me when she gets home."

"Yes, I will." Foster read the card. Ella was an investment banker. How far could Mary have gone in school if her parents had stayed together? The next time he went to the Internet Café he would look up night school courses. Mary could start one in September.

The old woman came to a window and shouted like a demented Cassandra. Foster looked at the Chudzik house. "It can't be easy with your mother."

Ella shrugged. "My sister could help more."

"Would your mother be more comfortable in another living situation?"

"A nursing home?" Ella shook her head. "I promised my father that would never happen."

As Foster drove back to the soccer pitch, he wondered if he should have told Ella the truth that sang in his bones. A promise is a tiger. A promise can eat you alive.

AT THE ATHLETIC centre, he parked the van and looked again at his watch. He was fifteen minutes early. If he caught the last of the game, would Shawna object? He worked his way up the bleachers and took a seat behind a woman wearing a Yankees jacket and a sunhat.

The lights were on, and Shawna's team came scooting down the field. And there was Shawna! The ball came to her. She wound up for a kick. Foster leapt to his feet and applauded. A lanky blonde — a natural at sports, Little Miss Perfect — stole the ball. But Shawna wasn't a quitter; she turned and ran with the play.

When the game was over, the girls gathered around their coach, cheered and waved their arms in the air. They broke from the huddle, and Shawna ran toward the bleachers and in a single breath shouted,

"We-won-I-blocked-a-shot-Gloria's-mother's-got-their-van-can-we-take-these-guys-home?"

"Sure we can. Absolutely." Foster trooped after Shawna and five of her teammates as they tore across the parking lot, jumping and spinning as they ran. He smiled as he unlocked the van, flipped up the tailgate, unfolded the third seat and watched the girls scramble aboard.

"Cool! It faces backwards!"

"I'm totally sitting here."

"Duh! Like, I didn't see it first?"

"What a great old car!"

"Want some gum?"

"Whatcha got?"

"Peppermint Ice."

"Their coach? He was like, keeeck it! Keeeck it!"

"Keeeck it! Keeeck it!"

"Is everyone buckled in?" Foster said.

"Keeeck it! Keeeck it!" The girls collapsed in fits of giggles. They were putting out enough energy to light a city block.

"Guys!" Shawna yelled. "Seat belts!"

Buckles clicked. Foster winked at Shawna and pulled the shift into gear.

On the drive back to the city, he remembered the day he had planted the apple sapling on the front lawn. A day like the one that was ending now. The shovel thrust into the earth. The root ball wrapped in burlap. Mary running from the shadows to stand at his side.

ON HIS WAY to Shawna's school, Foster stopped by the Internet Café. It was a hot day and he took off his suit coat and hung it carefully on the back of a chair. The teenagers sitting across the aisle gawked at him in his shirt and tie, as if he were an exotic sight. Something you don't see everyday, like a solar eclipse or a beached whale.

There was an email message from Cedric. "Working on something. Tropical island. Coconut palms. Bare-breasted maidens." Foster shook his head. Poor Cedric, marooned in his ex-wife's back garden like some digital-age Robinson Crusoe. Foster closed the email message and searched for jobs in the Middle East.

MRS. PATTERSON WAS running late. Strolling down the hall with his hands laced behind his back, Foster inspected drawings of cats, paintings of hockey games, photo collages of pop stars. Had he set foot in Mary's school? He didn't think so. Spoken to Mary's teachers? Not that he remembered. Kathleen had taken charge of such details. And, cards on the table, he had lost interest when Mary's grades had fallen. It was nothing to be proud of.

A young couple came out of a classroom nodding and smiling. A moment later, Mrs. Patterson came into the hallway and looked around with an expectant smile, a handsome figure in her brown linen slacks and silky, sand-coloured blouse. A string-of-pearls woman, the kind of woman who ironed everything. Foster's interest quickened. "You're my seven-fifteen?" Mrs. Patterson looked at him. "Mary called to say she couldn't make it."

"Grandpa to the rescue," Foster said. A bit too heartily, he felt, hearing his voice echo down the hall. "You look very nice tonight," he added.

Mrs. Patterson gave Foster a wary look.

In the classroom she wheeled out an office chair and sat behind her desk. Foster moved a straight-backed chair closer and sat down to take the measure of the unknown quantity who had charge of Shawna for six and a half hours each day. Mrs. Patterson opened a file folder, picked up a piece of paper and read for a moment. "Did you bring the interaction form?"

"Interaction form?"

"The one I sent home with Shawna."

"I'm afraid I don't …"

"Did you speak to Shawna about this meeting?"

Why would he speak to Shawna? "When I was that age," Foster said, smiling to put Mrs. Patterson at ease, "my grandmother would talk to my teachers, and I'd learn the consequences later."

"Consequences? What an odd thing to say. We take a proactive approach, Mr. Foster. Our aim is to build a strong team — child, parent, teacher."

Proactive. A strong team. They would be teaching the works of Gary Garth next. "Are those test scores?" Foster leaned forward. "How is Shawna doing in math?"

"She was coming along, but now she seems … confused. Argumentative."

"Oh? Can you give me an example?"

"We were doing pre-algebra — the objectives are number sense and patterning — and instead of making a chart and doubling values, Shawna tried to use some sort of formula."

"I showed her a better method. An algorithm."

"I don't understand."

"It's simple enough. You offset the value and sum powers of two." Foster pulled out a pen. "I'll be happy to show you."

"I understand the math, Mr. Foster." Mrs. Patterson said slowly. "I don't understand why you interfered. The rubric was designed by experts. It takes psychological development into account, and it's structured around teachable moments."

"Teachable moments?"

"Girls have trouble with math, traditionally."

"May I ask a question?"

"Of course."

"If you made math fun, wouldn't the students learn better?"

There was silence. Then Mrs. Patterson closed the file folder and said, "Do you have any other questions?"

"I didn't see Shawna's name on any of the art in the hall."

"There's only so much room. I'll put one of hers up another time."

"But she's doing well in art."

"She is slightly behind the developmental curve, but children often spurt ahead when we least expect it."

Rubrics. Teachable moments. Developmental curves. His granddaughter could disappear into this thicket of jargon. He didn't like Mrs. Patterson's indulgent smile. Had she written Shawna off? Shawna would go to university. He would make it happen.

Mrs. Patterson frowned. She opened the file folder and leafed through its contents. "Mary and I had such a good talk last term. I was sure we'd made a connection." She tapped her chin with her pencil. "Mr. Foster, did you say Mary is not in the home?"

"She's away at the moment."

A janitor clattered his cart past the door. The clock over the blackboard buzzed.

"Away? For how long?"

"She'll be back soon."

Mrs. Patterson looked at him. "The school has had concerns in the past. We consulted a social agency." She flipped a page. "The last home visit was four years ago."

Home visit? "Everything is fine," Foster said, in a tone meant to close the subject.

"How long does Shawna spend on her homework?"

"It varies."

"Ten minutes? Twenty minutes? An hour?"

"In that range." The truth was, he hadn't a clue. For all his bluster, all the schedules he had drawn up and posted on the fridge, he had trusted Shawna to make her own decisions.

Mrs. Patterson jotted a note.

Foster said, "I'll take the necessary measures."

"What a strange thing to say."

"Many thanks for this little chat." Foster got to his feet. "Very helpful."

[EIGHTEEN]

THE UNIT HUMS. Then the circuit breaker pops. Foster peered under the kitchen sink. The garbage disposal unit resembled a wasp's nest. It was a warm, rainy Tuesday in early June, and he had come home disappointed from the cattle call at IndTemps. There was no reason he couldn't fix the disposal unit; in Regent Heights, he had been a competent handyman. He went to the middle room and opened the closet where Charlie Anderson's tools had sat untouched since they had come into the house. Everything he needed was here, Foster saw as he sorted through the toolboxes, hefting adjustable wrenches, unwrapping rolls of chisels, lifting out trays of circuit testers and electrical tape. It was a melancholy task. Charlie had bought good tools, and they had outlasted him.

It took an hour to muscle the unit out. When it finally came free, Foster sat beside it on the kitchen floor, sucking the knuckle he had skinned when the wrench slipped. What would Shawna want for dinner? With country and western playing on the radio, he made himself a cup of Earl Grey, set the garbage disposal unit on the kitchen table, unscrewed a cover plate and probed the machine's innards with a pocket flashlight between his teeth. Were those white threads the remains of a gasket? Why was the flywheel jammed? He sniffed the shredder — and caught the odour of artichoke. Well, no wonder. You can't put artichokes in these things. He had learned that at Grandpa Camp.

When the phone rang late that afternoon, the disassembled machine lay arranged on the kitchen table in the meticulous order of a technical diagram, gears within gears, bolts mated with nuts, screws sorted by size. Absorbed in his task, Foster wedged the phone against his ear, picked up a screwdriver, said hello and scraped away at a crust of green crud.

"And when I ask you to be my bride," the radio sang. "You'll know my affection is bona fide."

"Foster? It's Cedric. Listen, something has come up. Are you still in the market?""

"Down the road of love we'll roll," the radio sang. "Two turtle doves on cruise control …"

Foster put down the screwdriver. "Yes, I am."

"I've been singing your praises to an outfit called APEAS."

"Appease?"

"No, dear boy. A-P-E-A-S. As in, All Pacific and East Asian Salvage. It does sound funny when you say it. Question for you: How many ships went to the bottom out there between '41 and '45?"

"During World War II? Hundreds, I suppose."

"Four thousand, they reckon. Hundreds of them were oil tankers. And here's the good news — they're leaking oil."

"Leaking oil. I saw something about that on television."

"You have telly in the colonies?"

"And indoor plumbing." Cedric sounded like his old self, Foster thought, confident and breezy.

"It's win-win, Foster. The locals will pay to get the oil out, and the oil can be sold. Which is where APEAS comes into the picture. They got their hands on a mid-range tanker, ex-Shell, Liberian registration, and they've cobbled together some mysterious pumping gear. All very high-tech and hush-hush. Could be a nice little earner. Smart people. Aussies, mostly. Problem is, they look like pirates and talk like lunatics. They scare the wits out of the authorities. They need someone like you."

Foster nodded. At last.

"Know anything about Micronesia?" Cedric said.

"The islands north of New Guinea?"

"Papua New Guinea, that's right. Six hundred and seven islands. Eighteen hundred miles end to end. Four island groups. Yap, Chuuk, Pohnpei, and Kosrae. You'll be based in Palikir, the capital. That's on Pohnpei. Foster, it's Dubai in the old days. Paradise before the punters came crowding in."

"Do they want me to set up a computer system?"

"No, no," Cedric said. "A monkey can work a computer these days. What they need is a liaison officer. Someone who knows the oil game and can talk sense to the government. Someone presentable. I had a drink with these people. They grunt a lot. They have chest hair spilling out of their shirts. Not the women, but you get the idea."

"What are they offering?"

"Three year contract. Renewable. Airfare out and back, annual. Salary —"

"Let me get a pencil." Foster was opening a drawer when Shawna came storming into the kitchen. She threw her backpack at him and shouted, "Patterson talked to the principal! Kayla was in the hall and she heard the whole thing!" The backpack scythed across the table, sending ring gears and springs and levers to the floor.

"Kayla?" Foster said.

"Kayla?" Cedric said.

"They'll tell Children's Aid! I'll have to go to a home!"

"I don't understand," Foster said.

"Who told you to understand? Who told you to come here? You drove Mom away and now you've ruined everything!"

"Cedric? Can I call you back?"

"They want to move fast. Can you come to London next week for an interview, hoist a glass, sign the contract? APEAS will cover the airfare. I'll send the ticket by email."

"Fine. And Cedric? Thanks."

"Foster?" Cedric's voice dropped to a lower register. "I need this one. APEAS will get me out of the potting shed."

"Send the ticket." Foster hung up and made a grab for Shawna's arm. She slipped away and ran sobbing down the hall. A door slammed. The house shook.

After a moment, Foster picked up the shredder ring, his mind reeling with images of oil tankers sinking through blue water with black oil trailing from their ruptured hulls. He crawled around the kitchen floor on his hands and knees, gathering parts and dropping them into a zip bag. It would be a miracle if he found them all. He zipped the bag, vaguely wondering why the neighbours were playing such dreadful music. It dawned on him that it wasn't music. It was a crashing cacophony, as if a giant version of the disposal unit had somehow roared to life. He hurried down the hall, shoved open Shawna's door and stared at the toppled shelves, the upended drawers, the clothes strewn across the floor.

"Go away!" Shawna grabbed a pop-up book and threw it at him. It was the castle book, Foster saw, the book she had shown him so proudly the night they went to Charlie's house. "I hate you! I hate you!" When she swept her dollhouse to the floor, Foster strode into the room, took his granddaughter by the shoulders and held her while she hammered him with her fists, held her until she collapsed against him and wept.

"WANT ANOTHER SLICE?" Foster felt like a man trying to disarm a bomb, wondering which wire to snip next.

"No, thanks." Shawna dropped a crust into the pizza box.

"I'm sorry. I've really messed things up for you."

Shawna looked wearily down the hallway. "I'd better start cleaning up my room. Children's Aid will send somebody."

"Shawna, listen. No one is going to send you to a home."

"Yeah, right."

The despair in her voice went straight to Foster's heart. She had written him off. "Tell you what. Bring me the dollhouse and I'll fix it."

"Are you kidding? I completely nuked it."

"I can try."

She pushed the pizza box away. "Nah. I don't want that baby stuff anymore."

Baby stuff. Was this a clue? Foster went to a drawer and took out a yellow pad and a pencil. "We can fix up your room any way you want it."

Shawna raised her head and looked at him. "Can we paint the walls a different colour?"

"Any colour you like." At Grandpa Camp he had attended a "Just Enough" session on interior decorating. Why hadn't he paid more attention? He trawled his memory for jargon. Emotional palette, the music of texture, the meaning of light … "I have some colour samples in my closet," Foster said, remembering the training manual from Grandpa's Toolbox.

"Jessica knows all about colours and stuff," Shawna said. "Can we get her to help?"

Can we get Jessica to help? Jessica wasn't speaking to him. "I'll phone her right now."

Foster walked to the kitchen and dialled the number.

"Hello?" Jessica said. "Hello?"

His courage deserted him. He couldn't ask this woman for help. He was off to Micronesia. He could say hello at least. But he couldn't. The word promised something.

The line clicked. "Foster?" Shawna said from her bedroom. "Hang up. I got it."

His hand shaking, Foster hung up the phone, picked up the pencil and made a list. Paint, brushes, rollers, trays, masking tape. Absent-mindedly, he sketched a map of the world. A Mercator projection, a flattened cylinder with straight rhumb lines. He drew the continents as rough shapes. Micronesia was on the Pacific rim, the island of Pohnpei a dot in all that blue above Australia. The town of Palikir would be small potatoes, but that didn't matter. Because you couldn't get much further from Mazurka Street. Not if you wanted to stay on the same planet.

"WHAT DO YOU THINK, Foster?" Dressed in a ragamuffin outfit of torn jeans, a paint-splattered middy, and a plaid shirt, Jessica looked at him over a fan of paint samples.

He squinted at the samples and saw yellow, yellow, yellow. "They're all very nice."

"Very nice, he says." Jessica gave Shawna a nudge; then she held one of the samples against the wall, looked at Shawna and lifted her eyebrows.

"Hey, yeah," Shawna said.

"We can get the paint on Dundas," Foster said.

Jessica stared at him. "We have to go to Grandpa's Toolbox."

"Why?"

"The samples you gave us are from their colour system."

"Oh. Right," Foster said. Grandpa's had fired him, a fact that rankled more now than it had at the time. "I'll get my keys."

They climbed into Charlie's van and headed north with Shawna snuggled against Jessica. They were friends. It had nothing to do with him. The weather had turned sultry; a cloud of ozone and particulate hung over Toronto. Once he was settled in Palikir, Mary and Shawna would come to visit and breathe the clean Pacific air. He turned on the A/C. Jessica glanced at him. Yes, he should have asked before turning on the A/C. The hell with it. He flicked the fan to high.

He felt like an imposter, walking into Grandpa's Toolbox in civilian clothes. And although he knew the way to Paint 'n Paper perfectly well, he was annoyed when a Grandpa strode past, ignoring him completely. Never walk past a customer. How many times had he heard Amanda Curtwell say that? As he crossed the aisles he saw people prowling around, searching for someone to meet their deeper need. He left Shawna and Jessica at the samples display and went to the mixing centre.

"Slumming, are we?" Grandpa McCrindle said over the roar of a paint shaker. "Brought the family, did we?"

Family. That was a stretch. Foster didn't feel up to explaining who was who. "How are things?" He looked up at the mirrors. "How's Amanda?"

"Fired," McCrindle said with a smile. "Peter Chen has the store now."

"Really?" Foster felt a sudden concern for the woman who had been his boss. Would she end up as one of Sam Skinner's telemarketers? *You're off script again, Amanda.*

On the drive home Foster thought about Palikir. There would be important meetings to attend. Royalties, concessions, permits would be at stake. It was time to dust off the old stone face and put on the tailored suit.

"DO YOU LIKE the colour?" Foster stepped away from the wall, brush in hand. Jessica had gone to the kitchen to put the kettle on.

"Think so." Shawna plugged in her hair dryer and played a jet of hot air over the patch of Etruscan Yellow. "Yeah, I do."

"Are you sure? Because we can take it back. Grandpa's has a mix guarantee."

"No, it's good."

"Are you sure?" Foster tipped a stream of paint into a shiny tray. He stopped in mid-pour and looked at his granddaughter. "I want you to be sure." Because I want you to forgive me. Because I'm going away to pump oil from sunken tankers and save the earth.

"The colour's awesome." Shawna drew a smooth yellow line along the top of a baseboard.

Lost in thought, Foster loaded a roller with yellow. Mary would be relieved when he told her about Micronesia. They could talk about an allowance later. The trip to Grandpa's Toolbox had almost cleaned him out. How would he get from Heathrow to the centre of London? Perhaps he could catch a ride. Or he would walk.

"You're doing fine, Foster."

Startled, Foster turned, and saw a child painting a wall, her eyes wide with concentration.

"HANDYMAN?" MRS. PARK said when Foster came to the cash register and began counting out the change he had gathered into a zip bag. It was his second trip of the day to Corner Convenience for bits of hardware. She pointed to a bulletin board and gave him her open-hearted smile. "Many people ask."

Foster shook his head. "I'm just helping my daughter." When Mrs. Park smiled at him again, his eyes watered. At that moment she seemed the only female in the Americas that he had yet to disappoint.

Social services called later that day, when he was in Shawna's room, putting a second coat of paint on the trim. The woman on the phone had a flat, insistent voice. "Are you in charge of Shawna?"

"Yes."

"What is your relationship to her?"

"I'm her grandfather."

"There's nothing in the file about a grandfather."

"Then put something in the file!"

"There's no reason to be rude, sir. The mother is absent from the home? Is this correct?"

"My daughter is visiting a friend."

"Who would that be?"

"Ella Chudzik." Foster winced. Why had he said that? Now he would have to call Ella, ask her to back up this lie.

"How long have you been in the home, sir?"

"Eight … No, almost ten months."

"Less than a year."

There are twelve months in a year. Foster resisted the urge to point this out. He imagined a box being ticked.

"With the mother absent, is there a regular source of income?

"Define regular."

There was a silence.

"Do you have a job, sir?"

"I'm self-employed."

The line went silent.

"Sir, I'm going to schedule a home visit. Will tomorrow evening between five and seven be convenient?"

"Fine." Foster hung up the phone. He dipped the brush into the paint, flicked off the excess and feathered in a thin spot above the door. Why couldn't people mind their own business?

"NOW, I DON'T want you to worry," Foster said. "Social services called. They're sending somebody over tomorrow night."

"Yeah, I figured." Shawna pushed away her dessert.

This was Tyler's fault, Foster thought. For knocking Mary off track. For luring her away when she was needed most. He looked at the phone and said, "Shawna, if you know a way to reach your mother ..."

"I already left a message on Tyler's cellphone."

"Oh, then your mother will be here tomorrow night."

"Don't count on it. Tyler's family? They live way up north. They have to drive, like, an hour to get a cellphone to work."

Digital signals travel by line of sight, Foster knew. Tyler's family must be quite a distance from a communications tower. What kind of people were they, living so far from civilization? Foster imagined a weather-beaten shack, a broken down stove on the front porch, a yard full of derelict cars.

"Never mind. You and I can handle it." Foster gave Shawna an encouraging smile. It would help to know what they were up against. "Who do they send? What kind of person?"

"Last time? We got Little Miss Moony. Total space cadet."

"Why are they snooping around?" Foster asked, trying to make the question seem casual.

Shawna shrugged. "They think Mom's a flake."

"I see." There was a history here, a story Mary hadn't told him. Or had she? He remembered a phone call he had taken at Duboco. Had Mary said something about getting Shawna back? "Shawna, this interview could be important."

"Yeah, I know. I'll wear my soccer uniform and we'll say you're taking me to a game after the interview. We should put some library books on the coffee table. When they come, I'll be doing my homework. Television's got to be off."

It worried him to hear Shawna speak with such calculation. He got to his feet, put a hand on her shoulder and stared through the patio door at the basket-weave fence. Nobody pushes Daniel Foster around, and nobody was going to give his granddaughter a hard time. Tomorrow night he would send Little Miss Moony packing.

AFTER SHAWNA HAD gone to bed, Foster sat at the kitchen table, staring at the swing set, wondering if he had done enough. It hurt him to see Shawna so afraid. Was the house ready for inspection? He thought for a moment, then went down the hall, opened the door to Mary's bedroom and switched on the light. The walls could use a coat of paint.

He had moved the furniture into the centre of the room and covered everything with a plastic drop sheet when he noticed a box on the floor. It must have fallen from a drawer when he had shifted Mary's dressing table. He picked up the box, stared at it — and felt a visceral shock. A pale green box from Tiffany & Co. on Fifth Avenue. The pearl necklace he had given Kathleen to celebrate Mary's birth. When Kathleen wore the necklace, light flowed through the pearls, as if they conducted some inner force. The clasp was tricky. Did Mary know how it worked? Foster couldn't make himself open the box. It contained more than the necklace; it held love and sorrow. He uncovered the dressing table, put the box in a drawer, pulled the drop sheet back and went to get the paint.

[NINETEEN]

EARLY THE NEXT morning, Foster rode the IndTemps van to a garden centre. He spent the day steering wheelbarrow loads of sand down a long aisle that ran between tables of marigolds. Buzzatti, the patriarch who ran the business with his sons and daughters, had a beakish nose and a fringe of snowy hair. Slip a toga on Buzzatti and you'd have Julius Caesar. *The fault, dear Brutus, is not in our stars, But in ourselves …*

After the workday, Buzzatti came walking over to the picnic table where Foster sat waiting for the IndTemps van with the other temporaries. Buzzatti opened a tin of biscuits, clinked down glasses, tugged a cork from an unlabelled bottle and poured out generous measures of red wine. "Salute!" Buzzatti said, lifting his glass. Foster took a sip. The homemade wine had a rich, dark flavour.

Like the other men at the table, he went home carrying a bottle of homemade wine. The little ceremony at the picnic table touched him. He would give a party for Shawna, he decided. Invite her soccer team. He pictured the living room bright with balloons, the furniture shoved aside, the children laughing and dancing. He would invite Jessica. They would pick up where they had left off, and then he would leave for

Micronesia. These last two propositions, Jessica and Micronesia, were contradictory, Foster knew. But accommodating contradiction is the basic skill of expatriate life.

Traffic was slow, and he arrived home later than he had intended. He bustled through the townhouse, cleaning and tidying and inspecting. In the bathroom he centred the mat and aligned the towels. In the kitchen he cleaned the patio door, polished the appliances and, for a finishing touch, set the bottle of wine on the counter. In the living room he ranked the glass animals on their shelf, lined up the books, fluffed the cushions. His eyes settled on the beanbag chair, and he carried it out the front door and around the house to the back lane where, to his great satisfaction, he tossed it in a dumpster. When he was overseas, he would send money to replace the rest of the furniture.

Pleased by this thought, Foster went back inside and strode down the hall. The doors should be open, Shawna had decided. He went to Mary's bedroom, hesitated, then opened the door halfway. One room left to check, the middle room he had occupied for almost a year. The sofa bed was folded away, the ironing board stored. Those toolboxes shouldn't be sitting there in plain sight. But where to put them? The closet was full; he had stashed the exercise bike in there, along with the rest of the stuff Tyler hadn't taken with him. Foster lugged his tools out to the van and covered them with an old blanket.

When Shawna came rushing in from school, Foster was standing in the hallway, triple checking the set-up. She dashed past him and disappeared into the bathroom. She was spending more time in there these days, he noticed. But tonight, with the Social Services appointment only a few minutes away, she didn't linger. He was in the living room, fluffing the cushions again, when Shawna came down the hall in her soccer uniform, brushing her hair as she went.

"Shouldn't I wear a shirt and tie?" Foster said, looking down at his jeans.

"Casual is better," Shawna said. "There's a soccer game later and you're taking me. Shows supportive routine."

"Supportive routine?"

"It's on the form they fill out."

"How do you know it's on the form?"

"I swiped a copy last time. When Moon Girl went to the can."

"Oh," Foster said. "Did I put a fresh roll of toilet paper in the bathroom? Is the air freshener on?"

"I turned it off. The pine smell made me puke."

Foster looked at Shawna with sudden concern. "You mean you actually threw up?"

Shawna pointed to the couch. "Maybe you should be reading my math text."

"I don't need to."

Shawna shook her head. "They don't know that."

The doorbell rang.

"I'll go," Shawna said, waving him back in his seat.

As Shawna walked to the door, Foster opened the math textbook and composed himself for the little drama they had rehearsed. Voices buzzed from the front door. He touched his forehead, ran his fingertips over the scar. He would mention the injury himself. Injured on the job. Shows responsibility. He glanced at the kitchen. The kettle was just off the boil. He would offer tea or coffee. What if Miss Moony asked for orange juice? There was a can in the freezer.

"Hey, Foster!" Shawna was pulling someone into the room. She was beaming. You're overplaying it, Foster thought. Take it down a notch. Okay, he told himself, you're on. Stand up, put on a smile, offer Miss Moony your hand.

But the woman at the end of Shawna's arm wasn't Miss Moony.

It was Mary.

With Tyler a step behind, carrying a shopping bag.

They hadn't rehearsed this scenario, he and Shawna, and Foster was taken aback. Did Mary know her lines? His daughter wore a white track suit that looked fresh from a store. She didn't look any different otherwise. No, the blond streaks in her hair were new. With Shawna clinging to her, Mary gave Foster a peck on the cheek.

"How are you, Mr. Foster?" Tyler said, with a deference that seemed as new as his shirt and tie. He was holding Mary's hand.

Mary looked around and gave Foster a puzzled look. The doorbell sounded again. Shawna hurried across the carpet and disappeared into the hallway.

"Somebody bop you one?" Tyler asked, looking at Foster's head.

Foster didn't have time to reply. "Guys?" Shawna said. "This is Regina."

The social worker stationed herself on one end of the couch. Mary took the other end. Shawna sat beside her mother. With the beanbag gone, they were one chair short. Before Foster could do anything about this, Tyler went to the kitchen, came back with a chair and offered it to him. Mary looked at the chair as if she were seeing it for the first time. Which she was. Yesterday, with the last of his ready cash, Foster had replaced the kitchen set.

"Well, now," Regina said brightly. The Foster family turned their heads in unison. They might have been posing for a photographer. "Why don't we go round the circle and introduce ourselves?"

"I'm Shawna's grandfather." Foster studied the social worker. She was tidily made and attractive in a smoky, Mediterranean way. Her summer dress seemed daring for the occasion. She had long, shapely legs. Foster raised his eyes. Grandpas weren't supposed to notice such things.

"Hi," Shawna said.

Mary gave Regina a curt nod.

"My name isTyler," Tyler said. "I'm Mary's fiancé."

Fiancé? Foster's heart sank like one of Cedric's tankers. Mary had come home. They would talk later. She wasn't going to marry Tyler.

"Oh, dear," Regina said, fumbling through her briefcase. "I know my notes are in here somewhere." She tucked her knees to one side, exposing a long slash of thigh. Foster raised his eyes.

"That's the wrong form," Shawna said.

Regina looked at Shawna shrewdly. Well, well, Foster thought. The Ditsy Miss Moonbeam bit was an act.

"Today at school?" Shawna said. "We got this math test back? I got a C+."

Foster tried to catch Shawna's eye. She wasn't sticking to the script. She was supposed to hand the math test to the social worker. "Shawna, that's wonderful," he said, not waiting for his cue. "What an improvement! I'm very proud of you."

"We all are," Mary said.

Shawna rattled off her speech about soccer. She seemed to have lost interest in the little play she had coached Foster through. She ran out of steam and was complimented by all.

"Got something for you." Tyler reached into the shopping bag, pulled out an expensive-looking soccer ball and handed it to Shawna.

Why hadn't I thought of that? Foster wondered.

"Hey!" Shawna said. "Neat!"

"What about you, Mary?" Regina said. "How was your day?"

"Fine."

Regina's smile tightened. "You're still with ..." A glance at her notes. "Secure-All?"

"Yes."

"And how long have you been there?"

"A while."

"Did you go to work today?"

"No. I've been on holiday."

"You've been away," Regina prompted.

Mary said nothing.

"You've got to see my room," Shawna said, taking Regina by the hand and tugging her to her feet. "It's awesome."

While Shawna was leading Regina down the hall, Foster reached for the math test. What did Shawna need to work on?

"Where have I been, Foster?" Mary asked in a whisper. "What did you tell them?"

Did the truth matter? Not at the moment. In the face of danger they would erect a barricade of fiction. Like any family. "I said you'd gone to visit Ella."

"Ella Chudzik?" Mary stared at him.

Tyler gave the television a longing glance. Did they still ask that question at weddings, if anyone here knows a reason …? Foster imagined himself leaping to his feet, saving his daughter from making a terrible mistake.

Shawna came back into the room with Regina, who looked at Mary and said, "The room looks terrific. You and Shawna did a great job."

"Thanks." Mary glanced over at Foster with a question in her eyes.

"May I be excused?" Shawna said, addressing no one in particular. "I have a soccer game."

"Yes, we should be on our way," Foster said, though Shawna was jumping the gun by a good half hour. Glad of the chance to escape, he got to his feet and took his keys from his pocket.

"Tyler will take you," Mary told Shawna.

Shawna looked at Foster. Foster nodded. As he sat slowly down, he saw Regina's eyebrows lift, and he put on a stone face. Little Miss Sharpie was taking everything in.

"Got your stuff, Shawn?" Tyler said, laying a hand on Shawna's shoulder.

Shawn?

“Thank you for showing me your room,” Regina said.

The front door closed. “Fine host I am.” Foster said. “Would anyone like some tea?” He remembered the bottle of wine. “Or something stronger?”

Regina looked at Mary with sudden concern. An uneasy silence settled in. Foster was baffled.

“I’ve been clean and sober for five years, if that’s what you’re wondering,” Mary said. “Not that it’s any of your business.”

“That wound on your forehead,” Regina said, turning to Foster. “How did it happen?”

Why was she asking him this? “A shelf fell on me.”

Regina frowned. “How many drinks do you have each day, Mr. Foster? One? Two? Three? Five?”

One, two three, five. A Fibonacci series, Foster thought. Each number is formed by adding the previous two consecutive numbers. The next member was eight. Three plus five. And then he was very angry. “What gives you the right to ask me that?”

“Shawna’s safety,” Regina said flatly.

“Safety? What are you hinting at?” Foster wanted to throw Regina out on her ear.

The room echoed with thumping music. A car with a monster sound system going down the street, Foster thought as the sound faded.

“This is about Mom.”

Mom? Foster looked at his daughter, mystified. What did Kathleen have to do with this?

“Mr. Foster …”

“He’s not a drunk,” Mary said.

“But you drink,” Regina said to Foster.

“He has a beer sometimes,” Mary said.

“According to Mrs. Patterson.” Regina flipped through her file “You came to the school confused and disoriented.”

"I did no such thing."

"Are you willing to admit your behaviour was inappropriate?"

"Inappropriate?"

"The wrong way to act under the circumstances."

"I know what the word means," Foster said hotly.

"She says you came on to her."

Mary closed her eyes for a moment. Foster looked away, wondering why the conversation had taken this troubling turn.

"What did you say to Mrs. Patterson?" Mary said.

"I don't know," Foster said. His daughter was watching him skeptically. "Maybe I told her how nice she looked. It was just a little harmless flirting."

"Flirting," Regina said.

Yes, the word was quaint. Like court and woo, flirt had been put out to pasture long ago, replaced by tougher words that saddened Foster. Regina turned to Mary. "How often is your father in charge of Shawna?"

"Occasionally."

"And you have no concerns about that arrangement?"

"No."

Good for you, Foster thought, proud of his daughter for stonewalling this busybody. No one spoke for a moment. The fridge cycled on. Mary folded her arms. Regina riffled through her papers, sat in thoughtful silence, then said, "From what your father said, Mrs. Patterson thought you had been away for some time."

"He gets confused," Mary said.

Confused? Foster sat in angry silence while Regina asked more questions and Mary answered them in monosyllables. He was out of the loop. It was as if he were no longer in the room. He had become a non-person, a piece of baggage, a candidate for a nursing home. An appalling thought came to him. *Serenity Lodge phoned*, Mary would tell Shawna someday. *Grandpa passed away in his sleep.*

"There seems to have been a misunderstanding," Regina said, breaking another silence. Her expression suggested that she did not believe this to be the case. Gathering her papers together, she turned to Mary. "I'd like to come again next month. See how you're getting along."

"Whatever," Mary said.

"Goodbye, Mr. Foster," Regina said, leaning forward and raising her voice. "It was nice to meet you."

Mary looked at Regina and in a firm voice said, "I'll show you to the door."

Foster said nothing. Alone for a moment, he wondered what other secrets Mary had kept from him. "What was all that about Kathleen?" he said when Mary came back into the room.

"I was going through a rough patch. Mom moved in. She was drinking ..." Mary sat down and ran her hand over a cushion. "I fell off the wagon. They took Shawna away until I got my act together."

While I was under a beach umbrella, Foster thought. Another rueful truth had come his way. And here was another reason to accept Cedric's offer and get out while the getting was good. Because if you hang around here, fella, one morning you will look in a mirror and ask, is that broken old failure really me? That's you, baby, the caregiver will say, steering your wheelchair through the corridors of Serenity Lodge. And there's Jell-O for dessert.

Mary was looking at the chair Tyler had brought into the room.

"If you don't like the new kitchen set, you can take it back," Foster said. "I set up a filing system. Let me show you." They went to the kitchen. Foster opened a drawer and dealt file folders on the counter. "Red folder, unpaid bills. Green folder, paid bills and receipts. Purple folder ..."

Mary opened a cupboard door. "You've changed everything!" She closed her eyes for a moment. "You were trying to help." She went back to the living room and began picking up school books. She looked down the hall. "I should see Shawna's room."

They walked down the hall. Foster opened the door and switched on the light. "Shawna picked out the Etruscan yellow. Jessica suggested Sap Green for the trim, and I —"

"Jessica? That woman you were going out with?"

"She was glad to help," Foster said. "You weren't here," he added. And immediately wished he hadn't.

Mary stepped into the room and looked around with a troubled expression. "Where's the dollhouse? Where are Shawna's books?"

"I threw them out."

"You did what?! Garbage day is tomorrow. Shawna's things will still be around back."

"Mary," Foster began. How could he say this? "When Shawna found out that someone from social services was coming, she threw … well, a temper tantrum, and she wrecked her room."

Mary took this like a blow. "Tyler and I needed space," she said in a slow, precise voice, as if she were thinking aloud. "We had to get away. I didn't want to lose him. You'll like Tyler when you get to know him. I knew Shawna would be okay with you." Mary gave Foster a puzzled look. "Why did you go to see Shawna's teacher?"

"I found the letter about the parent-teacher night."

"Oh." Mary looked away. "I see."

They moved down the hall. Eager to make amends, Foster opened the door to the middle room and ushered Mary in. "Only a few changes here. I painted the walls."

"Where's Tyler's stuff?"

"In the closet."

Mary nodded. Foster couldn't read her expression. But then, he never could. They went down the hall to Mary's bedroom.

"What the hell? Foster!"

"The room needed painting. Jessica picked the colour and …" His voice trailed off. If Mary was angry about the change to her room, he would take the blame.

"You brought that woman into my house?" Mary put her hands on her hips and glared at Foster. "Was she looking after my daughter?"

"Jessica and I aren't together," Foster said, offering the fact as an excuse.

"So you come on to Mrs. Patterson. Don't give me that look. Mom told me plenty."

"Kathleen?" Foster said, taken aback. "What did Kathleen tell you?"

"Anything in a skirt," Mary said in an uncanny imitation of Kathleen's lilt. "That's our Danny."

"That's not fair," Foster said, angry now. "And I did not come on to Mrs. Patterson."

"Why did you say I was staying with Ella?"

"Shawna had a soccer game. Out in the suburbs, near where we used to live. I left Shawna at the game and I drove to Regent Heights. Ella was there and —"

"You left Shawna at the game? You didn't stay?" Mary threw up her hands. "You went on your merry way. Just like you dumped Mom. Other people aren't real to you, Foster. You only care about yourself."

"Listen," Foster began. His anger had given way to a heartsick fatigue. He looked at Mary. The argument was pushing them to the edge. He had known many expatriates who were estranged from their family. It was a heavy loneliness to bear. He might as well get straight to the point. "You don't have to marry Tyler right away. Why don't you wait, think it over for a while?"

"We have waited." They were in the living room now, Foster standing in the doorway, looking at his daughter, Mary sitting on the couch, staring down at the carpet. "Tyler and I talked a lot while we were away. He wants to be a policeman. He's going back to school. There's a police studies program at a community college. I'll keep working and —"

"You're going to put that freeloader through school? Mary, he's just using you. Can't you see that?"

Mary took a deep breath, let it out slowly. "The wedding is at Secure-All. Saturday afternoon at four. You can bring your lady friend if you like."

"Secure-All? Because Tyler can't afford a banquet hall, I suppose. No. I won't come to the wedding."

Mary seemed not to hear this. "You're good with Shawna. I never knew my grandparents. I want her to have that. I want you to have that."

"Marriage is a big step. Tell Tyler you want to think it over. Once I'm set up in Micronesia —"

"Micronesia?" Mary stared at him.

"A job has come up. A job that pays well. Once I'm set up, I'll send money."

His daughter looked at him for a long moment. "You don't play fair, Foster. You didn't want us in your life, not really. You were only passing through." She waved a hand at him. "Get out. Go."

Stunned by his daughter's dismissal, Foster walked out the front door and into the summer night. A cat sprang from the darkness, leapt onto a fence and stared at him with blazing eyes. A train rumbled in the distance. The distant, shuffling rhythm carried Foster into the past. For a moment it seemed that his life lay ahead of him, its promises intact, its paths unexplored. He stood beside Charlie's old van, wondering if he should go back inside and talk to Mary — I've come for my things, he would say. But then he looked into the van and saw his tools sitting in the cargo area, covered with a blanket. There was nothing to go back for.

THE WORLD SHRINKS when you're broke, Foster thought as he started the van. Your options dwindle. Where could he go at this time of night with thirteen dollars in his pocket and the gas gauge knocking on empty?

Jessica stood in the doorway with her arms crossed. She heard him out, and then she said, "So you cut and ran."

Foster stared at her. Cut and ran? On the drive to Jessica's loft, he had convinced himself that he was the injured party, that the argument had been Mary's fault.

"I can't do this, Foster. Bail you out when you're in trouble, then get pushed away."

It would always be like this between them, Foster thought. Jessica tossing jabs that he would try to block. He couldn't block them all, though. Sometimes she would land a good one. Such as the truth she had just spoken. It was just as well that he was heading off to Micronesia. "It's just for a couple of days. Until I go to London. I'll sleep on the couch, stay out of your way."

Jessica sighed. She closed her eyes for a moment, then nodded. Foster had let his guard down, and the fact that she was taking him in hit him hard.

[TWENTY]

WHY WAS EVERYTHING made of marble? The floors, the walls, sure, that made sense, but the light bulbs? The windows? The furniture? How did they expect him to run programs on marble computers? Print reports on marble paper? Foster's long strides carried him through a palace as big as Grandpa's Toolbox. *Action!* someone cried. A dozen doors opened at once and women came walking toward him, women without faces. *You don't play fair*, they said. The cameras turned his way. The next line was his. What was he supposed to say? A telephone rang.

"But you promised," Jessica said. "Jerk!" She slammed down the phone.

Foster got up from the couch and belted his robe, pondering the dream. He had played fair, told Jessica about the job in Micronesia, stayed out of her way. Tomorrow he would be off to London.

"Foster? The gallery guy won't pick up my stuff. Can you drive me?"

"Yes."

"Can we take your van? I'll pay for the gas."

"Okay."

"Look, if you can't take me, it's okay. I'll rent a truck." Jessica looked around frantically. "Have you seen the phone book?"

"I said yes! I'll drive you to the gallery."

"The gallery is in Walter's Bay. Do you have a map? I'll find a map."

"I know how to get there."

"Can we leave before rush hour?

"Yes."

"Can we leave right away?"

"Yes."

"Listen. Are you sure about this?"

"Stop saying that. Okay? Just stop."

"Why are you so angry? I can't deal with your — what's wrong? Why are you staring at me like that?"

Jessica stood by the windows. She had on a pair of raw silk trousers and a peasant blouse of rough-spun cotton. He shouldn't have come here. But what else could he have done, with so few dollars in his pocket?

"I can rent a truck."

"Make coffee."

"Coffee? I've been drinking coffee all night. Oh, for you. Right." Jessica rushed into the kitchen.

Foster flat-footed his way around the wrapped canvases, stumbled over a toolbox and stared gloomily down at the clothes he had brought in from the van. What does the well-dressed human failure wear to an art gallery? He put on a pair of jeans, pulled on a black T-shirt, scooped a handful of coins and dumped them into his pocket. The coins rained down on his foot. The pocket had no bottom. He had forgotten about that little problem.

"Here's your coffee. Look, if you —"

"I'll unlock the van." On the way to the door Foster caught his reflection in a mirror. Life is a movie. He was playing the role of Frankenstein's monster. The scar on his forehead was the crowning touch.

THEY MADE THEIR way out of the city, speeding past the commuters trapped in the heavy traffic heading the other way. You don't play fair. The accusation gnawed at him. Did Jessica think it was true? A sideways glance convinced him not to ask. She was in finger-in-a-light-socket mode, fidgeting on her seat, staring through the windshield, then out the side window, then through the windshield again. Hearing a muffled rattle, he gave the dashboard a worried look. Was something wrong with the van?

"Your cellphone is ringing."

"Oh, shit, shit, shit, shit!" Jessica pulled out the phone, looked at the display, threw the phone into her purse and slammed back in her seat. She crossed her arms. Uncrossed them. Threw down the purse and kicked it.

After a moment Foster said, "Was that Mary?"

"What? No!" Jessica brooded for a moment. "It was the gallery."

They drove along in silence. The traffic thinned. Four lanes narrowed to two. They were rolling up Highway 10, retracing one of Irv's sales routes. Shelburne. Flesherton. Markdale. Berkeley. Holland Centre. Chatsworth. Hardware stores with tin ceilings. The scent of kerosene and galvanized metal. *Take a walk, Danny. I've got a story to tell Mr. Lomax, and it's not for the innocent.*

In the ditches, loosestrife and lupine wove a pattern of purple and blue. The fields were a patchwork of yellow and green. It would take time to adjust to Micronesia, with its year-round rain. It didn't matter. As long as there were places to walk.

JESSICA GRABBED HIS arm. "There's the turn off!"

"I see it." Foster yanked his arm free.

"Over there!" Jessica shouted when they were halfway down Main Street. "Beside the antique store!"

"Yes, I see it. Wait!"

Too late. She was out of the van, thumping on the back window. The moment he snapped the locks she threw up the tailgate, scrambled into the storage area and ran her hands over the cargo. "It's okay. Nothing's damaged. It's okay. It's okay."

Why would anything be damaged? Did the woman think he couldn't drive properly? Trooping after Jessica with a blanketed picture in his arms he wondered idly what she had been painting all these months. More blurry flowers?

The art gallery had windows of wavy glass and a front door of tiger oak. A bell jingled as he walked in.

"You're in the back." The sleekly groomed man had a three-day beard and a lot of attitude. Jessica gave him a miffed look and marched past. Foster followed her over a floor of honey-toned pine, blackened where store fixtures had once stood. The sidewalls — rough brick on the right, wallboard on the left — ran to an end wall covered in cork. The big room was lit by track lights. In its centre stood a dozen chairs. Foster looked up at a pressed tin ceiling, saw a pattern of roses, and knew the art gallery had been Lomax Hardware, the northern terminus of Irv's Grey-Bruce swing. Clifford Lomax had blown the whistle on Irv and testified against him at the trial. Grandma had pressed the newspaper clippings like flowers in her Bible, preserving them between the onion-skin pages of the Book of Isaiah. *The wilderness and the solitary place shall be glad for them,* she would declaim while her son served time in the slammer, *and the desert shall rejoice, and blossom as the rose.*

"Can I help?" Foster asked Jessica after they had unloaded the van.

She shooed him away. "I'll hang the show myself."

"Fine." Foster was glad to escape. On his way to the door he took a brochure from a literature rack: *A Walking Tour of Historic Walter's Bay.*

He stood outside the gallery. Mist rose from the roads. A cardinal called. The wheet, wheet, wheet came from a side street, and Foster set off in that direction. He had walked the town often as a boy, but there was always another path to explore.

The Georgian manor on the right was Harkness House, Foster learned as he walked along with the brochure in his hand. The Harknesses, founders of the Thistle Line, had come here from Strathclyde in 1852. The *Nyaw* and the *Nyanin* were the last ships to fly the Thistle flag.

At the intersection of King and Queen he stopped to inspect a church, a barn of a building with a bell tower and lancet windows. Beside the church, in a cemetery shaded by maples, monuments occupied the high ground. Did Clifford Lomax, whistle-blower and witness for the prosecution, lie under one of those obelisks? The maples had undermined the monuments with their roots, tipped the marble into comic angles. Foster looked at the brochure. During the town's long-ago boom the Lomaxes had made out like bandits. Barnabas Lomax, an Evangelical from Pennsylvania, had made a killing in lumber, cutting down the first growth forest. There was a different name on the mailbox. The Lomaxes had been cut down in turn.

Foster followed a path that led down to the river and into Jubilee Park. Near the bandstand, a wedding party struck a pose. He would hurry over, get into the picture, stand beside Mary. A photographer stepped to a tripod and the men in tuxedos and the women in gowns became strangers. It had poured rain the day he married Kathleen, despite the rosary she had hung on a clothesline to ward off the clouds. Foster walked on to the harbour and found it empty.

Tea & Thee had been the Union Bank, Foster remembered as he walked up Main Street. The rambling structure on the left, the offices of an accounting firm, had been the Victoria Hotel. There was a gap in the street where the McKenzie Department Store had stood, with its waxy mannequins and its overhead change trolley that ferried money to a central cashier. He stared into the window of a bookshop. A man with a high-water haircut and a starched white jacket seemed to stare back at him. Dexter's Drugs had stocked hemorrhoid remedies and hot water bottles, ice cream and comic books. The door swung open and a woman emerged carrying a basket of books. She was Jessica's age, or a little younger. She wore a denim dress and she smelled of patchouli. Setting the basket of books beside the door, she invited Foster to come in and look around. Dexter's aspirin and smelling salts had vanished; his gold-lettered displays (*Dental*, *Health*, *Beauty*) were covered with flimsy cardboard signs (*Fiction*, *Non-Fiction*, *New Age*). Next to the cash register was a stack of business books, with Gary Garth's *Never Business as Usual* on top, and in front of the cash stood an antique wheelbarrow loaded with romance novels. Foster picked one up, remembering *Larissa's Longing*, the novel he had tackled after Mary went off with Tyler.

"You'd be surprised how many men read them."

Foster nodded, flipping the pages while the woman in the peasant dress talked on. Her name was Vera. She had opened the store a year ago. She didn't miss the city. She loved Walter's Bay. It was wonderful that Foster was a reader. This wasn't true, but he let the impression stand, smiled and said how much he liked the store. When she smiled back at him and patted her hair, he wondered if he was flirting with her.

"Were you looking for anything in particular?"

He had to say something. "Books about Micronesia."

Vera went to a shelf and came back with a thin volume. Its title was *Oceanien*. The text was in German; the book had been published a hundred years ago. Foster leafed through a series of sepia images. There was a picture of a sand beach with palm trees in the background, a picture of a family, three generations posed stiffly before a house with a thatched roof. The women were bare-breasted. They wore grass skirts. In another picture a woolly-haired man with a round belly strolled down a path with a pig at his side and a stick in his hand. *Der Konig*, the caption read. Foster had to smile. The king with the pig and stick looked like a happy man. Though he couldn't spare the money, Foster paid for *Oceanien*, tucked it under his arm and said goodbye to Vera. And goodbye to you, Mr. Dexter, he thought as he went through the door. Give Mr. Lomax my regards. I'm off to paradise.

There were racks of DVDs in Tea & Thee, and movie posters on the walls. When Jessica burst into the café, Foster was sitting at a marble-topped table, studying the contract Cedric had sent by email. She dropped heavily into the opposite chair. "The bastard gave me the back wall."

"The one with cork on it?"

"Yes, the one with fucking cork on it!" Jessica made a face. "Know what you see when you walk in? Seascapes on the right, barnyards on the left."

Cannon to right of them, cannon to left of them, Foster thought.

"If you walk, oh, about a mile, you get to my stuff. It's like the bottom of a well back there."

"As bad as that?"

"Bad? It's a disaster. The light's all wrong. You can hear the fridge running." Jessica picked up a little package of sugar and worried it to pieces with her fingers. Sugar drizzled onto the table. "And that fucking cork ..." She slouched in her chair like a boxer who wasn't coming out for the next round. "What do you think? Should we pack everything back in the car?"

She was asking him, Mr. Cut and Run, the man who wasn't going to his daughter's wedding? Lady, you got the wrong guy. I hired on as a chauffeur, not a life coach. Gary Garth was right. People want you to fix them. "Let's go for a drive."

Jessica followed him dejectedly to the van. They drove past a row of antique stores with flags on their porches and flower boxes under their windows, cruised through a landscape of rolling hills and stony beaches. The sun dazzled the bay. Poplars lined the road, spinning their leaves in the wind.

"How's Shawna?" Jessica asked out of the blue. "You said you called last night."

"They were doing the dishes. They had Shawna's music on. Shawna was giggling. I think they were bumping hips. Mary wouldn't come to the phone. Not that it matters. She wouldn't listen to me anyway. Tyler has her wrapped around his little finger."

"Know something?" Jessica said, in that decisive, classroom tone of hers. "You're jealous."

"Don't be ridiculous."

"Okay, I'm ridiculous. I can't paint for shit and I'm ridiculous." She looked out the side window. "Maybe I'll paint a picture with a cow in it." After a moment, Jessica said, "Has it ever occurred to you that she loves the guy?"

"Love has nothing to do with it."

"Right," Jessica said. "Of course. Silly me."

They drifted along back roads, Jessica staring at the passing scenery, Foster making mental notes on the contract. Remuneration: Adequate. Annual leave: Sufficient. Housing: Unsatisfactory. Suitable accommodation provided, the contract said. You might slip that vague promise past a rookie, he thought as he turned onto a concession road, but he knew the ropes. He would stipulate a villa. Something suitable for Mary and Shawna when they came to visit. He glanced at Jessica. She was staring at the sky, her hair lifting in the breeze. He would need a Land Rover to take him to the walking trails. It wouldn't have to be new; a recent model would do. The road rose, swerved, dwindled to a circle of yellow earth. He had wandered into a dead end. He switched off the ignition and sat gripping the steering wheel. After a moment he got out of the van and walked over to a guardrail.

Beyond the guardrail, the ground fell away sharply. They were on the edge of a cliff. Foster shaded his eyes and peered into the distance. It was a northern landscape, an expanse of blue and grey and green. A landscape of layers — plateau and pine, horizon and cloud. The changing light gave it an elusive quality, a beauty that defied possession.

"Have you seen my sketch pad?" Jessica asked. She was standing by the van. The tailgate was open.

"I put it under the floor. In the storage bin."

"Under the packing blankets?"

"Wait, I'll show you." By the time Foster reached the van, Jessica had crawled into the cargo area.

"How does the floor come up?" Jessica asked.

"Pull that tab."

Jessica yanked at a loop of red vinyl. "It doesn't come up."

"You've got your weight on it."

"I don't have my weight on it."

"Lift your right knee. No, lift your — never mind." Foster crawled in beside her. "Pardon me."

"Uh-huh," Jessica said, pawing through a pile of quilted blankets.

To steady himself, Foster put his hand on the small of her back. His hand travelled over silk, spread its fingers, slid under a hem. His hand had a will of its own. The part of his mind that was still making notes found the phenomenon interesting. Jessica grew still under his touch. Their eyes met. Wanting her desperately now, Foster tugged down the tailgate. He turned to see Jessica reclining on a makeshift bed of packing blankets, a woman waiting to gather him in.

AFTER THEIR LOVEMAKING, Jessica settled against him with her head on his chest and her leg angled over his thigh. Foster cupped a hand around her shoulder, felt her relax — and wondered if the last half hour of his life was the sort of behaviour Mary had in mind when she had accused him of not playing fair. A shadow crossed his line of vision. Was there an airfield nearby? Turning his head he saw a Cessna coming in for a landing, its engine murmuring as gravity brought the little monoplane gliding down.

Neither spoke on the way back to town. Foster glanced at the dashboard clock, and then at the cloudless sky. Only a few hours to Mary's wedding. It wouldn't rain. He was glad of that. When they reached the art gallery, he nosed the van in front of a silver BMW, parking with the front wheels angled toward the highway and nothing between the van and the open road, a trick he had learned from Irv, the master of the quick getaway.

Jessica gazed at the art gallery. "Foster, I don't know."

"Oh, come on," Foster said with sudden impatience.

They stepped through the front door and into a buzz of talk and jazz. Jessica squared her shoulders and marched toward the back wall with her head held high. Alone again, Foster took in the scene. These were cottage people, he thought, rich retirees spicing their summer with a dash of culture. The women wore party dresses, the men cargo pants and safari shirts, or, Foster was amazed to see, ragtag costumes like his own mismatch of jeans, T-shirt, and suit jacket. Shawna's thrift shop look was in. The bar was on the other side of the room. He sidled his way through the crowd.

"Club soda," he said to the bartender.

"Ice?"

"Yes." It had been hot in the van.

"Now, I'd have thought we'd had enough ice, kind of winter we had," said a hearty voice.

Foster turned his head. The owner of the voice had a tanned face and a golfer's squint. "Gabe Petrie," the man said, clasping Foster's hand in a delicate grip.

"Now, don't tell me," Petrie said after Foster introduced himself. Petrie frowned thoughtfully at Foster's palm. "You live in the city, but you're sick of it. So you're going to move up here to God's country, buy a house from Gabe Petrie and live happily ever after."

When Foster took back his hand, there was a business card between his fingers. "I'm not in the market for a house." He gazed over the crowd, looking for Jessica. He should keep an eye on her, just as Sal and Tom and Charlie had kept an eye on him at Grandpa Camp.

"Then you're here to buy a picture." Petrie led Foster to a wall where small canvases hung at eye level.

How many hours had he spent leafing through Jessica's art books? Enough to learn the basics: the rule of thirds, figure and ground, harmony, negative space. Under the pressure of Petrie's gaze, Foster studied a seascape. A cliff. A shore. Streaky waves crashing on doughy rocks. Seagulls soaring picturesquely. The paint had been applied in light, fussy strokes. Foster nodded. He might not know what he liked, but he knew bad art when he saw it. Shawna had done better, Mrs. Patterson be damned. Foster peered at a display card. "Beach Idyll." Jane Petrie. Two hundred and fifty dollars.

"Quite the little artist, isn't she?"

"Um." Foster felt a tingle of interest. In his role as liaison officer for Cedric's band of oil-pumping pirates, he would need his diplomatic skills. "The allusions to postcards are playful."

Petrie looked at the painting and then at Foster.

"I like this one best," Foster said, moving to a view of a lighthouse. "It has a sense of moment, a balance of mass and colour." Also, it had fewer seagulls.

"You're too late," Petrie said. "It's sold. See the little red dot?"

"Well, that's good."

Petrie studied Foster, his eyebrows lifting skeptically. He has seen through me, Foster thought; if I can't beguile this back country wallah, what were my chances of snowing the bigwigs of Palikir?

"You're the man in the pictures," Petrie said.

Puzzled by this remark, Foster followed him to the back of the room. The two men stood before one of Jessica's paintings. As Foster stared, the male nude seemed to detach itself from the wall and advance toward him. Painted in pastels, the composition had an affecting rhythm. Lines flowed from the chest to the feet like grooves in bark. Twigs sprouted from the fingertips. The painting reminded Foster of a sculpture he had seen in one of Jessica's books. He thought for a moment and came up with the reference. Bernini's *Apollo and Daphne.* Pursued by Apollo, Daphne took root, changed into a laurel tree. Jessica had turned the tables, given Foster the tree treatment.

"Makes me glad Jane sticks to seagulls."

"Um," Foster said. Although its face was in shadow, the figure was unmistakably him. Small things define us: the curve of a shoulder, the angle of a thumb. Jessica had changed her style completely. No more vague flowers. It was a gutsy thing to do. Foster peered at a white tag. "Man #3" had sold for six hundred and fifty dollars.

"Interesting use of mass and colour," Petrie said, with a sidelong glance at Foster.

They moved to the next painting. In "Man #7," the figure had morphed into a manatee. Its wide flat tail and paddle-like arms were comic. And yet there was something tragic in the figure's expression. Manatee or not, this was recognizably him as well. Foster tried to work out Jessica's intent. Manatees were facing extinction; wounded by propellers, they bled to death while pleasure boats whizzed by. Did Jessica see him as an endangered species? Or was the creature's thick skin the clue?

"I like the way the artist thinks," Petrie said, studying the next painting. Foster looked at Petrie. He seemed sincere. "Man #1" was composed of math symbols. The figure's eyes were minus signs, its nose a plus sign, its mouth a pair of set brackets; its skin was covered with numbers. It had a demon's tail and a saint's halo, and over its private parts it clasped a software manual.

"Nice to meet you," Petrie said, starting for the front of the room, where a couple was browsing the seascapes.

Grateful to be left alone, Foster scanned the rest of Jessica's work. *I like the way the artist thinks.* Did these visual puns constitute a logical system? The idea made Foster dizzy. He looked across the room. Jessica was watching him.

"YOU'RE JUST A donkey they've rented," the tea boy had whispered when the sheiks cut Foster loose. An expatriate lives by maxims — keep your passport handy, know the fastest way to the airport — but the bit about the donkey trumped them all. After the axe had fallen that September morning, Foster had taken a pad of paper and made a list, a task he was starting again, in a defunct bank in a declining town on the other side of the world.

There were no other customers in Tea & Thee, and the mood music, a tranquilizing mix of harps and pan pipes, had lapsed into silence. He put a check mark next to "review contract." There was the villa to ask about, and there was nothing in the agreement about a death benefit, in case he died overseas. Foster noted these points. A young woman shoved a stroller through the doorway of Tea & Thee. A blast of wind lifted the papers on his table. Taking *Oceanien* from his pocket, he put it to work as a paperweight. He stared at the book, wondering why he had bought it. Possessions weigh you down. Under "Disposables," he wrote "van" and "tools."

The clock on the wall struck the hour. Soon, Mary and Tyler would walk down the aisle. It would be easier once he was overseas. How many times had a fellow expatriate shared a calamity unfolding far away — a nephew struggling with addiction, a sister going through a divorce — and said, well, there's not much I can do about it from here. You wrote a letter and enclosed a cheque. A letter. He would write Mary a letter.

He was starting on a fifth page when Jessica came walking in. She sat down and shucked off her shoes. "Michael's okay."

Michael being the owner of the gallery. Foster glanced at Jessica and went back to his writing. It worried him, the way their communication had become a kind of shorthand.

"Did you know he was a nurse? All that training, poof, gone! He was a travel agent for a while. He knows this terrific little hotel in Paris near the … What are you doing?"

Foster said nothing.

"Don't tell me. You're writing me a love letter."

Love letter. Foster lifted his pen and looked at the woman who had come into his life so accidentally. If he were to compose a billet-doux in his memorandum prose, what would he say? *I love you, in so far as I understand the concept?* "I'm writing Mary a letter."

"Why don't you just call her? You can use my phone."

"I want to be clear about everything."

"What's everything?"

"Everything I've done. My motives for acting as I did. So far as I can recall them."

"You're kidding."

"No."

"You're writing your life story."

"In point form. Some of the dates will be approximate."

"And Mary will read your letter and everything will be peachy."

"Something like that." Jessica stared at him. Foster felt a malicious satisfaction. For the first time since he had known her, she was at a loss for words.

Jessica got to her feet. "I need a cup of tea."

His attention drifting from the letter, Foster watched Jessica walk to the counter and place her order. The counter was authentic, a relic of the building's original purpose as a bank. The inkwells held stir sticks, the slots for deposit slips, napkins. His gaze drifted to the vault, the massive door and its spoked wheel. What did they keep in there, cream and sugar?

"When do you plan to spring this on her?" Jessica set down two cups of tea. "Are you going to leave it in the mailbox and run?"

"She's not home. They're all at the wedding."

"Wedding? Who's getting married?"

As if it wasn't obvious. "Mary and Tyler."

"Why aren't you there. Did Mary tell you not to come?"

"Not in so many words."

"Foster, look at me. What … did … she … say?"

"She wanted both of us there. But I wasn't sure that —"

"We? As in, you and me?"

"Yes."

"Sure about what? That she should marry this guy? That you wanted to bring me?"

"Um …" Foster stared at a movie poster, pondering the points Jessica had raised. If his life was a movie, he wanted a word with the director. The story was hard to follow. He looked at Jessica and saw tears running down her face. He stared at the pages he had filled with his neat script. He had left her out of the equation.

Everything can be measured. Tears, for example, exert a measurable force. From behind the counter came a hiss of steam. Foster gazed across the room. A cappuccino machine has a working pressure of ten bar — approximately ten times the atmospheric pressure at sea level. He had read that somewhere. Water pressure increases one bar for every ten metres of depth. He had read that somewhere as well. The Pacific was very deep in spots. The Mariana Trench had a depth of more than ten thousand metres, if he remembered correctly. How far down did those leaking tankers lie? More to the point, why was he thinking about sunken ships? His eyes drifted back to the movie poster. A romantic comedy. He had seen that sort of movie from the beanbag chair, dozens of them, in fact. The plots were unlikely. Just when all seemed lost, the characters would make a mad dash, jump in a cab, or run through traffic to declare their love.

What if he and Jessica went to the wedding after all, came through the doors at the last minute? They would have the element of surprise going for them. And, perhaps, a truth about family that Irv, that domestic disaster, had understood perfectly well: The inalienable right to keep showing up.

Foster put down his pen. "We should be there. Let's go."

Jessica gaped at him.

It was a loony idea. But it beat sitting in an obsolete bank with a woman you had reduced to tears. He got to his feet and took out his car keys. Showing up at the wedding would almost certainly create further difficulties. However, the immediate one, he thought as they sprinted to the van, was getting there in time.

THE VAN CLIMBED steeply between high stone walls, turned abruptly and sped down a narrow stretch of blacktop. Irv had always known the fastest way out of town.

"Where are they getting married?" Jessica asked.

"At Secure-All. Where Mary works. It's near the airport."

"Foster, if we can't make it, we can't. There's no sense —"

"Look for a barn with two silos."

"There are two silos coming up on the left. But that's a dirt road."

"And a straight shot to the highway." Foster swung into the turn. The sudden manoeuvre spooked the van, and it swung its tail alarmingly, the steering wheel shuddering in his hands. He countered the move and they went fishtailing past a dairy farm.

"Foster? There's a cow on the road. Shouldn't you blow the — Oh, my God."

A cow on the road was a good omen, Foster thought as he steered around the startled animal. It was the sort of thing that happened in a silly movie. A wheel caught the ditch and for a nervous-making time they shot along, pulling a rooster tail of dust behind them, Foster fighting to keep the car from turning over, Jessica bracing herself against the dashboard.

"You're driving awfully fast," Jessica said when they were on the highway.

"This isn't fast. When I lived in Dubai I'd hit two hundred on the way to Abu Dhabi. And a national would get on my tail and flash his lights until I let him by."

"We're coming to a town. You should slow down."

"There was a hardware store over there by the post office. My father went to jail. Did I tell you that?"

"What? Concentrate on your driving."

At highway speed his lost Mercedes would convey him down the road with a Teutonic competence. Charlie's van seemed to lift its head and break into a high-kneed gallop. Foster glanced at his watch. They had made up ten minutes. It occurred to him that he had left *Oceanien* in Tea & Thee. It didn't matter, because he wasn't going to Micronesia. When had he made this decision? It worried him that he didn't know. It was simply a fact. A given. The realization puzzled him, and he wasn't particularly happy about it. There would be no last dip in the fountain of youth.

They sped down Caledon Mountain. Four lanes now and a fast connection to the big roads. Foster wove through the traffic, gaining ground. They were on the expressway. *You need the luck, son.*

"Is that a police car over there?" Jessica said.

Foster glanced at the speedometer. He was over the limit. There would be consequences, if anybody was watching. God, or whoever monitored the traffic cameras. There should be consequences, he decided. Life should matter. He could take this line of thought no further.

They raced through an industrial district, swung around a factory and jerked to a stop in front of Secure-All. A road map fell to the floor of the van. Foster picked it up and for a moment he was back in the Emirates; it was the first day of the weekend, a day to lace on a pair of boots, stick a map in your pocket and head for the desert. A catering truck pulled into the parking lot and blew its horn, startling him into action. He threw open the doors of the van and hurried with Jessica toward the entrance.

The lobby was transformed. Garlands of silver foil stretched from wall to wall, swaying in the breeze of an oscillating fan. Someone — Shawna? — had drawn a pathway of rose petals and wedding bells on the floor. The ceremony was in the briefing centre, the security guard on duty told them, pointing at an archway of white balloons.

Buttoning his jacket, Foster walked under the balloons and through the door with Jessica at his side. An anthem began, the signal for the bride to go down the aisle on her father's arm. The processional was, of all things, Cedric's favourite hold music, the "Canon in D Major" by Pachelbel. Foster felt a surge of hope. He would reconcile with Mary, bury the hatchet with Tyler, build a life with Jessica.

He took in the scene. Mary's boss was here in his fancy uniform, flanked by two rows of security guards. Ella Chudzik was here, supporting her mother by the arm. Kayla and Benny were here with their parents. Percy the cop was here, standing with a dozen other policemen, all of them in dress blue. Foster turned his attention to the front of the room. The wedding party stood facing the congregation, facing him, suspended in the moment as if posing for a photograph. He had come too late, missed his chance to take Mary down the aisle. Tyler wore a tuxedo, and his usual grin. Shawna wore a velvet gown. A thrift store treasure, Foster supposed. He remembered the school portrait of Shawna he had studied in the Elite Restaurant almost a year ago, the day AMEB went down. His granddaughter had grown taller, acquired a coltish grace. She was travelling on, continuing a journey that would leave him behind.

He turned his gaze to his daughter. He scarcely knew her in her wedding dress. Her mother's pearl necklace from Tiffany's counterpointed her undeniable beauty. Pachelbel played on. Mary tilted her head, listening attentively, as if she were hearing frequencies beyond his ken.

She doesn't need you. You're just in the way. Leave. Leave now. Fly west, against the clock. Take up residence in the tropical paradise Cedric found for you. Wear the big suit. Walk the beach. Watch the tide ebb and flow. Wait for death to track you down.

Mary caught his eye and extended her hand.

Foster turned to Jessica.

Jessica looked at him and said, "Are you sure?"

The question annoyed Foster. Of course he wasn't sure. He was faking it, blowing smoke, pulling an Irv. It would be easier to live out his days among strangers. But the path he was following had led him here, and he took Jessica's hand and stepped forward to stand beside his daughter.

[ACKNOWLEDGEMENTS]

WITHOUT THE GENEROSITY of friends and mentors, this book would not exist. Kelly Dwyer, Bret Anthony Johnston and Sandra Scofield, my teachers at the Iowa Summer Writing Festival, shared their wisdom and provided inspiration. Karen Carney, Kenneth Sherman and Philip Marchand, true friends on this side of the border, read early drafts and made valuable suggestions. Special thanks go to Susan Walker, friend and editor, and to Beverley Slopen, my literary agent, for their belief in the book and their unwavering support of its author. I owe a debt of gratitude to Marc Côté, my editor and publisher, who revealed the heart of the story to me. The debt I owe Donna, first reader and life partner, is beyond reckoning.